GUNNER

GUNNER

ANNA

When Zach "Gunner" Cooper rode into my life ten years ago, he turned me inside out with a single kiss. Then he discovered who I am—his best friend's little sister—and he never touched me again.

Now he's the Hellfire Riders' sergeant at arms—sexy, dangerous, and still the only man who's ever set my body on fire. I've tried to stop wanting him. I've tried and tried. But this time…I have to get over him. Because everything I feel for him is killing me inside.

GUNNER

For ten years, I've pretended that I don't think of Anna Wall as anything other than our enforcer's little sister. Because the blood running through my veins is poison, and getting close to Anna will only destroy her.

But when her brother goes missing and the past comes calling, and a threat to her life waits at her front door…there's no pretending anymore. She's mine. She'll always be mine.

And I'll do anything to break through Anna's defenses and make her believe it.

LOOKING FOR CONTENT WARNINGS? FLIP TO THE END!

If you are browsing through a "Look Inside" feature and can't flip to the end, please feel free to visit my website and look for the content warnings link in the menu.

www.katiwilde.com

GUNNER

THE HELLFIRE RIDERS

KATI WILDE

GUNNER

(Turn the page for more...)

The Dead Lands
Fantasy Romance

THE MIDWINTER MAIL-ORDER BRIDE

THE MIDNIGHT BRIDE

PRETTY BRIDE

THE MIDSUMMER BRIDE
(COMING SOON)

Wolfkin & Berserkers
Shapeshifter Romance

BEAUTY IN SPRING

HIGH MOON

TEACHER'S PET WOLF

SHERIFF'S BAD BEAR
(COMING SOON)

Other Romances by Kati

GOING NOWHERE FAST[1]

SECRET SANTA

THE KING'S HORRIBLE BRIDE

ALL HE WANTS FOR CHRISTMAS

THE WEDDING NIGHT

EVIL TWIN[2]

---

[1] Includes cameos by the Hellfire Riders
[2] Set in the same world as the Dead Lands

CONTENTS

...

FOREWORD

This book is not like the ones that came before! Instead of a collection of three novellas that tell a full story arc, Gunner & Anna's story was written as a novel from the beginning.

Why the change?

Well, gather 'round, dear readers, and I'll tell you the story of the Motorcycle Clubs romance series. In the foreword for **Saxon**, I mentioned how I'd written that story for myself—no deadlines, no plans, all fun. But me being me, I also made up a cover and a website for Kati Wilde. Then at some point in autumn of 2014, I mentioned to my BFFs Ruby Dixon and Ella Goode that I was planning on publishing the story through the new subscription service that Amazon had just rolled out: Kindle Unlimited. And they said, "We should write a branded line of motorcycle club romances! Just novella length stories, so readers can finish them quickly...but they all have to finish happily, so readers are left satisfied."

We planned it all out. Ella would write the Death Lords MC, Ruby Dixon would write the Bedlam Butchers

MC, and I'd already begun the Hellfire Riders MC series. We all stayed in our own lanes regarding the characters and clubs themselves, but we had a small amount of crossover and shared world (for example, Lily's custom bike that was destroyed had been built by Judge from the Death Lords, and some of the Bedlam Butchers show up in this book.)

So I wrote three novellas for Saxon & Jenny, followed by three novellas for Jack & Lily. But by that time, Kindle Unlimited had changed their payment terms, so we were free to write the stories any length we wished. And some stories —like this one—just need to be longer and for the plot to build more slowly than it can in a novella.

Although eventually Ruby, Ella, and I wrapped up the Motorcycle Clubs series and republished them under our own brands instead of a shared brand, you can still find them online! Ruby's Bedlam Butchers are linked on her site, and Ella's Death Lords are available on hers. For more info, visit **rubydixon.com** and **ellagoode.com**.

—Kati

A NOTE ABOUT READING ORDER

In the course of writing Gunner & Anna's story, I had several revisions and restarts. One of my early starts included chapters from when they first met, ten years before the Hellfire Riders series begins—and those chapters are available as bonus material in the discreet cover edition of *Blowback*. You don't need to read those chapters to understand their backstory; it's just a little something extra for those of you who enjoy a peek at the characters before this story begins. And if you are a reader who prefers your hero and heroine to have interactions right off the bat, that might also be a better place for you to start, since the first chapters of this book have plenty of longing, but the hero and heroine are apart physically.

Don't have that edition? You can also find it on my website at katiwilde.com/bia-prologue. Happy reading!

GUNNER

ONE

GUNNER

My brain's about twelve hundred miles away—in some restaurant in Pine Valley or Bend, or wherever the hell that smug fucker Mark Miller is taking Anna Wall out tonight—when her brother abruptly sits up in the passenger seat of our rented Escalade and yanks me right back to a deserted highway in Arizona.

"Twenty-four *goddamn* hours," Stone spits out like he's been chewing on it for a while.

I tear my gaze from the dark road ahead. Stone's

staring out the windshield, sitting straight up though his seat is still reclined. Not a word has passed between us the past hour. I assumed he was asleep. Maybe he still is. Or maybe he took a few too many hits to the head today, because I have no fucking clue what he's talking about.

I've usually got a good idea what's going on in his thick skull. But my body's too damn tired and the day's been too damn long to try figuring it out. Especially when my brain's too damn busy imagining his sexy little sister on a date with a pompous prick.

But I can't say a word about that. Anna's not mine. She can't be. So I don't say anything at all, because Christ knows what would shoot out of my mouth.

Nothing her brother wants to hear, that's for goddamn sure.

Stone scrubs his palms over his scarred face and up over his short blond hair. Yup. Tired as fuck and trying to wake up. Roughing his hands over his swollen jaw probably does the job better than the scrubbing does. He winces and prods at the bruise blooming under his eye before shaking his head.

"Twenty-four hours," he says again. "We come all this goddamn way. And not a fucking thing to show for it."

Not true. "You got a busted lip to show for it."

His eyes narrow. "Your mama got a busted lip trying to fit her mouth around my dick."

I know he's still half asleep if he's pulling out the mama jokes. "My mama would bite that shit off."

"That's not funny, brother." His hands drop to his lap, as if protecting his junk. "Teeth are never funny."

Maybe not. But making him cringe is always entertaining. "You ever hear about vagina dentata?"

"Have I *heard* about it?" His full-body shudder is better than a cringe. "When I was sixteen, Anna tortured me by telling me all about that shit. Then she found my porn stash and drew teeth on the crotch of every centerfold. I had nightmares for a year."

My chest tightens up when he mentions his sister. He always makes a young Anna sound like a terror. She probably was.

She still is. A terror who can reach into a man's chest and squeeze his heart in her little fist without even trying. But even though the simple mention of her name aches like a motherfucker, I can't stop myself from wanting to hear about every single horror she unleashed on him.

Better than the shit my family liked to unleash. "Did she do it on purpose?"

"Probably. That was back when she started reading about Freud—thirteen years old, with full access to my mom's shelves, and my mom willing to discuss anything she read there. Jesus, those were terrifying days. You wouldn't believe some of the things she asked. But that vagina dentata stuff, it was probably an experiment so she could play psychiatrist and analyze my fear. Or it was a subtle way of trying to make me become a dentist, I don't know." Digging his phone out of his pocket, he starts scrolling through messages. "But it stuck. Last year, this one chick asked me about the scars. I told her my face got chewed up by vagina teeth while my mom was giving birth to me."

Jesus. "Were you trying to scare her off?"

"Hell no. This girl had the sweetest ass. Not the brightest bulb upstairs, but a sweet ass. I was just too wasted to think of another story and said the first shit that came to mind. Anyway, it worked. She invited me to stick my dick into her pussy and check for teeth. But I'm not stupid, man. I used my fingers first."

Grinning, I shake my head. "Shit, you're like the second coming of Einstein."

"Laugh it up, pretty boy. I'll take pussy teeth over the nothing you've been getting." He pauses on a message screen. "The prez says to stop by the Den tomorrow."

When we get back to Oregon. No problem there. I'd planned to stop by the Wolf Den anyway. Anna should be working the bar by then.

Unless she's sleeping late in Miller's bed.

Fucking hell.

A red haze swims in front of my eyes like I've taken a blow to the head. My fingers clench on the steering wheel. I've got no goddamn business caring if she hooks up with that prick. And the day will come when she hooks up with *someone*. Someone who can't be me.

I've always known that. I've got no business letting it tear at me now.

But I can barely make myself focus on the shit that *is* my business. "You already told the prez that Shaggy was a no-show?"

"Yup. But I expect he wants the full report."

Except we don't have a damn thing more to tell him. The point of traveling here was to get some info, but our contact from the Desert Kings MC failed to show.

Instead we spent three hours at a truck stop café, eating greasy steak and slurping coffee like aimless dickheads before giving up. That was an hour ago and our flight doesn't leave until noon tomorrow. "Maybe we'll pick up some chatter at the bar tonight."

Stone's wordless grunt gives his opinion of that. *Not freaking likely.*

Frustration bites at me. He's not wrong. Every weekend for over a month now, we've been bouncing around the western U.S. searching for goddamn shadows. The Hellfire Riders' warlord, Blowback, is doing the same, following leads he dug up in Vegas. And we haven't heard anything more concrete than what we started with: rumors that bikers are disappearing after they participate in underground fights. They get into the ring, they vanish, and everyone assumes they took their prize money and rode for sunnier climes.

That's what I assumed, too. On the rally circuit, a few Hellfire Riders are regulars in the ring—including Stone and me. I've fought some of the guys who supposedly took off and nothing I knew about them made me doubt that's what happened.

Until about a month ago, when the Devil's Hangmen nabbed a Rider. Our girl Zoomie had taken down their president with her fists. In retaliation, they were going to hand her over to some slick motherfucker who intended to put her in the ring.

Not just any ring. No, she was heading for the Cage. Blowback's source in Vegas says the Cage is some black market pay-per-view, fight-to-the-death shit that starts at a million dollars per ticket, but the real cash comes from the assholes who are placing bets online and laying odds on which fighter survives. Money from a cartel is twisted up in there somewhere, too. A network of MCs, including the Eighty-Eight and the Desert Kings, have been running merchandise for the cartel—merchandise like guns, meth, and girls. It's not a long jump to thinking those clubs are picking up and transporting the missing fighters, too. But we don't know who's really calling the shots or where the Cage is, or where the men are being held between fights. So we've got questions.

No one's giving answers. Not the families of the men. A few don't seem to know anything at all, but there have been others who clammed up fast, which tells us they're scared shitless. Some of the MCs we're friendly with *want* to talk—it's their brothers who are going missing. But they know less than we do and no one noticed a damn thing odd before the men vanished.

They won their fights at the rallies or their regular

joints, they partied afterward, they got laid. No different from any other Saturday night.

Except the next morning they were gone.

Zoomie's situation was different. She won a fight, yeah. But it wasn't at a rally. Instead she pissed off the Devil's Hangmen, who were all too happy to hand her over to the motherfuckers running the show.

According to Blowback's source, that's another way to end up in that ring: piss off the wrong people and they'll make an example of you.

Anyone who knows more about the Cage is probably either too wrapped up in the business or too fucking scared to open his mouth. Because with the kind of money they must be pulling in, cartels won't dick around. Most MCs won't either. Talking means a bullet in the head.

And *asking* could mean a target on our backs. But the Riders don't give a fuck. Those bastards went after one of our own when they went after Zoomie. So one way or another, we're shutting them down.

As soon as we find them. Which isn't happening today.

God damn it all. A whole fucking weekend wasted, with the two of us stuck flying around and spending half the time in a cage.

I roll down the window. Cold desert air blasts my face at eighty miles an hour. It's not like riding, with a bike between me and the asphalt and my back to the sky, but an open window's better than sitting on a damn cushy seat in a pocket of stale air.

Stone's voice raises over the noise of the wind. "Where the hell are we?"

As if in answer, the headlights catch the reflective paint on the sign ahead.

Now entering CACTUS GULCH. Population 14,598.

Except this weekend, about three thousand bikers have been added to that number—mostly regional riding clubs raising charity money with their holiday swaps and turkey runs. But there's a showing of one-percenters who come for the booze and the bikes and the fights.

The Desert Kings aren't among the one-percenters here, but our contact has family in the area and the holidays are coming up. So if he'd been spotted locally, no one would be asking why one of their members would show his face at an event like this.

Except Shaggy didn't show.

Stone must be thinking about the same thing. "Do you figure he chickened out or he's dead?"

Hell if I know. Both seem equally likely. But I'd put my money on dead.

Stone and I have worked together long enough I don't need to voice that answer. His expression is grim as he looks forward. "Yeah," he says. "Someone got wind."

"They got a sniff. But no details."

He glances at me. "Or we'd have had a meet up?"

Yup. Someone would have been waiting for us in Shaggy's place, ready to take us out. Or they'd have gotten to us on the highway as we left. So if Shaggy *is* dead, they didn't bother digging out any information from him first. They just shut him up.

"Better pass that on to the Butchers," I tell him.

With a nod, Stone pulls out his phone again. I hear the "fuck" he mutters under his breath as he starts typing. This isn't the kind of news we want to pass along.

Stone and I have ties to a few members of the Bedlam Butchers; those ties go back to our years in the Marine Corps. But Shaggy has personal ties to the Butchers, not to us. Specifically, he has a family connection to Crash, one of two Butchers who recently disappeared.

Needless to say, the Butchers have been real fucking interested in finding out what happened to their brothers. They knew Handlebar and Crash hadn't just up and gone. They found the remains of Handlebar's custom chopper and his kutte in the possession of some shitstain patch in the Hard Nine, who confessed he'd gotten them from someone in the Eighty-Eight—a skinhead club with chapters in practically every goddamn state. But that was as far as their trail led until we flew down to New Mexico and told the Butchers what happened to Zoomie. Then all signs pointed to the Cage.

But those signs might as well have pointed to Stone's ass for all the good that did. We've gotten our hands on a few low-level skinheads in the Eighty-Eight and had a few friendly conversations—it's fucking amazing how polite a racist piece of shit can be after you've put a bullet in his knee—but the grunts don't really know anything.

They can tell you how far they escorted merchandise, and which club was waiting at the end of their leg when they passed the merchandise on, but they don't know what the hell they were escorting each time or who set up the runs.

And getting to the higher-ups in the Eighty-Eight or the Desert Kings? Fuck. Stone and I used to dig terrorists out of caves and infiltrate compounds guarded by suicidal fanatics. Yet even we aren't thinking of trying to lay hands on the assholes running the national chapters of either MC.

We're not afraid of dying. Dying stupid is something else.

Besides, something will shake out. It always does.

Something like Shaggy.

Stone and I don't know him. That's why we're here. A member of the Desert Kings, he was too skittish to meet with the Butchers, though they were the ones he contacted—it was just too damn risky, considering that he has family ties with Crash. If anyone was watching him, it wouldn't be a stretch to put two and two together. But there's trust between Stone and me and the Butchers' co-presidents, so they persuaded him to meet up with us, instead.

And explaining our presence here? That one's simple. Stone and I are regulars on the rally fight circuit. Considering that we both recently invested in a gym and we each wiped out our savings, picking up some money in the ring is a no-brainer.

The guy I was up against earlier today looks like a tank—and he moves like one. I had him laid out before the first round was over. Stone matched up against a tougher, faster fucker from the Iron Blood MC. He'll be feeling the bastard's fists for a few days, but he still came out on top.

All at once I'm grinning.

Stone looks up from his phone and gives me the side-eye. "You losing it?"

"Just wondering when we became such dickheads that, between us, we pick up twenty grand in twenty-four hours and say we've got nothing to show for our time."

He blinks, which tells me he's forgotten about the money, too, then shakes his head. "It's only nineteen thousand. Because I put a grand in that toy drive box."

Shit. I almost choke laughing, because of course he did. Stone's road name fits him well—as the Hellfire Riders' enforcer, he's cold and hard as stone. But he's a toasted marshmallow when it comes to three things: kids, dogs, and any girl in trouble.

"But I'll tell you what," he adds, as generous as a slick salesman on late night TV. "We'll split the donation. That way Old Timer will only tax you on ninety-five hundred instead of your ten K."

Old Timer, the Riders' treasurer. We don't report our fight money to Uncle Sam—all that money flowing under the table is part of the reason the underground fighting is illegal—but we still pay taxes on it. Thirty percent of our prize money goes into the club's coffers to help cover expenses like travel and entry fees. The tax doesn't bother me any more than Stone's donation does. The club gives me back a hell of a lot more than I can count in dollar bills.

That doesn't mean I won't grumble about both. "So I claim half the donation and go home with ninety-five hundred. Then I let Old Timer take another twenty-eight fifty on top of that? That means we both come out with sixty-six fifty. But if I just have him tax my ten K, I come out with an even seven thousand. And you'll have…sixty-three hundred."

He's mumbling something and poking at the calculator app on his phone. I know my numbers are right but his "God damn it, you heartless bastard" when he arrives at the same answer has me grinning again.

"You should still split it with me," he says. "It's for Baby Jesus and shit."

I'll split it. But I'm sure as hell not going to tell Stone that until we're handing in our reports to Old Timer.

Instead I flip open the console between our seats. "How about this? Here's my own toy drive box. How about you drop a few K in there?"

"You ain't that pretty."

"Yes, I am."

"Yeah, you are." He gingerly pokes at his black eye and works his swollen jaw from side to side, as if testing how much it'll hurt. His resulting groan is as pathetic as what he says next. "This fucked-up mug is going to scare away any woman worth having tonight. You'll have to reel one in for me."

We both know I won't have to reel one in. I don't have to go fishing at all. I just have to sit there. But I'm not interested in catching anyone and he's usually not interested in catching what I toss back. He's not really interested now but I'll still give him shit for it.

"That's fucking pitiful," I tell him.

He grins, then grimaces when the scab on his busted lip splits. With another pathetic groan, he grabs a napkin and holds it to his bleeding mouth. "I'll take pitiful if sweet, sweet pussy comes with it."

"You didn't say pussy. You said a woman worth having. Are you telling me a woman who falls for a bait and switch is worth having?"

"I'm not looking for brains, brother." A hand over his heart, he gravely says, "Throw beauty and brains at me, and I'd be a goner. So reeling in the dim ones is an exercise in self-preservation."

Fuck. He's joking—but it's not a joke. Ten years ago, I met beauty and brains when I stopped to help her change a tire.

Five minutes later, she flashed me her tits and I was a goner.

There's no self-preservation after you're gone. No wall you can build around your heart. The only thing you can do is accept that you're fucked. You can't protect yourself anymore.

So you protect her, instead.

You protect her by doing nothing but watch her. And all the while, you're wishing for more but knowing you can't have it. You're pretending you don't think of her as anything other than your friend's little sister. You're telling yourself it's for the best when she starts dating again, because staying away from her is how she stays safe, and if she's happy then you should be real fucking happy for her, too.

Except you're already fucked. So you can't protect yourself and your armor is gone, and the thought of her with someone else is a blade that slides right in.

Maybe you walk while you're thinking of it. Maybe you talk. Maybe you laugh. Maybe you do your goddamn job and search for goddamn shadows every weekend, but there's not really anything left. Because you're a fucking goner.

And every day you don't have her, you might as well be dead.

TWO

GUNNER

Stone's grumbling again as the highway turns into main street. "This rig is a goddamn embarrassment. You know who comes to a bike rally in a cage? Prospects who've been told to drive the clubs' vans. Or assholes who drew the short straw."

Despite his bellyaching, Stone isn't embarrassed. Whether we ride in on motorcycles or in a clown car, no one with half a brain will fuck with us. Sure, sometimes these rallies are populated by fuckers with less than half a brain, but even they know to steer clear after getting a look at our kuttes. And if they aren't smart enough to do *that*…well, usually that's when shit gets really fun.

So I only point out, "You *are* an asshole," and he nods. "True."

He's an asshole, but the short straw belongs to me, because I've got to find parking for this beast. Chrome shining under the streetlights, motorcycles line the main drag of this small Arizona town as far as I can see. About a half mile down the road, there's a stretch of desert packed full of more hogs and RVs. Space is at a premium this weekend.

Considering our last-minute planning, I would call it a miracle that we got a motel room, but it's not. The Hellfire Riders have pull where we need it.

But no amount of pull reserves a parking space. The motel lot looks like a Harley-Davidson dealership during a Memorial Day sale. Three blocks from the main road I finally find a spot off a side street, in front of a run-down bungalow with a rusted chain link fence surrounding a yard full of yellow rocks.

His leather kutte in hand, Stone bails from the rental and slams the door. I grab my own vest and slide my ass out of plush seats. The Escalade is a nice ride, for a cage. Better than the work truck I've got sitting at home. But I'm not sorry to leave it.

The nighttime air's got a bite. It's cold and clear, and even three blocks over, the noise from main street breaks up the midnight quiet.

The chirp of the Escalade's alarm sets off a dog barking inside the bungalow. Stone shrugs his kutte on over his button-down flannel and gives the vehicle a considering look.

"Are we leaving that shit in there overnight?"

By 'shit' he means the two HK416 assault rifles and the four handguns tucked behind the front seats, courtesy of the Bedlam Butchers. We couldn't fly into Phoenix with any weapons and we sure as hell wouldn't go unarmed to a meetup with Shaggy. So the Butchers hooked us up by securing a stash at a public locker that we could collect on our way to the rally. Tomorrow we'll be locking them up again on our return trip to the airport.

"Might as well leave them," I decide. "They won't be any more secure in the motel room and we'll just be hauling it all back out in the morning." Our fight money is in the room, but the cash fits into a safe. The weapons won't. "You want to carry now?"

He shakes his head. "Not worth the trouble."

The trouble would be trying to enter any Cactus Gulch establishment with a weapon. Most places pat you down before allowing you in, because the rally organizers and the bar owners like everyone to play nice. Playing nice won't happen—as sure as shit, there'll be fights going down outside of the ring—but if no one gets shot or stabbed, everyone involved can call it a win.

As the Hellfire Riders' enforcer and sergeant at arms,

respectively, Stone and I don't go many places without a few weapons strapped on. But walking into a bar unarmed doesn't worry me. If shit goes down, I've got my fists. And if I don't feel like bruising my knuckles, there's always plenty of things close at hand — tables, chairs, beer bottles. The prez wouldn't have appointed us to our positions if we couldn't take care of problems without reaching for a gun.

I feel like bruising my knuckles tonight. Stone got in a good fight today, but me, I might as well have gone up against a tube of ground beef. Now Shaggy didn't show, we still don't know where the fuck all these guys are disappearing to, whether Crash and Handlebar are even alive, and Anna's out with one of the biggest pricks in all of Pine Valley.

My gut's twisted up, thinking about how that might be going. What time is it? Just past midnight, but an hour earlier in Oregon. About the time a dinner and a movie would be over. About the time Miller might be making a move on her, kissing her luscious mouth, sliding his hands into her dark hair.

I know the sweet, hot taste of her. Ten years ago, I took a kiss in exchange for helping change her tire, and I know her hair feels like thick silk between my fingers. I know how she moans and lifts up on her toes. I know the soft press of her body against mine. That knowledge has haunted me for a decade. Maybe Miller knows it now, too.

Jesus fucking Christ, I need to pound some bastard's face in.

Maybe Stone's face. I love the asshole like a true brother—and a hell of a lot more than I love my own brothers—but when he starts chuckling as we're walking along, the sound is like ragged fingernails scraping over my brain. His sister is out with a pompous dickbag. And he's laughing?

I glance over. His scarred face is lit up by his phone and he's wearing a shit-eating grin.

Like there's something to be happy about. "What the fuck you laughing at?"

"I'll send it to you."

A picture. There's only one kind of photo he sends to me.

Anna's.

I've got my phone out even before it vibrates in my hand. Sweet Christ, and there she is. Looking straight into the lens, her golden brown eyes narrowed and her mouth firmed, like she's annoyed as hell and making sure her brother knows it.

I spend a long second studying her eyes before letting my gaze drift over her sharply angled cheekbones, sliding down to her pointed chin. Small and delicate, she's got a sweet face, like a pixie's. But, Jesus. There's nothing sweet about her aside from her taste.

She made herself up for her date. Working at the Wolf Den, she usually doesn't do much more than put her long brown hair up in a ponytail. But now her eyes are dark and smoky, with gold glittering over her lids. Her glossy hair is loose. Her plush lips look like red velvet.

That's a mouth that could drive a man insane, wondering when he'll have a chance to kiss it. That mouth can stiffen a man's cock the second he looks at it.

Or at a picture of it.

Fuck.

With my dick an iron bar lodged against my zipper, I tear my gaze from her face. I don't know what to make of the rest of the photo. Anna's selfies are rarely just selfies. In this one, her middle finger is self-explanatory. But she's lying on a red rug I recognize from her living room with Stone's boxer, Daisy, in the photo beside her. A message is spelled out in dog biscuits over the top of her head. The same message she adds to every picture. Sometimes it's hard to find. Not this time.

Anna was here.

"She's pissed." Stone sounds amused by that fact. "Miller asked me for advice about where to take her. So I told him she loves the Rock'n Bowl."

That's a punch to the throat. She *does* love the Rock'n Bowl. She loves the noise and the neon under the black lights and the cheesiness of it all. If a guy wanted to make sure she had a good time on a first date, there's no better place to do it.

And Stone gave that advantage to *Miller*. It feels like a fucking betrayal. It shouldn't, but fuck me—it does.

Not betraying me. Betraying her.

It's all I can do not to swing my fist at him. I can't

have Anna. But, goddammit. She deserves better than this. "You told him that? He's a fucking tool."

"Exactly." His expression is as smug as fuck. "And he's the sorest loser you ever saw. He has been since high school."

Ah. The rage boiling through my blood cools. Anna's just a small thing, and she doesn't take the bowling part of the game seriously, but she's got a magic touch with the ball. What she doesn't have is much patience for assholes.

Her brother is an exception.

"I bet her that Miller would fake an injury halfway through the game—as soon as she started winning." He's grinning again, talking and texting at the same time. "Guess who told her he sprained his wrist while working out yesterday, and it just happened to start acting up on their date?"

Good. "Why bring Daisy into it?"

"That was the bet. If I was right, she has to give Daisy a bath before I get back."

I shake my head. I've seen Stone try to get the boxer into a tub before. The house he and Anna share was a muddy wreck by the end. "Because babysitting your dog every weekend we're gone isn't punishment enough?"

He blinks hard and sniffs, as if his feelings are wounded. "Daisy's not a punishment. She's a gift."

"A gift who rolls in shit every chance she gets."

"And that's why she needs a bath. See? I'm a mastermind." But his expression turns serious as he pockets his phone again. "Anyway, Anna needs the distraction."

"From what?"

"From Red."

My gut twists right up again. Red Erickson isn't just a Hellfire Rider. He's also the father of Anna's best friend, Jenny, and thanks to the cancer eating up his chest, he's got—I don't know, maybe another few weeks left. *Maybe.* This past month, he's been heading downhill fast and I don't think he'll wait for the cancer to take him. He'll go out his own way.

That would be rough enough for Anna, losing a man who's like an uncle to her and serving as emotional support for Jenny Erickson. But when it comes to cancer, Anna's got her own demons.

I should have seen it. We don't talk much, but I keep an eye on her when she's working at the bar, and she's been quieter lately. When she's not quiet, she's sharper. Like every word is lodged in her chest and she uses a razor to slice each one out.

But until Stone just opened his mouth, I hadn't put it together. I should have. She was sick with leukemia as a kid. The first time I met her, she'd just come off a new cancer scare—a lump in her breast. It turned out benign, but the scare rattled her so much she sought reassurance from the stranger who stopped to help change her tire. She flashed her tits at me and asked me to tell her they weren't perfect, so she wouldn't feel like she lost something in the surgery.

I couldn't lie; they were a pair of the prettiest breasts I'd ever seen. But I told her the scars wouldn't matter. That 'perfect' for her meant 'healthy.'

I meant every damn word. Because right there, seeing her courage and her fear and her determination, I knew I'd never be the same. I didn't know her name yet but I knew this girl had just fucked me over—and that there was nothing more important than knowing she was healthy. That she was alive.

And that feeling spooked the hell out of me. I tried to run—but I didn't get far. The girl I met and kissed on the side of a road turned out to be Stone's sister, and I was staying at his family's house for a week. At that point, Stone and I been serving together for four years and he was already closer to me than most of my family had ever been. On missions, we all but shared a brain and there was no one else I trusted more at my back.

So I was fucked…but after that sank in, knowing I was fucked didn't bother me so much. There's a lot worse things that could have fucked me over. Worse things, like seeing her hurt. Or killed.

Just like my brother's girl had been. After losing her, David was a dead man walking—and before long, just a dead man.

So maybe I was always meant to be fucked. I can accept that. Maybe meeting Anna was inevitable. I can accept that. But if I'd touched her, seeing her hurt might have been inevitable, too.

I could never accept that.

Now Anna might be fighting her own sense of inevitability. Ten years ago, she was terrified of getting sick again. Terrified of never seeing the world or doing anything with her life. Maybe watching Red go through this brought that terror back around.

I say, "Is that what this thing with Miller is—a distraction? Because it used to be, she didn't want to waste her time dating."

Or as she put it—*I've got better things to do with my time than sorting out the dickheads from the good guys.*

Stone shrugs. "I told her he was a dick. She said she knew."

"Then why go out?"

"She says it's because he asked her."

"Miller has asked her before." A hundred guys have. For the past six years, I've sat at the bar at the Wolf Den and watched every move they've made, seen every asshole who's flirted with her, my fists clenched and wishing I could beat the shit out of them.

Knowing I don't have the right.

But if I did… Jesus. I look at the picture, at eyes like a starburst of caramel and whiskey, at her dark hair spread out on the rug. I'd give anything to see those long strands spread out on my pillow and tangled by my hands, her red lipstick smeared all over her mouth. Then all over my cock.

At least Miller won't see it. "Why would she say yes to him now?"

Stone shrugs again.

Jesus fucking Christ. He brought up the topic of Anna needing a distraction from cancer and now he's shutting it down?

Fuck that. I'm not done with it. Not if Anna is afraid of dying.

And not if she's dating pricks like Miller because of it. What's she doing with him? Trying to cram in as much living as she can?

She's done that before. Not long after I visited Stone that first time, right after Anna had the scare with the lump, she took off. She'd just finished up four years of college, but instead of heading to med school like she'd planned, she started traveling. I didn't see her in person again for more than four years, but I saw the photos she e-mailed to Stone. Pictures from New Zealand and Bangkok and some white sand beach in the Maldives where she was wearing a bikini that I've jacked off to so many times it's a miracle my dick isn't broken. She backpacked through Europe and took a picture in front of pretty much every church and bridge ever built. She was in South America while Stone and I were heading back from Iraq, and eighteen months later, she saw the pyramids the same day we flew out to Afghanistan. She sent pictures of it all, and every single photo had the same message scrawled across it.

Anna was here.

Anna once told me it was something her mom taught

her to do when she was younger—to put her mark on the world around her, so it didn't feel like she could fade away so easily.

She still does it. Smartphones and apps have made taking the selfies easier, and most of the pictures are of her making funny faces or are a joke for Stone, but sometimes she sets up elaborate scenes. Sometimes finding *Anna was here* in the background is like a game of "Where's Waldo?" But every one still says the same thing.

And in the past six years, they've all been taken close to home. She went back to Pine Valley a few months before Stone and I left the corps and headed in the same direction. She's been working the bar at the Wolf Den ever since and she seems content to stay, aside from a couple of short trips during her vacation days. Most of her free time she spends remodeling her part of the old Victorian farmhouse they share.

Maybe that's about to change.

The inside of my throat feels like a raw blister when I ask, "You think she'll take off again?"

Stone's quiet for a long second before he says, "I don't know."

But that quiet moment tells me he's worried she will. And in that quiet moment, one thing becomes crystal fucking clear.

I need to kiss her at least one more time before she goes. I need to taste her again. And pray it'll get me through the next ten years.

If she wants a distraction, I'll give her one. Nothing demanding. I'll ask her out, take her to dinner, take her home. All aboveboard, friendly—nothing different from the date she suggested to me when I first met her. Just go out, grab a bite to eat, maybe fool around a bit.

Ten years ago, saying no to her was like slipping a knife into my gut. But she just shrugged and smiled before carrying on like she had before. No big deal.

This won't be a big deal either. Just a good time with her brother's friend. Her brother's good-looking friend. My face is a point in my favor with her. A couple of months ago, there was some trouble at a bar where she and Jenny were hanging out, and I ended up taking a drunk Anna home. She tried to kiss me then, slurring over a *Jesus, you are so damn beautiful,"* as she moved in.

The touch of her lips, heaven. Pushing her away, hell.

For me. When I pointed out she was wasted, that only an asshole would take advantage of her, she just shrugged before turning away. The next day it was like nothing happened.

No big deal. Just a kiss that I'd have killed for.

My voice is rough as I say, "I'm going to take her out before she goes."

Stone gives me a long look.

He knows why I've stayed away from her all these years. And he knows I want to get close. Not much escapes him. I never let myself be alone with Anna, because it'd take a fucking miracle for me to keep my hands to myself.

But whenever I'm at their house or sitting at her bar in the Wolf Den—which is pretty damn often—I watch her a little too much.

That's never been an issue between Stone and me. Ten years ago he gave me a warning—a warning he's repeated every year since we came back to Pine Valley. *I won't kill you if you go after my sister. I'll kill you if you hurt her.*

I'd kill myself before hurting her. But it was never me I worried about.

"What about your family?" he asks.

"It'll just be the one time." No reason for them to fixate on her. "And I'll downplay it. I'm just doing her a favor or I owe her a dinner or something. She's fed me often enough at your place."

"Still, you asking any girl out is damn remarkable."

Fuck. That's true. A hot knot winds in my stomach. "I'll settle shit with them first, then. Maybe they'll just let it all go."

If they did… Jesus. I wouldn't have to stop at just one date. Or just one kiss. I'd take however many Anna was willing to give.

I'd take *anything* she was willing to give.

He nods. "How long has it been since you've been home?"

"Six years. Maybe the futility of their plans for me finally sank in."

Stone winces, as if thinking of the operation I underwent before that last visit. The vasectomy was a last ditch attempt to sever ties between me and my family. That didn't go as I hoped but I don't regret the sacrifice. "Or maybe they'll chain you down and try to keep you this time."

"Maybe." In truth, I'm surprised they haven't already tried it.

"Watch your back, then. And if you need me to mount a rescue, guns blazing, I will."

Stone's tone suggests it's a joke, but he means every word. He'd put bullets in my brothers, my mother, and maybe he'd say sorry after. But the sorry would only be because he couldn't see another way to settle it.

I can't see another way to break their hold, either. And maybe one day it'll come down to bullets. That'll break every bond between us, once and for all.

But it won't be necessary if they just let me go.

"Heads up on your ten," he says quietly.

"I saw them." A few members of the Iron Blood, including the patchholder Stone took down in the ring today—Paladin. I spotted the wiry bastard and his brothers as soon as we hit the main drag. Even this late, the street's a mess of people—some coming and some going, some standing around and talking. Bikers and their women, most of them minding their own business, and a whole lot of them loud and drunk.

As far as I can tell, the Iron Blood are minding their own business, too. Paladin clocked our presence as soon as we stepped out from the side street, but although he's watching us, I can't read anything in his narrow, fox-like face.

"You expecting trouble?" I ask Stone.

Some assholes don't lose well. And sometimes the assholes who don't lose well get real fucking brave when they're surrounded by their brothers.

But even if Stone hadn't thrown down with Paladin in the ring today, we'd still be keeping an eye on them. Since they're centered in northern Nevada and the Riders are in Oregon, we don't often run into the Iron Blood. But we keep our ears to the ground and know their reputation. They're a young club, hungry and growing fast.

Most outlaw clubs don't grow fast. There are always stronger one-percenters in an area to deal with, politics to play and territory to sort out. If an established club feels threatened, it'll step in and crush the new one — or at least teach them their place.

That the Iron Blood hasn't been crushed yet suggests they've got some powerful friends looking out for them.

"Not especially expecting anything." Stone stops, crouching low as if he's checking out the custom chopper sitting next to the sidewalk. In truth he's scoping out the Iron Blood from a better angle. "There was just the usual shit slinging."

"You must have made a hell of an impression, because they're suddenly real interested in looking our direction." Not only Paladin anymore, but all of them.

"Probably because you're so damn pretty. I can't take

you anywhere without attracting some asshole's attention." On his feet again, Stone tilts his head toward the Ponderosa bar—our destination. Asking without words if we still want to head that way, since it means turning our backs to the Iron Blood. "It's that girly mouth you've got."

"Fuck that. My mouth is *manly*." I start toward the Ponderosa, my gaze sweeping the businesses lining the road until I see what I need: a window that offers a faint reflection of the street behind us. "Just yesterday, my lips wrestled a grizzly bear while barbecuing a giant squid they dragged out of the sea after skydiving from an exploding rocket."

"That is, indeed, pretty fucking manly."

"Hell yeah, it is." The back of my neck tenses. "That idiot."

Paladin takes a step in our direction—but before I finish calling him an idiot, a big hand on his shoulder stops him. He goes to shrug it off before his body stills, as if he realizes that isn't a hand he should shake off.

"That's their enforcer," Stone says. "They call him Chef."

He's a heavy, barrel-chested fucker with a shaved head and bushy black beard. I had a good look at him earlier today at the fight. Long sleeves cover thick arms but the tattoos on his hands are visible. Inked across the fingers of his right and left hands are two words. RIDE FREE.

That's a sentiment I can get behind. "Looks like someone in their outfit's got brains, then."

"Good sense? That's just no damn fun," Stone declares, then heads through the crowd lingering outside the Ponderosa's front doors.

Inside, it's standing room only, with bodies three deep around the bar. Despite the size of the place and the high ceilings, the odor of beer and sweat is so thick I can almost drink it, the voices and the music so loud I can't hear a damn thing. Automatically I scope the faces, the kuttes and the colors, seeing who's sitting and who's standing where. We were in here this morning, making arrangements for tonight, but a few tables have been moved and I memorize their new locations. There's so many women crammed into the hall outside the bathrooms that the emergency exits are blocked by a wall of shapely flesh.

I catch Stone's eye, flick my gaze to the bar. He nods.

If shit goes south, we go that way. There's a door behind the bar that leads to the kitchen.

We make our way toward the southwest corner. I ignore the double-takes and stares from the woman I pass. That shit's just a distraction. Anna's not mine, but I'm hers. And I've got no interest in fucking another girl just to get my nuts off.

For that, I've got two hands and a damn good imagination.

Fortunately at rallies like this one, the attention my face draws usually stops at the stares. Most of the women here are already with a man—primarily old ladies and club pussy who came along for the ride. The first will stay with the biker who brought her and the second knows it's best not to cross club lines. They'll look, maybe even smile and flirt, but they won't risk riling tempers by offering me an invitation.

Stone prefers events where free range pussy is thick on the ground. There's not much of that here.

The crowd thins slightly in the southwest corner, where a section of tables is cordoned off and a 'Private Party' sign taped to the wall. It's not really private but I don't give a shit about that. When I reserved the space this morning, I expected the crowd to push into the area. That doesn't matter. What matters is most of the guys who were up in the ring today are here.

"Gunner, you fucking asshole!" The tube of ground beef I went up against breaks into a grin when he sees me. Buster's cheerful as hell for a guy who lost two teeth today. The left side of his jaw looks twice the size of his right and his grin is just as lopsided. "You're late!"

Waiting for a contact who never showed. But that's past. Maybe we'll get information here, instead.

I return his grin and bump his fist in greeting. "Worried I was going to leave you with the tab?"

"Not yet." Buster waves toward the bar, then toward the tables, piled high with empty beer pitchers. "Waitress said you paid some up front." He leans in all confidential-like, his breath almost as potent as the beer in his grip. "But she said your deposit was about to run out and that got me scared, because I'm not done drinking yet."

"About to run out? Hell, no. We'll take care of that." I glance at Stone and he nods, heading toward the bar. I gesture to Buster's jaw. "You're a goddamn tank, walking around with that. I'd be laid up, crying and popping Vicodin."

"Free beer." He lifts his pint. "It's the best medication."

And the best way to ensure the guys we want to talk are close enough for us to hear them. Not all of the men who fought today are regulars on the circuit, but enough of them are. Someone might have heard or seen something when the missing fighters disappeared. So we let all of them know there'd be free drinks for anyone who got up in the ring. The liquor will bring them in. Enough of it might loosen their memories and their tongues.

Missing fighters or not, though, this arrangement is something I've done dozens of times at dozens of rallies. As the Hellfire Riders' sergeant at arms, part of my job is checking out every establishment my prez walks into—and making sure that as soon as he gets there, he doesn't have to stand around waiting for a table.

Over the years, I've tossed a few assholes out of their seats to make room for the boss. But it's easier—and builds up a hell of a lot more respect—to create a situation where people offer up their place. Even in a joint as crowded as this.

Sure enough, a few seconds later Buster offers me his spot. But the prez isn't here and my purpose is to gather info. That's best done on the move, like picking berries from a bush. Delicately picking. Coming at the question straight might do more harm than good. So instead I say good-natured shit like, *You seen Airbag around? The fucker told me he wanted a rematch in Kalispell but word is, he took off. Running scared, maybe.*

Buster's heard rumors but has seen nothing. So after a while I move on to someone else, use another approach.

An hour later, my berry basket is still empty despite shaking almost every available bush, and I haven't seen scarred hide nor blond hair of Stone — although he must have made it to the bar, because the waitress showed up with a tray weighed down with pitchers of beer, and those trays kept coming. I'm about to text him when he finally shows, wearing both a grin and a woman.

That figures.

He makes his way through the bodies to my position against the far wall. His grin widens when I let my expression tell him exactly what I'm thinking.

"Sorry, brother," he says in his so-not-sorry voice. "I miss anything?"

"Not a damn thing."

"Then it sounds like I had a more productive hour." He wraps his arm around the woman's waist. "I ran into Cherry up at the bar."

Cherry? Jesus. I suppose she gets the name from her flame red mane, but if Stone can't see she's sporting a wig, I'm not going to ruin the surprise for him. Or maybe he can tell and he just doesn't care. She's a looker under all that fake hair, though she's a scrawny thing. Not slender like Anna, but on the edge of strung out, with hipbones and ribs showing clearly through her skintight dress.

Then her emerald eyes meet mine and my stomach drops, heavy with sudden dread. Not because she seems interested in me after getting a look at my face. That happens sometimes with the girls Stone hooks up with.

This time it's because I've seen eyes like hers before. Stone's got a real soft spot for a girl in trouble. This one, though. I've seen eyes like that in Afghanistan, in women who lost their families, their homes, and who don't believe help is ever coming. I've seen it more recently in one of the women we found when we raided the Eighty-Eight's compound near home—after she'd been chained, sold, and raped God knows how many fucking times.

Shit. Stone does *not* need this.

Eyes locked with mine, her body seems to tremble before she looks up at Stone. Her face softens and the shattered expression blinks out, replaced by something like desperate hope. Then even that's gone, and she simply looks bright and vapid, with a smile curving her cherry red lips.

She curls her fingers around his empty glass. "You want me to get you a refill before we go, baby?"

"I sure would, darlin'." His hand lingers at her hip as she moves away, his eyes following her when she walks out of reach.

"Jesus." I lean back against the wall, shake my head.

"You gotta be careful with that one, man. She's broken."

"I know." His voice is grim, his hard gaze steady on her back. "But if she believes my dick might fix her, I'll happily give it my best shot."

And tear out a part of himself when there's nothing he can do to really help her. Especially not before we take off tomorrow. "Maybe you don't know this, but the white shit that shoots out of your dick isn't glue."

"You sure?" He flicks a surprised glance my way. "Because I was hoping to make Christmas cards this year by jacking off all over some paper and throwing down some glitter."

"And sending one to your mother?"

He grimaces, looking suddenly sick. "Sweet baby Jesus, that turned around on me quick."

Bringing his mom into it turned around on me, too. My skin crawls, thinking of Clara Wall touching a card covered in glittery jizz. She's a hell of a woman—and Stone's one lucky asshole, getting her for a mother.

He shakes his head as if to get rid of the image. "You don't have to worry, brother. I'm not walking into this blind. You think she came straight up to me because she liked the look of my face?"

"Maybe." After all, he likes girls in trouble. Some women like scars.

"Nah," he says easily. "She told me she saw me at the fight. So I figure she's looking for protection from someone she knows can handle his own. You see how jumpy she is?"

It's hard to miss. She's tense, her gaze darting around. My first thought was drugs—maybe meth—but although she's scrawny, her skin is clear and her teeth are fine. No track marks mar the pale, bare skin of her arms. If she uses, it's probably not habitual, or what she's using isn't the really hard shit.

So, maybe drugs. But scared fits, too.

"Protection from whom?"

"'Whom?' Your nerd is showing."

"Fuck off. Who's scaring her?"

Stone shrugs. "Don't know. But I'll get it out of her."

"Then what?"

"Then I figure if she's afraid of someone local, a bus ticket and enough cash to see her through a few months might fix what's broken. And if I give her money, I can call it a donation and ask Old Timer to deduct it from my taxes."

A goddamn marshmallow. "You heading back to the motel?"

He tears his gaze from Cherry to give me a wry look. "She knows how much I won."

I huff out a short laugh. It doesn't take a genius to figure out we've probably got the prize money stashed in that room. Even locked away in the safe isn't always safe enough—and it wouldn't be the first time some sweet pussy set a guy up, either cleaning him out herself or using her body to get into the room and letting a boyfriend hold a gun to the sucker's head until he gives up the combination to the safe.

Stone would probably give her every dollar, if he thought she really needed it. He wouldn't care about the money itself. But he'd care if she stole it or if she fucked him over. So he'd rather not even risk it.

"She mentioned a room she's staying in," he says.

Shit. That's not much better. I dig the Escalade's key fob out of my pocket and hand it over. Better for him to swing by and grab a weapon before he heads off to her place. But that reason goes unspoken.

"You can fold the back seat forward and the cargo hold is about as big as a bed," I remind him. "Might be better than holing up in a room where some asshole might come knocking."

"True that. I've got enough scars."

Which he got after going home with another girl in trouble. Except that one had an ex-boyfriend who liked using his fists on her. And that ex-boyfriend brought friends. Stone can fight like the devil, but he barely made it out of there alive—and he went out through a window, not a door.

He'd have bailed before it came to that, except he was still trying to protect the girl, who turned around and accused him of raping her to save her own ass from the jealous bastard who was going to kill her for straying.

Considering the circumstances, how terrified she was, Stone forgave her that. But he's been wary ever since.

Even now, there's caution in the way he watches

Cherry return, drink in hand. Her smile falters, emerald eyes searching his expression as she gives him the beer. "Are you all right?"

"Better now," he tells her. "Just discussing the perils of defenestration."

Her eyebrows rise. "Being thrown through a window?" She hesitates, her gaze lightly touching on his jagged scars. "Is that what happened to you?"

His body stills and I've got the sudden feeling there's going to be three of us on that flight home tomorrow.

"Don't you be pretty *and* smart," he warns.

"I'll try." Humor flashes in her eyes before it flickers out. "I'd rather be something else, anyway."

"What's that?"

With a shake of her head, she seems to draw into herself, and all at once there's that broken woman again. Her face is a mask of hopeless desperation as she gestures at his beer. "Why don't you finish that up and we'll head out?"

His eyebrows pull together in a frown, but he obediently chugs, watching her over the end of the glass. She's shaking again, her emerald eyes bright as she looks everywhere but Stone.

I can't hear his heavy sigh over the noise in the bar, but I see the deep rise of his chest and read the beleaguered look he gives me as he turns to set down his empty glass.

I'm laughing at his expense even as he slings his arm around Cherry's shoulders and leads her away. He's screwed. Not in the fun way. Cherry is so desperate, having sex with her would be like fucking a woman in chains. Stone's an asshole, but he won't take advantage of a girl who obviously needs more help than a dick can give.

So that's two of us who won't be getting laid tonight. The difference is, I'm not sorry.

Hell. Even I wasn't hung up on Anna, I'd be too damn tired to get it up, anyway. Nothing sounds better than heading back to the hotel and hitting the bed, but I've still got a tab to close out.

But maybe not yet. Buster's still going strong and showing no signs of stopping. I find a seat by him and finally sit my ass down, stretching my legs out.

I watch in amazement as he downs another pint. Plenty of bikers are heavy drinkers, but he must be setting some kind of record for staying upright. He slams down the empty and regards me steadily, a thick foam mustache hovering over his upper lip.

"You heading out?" he asks, his tone forlorn, as if the prospect of no more free beer is almost too much to bear.

I tip my head to indicate his empty glass. "I'm waiting to see if it'll catch up with you. You should be on the floor by now."

Swollen cheek bunching like a squirrel's, he grins that lopsided grin. "A fist is the only thing that can make me go down."

"Your old lady must pack one hell of a punch, then."

His sputtering laugh sends the foam mustache flying.

Grinning, I turn my head to avoid it, and when I glance back he's blinking off into the distance.

"Maybe it's hitting me harder than usual," he says with a shake of his head. "Because now I'm seeing double."

I follow his gaze and my grin freezes in place. Icy tension stiffens every muscle.

He's not seeing double. He's seeing one of my brothers.

Jacob. The second of six sons in the Cooper clan. Spotting him is like spotting a glimpse in the mirror eight years into the future. The same angular face, the same pale blue eyes. Look close, he's a little thinner and shorter than me, with gray salting the black hair at his temples. But at first glance — even at second and third glance — a double.

We've got four other doubles, but one of them's rotting in the ground.

I look for Benjamin and Isiah — the eldest of us, Adam, is in prison, which is a hell of a lot better than he deserves — but the only other man I see sporting the Notorious Few's colors is a big bastard I don't recognize.

Careful not to show any emotion, I lock eyes with my brother again. I won't think of him as Jacob. He goes by Strawman now. Better to call him by his road name, because there's still a part of me that thinks *Jacob* and remembers the older brother I used to admire. Back when I was a kid who didn't know beating me to teach me how to be strong wasn't the sign of affection he claimed it was. Back when I thought a man was defined by how much blood he drew from his enemies and how many women he fucked. Back when family meant falling in line.

His smile appears as he sizes me up—pleased to see me in the same way a poacher is pleased when a tiger crosses his path. I can always tell what he's feeling, and not just because I grew up tagging along behind him. It's easy to read a face just like your own.

Keeping my gaze on Strawman, I lean closer to Buster. "You mind giving me and my brother some space?"

He rises to his feet, belching all the way up, then gives Strawman a once-over. "He's not a Hellfire Rider."

"He's not." Thank fuck for that. A club that patched in anyone sharing my blood isn't a club I'd want to be a part of.

"Well, I'll be over there just drinking my beer."

I nod. Unsaid is the promise to have my back if shit goes down. Part of that's simply because Buster's a good sort. We aren't from the same club and only see each other a few times a year, but making another man bleed forms bonds between you and him. Often those bonds look like anger and revenge, but sometimes spilling each other's blood leads to trust and friendship. Buster's so damn cheerful it's impossible to go in any direction but the second.

But the other part is that, despite me calling Strawman my brother, despite the similarity in our looks, Buster must recognize what else the other man is—a fucking atom bomb, walking around and pretending to be human. And like any nuke, it's not just the explosion you've got to worry about, but all the dirty radiation in the fallout.

I left home at seventeen and I still don't feel clean. That was half my life ago. But the dirty shit, it lingers.

Maybe Buster smells it. Maybe he can see it by the cold glee in my brother's eyes. Or maybe he recognizes the patches on Strawman's kutte—the white skulls, the gray skulls. There's more than a dozen, each one representing a man he's killed.

That's not so remarkable. I've killed more. Most in service to the country, and some protecting the Hellfire Riders. I don't slap a patch on my kutte or a tattoo on my skin to count them, though some Riders do. Plenty of bikers in other clubs do, too. But the boys of the Cooper family—and by extension, the Notorious Few—they've got their own system. The white skulls show how many *pure* white men he's killed. The gray skulls represent men of any other color, and that patch is smaller, because those men aren't worth as much.

And the blood running through my veins? Not pure, though they like to say it is. It's fucking poison. The only thing pure in this family is the bullshit they all spout.

"If it ain't my little brother, Zachary!" Strawman spins the chair Buster vacated and straddles the seat, wearing a big toothy smile. "Been a long time."

"Not long enough."

"Long enough for you to finish growing up, get some muscle on you. You're not such a scarecrow now. You're starting to look like one of the family. Well, almost. One detail's wrong." His gaze lingers on the shoulder of my kutte, where my road name sits below the HRMC patch and my rank. "Sergeant at arms? You could hold the same position as one of the Few."

Not a chance in hell am I joining them. But I just take a swallow of my beer, holding his gaze. I've got nothing else to say to him.

His smile fades. "Mama misses you."

My stomach tightens. The warmth and concern on his face—that's real. One thing the Cooper boys do well is love their mama.

We hate her well, too.

But I still don't respond and he heaves a sigh, then turns his face to the side. And fuck. *Fuck.* I'm so wound up I didn't even notice he had a girl with him. Dark hair, tight skirt, strappy top. I spotted her near him earlier but didn't realize they were together. She's not a threat but if she had been one, I'd be fucked right now. My focus is too tight.

She comes up to his side and skims her fingertips along his neck. "You need anything, gorgeous?"

"Just your mouth shut and your ass warming my knee." He pulls her down so she straddles the lower part of his thigh, her panties on display as his hand circles around to her belly and tunnels under her top. Playing with her nipples in the same absent way some men play with their keys, he regards me steadily. "Mama'll be happy to hear I ran into you. But you're not even going to ask how she's doing?"

I'm not. Because they tried to bring me home once by saying she was sick. *She just wants to see you again. She might not have that long to live.* But she's as hale and hearty as she's always been.

I know that for certain, because I learned my lesson. I don't visit but I keep tabs. Partly so I'll know if they're lying, partly so I might see them coming.

But I didn't see this. So it's the one question I'm interested in asking. "What brought you here?"

"Club business," he says and triumph flashes across his expression. I'm talking; that's a victory to him. I'll let him have it because it's the only one he'll get. "Which I would tell you about if you were wearing the Few's colors."

I'm not that interested. "Is Muncher here, too? Six-Point?"

Benjamin and Isiah. I don't care about seeing them — I just want to know how many of my brothers I might be up against if they force the issue of bringing me home.

Strawman shakes his head. Her face flushed, the girl squirms on his knee, but she might as well be a dog at his feet for all the attention he's paying her. "This is an opportunity I'm cultivating on my own."

"Mama must like that."

She likes her boys to take the initiative. But only when their purpose falls in line with her own.

"She'll like it when the money starts rolling in. But what she'll like most is if you come home."

"Not happening."

"It will," he says as if it's a foregone conclusion. Not angry, not frustrated. In his head, my return is inevitable, so my answer doesn't upset him at all. "You want a piece of this?"

Of the girl riding his leg. "No."

"Bullshit." He laughs because it truly doesn't cross his goddamn mind that I wouldn't. So I can only be lying. "Hey, girlie. You want to suck my brother's dick?"

Surprise flares across her face, cutting through her heavy-lidded arousal when she looks at me. If that question shocks her, she hasn't been with my brother long. Probably not more than a few hours.

Then interest narrows her eyes as she gets a good look, and her tongue darts out to lick her full lips. "I think I'd like that." Her gaze slips to Strawman before returning to me. "I've never been with brothers. Are you twins?"

Twins. A hot blade slices through my chest. I had a twin. It wasn't Strawman.

"No," I tell her flatly. "Not twins. And you stay right there."

"I guess he prefers to watch," Strawman tells her, but although his mouth is smiling I know his thoughts went straight to David, too. His death still festers deep, a wound the entire family feels—and they feel it all the deeper because it was their goddamn fault. That pain darkens Strawman's eyes now and his voice is somber as he says, "Adam's getting out."

Rage stiffens every muscle. "Bullshit."

"It's true." It's not rage I see on Strawman's face. It's satisfaction. "He goes up before a judge this week and the lawyer says there's precedent for getting his conviction overturned. Turns out the lead batch evidence they used to match up his bullets is bad science. So when Adam comes home, he'll be taking his place as president—and Mama wants *all* her boys to come home."

"I've got a home." One I don't intend to leave. Everything I want is there.

He dismisses that response like it means nothing, but the sudden intensity of his shark's gaze puts my back up. He smells blood in the water.

"You got a girl, too?"

Brittle ice scrapes up my spine. I don't show the fear that question brings—I don't show a fucking thing.

And I don't think about Anna. She's not mine.

"No."

"No?" A lazy smile curls his mouth. The girl on his knee gasps in pain, her brows knitting, her body going still. His hand under her top isn't moving—pinching her flesh or her nipple. She'll be bruised tomorrow. He likes to leave a mark. But she's not protesting or trying to get away, so I'm not going to stop him. "Because you know Mama worries. So sometimes she sends the boys to check up on you."

The boys. Members of the Notorious Few who come from outside the family—the ones I wouldn't recognize.

"I know she does." I usually don't know when or who,

but it is not surprising news.

"Well, it seems there's one girl in particular you pay attention to. And spend a significant amount of time with her at work, at her house."

I play so fucking dumb that my brain might as well have crawled up my ass. But it's not all acting. I *am* stupid. So goddamn stupid for ever taking any kind of risk with Anna. For watching her. For not fucking every girl in sight, just to throw my family off the scent. Hell, stupid for befriending Stone and for joining the Riders. I should have kept running.

But that's all just bullshit now. All that matters is keeping Strawman from believing Anna means anything to me.

Frowning as if I'm confused, I ask, "Whose house am I supposedly visiting?"

"A pretty little bartender's."

In an instant, my rage and fear go from hot to cold. So cold. I think about snapping his neck. It'd be easy. His hands are trapped under the girl's shirt, his leverage gone thanks to her weight on his knee. He couldn't even ward me off.

And if I was in prison for killing him, I sure as hell wouldn't be going home and granting Mama's wish.

But that'd only protect me, not Anna. Because my family might guess exactly what set me off. And I could get a warning to Stone, ask him to take them all out before they come for her, but there's a more efficient way to make

Strawman believe Anna's nothing to me.

So I let my confusion ease into a smile. "You talking about Stone Wall's sister? No." I shake my head, chuckling. "She's just around. They share a house, and the Wolf Den where she works is the prez's bar."

"Word is, she's a looker."

"Cute as hell," I agree because no one would think anything different. "But she's damaged."

His eyes narrow. "Damaged how?"

I raise my fingers as I count off the reasons. "One—she had cancer. And she carries that disease in her blood. Two—the treatment left her barren. She's never giving birth to any kids. Three—she was adopted. Doesn't have a fucking clue who her parents are. Her mom could be a Mexican crack whore for all she knows."

All those reasons don't mean anything to me. But to Strawman, they're everything. And he's not good at imagining other people thinking differently from him. Especially if those people are his kin.

Slowly he nods. "You ain't lying?"

"No."

Because if he checks on those statements—and he will—a lie would fuck everything up. The only lie is pretending I give a shit about any of it.

"Good thing." His hand slides under the girl's skirt. "Mama's got a woman picked out for you. Real pure. And still a virgin, at least in the ways that count."

"Just what I asked for from Santa," I say dryly, then

glance pointedly at the girl's lap, where his fingers between her legs are working her up. "How's your wife?"

He grins. "Real good. About to have our fourth kid. Doc says another son."

"Only four?" Not the way he fucks around.

"I always wrap up my dick with pussy from off the farm." He nuzzles the girl's brown hair before spearing another look at me. "You really got snipped? Mama says she's sure you faked that report with your sperm count."

Of course she did. It's beyond her to think any Cooper might willingly sacrifice his legacy and future children. "I didn't fake it."

"I don't believe it, man." Laughing, he shakes his head—but his reason for doubting is different than my mother's. He can't imagine any man voluntarily undergoing the operation, because he never would. "But it doesn't matter. Mama made sure those conjugal visits between Adam and his wife bore fruit. Benjamin and I took care of that; we can do the same for your woman."

Just stand back and watch my brothers breed my wife. Jesus. Sometimes I think my family can't sink any lower, then they surprise me by digging the hole deeper.

And I'm done here. I finish my beer, get to my feet.

I stop short when he reaches for my arm, his fingers wet with the girl's pussy juices. Quickly he grins again, pulls his hands back in a placating gesture.

"Just a heads-up," he says and I pay attention, because his amusement's gone—and no matter how fucked up our family is, maybe because of *how* fucked up our family is, he'll look out for me. A heads-up means there's a threat lurking. "These fuckers I'm doing business with, they told me you were up in the ring today. You won your fight?"

"Yeah."

"You ought to stop doing that. Winning, I mean."

The back of my neck tightens. "Why?"

"You'll need to wear a different kutte before I tell you that." His smile is hard. "You come home and maybe we'll talk."

Fuck that. "Who you doing business with?"

"Blind fuckers, that's who." Now his amusement's back. "But I guess I've got to thank them for that. They mistook you for me a little while ago and tipped me off to where you were."

"Who?"

He shakes his head. "Come home."

That's not a price I'm willing to pay. And I'm giving him too much by pressing for the club's name. It's never smart to let the family know you want something.

I'm pretty damn sure I already know which club it is, anyway. All at once, my memory of the scene on the street with the Iron Blood starts playing another way. Paladin doesn't watch us because he wants to fuck with Stone after losing to him in the ring. No, he's looking at me, thinking I'm Strawman. And Chef doesn't pull Paladin back because he's smart enough not to start a fight. Instead the enforcer recognizes that I'm not wearing the right kutte.

Shit. It could be nothing.

But it doesn't feel like nothing.

Still, I'm not giving Strawman any more of my time. Stepping around him, I head for the bar.

His farewell follows me. "See you soon, little brother."

Not if I can help it.

My brain's working over the heads-up again as I close out the tab. Old Timer's going to have our ass when we turn in the expense report, but if my gut response to this info about the Iron Blood pans out, it'll be the first new lead we've had in connection to the Cage. Well worth the cash we spent.

The motel lies a short hike up the main drag. Inside the room, the featured amenities are a shag carpet and a sagging mattress. I've slept in worse. And a short time ago, I wanted nothing more than to get my ass into bed, but my adrenaline's still coursing after meeting with Strawman. My body's not ready to settle, though the crash will come soon enough.

I don't want to sleep with his filth on me, anyway. I've done some questionable shit in my time—hell, I even *crawled* through shit during a few combat operations—but nothing leaves me feeling dirtier than crossing paths with the family. Not because they rub off on me but because I remember how I used to be exactly the same. And how some part of me still is.

That filth doesn't wash off, but I've spent seventeen years trying.

In the bathroom, the ancient pipes shriek and groan when I turn on the shower. Waiting for the water to heat, I grab my phone with the intention of texting Stone.

Anna's face pops up after the security screen. The photo Stone sent me earlier.

My chest tightens. Jesus. What if I'd pulled this out while my brother was looking? Nothing I said about Anna would have made a goddamn difference if her selfie was right there in my hand.

So fucking careless. I always delete every photo Stone sends right after I get it. I look, I memorize, I erase. No matter how much I want to keep every single one. But I didn't erase this.

What was I thinking? I *wasn't* thinking.

Or maybe I was thinking that if I could take her out just once, if I could have one kiss, maybe I'd get to keep this photo, too.

But I won't get any of those. Not with my family watching. Not with them already focused on her.

Fucking hell.

My throat's a solid ache as I step into the shower and stand under the hot stream, head bowed, fists braced against the plastic tile. Eyes closed, I hold that image of Anna in my mind, slowly letting all the other shit go. I see her brown eyes, striated with gold and sparkling with irritation, her hair spread out on that big red rug.

A few months ago, she brought that rug home from an estate sale by tying it to the top of her Prius like a canoe, then she recruited Stone and me to carry it into the house for her. She's never afraid to commandeer the use of our muscle in her renovation project. Over the years, we've hung drywall, wrestled solid oak furniture up the stairs, installed kitchen cabinets, and held steady a dozen big picture frames while she leveled them off. Each time she thanked us with a beer or a meal—or both, depending on how hard the job was and how much time it took.

Each time I imagined her thanking me a different way.

And it's so easy to slip into that now, fisting my stiffening cock in a soap-slicked hand. Holding her image in my head, watching her eyes go from irritated to soft. Watching her bite her lower lip, like she does when she's got something to say but isn't sure if she should say it. Watching my fingers slide into her thick hair, feeling the rough texture of that rug against my knuckles, then claiming her mouth, because she doesn't need to say anything. She sure as hell never needs to say 'thank you' to me.

But I'd take it. Because I'd take anything she gave.

I'd take her soft, breathy moans and the heat of her mouth. I'd take the grip of her hand stroking my thick cock, her palm softer than mine, her fingers teasing—not jerking on my shaft in the same rough pulls that I'm doing, savagely fucking into my fist, imagining her smiling up at me, knowing exactly how she's driving me crazy, and looking as if she's never needed anything more than she needs me.

Looking at me as if I'm everything.

And— *Fuck.*

The orgasm rips the image away, rips everything away. Abs clenching like I've been punched, I curl over, my left hand slapping the tile as I come hard enough to see spots behind my eyes, my cock jerking in my fist.

For a long minute, I stand under the cooling water, my chest heaving. Jesus. I didn't even get to the part where I'm buried deep inside her pussy. All because I imagined her looking at me as if she loved me.

With unsteady fingers, I angle the shower head down and rinse the cum away. The hell of it all is, as much as I want her to look at me like that, this is better. This torture—of wanting her, of knowing I'm just her brother's friend, of staying away from her—is better than the alternative. Because if she loved me? If she was hurting like this, dreaming of a single touch she knew she'd never have, praying for a single loving look from me? I don't know what the fuck I'd do.

Except that's a lie. I *do* know.

I'd go after my brothers. I'd go after my mother. I'd make sure they could never touch her. I'd break every single hold they have over me. I'd break them hard, I'd break them bloody.

And lose Anna anyway. To prison…or because she couldn't accept a man who killed his entire family in cold blood. Even if I did it for her.

So this pain—of not having her, of knowing I never

will—is better than the hell of losing her completely.

At least she's safe.

I wrap a towel around my waist and leave the shower. Without stopping to look at it again, I erase her photo from my messages, then dump the cache of recently deleted pictures. I check the cloud storage. Gone.

Anna isn't here.

And I've just got to keep living with that. Somehow.

THREE

GUNNER

THE ALARM WAKES ME AT WHAT-THE-FUCK O'CLOCK. Prying my eyes open, I roll over and message Stone.

Drag your ass out of bed. I'm checking out in thirty. Breakfast is on you.

Knowing Stone, that means the McDonald's drive-thru, but I don't care as long as there's coffee to wash it down. We need to be on the road in an hour to catch our flight out of Phoenix.

The phone chimes while I'm in the bathroom, lathering up my jaw with shaving cream. I finish up, haul on my jeans, and take a look. Not Stone's reply, as I expected.

It's from the prez and his message is as long-winded as usual.

Call me.

I do.

Saxon answers on the first ring. He doesn't waste time with greetings. "You heading back now?"

"About to." As soon as I drag Stone out of whatever hole he ended up in.

"When you get into town, head to the clubhouse instead of the Den. Red's taking his final ride this morning."

The air shoots out of my lungs and I sit down hard on the edge of the mattress. His final ride. I knew it was coming. I didn't think it would be this soon.

I scrape a hand over my face. "Jesus."

There's silence on the other end. I can't imagine how the prez feels, making a call like this.

No. I can imagine. He doesn't give a shit about this call or how I take the news. I'd bet anything he's only thinking of Jenny Erickson, and of how losing her dad is going to rip her apart. Just like I'm thinking of how it'll gut Anna.

My own gut feels like a lump of lead. "Tell Red it was a goddamn honor to ride with him."

"I'll do that," Saxon says. "Is Stone with you? I've been calling him for a fucking half hour."

Shit. "He hooked up with some girl. I'll find him,

shake him awake."

"Do that. Have him call Red direct."

"I will." Because the Wall family and the Ericksons are tight. Red's the one who put Stone on his first motorcycle—and Stone will never forgive himself if he misses this chance to say a few final words to the man.

I disconnect and put the phone on speaker, dialing Stone again and again while I finish dressing and transfer the cash from the safe into my pack. His battery's not dead. If it was, the calls would go straight to voicemail instead of ringing first. Maybe he's got it on silent but he's a light sleeper. Even the vibration usually wakes him. Unless it's buried under a pile of clothes and someone's ass.

God damn it. I didn't want to have to track him down. Thank fuck there's an app for that.

Logins and passcodes aren't a problem. He's got mine, I've got his. Most of the time, we use them to find out the other's location when one of us is on a bike and can't answer the phone. But it's insurance, too. Not everyone the Riders run into is friendly. It's best to know where to find him if he can't tell us himself.

I've never had to use it to haul him out of bed, though.

His phone shows up right around the Ponderosa—the same bar we were at last night. When the girl said she had a room, she must have meant close. Probably in one of those apartments above the shops flanking the bar.

I head out, then don't make any new friends in Cactus Gulch when I pound on those apartment doors while the sun's still rising. Stone and the redhead aren't in any of them.

The Ponderosa's next. The joint is still closed but I recognize the manager inside—the woman who arranged our reservations for the private party. She's behind the bar, prepping or tallying receipts, who knows. I tap on the glass door and she pokes her head out. Stone's easy to remember, what with those scars on his face, but the manager tells me she hasn't seen him this morning.

Which leaves me in the middle of fucking nowhere. Running around like a dickhole, chasing after him. That boy needs his ass handed to him for going incommunicado. And if I don't find him in about five minutes, I'll take great pleasure doing it.

I circle around behind the bar, scanning the houses across the back lot. Maybe one of those. Somewhere close enough his phone's picking up the wireless from the Ponderosa. That might be what's fucking up the locator, because according to this app, I should be right on top of him.

Fuck. I call again, hoping he'll answer before I start waking any more townspeople this goddamn early on a Sunday morning.

A muffled ringtone sounds nearby. The muscles in the back of my neck tighten to steel.

Slowly I turn, and the steel becomes ice. That ringtone's coming from a Dumpster.

I don't remember crossing over to it. Instead I'm

remembering that redhead and how she was so jumpy. Afraid of someone. And Stone can take care of himself, but there's some shit you can't protect yourself from. A bullet to the back, for one.

Overseas, at home—I've walked into some hairy situations. Not one second of combat was as harrowing as lifting the lid of that Dumpster.

No body. No blood.

Thank fucking God.

Breathing air stinking of piss and rot, I haul out the garbage bags sitting at the top of the pile inside—probably the trash they took out late last night or first thing this morning. Stone's phone is sitting under one.

So is the key to the Escalade.

What the fuck? I grab them both, checking out the phone. A handful of missed calls from the prez. A dozen new texts. The earliest unread message is from me—the one I sent after deleting Anna's photo, just before heading to bed.

If he didn't read it, the phone was probably already in the Dumpster by then. Maybe even while I was still inside the Ponderosa. But I didn't get wind of any fights going down out here last night. That kind of news travels through a bar fast.

No blood. No cracked screen. No scuff marks on the case. Stone would never go easy. If someone wanted to get these off him, there'd likely be some sign.

And no message to me, telling me what the hell

Stone was thinking. Is he out there playing the hero? If so, maybe leaving the key fob was message enough. He'd have known I'd find his phone. Maybe he thought whoever was after the girl might find them that way, too, but by leaving access to the rig he wasn't leaving me stranded.

I take off for the Escalade. Whatever was going on, he'd have grabbed a few weapons first. Maybe left a message there.

As soon as I reach the rental, I check the stash behind the front seats. My blood runs cold.

He didn't take a weapon. There's no scenario in this world where he wouldn't have grabbed one of these guns before heading off with the girl.

Which means the scene I'd been playing out in my mind—he heads for the Escalade, arms himself, then tosses the phone and keys somewhere I'll find them—just got blown to hell.

He never got as far as the Escalade last night. Maybe never got farther than the Ponderosa's back lot.

Fucking hell. Heart pounding, I strap on a .45 before double-timing it back toward the bar. A block away, a message comes in over Stone's phone.

Anna. I freeze in place, reading it.

Red called. He asked me to go out to the ranch to be with Jenny today. Does that mean what I think that means?

I close my eyes, teeth clenched. This is a line I shouldn't cross. But Anna won't know. And Stone will forgive me. He'd rather that I answer her than make her worry about why he's not responding—and it isn't hard to guess that she's texting instead of calling because she's crying. Something this important, she wouldn't leave to a message. So she must be hurting enough without me adding fear for Stone to it.

And I'll find him. She's got nothing to worry about.

Yes. I text back. *The boss called this morning. Red's taking his final ride.*

There's a long pause before her response appears.

I knew it. God. I should be heading out there but I'm just sitting in the car bawling.

A groan rips from me, reading that. Wishing I could say what I wanted to. *You're tearing me apart, sweetheart. Because I can't hold you. Because I can't make it better.*

My chest aching, I make myself say what Stone would. That's easy. I've seen them together hundreds of times. They tease and poke at each other viciously, but when shit gets rough, Stone's softer with her than I've ever seen him. The affection between them runs deep but it's not hidden.

You'll be all right. Just hang in there, pipsqueak. I use his favorite nickname for her.

I will, she replies, and I can almost see her pulling it together, wiping her eyes, drawing a deep breath. *Are you and Gunner coming back today?*

Just seeing her write my name twists me up. I wish I had something better to tell her than, *Don't know yet. Something came up here. We might be delayed.*

Hurry.

I'll try. With everything in me.

Let me know when you have an ETA. Stay safe and I love you.

God, those words. They hit me like a sledgehammer. And she says them so easy. Stone would say them right back.

My fingers hit the wrong letters a hundred times, but I finally get it out. *Love you, too.*

The first time I ever said it. She doesn't even know it's coming from me.

And I could stay here longer, reading her last text over and over, but now it's time to get moving. I pocket the phone and head toward the Ponderosa. They've got security cameras. One way or another, I'm going to find out what the fuck happened to Stone. Then I'm going to find him.

She's not losing her brother. I'm sure as hell not losing my friend.

And I won't stop until I bring him home.

FOUR

SUNDAY

Anna: Any idea when you're coming home?

Stone: Not yet.

Anna: Why?

Stone: Club business.

Anna: Yeah, yeah. You're okay, though?

Stone: Everything's all right, pipsqueak. Just taking longer than it should.

Anna: You got a second to call me?

Stone: It's a bad time to talk.

Anna: Boo. Okay. Try to call mom tomorrow, at least.
Stone: I'll try.

TUESDAY

Anna: Are you still up?
Stone: Yes.
Anna: Did you knock up Tiffany?
Stone: Tiffany?
Anna: Yeah. TIFFANY.
Stone: As far as I know…no.
Anna: She came into the Wolf Den today, crying and saying you're the daddy, and asking where are you? You never return her calls.
Stone: She hasn't called me.
Anna: Maybe you're just not answering. Considering that you don't even answer your SISTER'S calls.
Stone: Talking isn't as easy as texting right now.
Anna: Well, maybe you should text your baby mama.
Stone: Tiffany who?
Anna: OMG. You don't even remember her? She said it was true love.
Stone: I guess not.
Anna: She said you had a magical night during Halloween. She was dressed as a pink unicorn with fairy wings.
Stone: Gunner and I went on a run over to the coast on Halloween.

Anna: So did you hook up with a fluffy pink unicorn beneath a full moon atop a sparkling sand dune? She said the waves crashed and sang a lullaby as you cried out your love.

Stone: …are you just fucking with me?

Anna: Maybe. You should really come home. You've got a magical unicorn baby waiting to suckle at your manly teat.

Stone: If I wasn't laughing so hard, I'd say you just permanently shriveled the testicles of every man in a ten-mile radius.

Anna: And you're seriously having an off day. I expected you to be ready with pictures of a unicorn baby snuggled against your chest. Just in case I ever said you were going to have one.

Stone: I'll be prepared next time. A unicorn baby with rainbow tail.

Anna: And a glittery mane. BTW, I'm changing your name to Unicorn Daddy in my phone.

Unicorn Daddy: It's unfortunate any dirty jokes about horns would be too inappropriate to send you.

Anna: Why?

Unicorn Daddy: Because you're my sister.

Anna: That never stopped you before. So I guess things aren't going so well, are they?

Unicorn Daddy: Not as well as I'd like.

Anna: Put Gunner in charge. He knows how to get shit done.

Unicorn Daddy: Gunner's a useless fucking asshole.

Anna: Yikes. Trouble in biker paradise?

Unicorn Daddy: Just frustrated. Not getting the info I need.

Anna: Beat someone up.

Unicorn Daddy: I tried that.

Anna: Okay, well. Hang in there. The sun will come out tomorrow and all that crap. And speaking of the sun about to come up, I'm heading to bed.

Unicorn Daddy: I wish I was, too.

Unicorn Daddy: Heading to my bed, I mean. And sleeping. That won't happen for a few hours, though.

Unicorn Daddy: Goodnight, pipsqueak.

Anna: Get some sleep, dork.

THURSDAY

Anna: Red's funeral is set for Saturday :-(

Unicorn Daddy: I know. The boss told me yesterday.

Anna: You'll be coming back at least for the weekend, right?

Unicorn Daddy: Maybe.

Anna: Maybe? It's Red.

Unicorn Daddy: I know. But if I leave and something pops up while I'm gone, the whole thing might be fucked.

Anna: Boo. Look at my disappointed face.

Anna: <attachment annawashere456.jpeg>

Unicorn Daddy: You look tired.

Anna: Gee, thanks.

Unicorn Daddy: Damn autocorrect. I really typed, "You look beautiful."

Anna: Who the hell are you? What are you doing with my brother's phone?

Unicorn Daddy: What did you use to write ANNA WAS HERE? Because it looks like elephant jizz.

Anna: There you are. Phew. And it's whipped cream.

Unicorn Daddy: Does the boss know you're squirting whipped cream all over his bar?

Anna: It wouldn't be the first time. But Saxon's out at the ranch with Jenny.

Unicorn Daddy: How is she?

Anna: Feeling about as shitty as you'd expect.

Unicorn Daddy: And you?

Anna: You're really asking how I am?

Unicorn Daddy: Yes.

Anna: Well, I'm also about as shitty as you'd expect. On the upside, though… No, there's no upside. Unless you count the upside of Burnout's ass, which is currently hanging out of his pants. I'm not sure who he's banging but he's got her bent over the pool table.

Unicorn Daddy: Look away. Trust me. I've seen that nightmare before. Still have PTSD thanks to it.

Anna: No kidding. His ass is so hairy you could French braid his butt crack.

Unicorn Daddy: You could. But a ponytail would be more symmetrical when observed from the side.

Anna: He's got so much hair, I'm pretty sure the ponytail would be longer than what he's got in front.

Unicorn Daddy: Maybe a bun? Or is that redundant, given the placement?

Anna: It could be the new man bun. And those suggestions had to come from Gunner, because you'd never think about whether something is symmetrical or redundant.

Unicorn Daddy: Guilty.

Anna: Well, tell him Hi. And also tell him thanks a lot, since now I'm picturing a swirly ass-bun and giggling harder than is appropriate, considering A) Burnout is humping someone in front of me and B) Everyone else is drunk and grieving. So I'm putting my phone away and getting back to work.

Unicorn Daddy: I'd better get back to work, too.

Anna: Yep. Be careful down there, and I love you, and all that crap.

Unicorn Daddy: All that crap right back to you.

FIVE

ANNA

If the Guinness Book of World Records had an entry for "witnessed the most badass bikers sobbing," my name would be written there. It's a job hazard for every bartender. Some guys, I only have to pour them a couple of drinks and it doesn't matter if they're weekend warriors or hardened criminals. The tears just start flowing.

But if Guinness ever tries to immortalize me with a world record, I won't include the tears I'm seeing on a few of the Hellfire Riders' cheeks as Red Erickson is laid to rest on the hillside behind his house. There's no drunken blubbering from these guys now. Just deep, quiet grief.

If I hadn't already cried myself dry, my tears would be joining theirs.

On my left, Jenny Erickson stares blindly at the coffin, her face white and her eyes red. She's all cried out, too. Now she stands rigidly, her arms wrapped around her middle, and I know she's not hearing any of the words being spoken over her dad. I know the only thing holding her up is sheer willpower and the strong support of Saxon Gray, the Hellfire Riders' prez.

I also know she'll make it through. She always does. Because she's as stubborn as Red was and it's one of the reasons we became friends so many years ago—she just didn't give up.

Jenny often calls me the stubborn one. I'm not. Not really. I just never know when to quit. Lately I've realized that's something I need to learn.

My reason is standing on the opposite side of Red's coffin. Zach Cooper—my brother's friend. For years, they fought together as Marines, and my brother called him 'Zed.' Now they ride together as members of the Hellfire Riders MC, and he goes by 'Gunner' instead.

I would call Gunner my friend, too…but it's not that simple.

I wish it were simple. Maybe seeing him would hurt less—and despite every promise I make to myself, I can't stop looking.

When I met him ten years ago, I thought he was the most beautiful man I'd ever seen. Although time has hardened each of his features, and although he looks like he hasn't slept or eaten much the past few days…he still is.

I'm not the only one who thinks so. Even here, where the atmosphere is heavy with grief, some of the women are stealing glances at him. I can't blame them. The first couple of times I laid eyes on Zach Cooper, I couldn't stop staring. He just didn't seem *real*. People just aren't that beautiful outside of movies or magazines — and everyone knows that's makeup and lighting, not real life. Yet there he was. So I kept looking, until looking wasn't enough. Until I needed to get deeper.

But he never let me in, and I never got much deeper than his skin.

Sometimes that's deep enough, though. Small changes on the surface often betray what's going on below. Ten years after our first meeting on the side of a highway, his cold is colder. His edges are sharper.

His hot is hotter.

His glossy black hair is slick with rain, his head solemnly bowed — but he's tall, so despite his downturned head, his face isn't hidden. Every breathtaking feature is laid bare before me. A few days' growth of beard shadows his sculpted jaw, his decadent mouth firmed against grief. Thick lashes fan across wide, angular cheekbones. Beneath winged eyebrows, his pale blue eyes are downcast, his focus turned inward. Not praying. He doesn't have faith in anything but his fellow Riders. Not crying. The only moisture wetting the stark planes of his cheeks is from the rain.

The downpour softens to a cold drizzle as the Riders' old timers carefully lower Red into the ground. Red's granite headstone is already here. He ordered it months ago, after he learned about the cancer. An older, matching headstone stands beside it—that one was for his wife. Over the years, Jenny and I have been out here on the hillside countless times, laying down flowers and weeding her mother's grave. Now she'll have two graves to take care of. I don't intend to change the part where I'm helping her do it.

I slide my arm through hers. She glances at me, and judging by the glistening in her eyes, she's not really cried out yet.

Judging by the painful lump clogging my throat, I guess neither am I.

Maybe that's why Guinness doesn't have a world record for number of tears shed. There's no limit when you love someone. When you lose someone. There's always more pain to feel. Even when you know the end is coming.

Red knew it was coming. So did Jenny. We all knew. So when Red called me up on Sunday morning, telling me Jenny might need me with her that day, I was crying before I made it out to my car. Because I knew what he wasn't saying—he didn't intend to come back.

Red held on for as long as he could before he took that final ride. Not a single Rider questions what he did.

Though it gutted Jenny, neither does she. By the time he found out about the cancer, there was nothing to do. He couldn't have it removed. Chemo wouldn't stop it. So these last couple of months, the cancer killed him slow until it started killing him fast. By the end, he could barely breathe. He could barely ride. Pretty soon he wouldn't have been able to get on his motorcycle at all. So he went out before that happened—and went out on his own terms.

I've been doing the same thing for more than a decade. Trying to go out on my own terms, cramming as much living into my life as I can. But in the past few months, I've realized I'm really just waiting for death to sneak up on me again and take what it didn't take when I was a kid. I've been waiting for death to get down to business instead of just playing with me, like it did ten years ago, when I found a lump on my breast.

It has to stop. No more waiting for death to catch up to me. I'm not good at quitting anything. But I need to quit living as if I'm about to start dying.

And I need to let go of what's killing me.

So these tears aren't going to dry up yet. There's always more hurt to come. Today I'm crying for Red, and for Jenny—and because of the pain in my chest that threatens to explode every time I look at Gunner.

I should just quit looking. But I can't.

And all those other women are stealing glances, too, but when Gunner looks up, it's directly at me—as if he felt my gaze on him. My breath stops in my chest. If his face is beautiful, then his eyes are something beyond that. Something indescribable.

Crystalline blue, those eyes should appear cold. Glacial. But they're warm, instead. Intense, burning with concern—as if he's silently asking whether I'm all right.

I'm not. I don't know when I will be again. I'll try to get there, though. To 'all right.'

But I'll settle for not hurting so damn much. This pain started out small. Just an ache. But it's been growing for ten years.

And I can't bear the agony anymore.

So I know what I have to do. When something is killing you—if you can, you have to cut it out. No matter how much it hurts. No matter how big the scar. You have to be brave, cut it out, and try to survive without it.

It's just a heart.

SIX

ANNA

An hour after the funeral, I'm in Jenny's kitchen A) working through a pile of dirty dishes and B) desperately trying to think of something I don't like about Gunner, so I can make myself *stop* thinking about him.

That's the problem, though. I've tried to stop wanting him before. Of course I have. It just doesn't work.

I have to cut my heart out…but first I have to find some way to sharpen the knife. Because just getting over him?

Been there. Tried that. Have the T-shirt that says, *Anna failed spectacularly.*

Okay, and also C) I'm hiding a little, because I keep crying over Red, and I *really* don't like showing my hurt to anyone outside my family.

But I can't pretend losing Red doesn't leave a big, gaping hole in my chest—and my mom keeps touching my shoulder or my back every time she passes through the kitchen. I'm not sure if she's comforting me or herself. I just know I had to tell her "No more hugs," because every time she wrapped her arms around me I teared up again.

As a therapist-turned-high school counselor, my mom's a big fan of crying. It's cathartic, cleansing. But she's just as much a fan of respecting personal and emotional space.

Her emotional space is usually thick. She lets a few of us in—my dad, my brother, me—but considering how often she slips quietly into other people's heads and hearts, she doesn't let many of them slip close in return.

Today that space seems thinner, her emotions showing more easily. I don't think it's just the ache of losing Red or hurting for Jenny. This is more like the quiet fragility that sometimes came over her when my brother was deployed overseas, during those long days between hearing about a marine's death on the news and hearing from Stone himself.

But my brother's fine. I'll admit the past week had me a little worried—he's only been texting at weird times and he sounds *odd*. Not just stressed and frustrated but barely like himself. Gunner's back, though, and the way they're joined at the hip, that means Stone will be around here somewhere, too. I wasn't sure they'd make it to the funeral at all but they must have flown in at the last minute.

So my mom has no reason to worry about Stone. Not that being the Riders' enforcer isn't dangerous, because it is. I don't think my mom knows all of what goes down in the club, though.

It's better if she doesn't know. And even if she guesses, it's better if she isn't aware of all the details.

I shouldn't be aware of all the details, either. But that's another side effect of working at a biker bar. Some of the Riders talk when they're drunk. But even when they aren't drunk, some speak in louder voices than they should, simply to be heard over the music—and sometimes they talk about problems my brother has taken care of.

But Mom knows Stone can handle himself. And a threat that could stop someone like my brother? I can't even imagine. It'd have to be something huge. Terrifying.

There's nothing like that threatening him.

So I think my mom's current fragility stems from worry about me, instead. Maybe thinking of how I could have been the one they buried today. I'm high-risk for new cancers, after all. And ever since I heard that Red was sick, I've thought about it more and more.

My mom might be thinking of it, too. But I won't ask if she is. It's possible that I'm wrong and she's simply grieving Red. Our families were close. Jenny is almost like another daughter.

Bringing up my old sickness would only make her worry more, anyway. There's something she taught me a long time ago: Whenever someone assumes to know what you are thinking about, that person usually reveals what is occupying her own mind. So I'm not going to mention the leukemia now and make her think that I'm obsessing over how long I have to live.

Because I'm not. I'm quitting all that, too.

I'll continue doing all the healthy crap that I've been doing for years. But I won't keep expecting death to jump out of the shadows. Instead I'm going to assume that I'll get the typical eighty years—and start living like it, too. And if I get sick again…well, I'll deal with it then.

The kitchen door swings open and my mom comes in carrying another empty platter from the buffet set up in the dining room. A burst of conversation follows her through before the door muffles the noise again.

"Megan's rounding up some of the other ladies," she announces. "They'll take care of the remaining cleanup."

The kitchen counters are empty. All I have left to clean is the platter she's holding. "It's pretty much taken care of."

"You're only saying that because you haven't seen what's left."

I can imagine. Almost all of the Hellfire Riders are here, along with their wives and old ladies, but Red wasn't just part of a motorcycle club. He co-owned a construction company and had enough employees to fill another house. Then there are neighbors and friends, like my mom and dad. He was well-liked in Pine Valley, and in addition to paying their last respects, many visitors are bringing food to share.

While she slips the platter into the dishwater, I grab a towel and start drying my hands. "How does Jenny look?" I ask.

"Guess."

I smile a little. I can't remember exactly when we started doing this, but it's a game we've played for a while: Take everything you know about someone and guess what their reaction will be to any given scenario.

With Jenny, it's not really guessing. I know exactly what's going on out there. "She's holding up, because she's got something to occupy her with all these people here. And if I told her that we're back here washing dishes, she'd freak out and feel guilty because we're cleaning."

The arch of my mom's eyebrows and the curve of her mouth says that I got it in one. Stone claims I often wear the same expression — except that, on my face, it just looks smug.

I don't look a thing like my mother, despite wishing fervently for her genes when I was younger. Wishing didn't turn my hair blond or my eyes blue. It didn't make me any taller, either. I've been called an elf more times than I can remember.

Which…all right, I can't really argue that. And I'm

not like one of the majestic elves from *Lord of the Rings*, unfortunately. My mom might pass for Galadriel; stick me in green tights and add pointed ears, and I could pass for one of Santa's helpers.

I don't have any of my dad's genes, either, but—personality-wise—I probably resemble him more.

She sighs, then looks around at the counters as if searching for something to do. "Have you seen Aaron yet?"

Unease skitters up my spine. I understand why I might not have seen my brother yet, considering the crowd and how I've been holed up in the kitchen, but I can't imagine why he wouldn't have sought out our mom for a word and a hug.

But he's been gone a week, chasing down God knows what. Maybe he's holed up, too, filling in a few of the Riders about what's going on.

"I haven't, but I saw Zach," I tell her. My mom doesn't refer to either my brother or Gunner by his road name. "So Aaron's probably around somewhere. But good luck trying to text him and telling him to get his butt in gear."

Not with the bad reception out here.

"It's a miracle if he answers promptly even *with* reception," she says with dry amusement. "I usually have better luck going through Zach."

God, that shouldn't hurt, hearing how easily she communicates with Gunner. From practically the moment he arrived in Pine Valley—way back when he and Stone were still in the Marine Corps, and he was visiting my brother while they were on leave—my mom and dad treated Zach Cooper like he was another son.

But, me. Jesus. Unless Stone or someone else includes me in a conversation with him, Gunner barely even speaks to me. I've never texted him. Yet my mother does all the time.

"Oh," I finally say, but I can't really remember what I'm responding to.

Her voice softens. "Anna. Do you want to talk about it?"

Yes. But if I do I'll just start crying again. "I really can't."

"All right."

Her reply is so accepting, so easy. Because she probably knows I'm going to spill my guts to her, anyway. And she probably knows exactly what this is all about.

I blurt, "Tell me something bad about Zach."

Her brows shoot up. "Bad?"

"Yeah."

"Why do you believe I know anything bad about him?"

"Because you know everything about everyone. You probably see right through him."

She regards me for a long moment. "Why do you believe there is something to tell?"

I notice she doesn't deny knowing everything about him. "Because there's *always* something to tell. He can't be as nice and as perfect as he seems—"

"Perfect?"

Oh shit. That word says way too much. But since I can't go back I go forward. "Everyone has secrets. He must, too."

"And those secrets must be bad?"

"Why would anyone keep good things secret?"

She gives me a pointed look. "Good things…such as caring for someone? Yes, indeed. Why would someone keep that secret?"

I groan in frustration. She always does this. You start talking with her about someone else and she flips it around and makes it about you.

But all right. She has a point. This *is* about me. "I need a kick in the ass. Something to make me stop. Seeing him all the time… I just can't. Not anymore."

She sighs a little. "I know, honey."

"But I don't…" My breath hitches in my chest. "I don't want to leave."

"I'm selfishly pleased to hear that."

Because she must have wondered if I would. "But what should I do? Just tell him I don't want him around anymore? Don't come to my house, don't sit at the bar? But it's Aaron's house, too. And at the Den, he sits at the bar to keep an eye on everyone." As sergeant at arms, that's his job—just like slinging drinks is mine. "I don't want to make things awkward for you and Dad, either."

"It wouldn't." Her steady gaze holds mine. "Unless you're asking us to choose between you and Zach? Or suggesting that we shouldn't invite him to our home anymore? No more Thanksgiving, no more Christmas?"

"I'm not suggesting that." I never would.

"Then whatever you do, however you decide to move forward, the only awkwardness will be between the two of you." Elegant brows arch over eyes sparking with sudden laughter. "Which will be no different from all the awkward silences of previous years."

God. "Thanks, Mom. I'm so glad my angst amuses you."

Though I know it doesn't really amuse her. She's just very good at helping me balance my emotions—and at pulling my head out of my ass.

She takes my hands, her expression serious again. "This will be good for you."

"Moving on?"

"Moving *forward*. It might be good for Zach, too."

I scoff at that. "I don't think it'll make a difference to him at all."

She gives me an unreadable glance. "I suppose you'll find out."

I don't think there's anything to find out. Nothing's different now than it was ten years ago. I'm just Stone's little sister. "Well, whatever. I'm just going to try to get over him."

"Yes. Try."

Oh, God. She's using her agreeable tone, which makes it impossible to tell whether she's actually saying, "Yes, you *should* try," or "Go ahead and try, but we both know it's futile."

To argue with her would be futile, too. Because she's not even arguing. She's agreeing. Maybe. But that problem I have with not being able to quit? Yeah.

"I'm not in love with him," I tell her.

"Of course you aren't."

Lord help me. There goes her *other* agreeable tone. And I should really, really quit.

But I can't. "I don't know him well enough to be in love with him."

"Now *that's* true." She kisses my forehead while I try to wrap my brain around what *wasn't* true. "Now stop digging your hole. Go on and check in on your father. You know how he gets when he's talking to Thorne, and I don't need a new motorcycle sitting in our garage."

"The motorcycle is never the problem," I tell her. "It's the kutte you have to worry about."

The kutte and all the obligations that come with it.

"The way your dad drives, I worry about the motor-cycle." She purses her lips and adds lightly, "I'd enjoy it if he just wore the vest."

Oh, Lord. I'm old enough to handle the thought of my parents getting their kink on, but…

Okay, no. I'm not.

And she likely said it to send me scurrying out of the kitchen that much faster. Guess how Anna will react to the sexualized image of her dad in a kutte? There's only one possible outcome: I skedaddle.

My mom knows me well. So she must know I'm not in love with Gunner. I'm *not*. You have to know someone before you can fall in love, and Gunner never let me know him.

I know some things. After almost a decade, of course I do. He's only lived in Pine Valley for the last six years, but he's been Stone's friend longer than that.

I know he went straight into the Marine Corps after high school, and that's where he met my brother.

I know he's a nice guy. Some women say nice is boring, but not me. I can't stand assholes who are dicks to everyone and who don't care if they hurt someone. And Gunner, I knew he was nice before I knew anything else about him—even before I knew how gorgeous he was. Because we met when he pulled over on a highway to help me change a flat tire. I didn't know who he was; he didn't know who I was. But he stopped in the middle of nowhere to lend a hand.

I know *nice* doesn't mean he's not really fucking dangerous. I've seen what his fists have done and I've heard his bullets have done worse.

I'm not supposed to know that, but I overheard it at the Wolf Den. What I've never heard? Anything that makes me think less of him.

I know he likes his job on the city's maintenance crew because he enjoys working outside. I also know his favorite part of the workday is lunch. Not because he eats, but because he pulls a paperback out of his back pocket or opens up the ebook reader on his phone and sits down with it for an hour. He's read more than almost any other person I've met—and every Christmas, he gives me copies of the books he liked best that year.

I don't know why he spends almost every holiday with my family. I mean, of course it's because my mom and dad have issued a standing invitation to him. But I don't know why he never goes home.

I know he has issues with his own family, because any time they come up in a conversation, he can't change the subject fast enough. I don't know what those issues are, and I don't think many of the Hellfire Riders do, either, because that's another thing I *haven't* heard them talking about at the bar.

But they do talk about how he never hooks up with anyone, and there's a bet going around about whether he's a virgin. Or married. Or gay.

I know he's not any of those, because he told me so the first time we met. But I also know a lot of the women who hang around the Riders don't call him Gunner. They call him the Damn Shame. As in, it's a damn shame all that prime male beauty is being wasted because he doesn't use it. I've never seen him with anyone. I've never heard of him being with a woman—and I *would* have heard about it.

I don't know why he doesn't sleep around. Heaven knows he gets enough offers. A couple of times, I was the one making those offers.

I know he can kiss like a house on fire, and I know the hot taste of his mouth, and I know the rough sound he makes in the back of his throat when I press up against him. But that was a long time ago, when he wouldn't let me buy him a drink as a thank-you for changing my tire. He took a kiss, instead.

Then he found out who my brother was and never tried to kiss me again. And when I tried to kiss him a few months ago—drunk off my ass—he gently pushed me away.

I know why. Or at least, I know what he said. That he'd be taking advantage of me. And, "It's better to keep things simple."

I don't know if he truly believes things are simple between us. I don't know what he imagines complicated is.

I know I never told Gunner how much his rejection hurt me. Instead I shrugged and pretended it didn't matter. I *always* shrug and pretend it doesn't matter.

But I'm not in love with him. How can I love someone who rarely talks to me, unless my brother's around? Who won't let me get to know him? No. If I love anything, it's the *idea* of him—and the hope of what could be.

But it's time to hope for more. I can't hold an idea close. An idea can't love me back. I know that for sure.

Just as I know Gunner will never be the one who gives me more.

But, oh my God. Knowing that *hurts*, as if every time I take a breath, a burning knife slices through my chest.

Luckily today is the one day it doesn't matter if that pain shows. Today, no one will wonder why my eyes are red and my mascara is gone. I don't like to expose myself when I'm hurting, but if my voice sounds thick and if my emotions seem raw when I see Gunner, everyone will assume it's just for Red.

Thank God, I don't see Gunner now.

From the kitchen, I make my way through the formal dining room and past the table loaded with food, slowly winding around a crowd of plates and familiar faces. I haven't been out of the kitchen since the funeral, so I'm stopped for too many greetings and hugs to count. Along the way, I steal Picasso's beer—he owes me one for driving him home from the Den the night before, when he was too smashed to ride—and finally emerge into the great room, where I spot Jenny standing in front of the fireplace.

She's still pale, and strands of brown hair are beginning to escape her French braid, but she's smiling and nodding at something Millie Wright is saying to her. Our third grade teacher has Jenny's hands clasped in her wrinkled ones, and I know the older woman probably has the same twinkle in her blue eyes as she did twenty years ago. Jenny was always one of her favorites. I…was a little more difficult.

But Jenny's in good hands right now. Which means I ought to go in search of my dad.

He won't be hard to find. Mom said he was talking to Thorne, and there's one of two places the Hellfire Riders' vice-president will be: in Red's garage or on the deck with the rest of the smokers.

Probably not the garage. Thorne and Red rode and worked together most of their lives. At the funeral, his face was like shattered stone. The garage would be too close to Red—and too painful because Red's not there with him.

And sure enough, I find my dad outside. It's not raining now, but the November night is cold enough to make my breath puff like smoke, and the cap sleeves of my black dress offer no protection against the chill. My dad sees me and pulls me in close.

I slide my arm beneath his tweed blazer, holding tight to his whip-thin waist, my throat one big lump again. *My dad.* I can't imagine losing him. And even though I don't see him every day, I can't imagine never again seeing his balding head and horn-rimmed glasses and infectious grin. He's not as big as most of the guys out here—at five-foot-four, he's barely taller than me—but he feels safer and warmer than a wall of muscle could ever be.

"Mom says you can't buy a motorcycle," I tell him.

He laughs and gives me a little squeeze. "Do you think she's practicing reverse psychology and that's her way of encouraging me?"

"No, I think she'd kill you."

"Then I'll suppress the impulse and live another day."

"Good plan." Smiling, I glance away from him to scan the deck. "Have you seen Aaron?"

"Not yet. But I've been hiding out here, so that doesn't

surprise me. How are you holding up?"

I shrug, because there's really no answer to that. He gives me another squeeze and looks to Thorne, who nods at me in greeting before crushing out his cigarette. Like the other Riders, Thorne isn't wearing a suit or his Sunday best. Instead he's wearing his leather kutte over his club best—black jeans, polished boots, a black button-down shirt.

I know some of the guests consider the kuttes disrespectful, especially the older vests that are beaten up by time and miles, but the kuttes represent the opposite of disrespect. All of the Riders have already sewn a patch with Red's name into their leather, declaring he's still their brother and he's still with them, and he won't be forgotten.

Thorne's eyes hold mine for a long second, his gaze searching my face as if there's something he expects to see. But he doesn't say anything, just looks away as Jeremy Marshall and Travis Jones join us, beers in hand. Both work for Red and Thorne's company—Travis as an engineer and Jeremy as a laborer, I think. I only know Jeremy by sight and by his preferred drink, but I went to high school with Travis, which unfortunately makes him think we have more in common than we really do. He's not my favorite person in the world, but he's not the worst. He's not an overt jerk or a creep. Mostly he's just always *too much*. When something is funny, his laugh is too loud. When he greets you, his smile is too big. And when the occasion calls for being upset, he's always the most upset, the most offended, the most ready to do something about it.

Right now, his sorrow is a physical weight on his face, pulling all of his features into a mask of grief. Except he wasn't really a good friend of Red's, so he's *too* sorrowful.

Especially since he's standing next to Thorne, who'd been Red's right hand for decades.

The older man bears it quietly, as he bears almost everything. An exchange follows between the men about what a damn shame Red's death was, and what a good guy he was, then Travis's attention turns to my dad.

There's his big smile, jarring after the deep display of grief. "How's retirement suiting you, Paul?"

"It suits me," my dad says, though he's not really retired. He's taking classes up in Bend, working on a second degree and eventually a second career, because real estate wasn't suiting him anymore — even though he did well enough he *could* retire if he wanted to. "My thumbs are more limber than they've ever been, playing Aaron's old Nintendo every spare minute."

I suppress a grin, because my dad sounds like he's kidding but he's not. He's become obsessed to the point that, just yesterday, Mom sent me a picture of him wearing a Mario T-shirt. I wouldn't be surprised if he pulled up the legs of his charcoal pants and exposed a pair of Yoshi socks.

But the mention of my name turns Travis's attention to me. "Since you're still working at the Wolf Den, Anna,

I guess nothing's opened up for you?"

For heaven's sake. No matter how many times I tell him… "I haven't been looking."

He nods like he knows exactly how that is. "Job market's rough. I guess I thought something would come up for you, though. Or maybe your mom could put in a good word for you somewhere."

"I'm happy where I am."

"I suppose you'd have to go back to school first, anyways. Take some refresher courses. I don't imagine those pre-med degrees last long. Though it might not be so easy to get into Stanford the second time around."

"It wasn't easy the first time." And it wasn't a 'pre-med' degree. It was a double major in psychology and biology.

"Heh!" Travis responds as if that's a joke—as if, because I was accepted, then it must have been easy. While I grit my teeth, he looks to Thorne. "I was real lucky you and Red had an opening for me right after finished up at Oregon State. Anna's not the only college graduate out there who's stuck waitressing."

Jesus. "I'm not waitressing."

And even if I was, he still wouldn't hear the main point of it all: My job suits me perfectly. I was on a pre-med track because I planned to head into psychiatry. Tending a bar sometimes feels like the same thing and the late hours fit into my life a lot better.

"Close enough," Travis says and looks to my dad again. "I guess Mrs. Wall must spend a lot of time pushing job ideas Anna's way. I remember in high school, we couldn't turn around without her pointing us toward an application or scholarship. A real go-getter. I can't imagine she'd give up on her own daughter."

"On Anna? Clara doesn't push anything on her." My dad glances at me, slightly baffled, then all at once he frowns. "I thought you liked working at the Den. Are you looking for another job?"

"I do like it," I reassure him. "And I'm not."

"Well, then," he says, shrugging.

And that settles it.

Every relationship in my family is basically that simple. Sure, we fight and push each other's buttons, but when we boil it all down, they love me and want me to be happy. I want the same for them. And somehow, we've managed that. Not that it's always been easy.

My dad calls himself a stumbler—whenever a bad situation comes up, he stumbles into something good from it. He claims his stumbling luck started when he met my mom, when he literally stumbled down a flight of stairs, breaking his leg and slamming into her when he reached the bottom.

Years later, about the time my mom and dad realized they couldn't have children of their own, one of his cousins was killed in a car wreck, leaving behind a toddler—Aaron, my brother. They adopted him, then adopted me not long afterward.

Then I got sick. Acute lymphocytic leukemia. I was

five.

The individual cure rate for children is high for that specific cancer, but not every family survives having a kid with leukemia. The stress, the fear, the medical bills… they can be as toxic to a healthy relationship as chemo is to healthy cells. Some parents look for more comfort than a spouse can give. Some siblings resent the family's focus on the sick child. For my family, the two year battle seemed to unite us, instead. I was just a little girl, but I felt it. Even though money was tight, even though my mom had to spend so much time away from her office that she lost half her clients, even though my dad lost his job as a property inspector—which meant his health insurance went bye-bye—it was as if Mom, Dad, and Aaron banded together and decided that as long as I was okay, all of the other hardships didn't matter. Even after the cancer went into remission, that never really changed.

And my leukemia was the bad thing that brought us here all those years ago. After losing his old position, my dad stumbled into a new job in real estate, we moved from Portland to central Oregon just in time for him to ride the local housing boom, and my mom began working as a counselor at Pine Valley High.

Everything since then has been pretty damn good.

I'm not a stumbler, but I know I've lived a charmed life—and it's all because of my mom, my dad, and Aaron. Because they brought me into this family.

So what if I get choked up about it now and then?

Like right now.

I simply can't imagine losing any of them.

SEVEN

GUNNER

"I guess Blowback didn't have to break your pretty little head open, after all," Zoomie says to me as we grab a couple of stools at the bar in the Erickson's rec room. "Good thing, since you can't afford to lose the brains."

I toss her a bottle of beer and sit. "You've been doing all right without any."

"When you're this fucking hot, you don't need brains." Sliding her hand over her pale blond buzzcut, Zoomie grins one of her dazzling grins. Her knuckles are roughed up, and a butterfly bandage at her hairline tells me that when she and Blowback went looking for info about the Iron Blood, they didn't always ask nicely. "But maybe Blowback's just deferring to the prez, so *he* can bust your head open."

Maybe. Three days ago, I put off the prez when he told me to come home in time to pay my respects to Red. Then Blowback showed up in Phoenix last night and told me I had two choices: to fly back to Oregon willingly or be dragged unconscious aboard the plane.

Coming from most men, that threat would be bullshit and bluster. Not when it comes from Blowback. And if most men threatened me, I'd change their tune quick. I'm good with my fists and feet. Damn good.

Blowback would wipe the floor with my bleeding corpse.

It didn't come to that, though. I'm stubborn but not stupid. In the past week I tracked down members of every single club that attended the rally in Cactus Gulch. If there was any trace of Stone to find, if there was anyone who'd seen what had gone down in the Ponderosa's back lot, I'd have found them. But by last night I was so damn tired, I don't know whether I'd have recognized a trace if I'd seen it. The few hours on the plane this morning was the first solid shut-eye I've had in a week.

I'm still tired as hell, but my head's on straight again. So it's the right time to sit down with the prez and the few Hellfire Riders who are aware of what's really going on with Stone.

There aren't many of us. The prez wanted to keep this quiet and I assume he's acting on the advice of Blowback, the Riders' warlord. And although a part of me wants to blow this shit wide open, hoping something will shake out, it's probably best to play it Blowback's way — because although blowing shit open sounds damn satisfying, we don't even have a solid target yet.

And, Christ. I don't want to see the look on Anna's face when we tell her Stone is missing. Seeing her standing over Red's grave, seeing all her hurt and grief…that's more pain than she should be feeling in a lifetime. Add on her realization of how I've been pretending to be her brother, texting her for more than a week? Jesus.

Better to just get Stone home.

Blowback settles back against the edge of the poker table. His posture's casual, his arms crossed over his chest, boots planted at shoulder-width. But you only have to look at his eyes to see there's never anything casual going through his head. They're empty, as if every emotion in him is dead.

I've killed. It's sometimes simple but it's never easy, even if it's necessary. For Blowback, killing another man is about as difficult as putting on a pair of socks.

His gaze warms slightly when it skips over to Zoomie, then flattens again when he glances toward the door. "We just waiting for Thorne?"

The prez nods and drags out a leather club chair from

beneath the table. Normally we'd be holding a meeting like this in the prez's office at the clubhouse, but Saxon doesn't want to head out there. I'm guessing he doesn't want to leave Jenny, even though her house is full of mourners and she's surrounded by people wishing her well. He doesn't want to be gone if she needs him.

It's the same reason Blowback had to drag me home. I wasn't going to leave Arizona, not without Stone—fearing that the second I looked away, I'd miss a sign pointing to where he'd been taken.

The prez sinks into the chair and slides a big hand through his dark hair, looking exhausted as fuck. It's not often he shows that. Hell, he rarely even sits his ass down, let alone sits low in a seat with his legs sprawled, rubbing his face and letting loose a heavy sigh.

He eyes me. "Glad you could finally fucking show up."

There's no answer to that and he's not really pissed. If he'd been the one with Stone last weekend, if a brother had vanished right beneath his damn nose, someone would have had to drag him home, too.

The door opens and the veep comes in. Thorne's got almost thirty years on everyone else in the room, but it's not just age sitting on his face today. Haggard and worn, he looks like the rest of us have probably felt since Stone went missing and Red took that final ride.

The difference is, I'll be getting my friend back. Red won't ever be making that return trip to Thorne's side.

"This it?" Thorne asks and claims the stool next to me,

bringing with him the scent of cold winter air and Marlboros—a scent that takes me straight back to a woodpile behind my mother's house, with my father sitting on a tree stump with a cigarette dangling from his fingers, wearing a grin on a face that looks just like mine.

Jesus. I rub my eyes, try to focus.

"This is it," the prez says, then looks to Blowback. "So where are we at?"

Where we are is nowhere new. Most of the intel Blowback has on the Iron Blood is essentially what we already knew—but he lays it out again, to make sure we're all on the same page before we move forward.

In the past week, he and Zoomie picked up a hell of a lot of details—the members' road names and real names, the location of their clubhouse, which MCs they're friendly with—but none of it's what we're looking for: the Iron Blood's connection to the Cage.

If there *is* a connection. We're making a lot of assumptions right now. But my gut says it all fits.

Quiet falls when Blowback winds up. We're all riding the razor edge of exhaustion and frustration, and for a long moment we just look at each other's grim faces, as if hoping to see some solution dawn bright in someone else's eyes.

But the only solution I'm beginning to see isn't bright. It's like a rotten virus worming into my head.

It's been squirming there all week. And it looks a lot like Strawman.

"Can we grab one of the Iron Blood?" The veep breaks the silence. "Make them talk?"

Blowback shakes his head. "If we did, we'd lose them. When the cartel running the Cage gets wind of a club fucking up, they cut all ties. That's what they did with the Devil's Hangmen."

After Zoomie was taken. The Devil's Hangmen were a pain in our ass before that, forming a new local chapter and taking over the Eighty-Eight's old territory in the next county over. Then they fucked up by grabbing Zoomie and not delivering her to the Cage—and the whole deal between their club and the cartel went sour when the Hellfire Riders quietly made the cartel's delivery man disappear.

The Devil's Hangmen folded their local chapter and crawled back to Las Vegas. Blowback's source inside their club says the Hangmen have been blacklisted. The cartel won't do business with them again.

But there's always another club that can take their place. With the kind of money a cartel throws around, finding assholes to do business with is never a problem.

The prez says, "We can't risk shaking loose the Iron Blood's connection to the Cage, not when it's the only connection we have—and not with Stone dangling out there." He eyes Blowback. "Can you pose as a prospect, get into their ranks?"

"With more time," the warlord says. "But we don't have enough."

Because if Stone's in the Cage, then every fight is a fight to the death. Every fight might be his last. So we need a way in, and we need it fast.

My chest suddenly weighs a goddamn ton. I don't know how it's so heavy when everything inside it feels so fucking empty.

"I've got a way in," I say.

They all look to me.

"The Notorious Few," I tell them. "They've already got ties to the Iron Blood. Their VP is working out a business arrangement with them. So I'll join up with the Few and find out more."

Zoomie narrows her eyes. "You said the Iron Blood saw you in Cactus Gulch. You don't have a forgettable face. They won't be suspicious if you suddenly show up in another club?"

"They won't know I'm the same person they saw wearing a Hellfire Riders' kutte. There are four members of the Notorious Few who look just like I do." I've never been glad of this before. For the first time, I am. "The Iron Blood won't know the difference."

"Jesus," she says, her flinty gaze raking over my face. "What the hell do they put in the water where you're from?"

"Their own special brand of Kool-Aid." Which probably isn't news to everyone here. Blowback's looking to the prez. I don't know how much the warlord knows about my family, but part of his job is knowing who and what might ever threaten the club and its members. So I wouldn't be surprised if he's aware of exactly who the Notorious Few are.

And I don't know how much he told the prez, but the way the boss is staring at me, I'm thinking Blowback must have mentioned some of it.

"I'd be wearing another kutte," I tell the prez, just so it's clear exactly what'll be required if I do this. "Going in and asking nicely won't cut it. They'll want me to fall in line before they give me anything."

"Then you think they will?"

"Yes."

His eyes are like steel. "And when you come back—will we have trouble then?"

They're not going to let me go again. If I try to leave, it'll come down to blood. Mine, Stone's, theirs.

But I'll deal with that when the time comes. For now I just say, "They'll be pissed. But they won't have much choice."

"Fuck." The boss spits the curse. He doesn't like this. But he probably doesn't see much choice, either.

Zoomie's wearing a frown. "Before you take off your kutte—are we sure this isn't *just* about the girl? We're assuming Stone vanished the same way those other fighters did. We're assuming we're up against something big. But what if it's something small? We run the danger of overlooking him if we're searching for the Cage when we should be searching for this girl and whoever she wanted protection from."

"It could be," I agree. "But that doesn't feel right. If we're speaking of assumptions, her needing protection was also an assumption Stone made. But the only thing Stone and I knew for sure was that she was scared off her ass. And if she was hoping he'd protect her, she wouldn't have drugged him."

The security feed from the Ponderosa showed that. Cherry slipped a roofie into Stone's glass—did it right in front of us. He chugged it down just before they left. After that, it must have been simple to get him out of the Ponderosa's back lot. No noise, no fight. A van could swing by and just load him right up.

"If she saw him fight, she had to know Stone could turn her into pulp," Thorne says. "So to drug someone like him, to risk pissing him off—that'd scare anyone. That says to me she was scared of something worse than what our boy could to do her."

"Something like a goddamn cartel," the prez agrees and looks to me again. "When you heading out?"

If I had a choice, never. But Stone can't afford for me to put this off. "Tomorrow."

Blowback says, "I'm heading out tomorrow, too. I'll keep circling the Iron Blood, dig up what I can from our contacts, maybe find a way to see these cage matches."

"Send me anything you find," I tell him. "I'll do the same."

The warlord nods.

"I want Zoomie to head out with you," the prez says

to Blowback. "No one operates alone right now. You eat together, sleep together, piss together—and take one of the prospects along as another pair of eyes." He looks to me. "Who you taking?"

"No one." When his jaw tightens, I tell him, "The Notorious Few will help, but not unless I say I'm all the way in and I intend to stay that way. If I've got another Rider hovering around, it says I'm not."

"What's the difference? You're going because of Stone."

"They'll allow my loyalty to a friend but not to another club. Because a club is family. And if they think I've got one foot out the door or if I'm relying on anyone but them, I've got nothing. But if I'm wearing their kutte, they'll have my back."

The prez still doesn't like it but he nods. "I want to hear from you every twenty-four hours. You miss two days, we're going in."

I nod. "I've got Stone's phone. I'll use it for updates."

"You've got his phone?" Zoomie's brows shoot high. "Is that how you've been keeping this shit quiet? What are we telling Anna? His family?"

"Nothing yet." It rips me up to think of them hurting, worrying. "We'll get him back and they won't even know he was gone."

Her lips flatten. "So we'll keep lying to her?"

"Yes," the prez cuts in and his tone tells her not to argue. "For now."

"The fewer who know the better," Blowback adds.

"We don't want the Iron Blood or the cartel wrapping this up tighter than they already have. Right now, they probably know we're asking questions, but because we weren't asking the *right* questions, they knew we weren't anywhere close to the truth. That'll change if too many brothers know—because even if we tell them to keep their mouths shut, they'll try to help and start asking their buddies about the Iron Blood. Before long it'll get to another MC, maybe one who's got a brother missing. Then they'll charge in and it'll all go to shit."

Zoomie's flinty eyes are sparking as she says, "Yeah, I got all that. But we need to make sure *none* of what's really going on with Stone goes past that door. Anna hears too much at the bar."

The prez frowns. "What's that mean?"

"Just what I said. Some of the brothers can't keep their mouths shut and they'll jaw off about club business right in front of her. Most of the time, it's about shit that doesn't matter. But this? It'll hurt her twice. Once because Stone's her brother and he's in trouble, and the second time because she had to overhear what happened to him from some assholes instead of hearing it from her friends." Zoomie gives me a look that says she'll lay an equal measure of pain on me if that happens.

She won't need to. I'll lay it on myself.

Hell, I'm laying it on myself *now*. There's nothing I enjoy about lying to Anna. Not even the messages we send to each other. Christ. Every goddamn hour I hope to see a new text from her on Stone's phone. Seeing her talk to me so easily…it's like being handed a piece of something I've wanted for almost a decade. But she's not talking to *me*. And knowing that, knowing how I'm deceiving her with every word is a rotted ache spreading inside my gut.

Frowning, the prez looks to Thorne. "Maybe you ought to have a word."

The veep appears almost amused. "A word with Anna or with the brothers?"

"The brothers, since she's apparently better keeping her mouth shut than some of them are." He eyes Zoomie. "Though maybe some Riders are a little *too* tight-lipped."

Zoomie shrugs. "Her loyalty to Stone is as strong as any Rider's. She's not about to go blabbing something she hears to anyone who shouldn't be hearing it."

"I'm not talking about Anna. She wouldn't be working my bar if I didn't trust her. But I'd have liked to know about the brothers. They should keep that shit in the clubhouse."

"Yes, boss," she says. "I'll tattle next time."

His gaze narrows as if he's about to tear into her, but he only shakes his head and says, "Shit. So that's how Jenny always knows more about club business than most of the brothers do."

He sounds a hell of a lot more amused by that than the prez of most MCs would be. Truth is, I'm more amused than I should be, too. But Zoomie's got it right. Anna's too loyal to Stone to risk opening her mouth to anyone other than Jenny—and betraying the Riders would be like betraying her brother. She never would. Just like Jenny would never betray her father or the prez. So everyone in this room trusts both women as much as we do any brother.

More than we trust some brothers, probably.

It'll have to change, though. Keeping club business quiet isn't just about covering our asses if shit goes south. It's about protecting Anna and Jenny, too. If they don't know about club business that crosses legal lines, they can't go down for lying to any cops who come asking.

But, Jesus. Thinking about how much shit Anna's probably kept silent about over the years drills the empty hole in my chest even deeper. Any Rider would be damn lucky to have a woman like her. Smart, loyal—and with just enough bite to her temper and her humor that a man can't ever rest too easy.

It's no surprise I'm a goner. The only surprise is that all the other brothers aren't scrambling over themselves to make her look their way.

The prez rubs his face. "All right. Nothing about Stone goes beyond this room. But we can't keep it all quiet because I'll be appointing Bull as temporary enforcer while Stone's gone. And since Gunner's going, I'll put Spiral in as SA."

Taking over my position. Jesus, even with the 'temporary' in there, that burns like hell. But Christ knows how long I'll be gone and the prez needs to keep order among the brothers.

"So what are we telling everyone?" Zoomie asks.

The best lie is always mostly true. I tell her, "Say Stone hooked up with a girl in trouble. The rest is club business we don't intend to share."

"That'll do." The prez gets to his feet. "Anything else we need to cover?"

Not here. The only business left to take care of is with Anna. I don't know what the hell I'll say when I see her—I can't trust my mouth when I'm with her. But after tomorrow, I also don't know when I'll be seeing her again. Or *if* I'll see her again. So I can't stay away from her tonight.

Just a few hours. And I'll pretend it'll be enough.

When no one brings up anything new, the prez heads for the door. Thorne gets up from his seat and I'm up right after him, until Zoomie catches my left biceps and steers me backward.

"Sit back down for a second, pretty boy." She waits until I do, wearing the same expression she does in the ring, and rolling her tongue over her teeth like she's already tasting blood. "You know, out of all the assholes in this club, you're my favorite."

Shit. She's buttering me up. I've been sparring with her for years and I know what that means. She butters you up right before she knocks your teeth out.

Wary, I watch her eyes. They're flat and gray and steady on mine. Not giving anything away yet. "Blowback's not your favorite?"

"I said 'out of all the assholes.'"

Damn. "I walked into that."

"Yeah." But she doesn't smile. Instead she clenches her jaw and looks away from me. "We've been friends a long time, Gunner. And it's a damn good thing. Because it means I know the way you're fucking with Anna by using Stone's phone isn't what it looks like."

My grip on the beer bottle goes from easy to white-knuckled. Zoomie and I *have* been friends a long time. It's the only reason I'm not forcing those words back down her throat.

Fucking with Anna? Is that what she calls it? Rage rolls up through my chest but I choke it down. "What does it look like?"

"It looks like you think she's just a piece of shit who can't be trusted with the truth about her own goddamn brother, even though she's been keeping her mouth shut for years. What you're doing is a kick in her face—and instead of backing off, you're lacing up your boots."

That speech is a knife in my gut. "I'm trying to keep her from hurting."

"I know that. *She* probably doesn't. She has no clue how you feel about her. So I'm telling you—it'll look like something else to her when she finds out the truth." Her gaze meets mine again. "And if Stone doesn't come home, your lie isn't the kind that can be forgiven."

I know it. But if I don't bring Stone home, Anna will be hurt by far worse than a lie. So not bringing him back isn't an option.

But the other bit Zoomie mentioned—*she has no clue how you feel about her*—that's catching right in my chest. Zoomie and I are friends but I've never said a damn thing to her about Anna. I've never said a damn thing to *anyone* about Anna. Yet Zoomie threw that out as if there was no question.

The same way Strawman thought he knew something, too.

Watching her face, I ask, "What exactly do you think I feel for her?"

An abrupt laugh sputters through her tightened lips. "Seriously? I'd say you think she hung the goddamn moon."

I do. But I didn't think it was that fucking obvious. "Everyone thinks this?"

"Not Anna." Zoomie grins slyly and takes a swig of her beer. "But I'll put it this way—the past two years, Beaver's been running a pool. Every New Year, he takes bets on when you two will finally hook up. But half the brothers think you two are already hooking up on the sly."

Motherfuck. I thought Strawman just focused on Anna because he didn't know I was close to Stone, and so he assumed my sitting at Anna's bar and being at her house was all about her.

But the other Riders know why I'm always around the Den. Why I'm always around Stone. So that shit doesn't fly. "Why do they think it?"

"Why?" She frowns, a line forming between her pale

eyebrows. "Or do you mean, 'Who noticed the way you watch her and started talking about it?'"

"That."

Her gaze searches my face for a long second. Finally figuring out this is a real problem instead of a joke. "The women," she finally says. "They've always got their eyes on you. You know that?"

"I know." And it never mattered.

Maybe it should have.

"When you don't hook up with anyone, they start wondering why—and they don't stop looking at you just because you turn them down. Not with that face. They watch you and they talk. Some of that talk reaches the brothers' ears."

Fucking hell. "And their talk reaches other ears."

Zoomie's eyes narrow. "Whose ears?" When I only shake my head, she adds, "If it makes you feel better, it took me about two years before I picked up on it, and that was only because I'm around you so much. The brothers probably never would have on their own. You hide it well."

It doesn't make me feel better. Not when Anna could have been hurt because of it. "Why didn't you say anything?"

"Because it was pretty damn funny watching you turn into a lovesick dick every time you saw her." She picks at the label on her bottle. "And maybe because I was never friends with her. But the last couple of months, that's changed. I've seen the shit she takes for it."

The back of my neck tenses. "What shit?"

"Uh-uh." With a slight smile, she shakes her head. "That's for her to say. If she ever wants to."

"You see this?" I flick the *Sergeant at Arms* patch on my shoulder. "It's my job to keep the brothers in line, so you're gonna damn well share it."

"I'm not talking about any Riders. The brothers know better than to fuck with her."

"Then who doesn't know better?"

Zoomie shrugs as if she doesn't see how I'm ready to bust some goddamn heads. Maybe starting with hers. "Anyway, none of it is quite so funny anymore."

"It was never funny."

She nods, watching me. "I always figured you held back because of Stone. Some 'I can't bang my friend's sister' bullshit. Or maybe you asked her out and she told you to fuck off, and you've been pining ever since. Because if it was Anna going after you, she'd still be going after you. She's like a bulldog with a bone as soon as she gets her teeth into something."

She is. And the thought of Anna getting her teeth into my bones is too damn distracting. Or maybe I just don't want to think about how easily she shrugged and went about her business after I turned down her invitation all those years ago.

"We agreed it was best to keep it simple."

Zoomie snorts out a laugh. "And she's the only one who held up her end of that?" Her amusement quickly fades. "But apparently you had your reasons to hold back."

"For all the good it did. So tell me—who's giving her shit?"

Zoomie just shakes her head.

Maybe because I just did the same damn thing to her, refusing to answer when she asked whose ears were hearing about Anna and me.

I can't afford to keep silent about that, though. She *is* Anna's friend. And there might be trouble when I head home.

"Do this for me," I tell her slowly. "If you ever see someone come around who looks like me—but who isn't me—you get to Anna's side real fast. And you watch her back."

"You know I will." She bumps my fist, sealing the promise. "Since Blowback and I are taking off tomorrow, maybe you ought to give Spiral and Bull a heads-up, too."

"I will." Along with the prez.

She nods, then purses her lips and gives me a pointed look. "Last I saw her, Anna was in the kitchen with her mom."

I won't be alone with her. But I'll take what I get.

I clink the neck of my beer bottle against Zoomie's and slide off the stool. As I head past her, she tosses at my back,

"Try not to fuck it up too bad."

Shit. I'll try.

But lately my 'don't fuck it up' track record is a damn sorry one.

EIGHT

ANNA

Eventually, the cold drives me back inside the house. I leave my dad and make my way toward the great room. A step through the threshold, I come to a halt.

By the fireplace, Gunner is standing in the cluster of people talking with Jenny—a cluster including my mom, who's right by his side. There's also Spiral, who's saying something to make Jenny laugh—probably by poking fun at Picasso, because he's scowling at Spiral and his "do you believe this bullshit?" expression is firmly in place on his uneven face.

My plan is to walk over there and say "Hi," to Jenny, give her a hug, and join the conversation. Gunner will fall quiet when I show up, because he always goes quiet around me. But I won't let myself wonder what he's thinking. I won't obsess over why he never tries to make me laugh. And when I notice him watching me in that silent way, I won't nurture any hope that his attention means there's something between us, or that the attraction isn't all on my side, or that I'm more to him than just Stone's little sister.

I'm quitting all of that. Right now. This is the moment when everything changes.

Except I can't force my feet to move. I stand immobile, my face flushed with heat, my heartbeat throbbing heavily in my ears. After the chill outside, the house feels suffocatingly warm. The conversations around me seem muffled, the hushed and solemn voices drowning in the thick, hot air filling the room.

Until one voice cleaves straight through. "Do I need to pull those two jokers away from her?"

I glance over…and up. Saxon Gray doesn't usually stand this close to me, so talking to him doesn't normally threaten to put a kink in my neck. And, considering that he's the owner of the Wolf Den and my boss, I talk to him regularly.

Never about personal stuff, though. It's kind of crazy—I've worked at his bar for six years, and I'm pretty sure part of the reason he hired me was because Jenny is my best friend. Not that he ever asked me about her. The whole Romeo-and-Juliet thing they had going on for almost fifteen years was one of those subjects we never touched. Saxon was my boss and our relationship was that simple. If he just happened to love my best friend…well, he wasn't ever going to mention it. Neither was I.

Red's cancer changed all that. Not right away. But when Jenny's dad found out he was sick, one of the first things he did was go to Saxon. Red had been president of the Steel Titans MC for decades, and before Saxon took over as Hellfire Riders' prez, the two clubs had some serious bad blood between them. But there wasn't any bad blood between Red and Saxon. Not after Saxon saved Jenny from being raped fifteen years ago, and got five years in prison for manslaughter after killing the biker who attacked her.

So Red went to Saxon and asked him for two things: to protect Jenny from the asshole skinheads who'd been hassling her, and to fold the Steel Titans and the Hellfire Riders into one club.

That was only a few months ago. With the club rivalry no longer an issue, Jenny and Saxon hooked up in two seconds flat, and they've been together ever since. It's kind of cute, actually. Here's Saxon, this big and gruff guy who can make a roomful of bikers quake in their boots simply by looking at them, and he's head over heels for my BFF—so much in love that she can make *him* quake.

Not that Saxon shows it; he's a hard man to read. But I've known him a long time and I've had a lot of practice deciphering his expressions.

To most people, the stone set of his face and the clench of his bearded jaw probably appear on the edge of pissed. But he's not angry. He's worried, his gaze fixed on the group across the room, and his entire being focused on Jenny.

And he's asking me whether to toss Spiral and Picasso out on their asses.

The president of the Hellfire Riders doesn't exactly go around asking advice. He probably listens to the club's officers behind closed doors, but under normal circumstances, he doesn't openly consult anyone before making a decision. He certainly wouldn't consult me.

Even after he and Jenny became a couple, my relationship with him didn't change. Saxon draws lines, and I was still his employee, so he still didn't talk about her with me. And that was the way I liked it, too. No need to make things awkward at work.

But that's all been turned around in the past couple of days. Losing her dad ripped Jenny apart, and Saxon's desperate to help her though this. So he's been crossing those lines, because with Red gone, I know Jenny better than anyone—and I was there when she lost her mom, too. Now Saxon and I are the closest two people she has left, so we've formed kind of a team, making sure Jenny has everything she needs.

I love him a little for that—for crossing those lines. For doing whatever it takes to help her. Because I would do the same.

Glancing back at Jenny, I study her for a long second, my heart pulling tight. Her face is drawn and pale. She looks so tired, despite her smile. Despite her laughter. That's what Saxon's picking up on. He's worried she's expending too much effort pretending to be amused by whatever antics Spiral and Picasso are pulling.

I don't think she's pretending, though. "She probably needs the laugh," I tell him. "And she might feel guilty about laughing after burying her dad, but it's also probably a relief. I mean…look at everyone."

So serious. So careful. A whole house full of people walking on eggshells, and there go Spiral and Picasso playing the clowns—maybe even deliberately. Considering who else is standing there, I wouldn't be surprised if my mom asked Gunner to recruit these guys in an effort to cheer Jenny up.

"And don't forget my mom is there to run interference," I add.

Saxon nods. His steely gaze touches my face for a moment before returning to Jenny. "What you said to me the other day, about not asking if she was all right—it was good. I told the brothers not to ask her."

I have to bite my lip against a grin. Stopping every Hellfire Rider from asking Jenny if she was all right wasn't exactly what I was thinking when I gave him the advice, but I should have realized he would take it a step further. Now he'll probably pound the shit out of them if they forget and do ask her.

Maybe it's for the best, though. My mom taught Stone and me a long time ago that "How are you?" can be one of the most unintentionally cruel questions to ask someone who is grieving. Sure, it stems from concern about that person. But it can place a burden on them, too—the burden of reassuring the other person that they're fine. The burden of lying if they're not. The burden of pretending the question doesn't hurt even though every emotion is raw and exposed.

And Jenny…Lord, I love her, but she'll bend over backward to help someone, to reassure them. She'll pretend she's okay until she breaks—and she'll especially pretend for Saxon's sake, because she won't want him to worry.

But he'll worry anyway. So it was best just to nip that in the bud, so he never asks a question that will force her to pretend.

His voice sounds a little rougher when he abruptly asks, "*Is* she all right?"

"No," I tell him and when despair suddenly wipes the steel from his eyes, leaving misery in its wake, I rush to add, "But she will be."

And look at me. Just like Jenny, reassuring him. But, God. Seeing that expression was like watching him take a slow dive into Hell.

I bump his arm with my shoulder, so I know he's listening to me instead of wallowing in a lake of fire. "Just keep doing what you're doing. Be there for her. Don't try to keep her from working"—no matter how much he probably wants to roll her up in a blanket and prevent anything from touching her until she stops grieving—"because keeping busy is how she copes when she's hurting. And don't ask her if she needs help with anything, because our girl will feel bad if you do things for her. So frame any help like, 'I'd love to do this thing for you,' because then it's about what you want to do, and it'll make her feel good because she's helping *you*."

Slowly he nods again. "I'll do that."

I know he will. If Jenny needed him to, Saxon would find a way to rip a hole in the sky. Even if it killed him.

It's all kind of…incredible. To be loved like that. I mean, I *am* loved like that. My parents, Stone, Jenny—I know they'd do anything for me, too.

That's not the same, though. I don't know why, but it's not. And, Lord help me—I want that kind of love for myself.

I don't know if I deserve it. But I want it.

And screw that kind of thinking, anyway. I *do* deserve it. I deserve someone who will cross every line, simply because he loves me. Because he needs me.

That's never going to happen with Gunner. He's never going to give me more. That's why I have to quit.

But I'll never be able to quit if I can't take a step

forward. So I take it. Then I take another. Soon I'm halfway across the room, and each step is harder than the last, but that's not the point. This doesn't have to be easy. New roads usually aren't. There are usually mountains that have to be climbed and deserts that have to be survived and rivers that have to be forded.

And I'm on my way to cut my heart out. So it's not like any of this is easy. It hurts *so* much.

Maybe Jenny sees it, despite my attempt not to show anything. Or maybe she's just being Jenny when she grips my hands in hers, her green eyes taking an inventory of my expression.

Her forehead creases with concern. "You okay?" she asks and I give a watery laugh, because really. She's the last person who should be caring about how anyone else feels right now.

Yet of course she does. So I squeeze her hands and nod. "I'm good," I tell her, and it's not even a lie. This pain is necessary—the surgical cut that has to be made so I can begin to heal. So I can get better.

But I can't even look at Gunner yet and the knife in my chest keeps slicing deeper.

"Anna." My mom links her fingers with mine, draws me close. Her tone is light but that touch isn't. She can see I'm hurting and is giving me all the comfort she can. "Zach found me in the kitchen, and told me Aaron had to stay in Arizona."

"Really?" They didn't travel to Arizona for fun. Instead

they've been trying to track down information about some crazy underground fighting ring. But this is more club business I'm not supposed to know. I'm curious what explanation he gave, though. "Why?"

There's a pause, and I realize Mom's waiting for Gunner to tell it. But he's quiet as usual. Because I'm here.

Smoothly, my mom fills in the silence with an amused, "There was a girl."

Oh god. My facepalm can't begin to convey the embarrassment I'm feeling on my brother's behalf. Always playing the hero, as if female helplessness acts as an irresistible pheromone, and he can't stop himself from rushing in to save them. It would be awesome if it wasn't so *sad*. "Is she in trouble?"

"Apparently," Mom says and although she's still wearing her soft smile, her tone is a little cooler now — the counselor side kicking in. "It might behoove him to seek professional help for this woman instead of trying to solve her problems for her."

"I'll point that out to him," Gunner says.

Lord, his voice. It slides right into me, sweet and painful — a low sexy rumble with a rasping edge, as if he doesn't talk much. But he does talk. Just not to me.

Except now, when he adds, "Don't worry, Anna. I'm going back tomorrow morning. I'll help him keep his head."

Everything in my chest clenches, a tight burning ache. He'll expect a response. I can't avoid looking at him now.

My fingers fall away from my eyes. Gunner's watching me, his pale gaze steady on mine, and it hurts so much to see him. Not because he's beautiful but because when he looks back at me, his eyes aren't empty or guarded. He looks tired, his features drawn—but those eyes are filled with warmth, as if there's more between us than just a brother. There's humor, because he likes poking fun at my brother as much as I do. There's expectation, because on a few occasions we've teamed up to make fun of Stone.

And—maybe for Jenny's sake—he's waiting for me to join in again now, with no idea how the warmth in his eyes rips at my heart. With no idea how a single word from him affects me. With no idea how much I want to hear his voice, rough and demanding against my ear, his skin hot against mine.

I should run away. Just get out of here. Because I love this. His silences hurt, but I feel so alive when he *does* talk to me—and that feeling is why I held onto hope for so long.

Hope isn't enough. But Gunner's look makes me hope all over again. And my heart can't survive this any more.

Only Jenny's face stops me from bolting. Because she's smiling, her eyes bright. Knowing Stone went into hero mode amuses her, too. And heaven knows, she needs that amusement.

So I swallow the lump in my throat. "You'll help him keep his head? Are you saying my brother is occasionally brainless when it comes to women?"

Gunner responds with a solemn nod. "Around a certain type."

"So what's his type?" I ask like I don't know. "Let me guess. Stray puppy?"

Amusement gleams in his pale eyes. "I would have said 'lost lamb.'"

"No lambs. The girls he hooks up with are rarely innocent. What about a sad monkey?"

"Monkeys are smarter than his usual type."

God, that's true. I catch my breath on a laugh. Jenny quietly giggles behind her hand while my mom just nods and heaves a deep sigh.

"Hey, at least a monkey's easier to nail than Picasso's type," Spiral throws in.

Jenny's eyebrows arch. "Which is?"

"Uh…" Picasso glances at my mom.

She pins him with her impassive stare. "One never quite escapes the high school counselor's office, does one?"

"Who is 'one?'" Picasso looks hunted. "Are you meaning me or you?"

"Which of us do you think I mean?"

It takes him a long second to answer, and as if he isn't certain whether it's a test. "Maybe…me?"

I hide my smile behind my free hand. She's not testing him. She's teasing him. But she still pulled something out of him he probably didn't want to reveal.

My elegant mother apparently intimidates the hell out of the big, tattooed biker.

"I see." Done torturing the poor guy, she slips her fingers from mine. "Well, I'll leave you young ones to discuss your types."

A brief silence falls as she moves away. As soon as she's out of earshot, Picasso declares, "A goddess type. Like this one woman we ran into a few months ago. Blonde, long legs, tits out to here."

He cups his hands in front of his chest to illustrate. I look down at my chest, then over at Jenny, who has a little more than me but is definitely not in the range he's suggesting. She catches my gaze.

"I think we're lowly mortals," she tells me.

Picasso shakes his head. "Everyone is lowly in comparison. This was one of those women who is everyone's type. Am I right?" He looks to Spiral, who's nodding, then to Gunner. "You remember. At the Pendleton rally. She came up to you first."

Gunner narrows his eyes, as if thinking about that. Abruptly he nods. "I remember. And you're right."

So she was ridiculously gorgeous. Like he is.

But Gunner's thinking of someone else. "She was like Zoomie," he adds.

Our friend Lily Burns—the only female member of the Hellfire Riders. And, yeah. That makes sense. Lily is stunning. Like, crazily so. Not just because she's tall and blonde with cheekbones that could cut glass and lips that could sell collagen injections by the thousands, but because she looks at the world like she's going to own it.

That attitude is sexy as hell.

Yet she's not quite like the woman Picasso described.

"Lily doesn't have tits out to here." I hold my hands out in front of me like I'm carrying two giant watermelons, then give them a bounce for good measure.

Gunner's grin sends my heart bouncing, too. Up, so far up.

But it'll come down. It always does.

And shatters when it lands.

His smile fades as I drop my imaginary breasts and wrap my arms around my stomach, trying to hold in the ache. His pale gaze searches my face but I force myself to look away, to pay attention to Picasso.

"Not like Zoomie *physically*," he's saying. "She wasn't quite that tall and probably couldn't kick ass. By 'everyone's type,' I mean she was the kind of woman who could tempt gay men for a night and make straight girls cross over."

All at once, Jenny's pale cheeks have a little pink in them. Probably because she *did* cross over with Lily. Kind of.

The rasp in Gunner's voice is more pronounced when he adds quietly, "But the question with this woman was: Would two straight guys cross over for *her*?"

I blink, trying to work that one out. "What?"

Spiral's laughing at Gunner. "So you do remember her."

"I remember you telling me how it crashed and burned."

"How?" Jenny asks.

Picasso's wearing his cheesy grin, a lopsided smile that almost evens out his features. "She comes up to Spiral and then looks over at me when she asks him, 'So are you together?' And I'm thanking God, because even though Spiral's prettier than me, my dick's bigger than his so I'll come out ahead—"

"What the— The hell it is!" Spiral sputters, trying to edge in, but Picasso's still going.

"—so I tell her 'Yes' before he can get a word in. The she says to me, 'I want to watch you guys go at it.'"

That wasn't what I expected. On a startled laugh, I glance at Gunner. He's smiling again, though it's more subdued. Just a slight curve of his firm lips, and a brooding weight to his gaze as he watches me.

Picasso's *still* going. "So I look to Spiral and I think, 'If she stays around after, doing him might be worth it.' Then I slam my beer down on the table and tell him, 'C'mon, man. Let's go for it! Right here!'"

Oh my god. My hand flies up to cover my mouth when my laugh shoots out. I have zero doubt he really did say that. Jenny's giggling and wiping her eyes. Probably because she can imagine Picasso saying it, too.

Though he's been shaking his head since the comment regarding his dick size, Spiral adds now, "So I tell him that I'd have to be a lot more drunk, or he'd have to be a lot prettier. Like SA here." He gestures to Gunner.

"Prettier?" Picasso scoffs. "Let me point

out—again—that if I'm drilling your ass, you don't have to see my face. And thank fuck I wouldn't have to see yours."

"And I told you I'd be giving, not receiving, because I'm a generous man." Spiral looks to Jenny again. "So that's why the goddess moved on and he struck out. She left while we were arguing over who gets to be on top."

I can't even answer that because I'm imagining them wrestling for the top spot, then desperately trying not to imagine it, and giggling helplessly all the way through.

"Generous, my ass." Picasso manages to sound both haughty and offended. "When I said you should always cover my back, I didn't mean that."

"If that's what covering each other's backs meant, we'd have an entirely different sort of club," Gunner says.

"Or not so different. A lot of you guys already wear leather chaps," I point out, and Jenny covers her face, her shoulders shaking. Gunner grins at me, sending my heart spinning dizzily upward again, but Spiral holds up his hands as if to stop us right there.

Smirk firmly in place, he looks to Gunner. "If you were in that club, it'd answer a hell of a lot of questions about *your* type."

Gunner tilts his head as if considering that, then nods. "I guess it would." He glances at me. "But it might raise new questions about Stone."

I snicker and shake my head. No, there's no question about my brother. Or Gunner, really. But it is funny watching these guys try to figure him out.

At least I'm not the only one trying to.

"Sheeeit, man," Picasso drawls. "You ain't fooling anyone. We know your type and she doesn't have a dick. She's brown haired, sassy, and can pour a dozen shots faster than—"

Abruptly Picasso goes quiet. My cheeks hot, I lock eyes with Jenny, who's stopped laughing. She's absolutely still now, watching my face, waiting for a cue from me—to shrug it off, to turn it into a joke, or to pretend we have no clue who he's talking about. But I don't know what cue to give. I hear this a lot—that Gunner's hung up on me. Usually I let whoever says it continue thinking it because A) it's not so terrible if people believe a big, sexy biker is crazy about me and B) what else am I supposed to do? Point out that I threw myself at him a couple of times and he turned me down? Not to mention, C) on the occasions when I *have* said that Gunner isn't into me, they don't believe it, anyway.

But they never say anything to me *in front* of him. This is the first time. And, Jesus. I have no idea what to do or say now.

I steal a glance at Gunner. He's not looking at me. Eyes glacial, he's staring Picasso down.

The other biker backs up a step. "Hold up, SA. You know I don't—"

"So you're spreading the old ladies' gossip about your brothers instead of dealing in facts?" Gunner's voice is soft.

Dangerous. "Because I've never said a fucking word about being interested in anyone."

Especially me. That's what I want to add, tossing the response out with a careless shrug and a flip of my hair, but a painful lump blocks my throat and I'm frozen in place.

"True. You never *said* a word," Spiral says and the lift of his brows suggests that Gunner didn't need to say a word because his actions have been talking for him.

If he'd seen Gunner shoot me down, he'd have seen words *and* actions.

Jaw clenched, Gunner turns that lethal gaze on Spiral. "You got something to say, brother?"

Spiral holds that gaze for a long second before flicking a glance at me. "I guess I don't."

"Good thing. Because I do and you'd best fucking listen. The next time it crosses your minds to shoot your mouths off, just consider who the fuck you're talking about. Consider whose sister she is, and how you're disrespecting her by talking about me climbing between her legs and by making bets about when I'm going to do it." Each word snaps like ice, his face a rigid mask. "You hear that shit going around again, you better put a stop to it."

"Will do," Spiral promises and reaches out to bump Gunner's fist. Picasso does the same. Just like that, buddy buddies again.

And me, I'm praying for a meteor to hit the house. Because, Jesus. *That shit going around* is Gunner being hung up on me. It's him getting between my legs. *That shit* is what I wanted for years. That *shit*.

Shit sums up how that feels.

I know Jenny's looking at me in concern but I can't crawl away now. I can't hide. The only thing I can do is suck it up and keep my chin high when Gunner looks to me and says,

"Just don't pay attention to these fuckers."

Suck it up. Don't show a goddamn thing. "I won't."

Not glacial now but warm, his crystalline gaze searches my face. "You all right? You don't let this shit get to you?"

This shit. "Of course not. We both know it's all nothing," I say and add a shrug, as if it really doesn't matter.

Gunner frowns at me, studying my expression for so long that I'm sure he realized how fake my shrug was. But if he was going to call me out on it, he loses his chance.

One of the Riders' prospects comes up on his left—Bottlecap, who was assigned to help manage parking. With dark hair plastered to his skull and his black shirt soaked, he looks like a drowned puppy. A thin, lanky drowned puppy.

Only his kutte is dry, but I'm guessing he probably took care to wipe down the leather as soon as he came inside. Now he hesitates slightly, looking from me to Jenny. Not because he's worried about talking club business in front of us, I realize—but because he's torn between acknowledging the ladies first or greeting Gunner, a club officer. Politeness versus the risk of having his ass kicked.

He opts for politeness, and considering where we

are—and Jenny's relationship to the club's president—that probably saved him an ass kicking from another direction.

"Miss Jenny," he says, "I'm real sorry about Red. You know he brought me in"—he gestures to his kutte—"and gave me a chance. I'll never forget that. Or let him down."

At the mention of her dad, Jenny's eyes dim a little but she still has a smile for him. "He thought you were worth that chance. And thank you."

He nods, then glances to me. "Miss Anna."

God, that 'miss' kills me. So respectful. So quaint. And such bullshit. Like many of the Riders, he's gotten into the habit of calling the girls who hang around the patchholders 'sweet butts' and 'club pussy'—it doesn't matter if those girls are screwing the bikers or not. Jenny and I aren't any different from those women. Bottlecap's just afraid Saxon or Stone—or Gunner—will tear him a new one if he treats Jenny or me like he does the other women. He respects the men, not us.

But I just smile back, because after six years of working the bar at the Den, I've learned to accept respect by proxy. It beats the alternative. And honestly, Bottlecap isn't so bad. He might say some stupid shit, but I've never heard of him being a dick to a woman.

I can't say that about every Rider.

"Prospect, you had something else to tell us?" Gunner prods.

"Reverend Powers is getting ready to go, and your bikes are between the reverend's Buick and the driveway,"

Bottlecap says to Picasso and Spiral. "I didn't want to move your rides without asking, so—"

"We'll get them," Picasso says, which isn't a surprise, because he'd be more likely to let another man screw his girlfriend—if he had one—than push his motorcycle a few feet. He and Spiral start to head off, then he turns around, pointing at me. "About the ride home last night. Thank you."

"You don't have to say it again."

"I was so damn drunk I couldn't remember if I said it the first time." He snaps his fingers before looking to Gunner. "And speaking of drunk—don't forget the kegs."

That's like a magic word to Jenny, whose brewery is located in a renovated barn a few minutes' drive from the house. As Spiral and Picasso take off, her gaze zeroes in on Gunner. "Kegs?"

He nods. "The brothers have food here, some booze, and no reason to go. So I figure it'll be easier to round them up and get them out of your hair if we promise to have enough beer at the clubhouse to get them shitfaced by midnight."

She frowns. "I don't care if they stay here."

"Maybe so, but it's my responsibility to see they stay in line," Gunner says evenly. "And I don't want to explain to the prez why I let a brother get drunk enough to break a window or to piss in a houseplant, or let one start a fight that scares the shit out of the good civilians here. Because with the brothers' emotions running high, you know it'll happen."

He's right. Jenny glances at me, as if looking for someone to help her be sweet and generous enough to leave her house open to fifty bikers and their old ladies all night. My wide eyes and a shake of my head tell her I'm not that person.

She sighs and nods, then scans the crowd. "Have you seen Hashtag?"

Who has been working with her at the brewery. I scan, too. I don't remember seeing the Riders' newest member in the house, but I know he didn't miss the funeral.

"Widowmaker sent him home sick." Gunner solves that mystery. "The kid was supposed to take care of this for us, but he could barely stand through the service. Picked up some flu going around."

"Oh. Well, I don't know if I can leave…" As Jenny glances around the crowded room again, uncertainty flickers over her face, followed by resolve. "It's okay. I'll head out to the barn and—"

I stop her. "I'll do it."

"But—"

"I know where all the stuff is." I've helped her out in the brewery's storefront plenty of times. But she's already looking guilty, so I add, "I'd actually like to go, because a little fresh air sounds really good right now. I'll take your truck, so I can load the kegs up in the back."

My body stiffens when Gunner says, "I'll go as muscle."

"I can do it—"

He cuts me off. "I know you can."

His eyes are hard when they meet mine, as if he's daring me to keep arguing. I wouldn't. Because A) loading those kegs is hard and I could use the help, and B) I'm hardly going to tell him what he can do while we're in someone else's house.

And of course there's C), which is: being alone with him will hurt—but I'm hurting now, so there's not much difference.

"Anyway, I could use some air, too," he says to Jenny, and I'm not sure if he means it or if he's following my lead, making Jenny believe she's doing us a favor by letting us go.

At least her guilt is gone, and she's smiling again as she nods—then her expression freezes, her eyes locked on mine and flaring wide. Her gaze flicks to Gunner and back to me.

Oh. That look was gone in an instant but I could read it. She probably knows I was grabbing onto any excuse to get out of here, especially after hearing about all *that shit*.

But it'll be okay. Because like the gossip, this means nothing. Gunner's simply not the kind of guy who will let me wrestle kegs into the back of a truck by myself. He's just being nice by offering to help.

Because if there's one thing the past ten years have taught me, he's sure as hell not offering because he wants to be alone with me.

NINE

ANNA

I CAN COUNT ON ONE HAND THE NUMBER OF TIMES I'VE been alone with Gunner in the past ten years. I don't even need to use all five fingers.

The first time was when Gunner stopped to help change my tire. Big, sexy, sweet—and he was the most beautiful man I'd ever seen, so I offered him my name, my number, and a drink that I hoped would lead to my bed.

He didn't want any of them. He claimed one night probably wouldn't be enough and he'd come looking for me. I didn't see the harm in that.

Gunner did, though he didn't explain why. So he only took a kiss and walked away.

A few moments later, he learned my name anyway. Before he could ride off, I got a call from my brother, and I discovered the man who stopped to help me out was the same man visiting my family for the next week.

He was the man who would be sleeping in the bedroom across the hall from mine.

The second time I was alone with him, we were in that bedroom. Well, we were in the bedroom for a few minutes, but mostly in the hall. I hadn't expected him to be home that Saturday night. My brother and Gunner had been to another funeral that day—standing with the Hellfire Riders, who were forming a line to block a hate group picketing a soldier's burial. My brother's plan for afterward had been to hook up with any willing chick. I assumed Gunner's plan was the same. I don't know if my brother scored that night but Gunner didn't, even though I would have been an easy shot.

I'd been out with Jenny, trying to have a good time and pretending that it didn't matter where our visitor spent the night. But when I came home I found Gunner already in the guest room, reading. We talked for a few minutes, then I asked if he wanted to grab breakfast with me the next day—an invitation that he could have taken any way he liked.

He didn't take it at all. Instead he said it was better to

keep things simple between us — because Stone was his friend, and I was Stone's sister.

That rejection sucked, but I accepted it. After all, he was so nice about letting me down. And he was just visiting, anyway, so I assumed I'd never see him again after he left.

And I didn't for four years, though Stone frequently mentioned him.

I never imagined Gunner would come back to Pine Valley. Certainly not to live. People don't move *to* this town. They move out. But he came, patched in with the Hellfire Riders, and was always around — at the house Stone and I bought, at the Wolf Den.

And since he was always around, it didn't take me long to figure out that he still meant to keep things simple. Because he didn't talk to me unless someone else was there to act as a buffer. Because he clearly made every effort *not* to be alone with me.

That's when it started hurting. But it was so stupid to feel that way — I knew it was. So I tried not to care.

I tried so hard. But of course, the next time I was alone with Gunner, I threw myself at him. Nine years of wanting burst through the dam I'd built of my emotions and I don't know if I could have stopped myself, even if I hadn't been drinking.

Sure, I *was* drunk off my ass. And sure, he's a decent guy, so he pushed me away. But the next day, I wasn't drunk. The next day, he *had* to know I wanted him. But instead of taking a step in that direction, he asked if things were still the same between us. So I shrugged and told him of course they were.

Simple. Like always.

Maybe that's why he's wary of being alone with me, though. What an awesome track record I have. The first time, I give him a clear invitation to my bed, but he only takes a kiss. The second time, I invite him to my bed again and he gently declines. The third time, I drunkenly throw myself at him and he pushes me away.

Even now, he's probably wondering how hard he'll have to fight me off when I inevitably jump him on our way to pick up the kegs.

But I'm not going to touch him. If I can help it, I won't even look at him.

I've never been able to help it, though.

My stomach has twisted into a nervous coil by the time I grab Jenny's keys, slide into my big puffy coat, and make my way out to the garage. The overhead door is rolling up, the motor a smooth hum. Gunner must have told Bottlecap we were leaving, because the prospect is sliding into the driver's seat of an SUV blocking the garage entrance. The rig's headlights cut through the dark outside, sparkling against rain mixed with bits of snow.

Standing by Jenny's pickup, Gunner glances up from his phone, slipping the device into his back pocket as I step through the door. Good Lord, he's beautiful. Halogen lamps glare down from the ceiling, but the harsh light seems to soften against the sharp angles of his face. The stark shadows below his eyebrows highlight the dazzling blue of his eyes.

I suspect those bright lights aren't as kind to me as they are to him. There are no tears now, but my face must be ravaged. Puffy, red. As I approach the truck, his hand lifts toward me—then he abruptly shoves his fists into the pockets of his black jeans, his shoulders hunching over. He doesn't need to tell me I look like hell. The sudden concern on his face says it for him.

But since I can't count on him to actually *say* anything, I opt for a polite, neutral, "How are you, Gunner?"

"Shitty." His voice is low and rough and it doesn't matter that his hands are tucked away, because his gaze moving across my face feels like the warmest caress. "I won't ask how you are."

A ragged laugh escapes me. Great. "You don't need to ask because I *look* shitty? Or you won't ask because Saxon told the Riders not to?"

"He told us not to ask Jenny. But you loved Red, too."

Yes, I did. For a long second, my throat hurts too much to get anything out, then I finally manage a hoarse, "He was her dad, but…I was here a lot."

"I feel the same way about your parents," he admits and I almost start crying again.

Because I know he does. The way my parents welcomed him in, he might as well be part of the family. Maybe it would have been easier if he was. If I could think of him like a brother. If he could just wrap me up in his arms like my brother sometimes does. Maybe this would hurt less if he talked to me as easily as he talks to Stone, so I wouldn't try to grab moments like this and hold them close.

But maybe it would be harder than it already is.

"Anna, no. Don't cry."

His command is a soft groan. He steps closer, obviously thinking the tears swimming in my eyes are for Red. Because if he knew the real source of my distress, he couldn't be backing away fast enough, telling me to keep it simple.

I desperately try to pull it together. This is not me. I'm *not* a weeper. I'm a laugher. I'm a snapper. But today nothing is normal. "It's okay. I'm not crying again."

"All right." Something in his voice says he doesn't believe that, and he's watching me so carefully. "But tell me if there's anything I can do for you."

There is. *Grab me and kiss me and tell me there's hope for us.*

I'm not stupid, though. There's pain, and then there's *pain*. Asking for Gunner's love and then hearing him say he can't give it would destroy me far worse than a broken heart could.

"You are doing something for me," I remind him, gesturing to the truck. "You're the muscle, remember?"

Over six feet of lean, gorgeous muscle.

He shakes his head. "Loading up the kegs isn't for you. The beer's for the club. If anything, you're doing this for us."

"For Jenny, actually."

A smile lifts the corners of his mouth, but his solemn gaze doesn't lighten. "I'd like to do something for you."

He'd like to do something. As if I would be doing *him* a favor by letting him. Oh god. He's managing me in the same way I told Saxon to manage Jenny.

I purse my lips. "You've been around my mom too much."

Because that's where I learned it from. I should have known Gunner picked up this kind of thing from her, too.

"Guilty," he says and this time his smile touches his eyes. "But that doesn't mean it's not true. I'm not used to seeing you…hurt."

Because I usually hide it from him. That won't change now. A long, deep breath helps to outwardly steady me. The ache in my chest still grows — but I won't show it.

Instead I arch my brows and jingle Jenny's keys. "All right. Let's head out, and on the way I'll think up some horrible task for you to perform on my behalf."

Interest narrows his eyes. "How horrible?"

"Really horrible," I tell him but the ideas springing to mind aren't so terrible. Ideas that involve his lips and his tongue and his fingers. Or my lips and tongue and fingers.

You know what you can do for me? Just stay still as I taste every inch of you.

Every hot, hard inch.

I don't know if what's running through my head is showing on my face, but his powerful body's gone still, his pale gaze locked on my lips. I want to believe he's thinking the same thing I am, that he's thinking of tasting me all over.

But he's already looking away, his jaw tight. So whether he read my expression or was imagining what I might ask him to do, he doesn't want any of it.

God. *Just pretend it doesn't matter,* I tell myself. Pretend that imagining his touch hasn't hardened my nipples and fired a low, liquid ache between my legs. Pretend I don't hate myself for desiring him, even now, like some idiot who rams head first into a brick wall, over and over and over again.

Pretend it doesn't hurt.

Shrugging, I say, "However horrible it will be, I'm sure you've done worse before."

His gaze flattens. "Yes."

With that brusque admission, he snags the keys and opens the pickup's door. Though he gestures to the seat, inviting me to drive, I head for the passenger side. Jenny's truck has a manual transmission. Technically, I know how to use a clutch but the ride will be smoother if Gunner takes the wheel.

Smoother—and quieter. Because his silence is back. By the time I've settled in and clicked my seatbelt, a familiar tension has slipped under his skin, holding his big body rigid. He stares straight ahead while starting the engine, and it's like a canyon separates us instead of eighteen inches of bench seat.

Throat tight, I turn my head away. My face is a shuttered, transparent reflection in the passenger window. I close my eyes so I don't have to look at myself.

Because what I see is a woman desperately trying to drag out these minutes alone with him. I need to move forward, but having Gunner to myself is such a rarity that I'm grabbing onto this chance like a starving woman grasping for the last crust of bread, knowing each bite only delays the end but too hungry not to devour it.

I rest my cheek against the cold window, and desperately try to think of anything but how close Gunner is. In my own way, I'm as pathetic as my brother when it comes to romance.

But at least Stone plays the hero. So even though I tease him about going for the girls in trouble, I admire him. He just throws himself out there, risking his heart every single time.

I've thrown myself at Gunner. Each time, he shot me down. Throwing myself at him again wouldn't be taking a risk—I know exactly how it will end. *Let's keep it simple, Anna.* The real risk will be moving forward. But I take a step back every time he smiles at me.

I have to quit this.

I close my eyes. *Just get the kegs and get away from him.* No more smiles. No more time alone.

No more hope.

Not that I have much hope left, especially now. I was searching for something wrong with Gunner, hoping to learn something bad enough to knock him off the pedestal I've built for him, yet all the while I've been dancing around the truth. But Picasso and Spiral aimed right at it when they asked about Gunner's type.

Because I *am* his type. Or I was. The first time we met, Jesus—he basically *told* me that I was. And the kiss we shared was insanely hot. It wasn't only the physical attraction, though. We just clicked. Everything he said, every joke he told. It was like he was made specifically for me. And I'm pretty damn sure he thought the same.

But still he told me he wouldn't see me again. I like to pretend the reason he stays away is because of what he said later—I'm Stone's little sister, and it's best to keep things simple—but that wasn't why he planned to ride away that first day. He didn't know I was Stone's sister then.

Anyway, Stone wouldn't care if his friend dated me. He'd care if Gunner acted like a dick or screwed me over, but my brother's not some stupid meathead guarding his sister's virtue.

And I've been looking for a reason not to want him. But the truth is, there's not anything wrong with Gunner.

There's something wrong with me.

Or if not something *wrong*, just not enough *right*. And because of that, he drew a line between us—the line that said, "Let's keep it simple." The concern in his eyes is genuine, I'm sure. But no matter what he feels for me, I'm not worth enough for him to cross over that line. Maybe the reason is my brother. Maybe it's something else. But whatever the reason, he doesn't want me enough to step over.

And every time I've thrown myself over that line — he doesn't want me enough to hold on. Instead he carefully pushes me back to my side.

God. I wanted a knife sharp enough to cut out my heart? Here it is. Knowing that Gunner's everything I want…but I'm not enough for him.

And after all these years, it's clear I never will be.

"You drove Picasso home last night?"

A hard note in his voice makes me lift my cheek from the window to look at him. I don't know why I bothered. He's staring straight ahead, wearing no expression at all.

My throat's a solid lump, so I just nod.

He glances over to catch my response. His jaw tightens. "I'll make sure it doesn't happen again."

The quiet anger in his reply makes me frown. "Why?"

"Did you close last night?"

"Yeah."

"And look at you."

"Look at me?"

"Half asleep over there. You're fucking exhausted, aren't you?" Gunner shakes his head. "You shouldn't be driving Riders home in the middle of the night. If they need a lift, they can ask a brother."

"There wasn't anyone else there." Friday night, usually there is. But not last night. Knowing today was Red's funeral, almost everyone else cleared out around midnight.

"Then they can call up a brother and wait until he arrives."

Yeah, they could. There's no reason to, though. "I was on my way home."

His frown darkens every feature, his profile like an angry god's. "Picasso's place isn't on your way—"

"Hold on. Jesus." I can't believe I'm hearing this. Even my brother at his most dickish isn't this overbearing. Now Gunner gets me alone and thinks he's going to be? "How about this? You want them to stop accepting a ride when I offer one? Then you tell *them* that. I'll keep doing what I'm doing when I feel like doing it. If I want to drive Picasso home, I will. Hell, if I want to drive him home and bounce on his drunk dick all night, I will. You can tell the brothers to do whatever, but you have no say in what *I* do."

His icy gaze flicks over me. A muscle jumps in his jaw. "You'd bounce on his dick?"

"Hell no. Picasso's an ass." Not as bad as some of the Riders, but for god's sake—I've seen him balls deep in more women than I care to think about. I'm not likely to add myself to that number.

"That didn't stop you from heading out with Mark Miller."

No, it didn't. A huff of laughter bursts from me. That date was a freaking disaster.

My laugh seems to dispel the anger building in him. He's quiet for a moment, before he asks softly, "Did seeing what happened to Red make you worry about that cancer stuff again? Like when you found that fibroadenoma?"

The mass in my breast. "You remember what it was called?"

"I looked it up," he says and that doesn't really surprise me. Not considering how much he reads. "But are you thinking the same thing now—are you worried you haven't lived enough, done enough?"

"The opposite, actually," I say. But he looks at me, as if waiting for more, so I try to explain. "Seeing Red…I *did* start thinking of it again. But in a different way. I'm trying to let go of the fear—and instead of assuming that I'll die young, I'm going to trust that I'll have a good, long life."

He nods and faces the front again. His throat works before he says, "So I guess you'll have time to sort out the dicks from the good guys."

He remembers that, too? It was a lie. Well, partially a lie. I didn't want to waste the time I had left, that was true. But what I really didn't want to do was waste my time being with any man who wasn't the one I wanted. Maybe it seems backwards. I think most people who are worried about how long they have to live grab pleasure where they can. Me, I didn't want to spend that precious time settling for second best.

But I have years to find a new best. No settling.

I just have to get over Gunner first.

"You didn't need to sort Miller," he adds. "Everyone knows he's a prick."

"Yes." And that's why going out with him was…safe. I wasn't jumping into anything that might hurt me. "But at least he didn't think hooking up with me qualified as 'that shit.'"

Gunner's fierce gaze snaps to mine. "Who the hell said that?"

Unbelievable. "*You* did. Ten minutes ago, talking to Picasso and Spiral." I lower my voice to mimic his. "'Yup, me hooking up with Stone's sister? That's shit. Don't talk about it.' And you gave them your *me big angry man, you listen good* caveman stare."

Which looks a hell of a lot like the expression he's giving me now. "You know I didn't mean it like that."

"Do I? Because I was right there and it felt like you did."

"I was talking about the fucking *gossip*. Zoomie told me people were giving you shit because of it."

That does spin it another way. "Oh."

"Any guy would be lucky to hook up with you."

Not lucky enough, apparently. "Okay."

"Spiral and Picasso damn well know that, too. So they knew exactly what I meant by it."

"Okay! I get it. I'm bangable." Even if Gunner doesn't want to bang me. "Thanks."

He nods tightly before looking at the road again. His strong fingers flex on the steering wheel. "So who's giving you shit?"

"What?"

"About those rumors going around about you and me. Who's giving you shit?"

"Oh." *God damn it, Lily.* She shouldn't have mentioned it. "Just, you know, guys being assholes."

"Who?"

"Just whoever. Some guys are like that. If you turn them down, it's never about them. It's always about the girl. I'm good enough to ask out but as soon as I say no, they're like, 'So it's true that you're really spreading your legs for Gunner on the side' or 'You're so hung up on that pretty boy, your pathetic ass wouldn't know a real man.' Because if I don't want them, there obviously must be something wrong with me."

"Who?"

His hands are white-knuckling the steering wheel, his lips flattened into a harsh line. Holy crap. He's really pissed.

I can't decide if that's funny or awesome or both. "What are you going to do? Beat them up?"

"Maybe" comes out of his mouth. His tone says, *I'll kill them.*

"I have a brother for that."

"You've got me, too."

No, I don't. Though I believe he'd come running to my rescue. But not the way my brother runs to the rescue of the girls he hooks up with.

My voice is a little rough as I ask, "Do you think Stone loves her—that girl he's helping?"

Gunner seems to grapple with that for a long second. Maybe not ready to abandon the pursuit of all the assholes he needs to thrash. Then, "I think he loves all of them a little. At least at first."

Yes. That's probably true. "But this one, she must be something more. I mean, he missed Red's funeral for her. I'm trying to imagine him missing any Rider's funeral, and I can't. But *Red's* funeral? I really, really can't."

Gunner doesn't answer. Maybe he has a hard time imagining it, too. Maybe he's disappointed in my brother for putting a woman before Red. But if he is disappointed, I don't think he'd ever say so to anyone but Stone.

I'm not disappointed in my brother. It's just…strange. "Do you know he didn't even ask about Daisy?" I tell him.

"What?"

"In his messages. He didn't ask how Daisy was doing. And lately his messages have been really odd. But I guess whatever's going on with this girl explains it."

"Yes."

"What *is* going on with her?"

His jaw clenches before he tells me, "I can't say."

"Club business?"

"Yes."

I blow out an exasperated breath, shaking my head. But it doesn't matter. If it's club business, it'll eventually reach my ears anyway. It always does.

Other things reach my ears, too. "Ray Peterson came into the Den the other day." Gunner's boss on the city maintenance crew. "He's pretty pissed that you've been gone all week."

"I know." His response is wooden. "If I'm not back tomorrow, I'm out of a job."

I gape at him. "For real?"

Gunner nods.

Holy shit. Stone doesn't have the same worry—he works with Widowmaker on his logging crew, and they're pretty much off for the season, anyway. "But you're still leaving tomorrow?"

"Yes."

Jeeeeesus. "That must be some seriously important club business."

"It is." By the grim tone of his voice, 'seriously important' might be an understatement.

"Is that why Blowback and Lily have been gone all week, too?" I know he won't answer me—freaking club business—so I just shake my head again. "I thought they were on their honeymoon."

His head turns sharply, his pale gaze catching mine. "Honeymoon?"

"Yeah." Doesn't he know? "They got married in Vegas a few weeks ago."

"The hell they did."

"They did." I have to laugh. He's stunned by the news. "I think they plan to keep it quiet. You know, to avoid the commentary of the club's assholes. But I assumed Lily told you and Stone."

"She didn't." His grin breaks through and he returns his attention to the road. The snow's gaining on the rain, but it's all melting as soon as it hits the ground. "Damn. That means we must be assholes, too."

"Well, now that you mention it…" I let that trail off, and he flashes another grin my way.

God, my heart. It just stops when he does that.

But nothing stops for him. He just says, "Good for them."

I nod in silent agreement. *Good for them.* Lily's the last person I expected to be married now—Blowback, too, but he's another breed entirely. Like some kind of unfeeling, inhuman killing machine. Maybe I shouldn't have been so surprised, though. When Lily goes, she goes all in, and in this case, she grabbed onto a future with Blowback in both hands and went for it.

I need to do the same. Not a future with Blowback. Just any future. And not by grabbing on. By letting go.

It won't happen quickly. I know that. Getting over Gunner isn't going to be as easy as going out on a few dates with other guys. I don't even *want* to go on more dates with other guys yet—the disaster with Mark taught me that. But that date was a step in the right direction. Because when I told Mark yes, I'd stopped hoping that anything would ever happen with Gunner.

Gravel crunches beneath the tires as Gunner turns into the lot outside Jenny's brewery, then reverses and backs up the truck to the front door. He glances over.

"Ready?"

"Hold on." I show him my phone. "I've got a bar of reception. What's her name?"

"Whose name?"

"The girl Stone is with."

"Cherry."

"Are you for real? *Cherry* and *Stone*? Is her last name Pit?"

"Oh shit." His eyes close as if in physical pain. "I didn't put that together before. That's terrible."

Beyond terrible. Giggling, I type out a message. *Gunner told me all about Cherry and your seeekrit speshul TRUE WUV. And Mom told me I'm her favorite kid.*

I hit 'send' and something inside Gunner's kutte vibrates and lights up.

Phone in hand, I go utterly still — staring at the slice of pale light, with a knot of dread unraveling inside me. "What is that?"

Gunner tugs the keys from the ignition. The overhead light flicks on. "My phone."

"No. Yours is in your back pocket. I saw you put it there."

"It's a burner. Every Rider carries one."

I know they do. But I also know the chances of a Rider texting Gunner's burner phone at the same instant I send a message to Stone is almost zero. They only use those unregistered phones when something illegal is going down — and all the Riders are back at Jenny's house, where the reception is even worse than it is here.

I quickly type a single letter and hit 'send.' In the shadows beneath his vest, the light flares again, followed by a cold spike of fear through my chest.

"Oh my god. You have his phone. *Why* do you have his phone?" When he reaches for the door handle, I lurch halfway across the seat, grabbing his kutte. The memory of all those odd messages stabs through my mind on another icy spike of terror. "How *long* have you had his phone?"

"Shit." His pale eyes locked on mine, Gunner catches my face in his big hands. Oh god oh god. Does he need to brace me for what's coming? "Anna—"

"Is he okay? *Is he okay?*"

"He's okay." His fingers tighten as if to hold me in place, as if to force me to accept the truth of those words. "He's okay."

"Then why do you have his phone? Why isn't he here?"

"There was a girl—"

"Are you lying to me?" On a burst of anger, I swat at his wrists, pull out of his grip. "Of course you are. *Cherry*, Jesus Christ. What kind of name is that?"

"Not her real name, I'm sure." Dragging his hands away, he viciously rakes his fingers through his short hair. Tension whitens the sculpted planes of his face. "Listen. There was a girl. Some shit went down. And it's taking longer than we thought to sort through."

"And he gave you his phone? Why not keep it? Is

he…I don't know—undercover in another club or something?"

His gaze holds mine, steady. Even. "Something like that."

Some of my fear begins to recede. Gunner's not telling me anything, but the fact that he's *here* says more than words could. If I know one thing for certain, it's that Gunner would never abandon Stone if he was hurt.

But he's going back tomorrow. So whatever my brother is tangled up in, it's still happening.

Quiet falls between us. The dome light clicks off and for a long second, I study him through the dark. He's angled toward me, one shoulder against the door and the other against the back of the seat. Shadows conceal most of his face but I can feel his gaze on mine.

He's so close I can smell the leather of his vest, his clean scent. I'm still halfway across the seat, just a few inches from sitting in his lap. I'm no longer holding onto his kutte but my fingers burn with the memory of his warmth. Despite the cold night, he's only wearing a black long-sleeved shirt under his vest. Beneath the thin cotton lay steely strength, solid muscle.

God, the *feel* of him. I curl my fingertips into my palms, holding onto the heat as long as I can. It's all I can do not to crawl closer, to fasten my mouth to his…and throw myself at him again.

I know how that would end.

Tearing my gaze from his lips, I scoot back a little.

"So what's really going on?"

He takes a moment to answer and when he does, his voice is low and rough. Just like I imagine it would be if I *did* crawl into his lap. "Club business."

"Really? That's still your answer? Club business?"

"Yes."

Goddammit. But I *will* find out eventually. "So Stone told you to text me?"

He's utterly still, watching me. "No one wanted you to worry."

I barely hear the answer because all at once, the full import of what he's saying strikes me. Stone's replies weren't odd—they just weren't Stone's.

Oh my god. What exactly did I text to Gunner this week? A few throwaway messages. A few conversations. I yanked his chain about a fake girlfriend with a unicorn baby. And joked with him about Burnout's ass hair—and Jesus, no wonder I thought Gunner was feeding Stone those replies about symmetrical ponytails and redundant man buns. *All* of that was from Gunner.

That's not so embarrassing, I guess. I always assume Stone shares some of my texts with Gunner, especially if they're about other Riders. But did Gunner scroll back through my brother's messages? Or—please God—did Stone delete those old texts? Because I've never had a discussion with my brother about Gunner over the phone or anywhere else, but Stone knows me as well as my mom does. And a few times, he's poked at me a little. Nothing like a big flashing sign saying ANNA'S HUNG UP ON GUNNER but still not anything I'd want him to see.

There's probably nothing to see. I never delete any messages, but I think Stone erases most of his. He doesn't like leaving easy-to-follow trails—even if those trails are legal.

But I still feel like such an idiot. Sick humiliation churns in my stomach. My face burning, I fumble for the door handle.

"Anna? Shit."

His door slams. He's around the back of the truck faster than I can get to the brewery's entrance, his big body blocking my way.

Gunner's got the keys, anyway, so I couldn't get inside even if I went around him. I lift my chin, hating how the floodlight over the brewery door exposes me. I can't hide the humiliated flush in my cheeks, but I can throw a hell of a lot of anger behind it. I meet his brooding gaze and wait.

When his reply comes, it's exactly what I expected. "I didn't like lying to you—"

"But you still *did*," I snap before he can finish. "So what's coming next—an apology where you aren't *really* sorry because you still think it was for the right reason?"

By the clench of his jaw, I know that hit right on the head. He's only sorry I found out.

Frustration vibrates through his deep voice. "I didn't want you to worry."

"So pissing me off is better than worrying me, huh? *Humiliating* me is better?" His body goes rigid and a tortured expression twists his hardened features. I hold up my hands, stopping his reply. "No, no. Let me be pissed off—and I'll let you wallow in how shitty it feels knowing you hurt me. You earned it. God knows I can't stay pissed anyway, so it's not like it'll last. So let's get these fucking kegs and get this done, and by the time we drive back everything will be hunky-dory again."

A muscle in his jaw works before he nods and steps back. He unlocks the door—but doesn't move inside, holding it open for me with his arm extended, so I have to brush past him on my way through. I feel his gaze with every step.

I'm already less angry. Shit. That's the problem with knowing he's a decent guy instead of an asshole. He might do asshole things. But everyone does at times. Even me. And he's a far cry from some jerk who simply doesn't give a fuck. His reason for doing that asshole thing was fueled by good intentions.

It's hard to stay mad about that.

Despite the chill inside, the storefront to the brewery smells like warm toast, as if the yeasty odor of the mash has permanently cooked into the air. Jenny's got a small tasting bar along one wall, flanked by shelves of T-shirts and pint glasses branded with her logo. Stocked with bottled ale and mini-kegs, two big glass-front refrigerators hum against the opposite wall. The cash register sits on a counter in front of the walk-in cooler, where the full-sized kegs are kept.

Gunner catches up with me at the door to the walk-in. I reach for a hand truck, but his heavy boot pins the blade to the floor.

"Leave it," he says. "I'll carry them out. You just point to the right kegs and tell me how many."

"For all the Riders and their old ladies? You're going to need at least five or six kegs." I tug on the dolly's handle. It doesn't move an inch. "They're like a hundred and fifty pounds each."

"One-sixty-two filled. So that's one hundred and sixty two reasons for you not to be pushing that over the gravel outside."

"So you're just going to lug them out?"

"Yup. I'm the muscle, remember?" His smile isn't quite all there but the curve of his mouth still shivers over my every nerve, prickling my skin with instant awareness. "Back in the day, I had a drill instructor who made us march ten miles with a barrel on our shoulders whenever he got pissed at us. He called it our penance for being pissant mealworms. So this is nothing. Twenty feet, back and forth."

I purse my lips. "As penance?"

"For being an asshole."

"But you just said it's no effort. Not much of a penance, if you ask me."

Humor flashes through his eyes. "You can flog me

along the way. Go medieval." Abruptly the intensity of his gaze deepens, the amusement burning away. "But a flogging wouldn't be much of a punishment, either."

My breath catches in my throat. No, it really wouldn't be. But before I can reply, his face shutters and he hauls open the walk-in door.

"Which kegs?" His voice is taut.

Because that look wasn't simple. But he still wants it to be.

With my chest aching and the rest of my body humming, I point to the stainless steel kegs lining the nearest wall. "Two of those. Then the rest from this stock over here. I'll track down her price sheet and write up an invoice for Old Timer. Jenny will probably say they're on the house, since it's for her dad, but you tell him not to let her."

"I will," comes his gruff reply.

I leave him to it, taking down the price list near the cash register, and not even looking over when he passes me with a keg braced on his shoulder. Any other time I might have watched every step he took. But I'm aroused and hurting and neither feeling will be helped by staring at a perfect ass and a strong back that aren't mine to touch, to hold.

I keep my head down as he comes back through. It only takes about two minutes to write up the invoice. On his third trip outside I pull out my phone, scrolling through the texts from the past week. Now that I'm looking for it,

I can spot the moment he took over Stone's messages. My brother's punctuation and spelling were never that accurate.

My "It was Sunday morning, yeah?" catches him as he comes through the door.

His gaze flicks to the phone before lifting to meet mine. "Yes," he says, then watches me with that brooding stare, as if waiting for me to ask more.

But I put my head down again, blindly gazing at the messages. Sunday morning. The worst fucking morning. The morning Red called—the morning I sat in my car crying, feeling hacked open with my guts spilling all over.

I feel that blade in my stomach again now. *Pipsqueak,* he called me. Did my brother tell him to use that nickname? Or did Gunner just know?

Love you, too.

Oh god. The words waver in front of me. I dip my head to conceal the sudden tears burning my eyes. Stone would have said that, no question. But knowing it's from Gunner?

It hurts. It hurts so much.

And I can't believe my brother did this to me. In no scenario I could ever imagine would Stone tell Gunner to pretend to be him. If I'd been playing the guessing game with my mom, I could have tripped her up on this one. "Hey, Aaron went undercover in another club and didn't want us to worry. So guess what he did?"

My mom would *never* say, "He asked Zach to text us

and pretend to be him, so that we wouldn't worry."

My heart thuds. A thick, heavy ball forms in my gut.

She'd never say that. Because my brother would never do it.

If Stone knew he'd be out of touch, he'd have said so. He'd have sent us a message like, *Going to be out of reach for a while. Don't worry about me. I'll contact you when I can.* Because he's sent that kind of message before while doing business for the club. So if he told Gunner to send any message on his behalf, it would be that same one.

And Stone would never let me believe I was texting him while I was really texting Gunner. Because Stone knows Red's cancer left me feeling emotionally vulnerable, and he knows how I feel about his friend. He'd never put me in a position where I might be exposed and hurt.

But I am hurt. And angry. I wanted to find something I don't like about Gunner?

I just fucking found it.

His deception might have come from good intentions. But only a few minutes ago, I asked him point blank if Stone was okay—and he lied to me. It *had* to be a lie. Because if Stone was okay, this wouldn't have happened.

And maybe Gunner really is trying to keep me from worrying. But it's one thing to keep me from worrying if my brother is fine. It's another thing to lie to my face when my brother is very likely *not* fine.

But what's Gunner going to say if I confront him? He'll just lie again. He might ask how I'm so sure. What should I tell him? *Because my brother knows how I feel about you and he'd never do this to me.*

I never imagined Gunner would do this to me, either.

But now…I don't even care. I don't even want to deal with him. I just want to get away from him and figure out where my brother is.

At least my tears are gone. My eyes feel hot and dry and hard as I look at his message again.

Love you, too.

Funny. Those are words I wanted from him more than any other. Those are words I believed would fill my heart to bursting. Instead those words are as hollow as my chest, and they're a clear declaration of what I am to him.

Nothing. Which is about as simple as it gets.

And I can't ever let myself forget it.

TEN

GUNNER

I'm such a goddamn asshole.

The cold bites my face as I load the last keg into the truck bed and slam the tailgate closed. I could have come out here to pick up the beer by myself. I know where everything is. When Jenny was in trouble last summer, the prez had me look at the security in the old barn, get familiar with the layout. And I've stopped by plenty of times since.

I could have done this alone. Instead I let Anna drag herself out here with me — even though she's exhausted as fuck and grieving so hard she looks ready to shatter into a thousand pieces.

Dragged her out here, then lied to her.

Lied to her even as my eyes consume her whole. She's wearing a coat that swallows her like a sleeping bag from her neck to her knees, but I know every slender curve hidden beneath. In the garage, in the truck, just keeping my hands off her strained my self control to the breaking point. Thinking about how warm she'd be if I hauled her over me and spread her sleek thighs. Thinking of her hot mouth and of sinking balls deep into her, holding on and fucking and pretending tomorrow won't come.

Because the only path ahead is the last route I ever wanted to take. But I'll do anything to bring her brother home—even if it means I won't be coming back again.

And now, maybe my last time seeing her, I've got the filth of these lies all over me. I want to kiss her. Want to hold her. But I'm covered in this shit and I've already hurt her with it.

So I watch her instead, taking what little I can. She looks so damn tired, fragile. And so beautiful, her dark hair coiled back and framing her fairy-like features.

I head back into the brewery. She's at the cashier's counter, staring down at her phone, her expression so brittle it's all I can do not to pull her into my arms, try to soothe the hurt.

The hurt I caused. I've got no right to touch her.

I don't know if I'd stop once I did.

Standing by the door, I clear my throat. "You helped Jenny decorate?"

Her gaze is blank as she looks up, then over at the wall I gesture to. A mural is partially concealed by the shelves of branded T-shirts and glassware Jenny has for sale. It's a simple painting of a field in the spring, but because I know what to look for, I can see how the wildflowers form a connect-the-dots.

Anna was here.

Not just selfies—she's done the same with paintings in her own house. I don't know a thing about art, but to my eye, she's damn talented with a brush. Anna doesn't agree. She told me once her artwork wasn't even as good as the stuff you can buy for cheap at Target. Maybe that's true, but they look good to me. And I fucking love the second I see the words I'm looking for in them.

She's staring blindly at the mural now, and the blankness of her expression slowly hardens, comes into focus. Finally her gaze slides over to me. "Do you still want to do something for me, even if it's horrible?"

"Name it." Anything for her.

"Remember when I found out I was having breast surgery, so I flashed my boobs at you and wanted you to tell me they weren't perfect?"

As if I could forget. I can't stop my eyes from drifting down now. Her coat conceals the soft curves of her breasts, but I remember those small, pretty tits. There's a scar now, I guess, though I've never seen it. But I've seen her breasts a thousand times in my mind. I've drawn her taut nipples into my mouth, imagined her moans as I licked and sucked those stiffened tips.

Fuck. My cock's about to tear through my zipper. "So my horrible task is to stand here while you flash me again? Shit. I'll try to bear the pain."

Seeing her mouth twitch with humor is like winning the goddamn lottery—then having the prize taken away when her smile quickly subsides. "No. I started down a new road that day. I was so worried about dying. But I've started a new road today. I'm starting it now. So I want to mark it with a picture. Something…to remind me why I'm doing this."

One of her selfies. Though by definition, a selfie doesn't need me. "I'll take a picture of you flashing me, if that's what you're asking."

"No. It'll be a picture of you." She points at my chest, flicks her finger upward. "Strip your shirt and kutte off."

This is so damn close to a thousand fantasies I stand motionless—brainless—just staring at her.

"Come on." Her eyebrows arch in challenge. "You said you'd do anything."

That's a boot in my ass. "I meant it."

Quickly shrugging out of my kutte, I fold the leather carefully before laying the Riders' colors on the bar. With my back to her, I yank the tails of my black shirt free of my jeans. This is a fucking problem. My erection bulges behind my zipper, aching to be buried deep inside her.

There's no way she won't see how hard I am.

Like some preppy fucker, I tie my shirt around my hips. The long sleeves dangling beneath the knot cover most of the evidence. At least I won't poke her eyes out with my dick when I turn around.

When I face her, she's utterly still, looking at me and holding her breath. Her bottom lip is trapped between her teeth, those warm brown eyes locked on my stomach, her gaze slipping over the ridges of muscle. A flush spreads up her pale cheeks and I remember her drunken *"You are so damn beautiful."*

Maybe so. But I grew up with five brothers who looked the same, so it's nothing.

The way she looks at me, though, like she could eat me up—that's everything. I'll take it with me. I can't have a kiss, I can't have her. I'll take this.

Grinning, I spread my arms so she can see all she wants and move in closer, adding an extra bit of swagger. Her sudden laugh fills me right up, makes every single hour busting my ass in the gym and fighting in the ring worth it. I'm almost sorry when she closes her eyes, like it's all a visual overload, but not sorry when she breathes, "That's just ridiculous."

"And it's all yours, baby." Only yours. Forever.

Something painful slides across her expression, scraping away her laughter and leaving a thin smile. Her brittle gaze lifts to mine before dropping to my chest again. "You know, the first time you stayed with us, I told my mom we should install hidden cameras in the guest room so we could sell the photos."

Considering how many times I stroked my dick while thinking of her just across the hall, it's a damn good thing there weren't hidden cameras in there. "You going to sell this picture?"

Her smile fades. "No. It's just for me."

I tap my forefinger beneath her pointed chin, making her meet my eyes again. "You aren't sending me a copy?"

She shakes her head before turning away. I barely stop myself from reaching for her, drawing her back. Hands clenched at my sides, I watch her circle around the bar. From beneath the counter she grabs a white hand towel. My gaze follows her as she returns, unfolding the towel on the diagonal and quickly whipping the terrycloth into a white rope.

I haven't seen anyone do that since a locker room in high school. "So it'll be a flogging after all?"

Her brittle smile returns. "No. I want you to put it on like a blindfold."

She holds the towel up for me to take. Hell no. I'm not passing up this chance. I play dumb as fuck, as if I think she's offering to tie it for me. I lower my head, close my eyes.

On a deep breath, she moves closer. And it's torture. Sweet torture. Soft, warm fingers brush against my cheekbones as she carefully lays the rough cloth over my eyes. Then she lifts up on her toes and her hands wind the towel behind my head, her chest pressing against mine, the soft coat pillowed between us. Jesus Christ, this is heaven. The whisper of her breath on my neck, the delicate fragrance of her hair.

And thank fuck for that big puffy coat or she'd know exactly how this affects me. Between us, my cock is a solid throbbing ache.

My voice is a thick rasp. "This is a lot kinkier than I expected."

Her breathless laugh against my ear almost snaps my control. Body rigid, I force myself not to grab onto her, to haul her up closer and claim her mouth, kissing her until that laugh deepens into a needy moan.

A tug at the back of my head tells me she's almost got the knot tied. The blood pounds in my brain, harder and harder, then her warmth disappears as she pulls away. I lift my head, tension straining every muscle. A rustle of cloth sounds, as if she's digging into her pockets, followed by the soft click of a cap or a bottle being opened.

"Okay, now—stay really still. And don't look."

She moves closer again, her sweet scent returning with her. I clench my jaw against a groan when her palm flattens against my chest. Steadying herself, I realize—one hand braced against my right pectoral even as something cool and wet swirls across my left pec. Something moist, but not warm enough to be her tongue.

She's writing on me.

Oh fuck. I know what she always writes. I know

without even looking.

Anna was here.

Sweetheart. You were always here.

The need to reach out to her is overwhelming. But that's not what she wants now. This is about her taking a new road, not about some asshole taking her into his arms.

She stops writing and begins drawing a line around the words. Every nerve in my skin seems focused on the wet path of her pen or brush or whatever she's using.

Not just a line around the words—a shape. Two curves at the top, the point at the bottom.

A heart. Right over mine.

I clench my jaw against the pain rising in my chest. Christ. The path of that heart seems to draw blood, knowing I'm leaving tomorrow. Knowing I'll never have her.

But I'll have this.

"Just a second," she whispers and her voice isn't right. Thick, as if clogged with tears. "I still have to take the picture."

Even though she's crying. As if this is hurting her. Gritting my teeth, I wait until I hear the click of her phone's camera. Fucking finally. I reach up to grab the blindfold.

Her hands catch my wrists. "Wait. I have to…"

Clean me off. Even as her voice trails away she begins wiping at the words on my chest—using tissues, it feels like.

"Shit," she whispers. "Shit."

"What?"

"I used lipstick. Now it's just smearing."

"It doesn't matter. Can I take this off?"

She rubs hard for another long second. Finally, she steps back. "Okay."

I glance down and fight back another groan. A blob of crimson darkens half my chest—the same color of lipstick she wore in the selfie she sent to Stone last week. I dreamed of having that lipstick smeared all over my cock. My pec is a hell of a long way from that, but I still love wearing Anna's mark.

She's not so thrilled. With a sigh, she gathers up the wadded tissues and heads for the trash bin. "It's going to stain your shirt."

"I don't care." I study her face as I untie the sleeves knotted at my waist. Though she's not crying as I thought, she looks wrecked—as if something inside her shattered and she's barely holding it together. "Are you all right?"

She doesn't answer right away. That's an answer in itself. And she's not ogling my body now. Instead her face is averted, as if she's waiting until I'm safely covered before looking at me again.

Damn it. I liked her looking at me.

But something's changing in her. Even as I watch, her expression slowly hardens with determination, resolve—as if she's gearing up for something. Or bracing herself. She moves to the bar and props herself against the edge of a stool, her shoulders hunched, her hands balled in her coat pockets.

Finally she looks at me. "There's something else I need you to do for me."

I finish buttoning my shirt, leaving the tails untucked to cover my erection, and reach for my kutte. "Anything."

Her chest lifts on a deep breath. "When you and Stone get back…I don't want you coming to the house anymore. Or sitting at the bar when I'm working."

I freeze with the leather dangling from my fingers. Is she joking? But she's not. Her eyes aren't sparkling in that way she has when she's jerking Stone's chain. Instead her gaze is flat and hard and steady.

She meant it. But I can't fucking take it in.

Slowly I shrug into my kutte, feeling like I've been sucker punched. Every thought is scattered and I can't catch my breath. "You want what?"

She doesn't repeat herself but just barrels forward. "I know it's Stone's place, too. And the Den isn't my bar, so it's not even my right to ask—"

Fuck rights. "Why the hell would you ask? You don't want me around?"

Her gaze remains steady but tension's starting to unravel her voice. "I need to start this new road—not being afraid of dying."

"Good. But what the fuck does that have to do with me?"

Now her eyes dart to the side, like she's looking for

a reason. Which tells me this won't be her real reason. "Remember you said a long time ago to keep it simple? You're just Stone's friend. I'm just his sister."

"Yeah."

Of course I remember. I did it to protect her. And it's killed me for ten goddamn years.

"Well, nobody thinks it's simple," she says, her gaze meeting mine again and her voice picking up, like she's convincing herself as she goes along. "And I need to move forward. But every time someone asks me out, they think they'll have to go around you. Like Mark, the other day he asked—"

"Mark's a fucking tool."

"I know." It bursts out on a short, sharp laugh, like it rips from her. "But you wondered about the shit I get because of those rumors about you and me. And Mark, he asked if he was going to have to fight you. They all ask. Because you're always there. And I know you don't do it on purpose. It's just what they think. And so guys who might ask me out won't, because they think they'll have to go through you. Or they think we're already together."

So I've been cockblocking some of those fuckers? I'm sure as hell not sorry about it. "Any asshole who isn't willing to go through me to have you isn't a man worth having."

Pain flashes over her expression. "So I need someone who'd risk anything to be with me? I know."

That pain settles into a sad, longing smile that about

rips my heart out. Jesus. Chest aching, I clench my jaw and look away from her, staring blindly toward the back of the store. I'd give anything to be with her. But to keep her safe, *being with her* is the one damn thing I can't have.

Especially now. Not with my family looking at her. Not when finding her brother depends on me joining the Notorious Few and falling in line.

"I know what you're probably thinking," Anna adds quietly. "You're practically a member of my family. So where do I get off telling you not to come around?"

My gaze shoots back to hers. "Oh, is that what I'm thinking?"

Her shoulders hunch over more, as if she's protecting herself from my anger. "I'm just saying. For holidays and stuff, of course you should still come to my mom's place."

"But otherwise stay the fuck away from you?"

Silently she nods.

Sick agony bursts like a blood blister through my chest. Stay away from her. I should. What she's asking is exactly what I should be doing to protect her. I should agree and walk the hell away.

Instead I stalk closer, driven by fury, by pain. "Would it be so fucking terrible if people think we're together?"

Her shoulders shoot back like steel was injected into her spine. Her chin lifts. "You tell me! Because it sure as hell wouldn't be *simple* anymore."

"Hell yeah, it would." My blood drumming heavily through my veins, I lean in and brace my hands on the bar behind her, caging her between my arms. "It doesn't get much simpler than a man and a woman fucking, sweetheart."

Her eyes widen. Not hard and flat now, but glowing with gold and honey. "Wh–What did you say?"

My fingers clench on the edge of the bar. It's the only control I've got left. If I touch her, if I feel her soft skin beneath my hands, Christ knows if I'll be able to stop. She's staring up at me, her lips parted. A hectic flush stains her pale cheeks. Deliberately I press closer, forcing her to sit back farther on the barstool and settling into the space between her thighs, watching her expression go utterly still. Her coat and skirt are wedged between us but there's no mistaking how damn hard I am, and how easy it would be to push all the barriers aside and thrust my cock deep inside her sweet heat.

"I said a fuck is real simple." Need roughens each word. A shiver races through her and I lower my head until I can feel her warm breath trembling across my lips. "As simple as you, me, and a bed. You won't need to sort through the assholes if I'm already inside you. And I'll make it so goddamn good for you, Anna."

It's already so fucking good. Being this close to her. Hearing the soft moan that escapes her throat before she bites her bottom lip. Feeling the sleek muscles of her thighs flex, pushing her hips against me as if seeking more pressure. I give it to her, rocking forward and grinding between her thighs. She sucks in a sharp breath through her teeth and the quiet evidence of her aroused response leaves my body shaking with tension, on the edge of coming.

For a taut moment we're breathless, motionless. Then a shudder wracks her slender form.

"I can't do this," she whispers.

Jesus, she's killing me. I close my eyes, my body in the grip of torturous need. But I can't argue. It's not the best time. Not when she's grieving and not when Stone's still out there.

I nod and lower my head, pressing my lips to the corner of her jaw, just below her ear. Arousal roughens my voice. "When I come back, then. You don't have to send me away, Anna. I'll give you what you need any time you want it."

And one way or another, settle the shit with my family, so I'll never have to stop.

"Goddammit, Gunner! I don't want a fuck." Her hands shove against my chest. "I want a future!"

Her push didn't have a lot of power behind it but her words strike hard. I stagger back a step, looking down at her. Determination tightens her jaw but her eyes are huge and soft, swimming with tears.

Her gaze searches mine, and the longing in her voice tears me apart. "I want what my parents have. What Jenny has. Someone who'll promise me forever. Are *you* going to give me that?"

I would. Oh Christ, I want to.

But I can't promise a damn thing. Not now. If I come back and don't bring her brother home…she sure as hell won't want to spend that future with me.

Unbearable tension squeezes at my throat and I can't say a goddamn word in response. But maybe she reads the answer in my face.

Her eyes close, spilling tears down her pale cheeks. "I want a future. But if everyone thinks we're fucking each other, if they think we're hung up on each other, I have no chance. Not in this town." Her voice breaks and she whispers, "I mean, Jesus. Even Jenny thinks I'm in love with you."

Her best friend. Who would know. Christ. My hands shake as I drag my fingers through my hair, trying to pull my emotions back under control. I shouldn't even ask if Jenny's right, because the question is a knife poised right over my heart.

But I can't stop myself. Hoarsely I ask, "Are you?"

Anna's shattered gaze lifts to mine. She says bleakly, "Truthfully? I don't think I even know you."

Her answer stabs straight through me. I can't think. Can't respond.

The silence between us stretches thin until she draws a shuddering breath. "Am I anything more than Stone's sister to *you*?"

What the fuck does she think? Since the day I met her, there's been no one else. I haven't touched another woman. Haven't even looked at another woman.

But if Anna has to ask…then she truly doesn't know me. I could show her what she means to me. Right now. I could push forward, take her mouth, and with one kiss she'd know every damn thing that matters.

But her eyes, Jesus. They're pleading with me, tears glittering in their shattered depths.

Pleading with me to say she's more than Stone's sister? But that's not what she's asking for. She's looking for a future. A promise.

I can't give her one.

Throat raw, I tell her, "You're not anything more to me," and shred my soul with the lie.

A lie she doesn't see through. She stares at me, her expression utterly blank—like she's not even seeing me. Like she's seeing nothing at all.

Then she turns her face away. And shrugs.

"See," she says. "Simple."

"Simple," I echo. My chest is completely hollow.

Her shoulders hunch again, her hands stuffed deep into her coat pockets. "So, yeah. And when you come back…I know it'll be inconvenient for you not meeting up with Stone at my house or not sitting at the bar, but"—she shrugs again—"we'll live with it."

This is living? A harsh laugh breaks from me, dredged up from the emptiness inside my chest. But it's not so empty any more. Agony is filling it up fast.

"Yup, we'll live with it." Each word comes out hard and bitter. "And you chose a damn good time to kick me out of your life. The renovation on your place is almost done. So no need for me to hang around, providing free labor."

She flinches. And fuck me, that was low. So fucking low, lashing out like that.

I've got to get the hell away from her before I do it again. Because the pain is still growing, building.

I thought I knew what hell was? I thought hell was being near her and not having her? That wasn't hell.

This is.

I can't breathe. I turn toward the door, not seeing a damn thing but her flinch and her tears. Blindly, I put one foot in front of the next.

I'll be putting one foot in front of the next for the rest of my pointless fucking life.

"The kegs are loaded up," I say roughly. "I'll drop you off at Jenny's on my way out to the clubhouse."

"Will you send Bottlecap here to pick me up, instead?"

Her voice is muffled and when I glance back, she looks so damn small. Tiny. Like she's folded up in that big coat, the bottom half of her face buried in the puffy collar, her wounded gaze making her eyes seem huge.

"Yeah, I'll send him," I tell her. "We wouldn't want anyone to see you've been alone with me. All the assholes in town will be too afraid to touch you. But hell. If a coward is what turns you on, I wish you the best."

I hear her quick draw of breath but she just stares at me, and that wounded gaze just gets bigger, deeper.

And that wasn't fair of me. Just not fucking fair. All she wants is a future. A life. Marriage. She deserves them. Deserves to be happy, to be loved.

But I can't say I'm sorry. Not when seeing her with someone else will kill me.

Swallowing hard, I nod and turn away from her. "All right. We'll make it real simple from now on. I said I'd do anything for you and I meant it. I'll do any goddamn thing you want. So here's me, heading right out of your life."

I throw open the door and hell is an icy wind, blasting into my eyes, making them burn, blurring the path ahead. I want to keep going, just disappear into the middle of nowhere, and wait for the cold to take me. Wait until I'm numb. Wait until none of this matters anymore.

But I've got a brother to bring home. And maybe Anna did me a favor, tearing out my heart.

Where I'm going tomorrow, it's best not to have one.

ELEVEN

ANNA

I wasn't afraid someone would see Gunner and me together. I was afraid that I'd do exactly what I did—break down and ugly cry on the floor of Jenny's brewery.

Fifteen minutes after Gunner walked through the door, Bottlecap pulls up in my Prius. I head out into the freezing rain to meet him. My eyes are dry, but every breath shudders with little hiccuping sobs that won't stop. I sound bad enough that he keeps giving me worried glances on the drive back to Jenny's. Poor kid. Stuck in a

little car with an emotional woman. He's probably terrified that I'm going to start bawling again.

I won't. I've got nothing left. I'm absolutely numb as
he stops the car. Dully I thank him and head around to
the driver's side. He glances toward Jenny's house, like he's
surprised I'm not going back in, but I just can't.

I've cried all day but it wasn't like *this*. I was hurting
during Red's funeral and afterward. But I was grieving,
not broken. And now…I'd scare the shit out of my mom if
she saw me like this. I'd scare the shit out of Jenny.

And Gunner would see how he shattered everything
inside me.

You're not anything more to me.

I knew I wasn't. So I shouldn't have asked if I was. But
even in the midst of trying to break the emotional chains
wrapped around my heart, I just couldn't quit.

I guess I paid for it.

The thirty-minute drive home passes in a blur of icy
rain and black asphalt. I pull into my driveway and sit
in the quiet and the dark, too exhausted to open the car
door. I don't remember ever being so worn out. Emotionally, physically.

I did the right thing, pushing Gunner away. I did.
Now I can move forward—and find out what's going on
with Stone.

Though now I wonder if there *is* anything going on
with Stone. I jumped to the conclusion that Gunner had
lied about my brother being all right. And why? Because

I didn't think Stone would ever let Gunner pretend to be him.

But growing up with my mom means that I don't ever get to escape myself. I never stop questioning my reasons for everything. I told myself that the reason I pushed Gunner away was because he lied to me about Stone, but really…it was all about me. Because what had I been doing all night? Trying to think of something wrong with Gunner. So I latched onto those doubts about Stone and used them as an excuse to tell Gunner not to come around.

Because I wasn't brave enough to just move forward. I wasn't smart enough to figure out how to get over him.

I haven't been *enough* of anything.

Slowly I gather my purse, stopping for a half second to look at my phone. Any other night, I'd be messaging Stone. *Guess who set a world record today for bawling like a baby?*

He'd reply with something to make me smile.

For the past week, Gunner made me smile, too. He made me laugh. But I can't smile and laugh now. Instead the memory of him slamming out of the brewery lodges in my chest like a jagged razor.

And the memory of his touch? God. I haven't even *begun* to work that through. All these years, nothing. He carefully stays on his side of simple. Then I piss him off and he's all over me? Furious and ready to fuck?

I should have pissed him off before. Just enraged him, so he wouldn't stop at pushing between my legs and promising to make it good—

No. Teeth clenched, I stop before my imagination takes it further. I can't *do* this.

No more "should have"s.

Only moving forward. And if that movement is slow, as if every part of me is broken? So be it. I'll go slow. At least it'll be in the right direction.

Though Stone's dog won't appreciate this snail's pace. As soon as I open the car door, the sound of Daisy's frantic barking reaches me from the second floor.

God, the poor girl. She's been locked in since I left for the funeral early this afternoon. And Daisy never barks; Stone taught her too well. She'll chew up furniture and roll in shit, but she doesn't bark. She must be desperate to be let out if she's making that much racket.

"I'm coming, Daisy!"

The toll of today's crying turns my voice into a hoarse croak. I'm so tired and numb, I just want to curl up in bed. But the dog demands to be let out—and curling up isn't a step forward. Hiding away isn't picking up the shattered pieces of my heart and getting on with life.

Letting the dog out is.

Wearily I trudge up the concrete path to the front door of my old farmhouse. There's an unattached garage beside the house but that's mostly Stone's domain. Technically, the property is only mine—my brother doesn't like leaving paper trails and lists the Riders' old clubhouse as his official address—but Stone pitched in a huge chunk of the down payment, so it's really ours.

Although, *really*, the house is mine. It's where I plan to spend the next fifty years, all the remodeling I've done was based on my designs, and I live in the main part of the house. Stone lives in the apartment that takes up half of the second level. Years ago, the old widow who owned the place renovated the house to accommodate a renter, creating a separate living area complete with a single bedroom, a bathroom, and a kitchenette. The old layout of the farmhouse included two stairways, so instead of building an exterior stair to the second floor, Stone has his own entrance on the side of the house that opens up into a shared mudroom. From there, he can turn left through a connecting door and step into my kitchen or head straight up the stairs to his place.

That connecting door's closed now, mostly so I don't have to heat the whole dang house. Okay, also — because sometimes Daisy gets bored, and if she's going to chew up someone's furniture, I'd rather she chewed up my brother's.

And if there's pee, I'd definitely rather sacrifice his stuff.

"I'm coming!" I call through the front door, then mutter, "Dammit, just hold on a second," when I fumble the keys in my gloved fingers.

She's still barking her head off. Usually if she has to go, she waits by the mudroom door — unless she had an accident, then she hides in shame under his bed. From the sound of it, she's running from room to room upstairs.

Maybe a squirrel got through the roof or something. Jesus.

Luckily we live far enough out of town that no one will be bothered with the noise. My nearest neighbor lives across the road, but their house is set back almost a quarter mile down a long driveway.

"Hold on!" I call and swing open the door.

A shadow moves to my left. It's big, far too big to be a dog, but still a stupid *How did Daisy get down here?* runs through my head just before pain explodes through my jaw and white bursts behind my eyes.

Daisy's still barking. Why haven't I let her out yet?

Dizzy and sick, I raise my head—oh my god, I'm on the floor and I don't even remember going down. Hot metallic fluid fills my mouth. Trembling, I lift a hand to my lips. I'm drooling blood onto the wood flooring, the red splatters appearing almost black in the dark. My jaw aches and the side of my thigh is on fire. Beside me, my antique side table lies belly up. I must have tripped and whacked my leg on the table, knocking it over.

I shake my head, trying to clear it. That's not right. Someone knocked *me* over.

Oh Jesus. Where's my purse, my phone—

"You stay right there."

The rough command freezes me in place. I don't recognize the voice. Someone tall. Big. A balaclava conceals his face, the mask darker than the shadows in the foyer.

Terror sends my heart into overdrive.

With a heavy boot, he kicks the door closed. His gloved hand twists the deadbolt. Locking me in here with him. A panicked sob catches in my throat. My gaze darts farther into the house. In the dark, I have the advantage. I know the layout. If I'm fast enough, I can get to the kitchen. Then up to Stone's place. He's got guns, he's showed me how to use them, and Daisy can slow this guy down.

"Uh uh." It's a warning. "Don't you move."

A flashlight shines in my face and I squint, raising my hand against the glare.

"Take off that big coat. I want to make sure you haven't got anything stuffed in there that'll make this difficult."

Nothing in my coat. But there's pepper spray in my purse. Averting my gaze away from the harsh light, I spot my bag farther down the hall, lying on its side with the contents spilled across the floor. My keys. My phone. The pepper spray is lodged against the foot of the storage bench sitting beneath the coat rack.

If I can just get to that...

Slowly I stand, gritting my teeth against the pain shooting through the muscle in my thigh. My shaking hands lift to the zip of my coat. The rasp of the zipper seems to drag down my spine like claws and I'm suddenly struck by a new terror.

I'm already vulnerable. And now he's asking me to remove clothing?

Stomach roiling, I face the light again. It's coming from a phone, the tiny flashlight bright enough to blind.

"Please just tell me—"

"Take off the fucking coat."

I do. Tossing it to the floor, I stand shivering.

The light travels down over me, slowly, as if he's liking what he sees. Oh god. Stiffly I wait, teeth chattering, the ache in my heart joining the throbbing agony in my jaw, my leg.

"The way your brother looks, I didn't expect his sister to be a fucking knockout. That'll make this a hell of a lot more fun than the usual."

More fun. Sick fear shrivels my skin as if my entire body is drawing in, trying to hide. His intent is obvious—but I can't make sense of the rest. "My brother?"

"Blond. Scarred. A real stubborn motherfucker. That sound right?"

I nod, my mind racing. I need to keep him talking. If he's talking then he's not hurting me.

And maybe it'll give me time to think of a way out of this.

"Well, he's *too* fucking stubborn." Dark humor laces his voice. "So we have to persuade him."

Persuade Stone using me? But why would they need to? Unless they'd already tried to persuade him…and couldn't.

Horror grips me. Gunner said my brother was okay but maybe something went down after Gunner left. It must have, because if any of the Riders knew this was coming, I wouldn't be here alone. "Have you hurt him?"

"Damaging the goods? Nah. We need him in prime condition. And this is more efficient. Lots of men can withstand pain. But hurt their women?"

The light switches off and spots dance in front of my eyes. Oh god. Oh god. I need to keep him talking so he won't come over here and do what I think he's going to do. "Persuade him to do what?"

"Fight." The shadow moves closer. I back up but the wall's behind me. His gloved hand roughly grips my chin and pain rips through my jaw. "I'm going to enjoy giving him a reason."

Sour bile rolls onto the back of my tongue. Desperately I try to focus on anything but the fear and dread clawing through me.

They want Stone to fight? I know what this is about. This is what Gunner and my brother were looking for—some fucked up cage match where the men fight to the death.

That makes so much sense. And it must be why my brother isn't here—that undercover thing Gunner said he was doing. He and Gunner must have found the connection they were looking for. Maybe that's why a girl was involved or maybe she was how Stone got inside? And now they want him to fight but he won't—because if Stone goes into the ring, he'll have to kill his opponent. An opponent who hasn't done anything to threaten the Riders or his family. Stone wouldn't do that. My brother has killed before but he draws lines.

So they're going to hurt me to make him step over that line.

"Hurting me won't do it," I rasp.

"Yes, it will." He fists his fingers in my hair. Pain tears across my scalp as he forces my head back. "It always does. Because if he keeps refusing, we'll tell him we'll come back and finish you."

"It won't work," I say and it takes everything I have to keep the terror out of my voice, to speak with firm confidence. "Not with Stone. He'll assume you already killed me. He doesn't know you're wearing a mask and gloves and I can't identify you at all." Oh my god, please let that be why he's wearing them—because he intends to leave me alive. "He'll assume that after you hurt me, you killed me to make sure I stay quiet. And then he'll have no reason at all to fight."

"You're just trying to save yourself."

"Yes, I am." Gaze unwavering, I stare up at him, at the dark eyes visible in the face of the mask. "But that doesn't mean it's not true. I know my brother. You want him to fight? Then promise him that he'll be able to call me and hear my voice. Tell him that if he fights and wins, you'll let him verify that I'm still alive, that I'm all right. He'll fight for that."

A long silence falls between us, as if he's weighing my words against what he already knows about Stone.

He releases me and steps back. Relief lifts through my chest, then abruptly crashes when he says, "Take off that dress."

"Please—"

"If he wins, I'll let him call. But I've still got to let him know we're not fucking around. So take off the dress."

The light blinds me again. Blinking against the glare, I turn my head, desperately trying to think of anything that might save me. But I've got nothing.

"Now." The easy humor is gone from his voice. "Or I go kill that fucking dog."

Daisy, whose barking hasn't stopped. Who tried to warn me that something was wrong. And I should have known. She doesn't bark. But I was too numb and tired to really think about why she was.

And I'm numb again. My eyes burn but there are no tears. My fingers shake so hard I can barely undo the buttons at the front of my dress, but slowly I manage each one—trying not to hear how heavy his breathing is, trying not to feel the weight of his stare or notice the way the light follows the path of my hands as I ease the dress down my shoulders.

"What the fuck is wrong with your tit?"

The flashlight beam spotlights my left breast, tracing the scar from my surgery. Pale silver against my light brown skin, the puckered line extends about an inch from the edge of my areola.

I force the answer past the lump clogging my throat. "I had a tumor removed."

"Jesus fucking Christ." Irritation deepens his voice.

"I'd screw you from behind so I don't have to look at it, but the whole goddamn point of this is videotaping your face while I'm fucking you. Now get the rest off."

Despair threatens to choke me. So they're going to show Stone a video of me being raped? That will kill him. And it won't matter that I'm numb or if I conceal how much it hurts, refusing to cry out. Stone will know. He knows how I hide when I'm hurting.

I toss the dress aside — covering the pepper spray. If I get lucky, maybe I can grab it and he won't realize what I'm really reaching for.

"Those granny panties, too."

The light moves downward and focuses on the juncture of my thighs as I push my underwear over my hips. Hot vomit fills the back of my throat. Now that the flashlight isn't shining into my eyes, I can see him better. His right glove is off and his jeans unfastened. He spits into his palm and strokes his erection.

"Oh fuck, yeah. Your cunt's nice and smooth like I like. Now spread those legs — What the fuck is *that*?"

The abrupt, angry disgust in his voice scares me more than taking off my clothes did. Everything before was playing with me, a predator with his prey. But that disgust. It's like he's taken personal offense to something I've done.

He shines the light down — at my discarded underwear. A few red streaks stain the pantyliner adhered to the gusset.

"That mess in your panties. Are you bleeding up there?"

Barely. My period is almost over.

But I nod for all I'm worth.

"That's some nasty shit," he spits, and I cringe as he turns and roars, *"Shut up!"*

Daisy only barks louder.

The light returns to my groin. "God damn it. I'm not going to fuck that if it's bleeding. Makes me as limp as a priest."

He's not lying. Roughly he shoves his flaccid penis into his pants, then jerks the light to the side. "You get into that room over there, sit your ass down in that chair. Don't do that"—he stops me as I reach down for my dress and the pepper spray beneath it—"just fucking move your ass like I tell you."

Naked and shivering, I head for the chair. He follows and the rip of duct tape joins the staccato barking from upstairs. I sit, shaking uncontrollably as he leans in close, taping my ankles to the chair legs and my wrists to the armrests.

He sits back on his heels, lifts the phone. The flashlight abruptly blinds me again. "Say something to your brother, Anna."

Recording a message to him, showing me bruised and bleeding and naked. My voice is a hoarse whisper as I tell Stone the most important thing he needs to know. "I'm okay. Don't freak out. I'm all right."

"A little roughed up," is the bastard's cheerful addition. "But it could be worse. This could be my fist."

His palm explodes across my cheek, whipping my head to the side. I stifle my scream but can't stop the tears filling my eyes, instantly watering from the stinging pain.

"Now, Stone, here's the deal. You fight, you win, and you'll get to call your pretty sister and hear how alive she is. In fact, you can call her after every fight you win." His tone hardens. "Anna—do you know what happens if your brother doesn't call?"

The answer almost chokes me. "It means he lost."

And in a cage match to the death, that means he's dead.

"It means something else, too." His fingers lift to my bruised cheek and I barely stop myself from flinching away. "Because for everyone else, the threat to their family is enough to make them fight. Then we leave the family alone, even if he loses. And they keep their mouths shut so it's a win-win for everyone. Yeah?"

No. The fighters lose, the family loses. But I know better than to say that.

Mutely, I nod.

"But with your brother, and because he's so fucking stubborn, we'll be doing something different." His voice hardens. "Because as soon as you lose, Stone, I'm coming back here to finish what I started. I'm going to fuck your sister's sweet ass, I'm going to tear that pussy apart with my cock, and then I'm going to put a bullet in her brain. So as soon as you lose, motherfucker, your sister loses, too."

The light abruptly turns off and I know the last image

Stone will see is the horror on my face.

Quietly, the bastard in front of me says, "You didn't win, honey. You just bought yourself some time. A few weeks, a few months."

A short, raw laugh escapes me. A few weeks to live. Those are words I've always expected to hear. But not like this.

He rises to his feet and returns a few moments later with my phone in hand. "What's your number?" He enters the number I recite into his own phone, then says, "Your brother will call if he wins. Now close your mouth."

Panic tears through me as he leans forward with a strip of tape. He seals my lips and every harsh breath through my nose feels clogged, restricted. His hands are gloved again and I whimper as he grips my fingers, thinking that he's going to smash them and get a last bit of torture in, but he simply presses my thumb to the home button on my phone, unlocking the security screen.

He lifts the device, snaps a photo of me. I blink away the afterimage of the flash and stare up at him in confusion.

"We don't want you starving to death here. Now, I don't need to tell you that going to the police will get you killed a lot faster, do I?" He waits until I shake my head before continuing, "So who's in your contacts? Should I send this to your mommy—?"

"No!" It's muffled by the tape but I try again. "No!"

My sharp desperation makes him chuckle. His thumb

swipes down the screen of my phone. "All right. Unicorn Daddy?"

Stone's phone…but Gunner has it.

My terror disappears and I look up at the masked fucker who's getting so much enjoyment out of this.

Gunner will come. And maybe this asshole will get away tonight, but as soon as Gunner knows what happened to me, as soon as my brother and the Riders know how he's hurt me, there will be *nowhere* far enough for him to run.

I nod and hear the swoosh as he sends the photo. That sound is his death knell.

He just doesn't know it yet.

TWELVE

GUNNER

IT'S HEADING TOWARD MIDNIGHT WHEN I LEAVE THE clubhouse—sober as hell, though I wish I wasn't. Any other night, I'd have stayed and drank myself numb. But I've got somewhere to be tomorrow and there's no avoiding it.

Even layered up and with my handlebar warmers going, it's a shit night for riding. The asphalt's as slick as snot. But unless they're transporting the body or unable to sit on their bikes, any brother who arrives at a Hellfire

Rider's funeral in a cage doesn't deserve to wear the club's colors. Red can't ride anymore. So for the rest of us who still can, it's ride or die.

Right now, riding and dying feels about the same.

Stone's phone vibrates against my chest as I hit the main road and get reception. After a week of answering Anna's messages, I'm like one of Pavlov's drooling dogs—my heartbeat picking up, my hand automatically reaching for the device.

But I'm so damn layered up I can't get to the phone without steering one-handed longer than any man ought to on a slick road.

So I keep on riding. It won't be Anna, anyway. Not now that she knows who's got the phone. Most likely it's one of Stone's regular hookups. Christ knows they've sent him plenty of texts this week.

Anna doesn't want to see me or talk to me again. And, Jesus. The shit I said to her on my way out, I don't deserve to see her.

But I'm so fucking pathetic I only last a mile before pulling over and reaching for the phone. My chest tightens when the screen lights up.

It *is* from Anna. A photo, a tiny thumbnail on the notification screen. A selfie? Did she send me one of her selfies? Maybe the one she took in the brewery.

I've never swiped so goddamn fast before.

And it's wrong. All fucking wrong. For a second I stare at the picture, telling myself that it's a joke, that she's just fucking with me, because she's sent pictures like this to Stone before. Over the years, she's dressed up with fake blood and posed with rubber vampire bats and Gremlins and all kinds of crazy shit. But the light's too bright, her golden brown skin washed out white. As if taken in the dark with a powerful flash—and the camera's too close, like something out of *The Blair Witch Project*. Anna doesn't give much credit to herself but her photos are never poorly lit or framed. And that blood looks too damn real.

And there's no *Anna was here.*

Christ, no. My chest turns inside out and I rip the throttle open. The engine roars. The bike shoots ahead, fishtailing before gripping the blacktop.

The road unravels ahead but I only see her eyes. Tear-filled, terrified, angry.

An image that will haunt me for the rest of my fucking life.

THIRTEEN

GUNNER

I never should have kissed her. Never should have moved to this fucking town. Never should have given my family any reason to look at her. Never should have let my brothers live after discovering they knew about her.

But now it's just too late.

Her car's out front in its usual spot. Gravel spits out from beneath my tires as I race past it, practically riding up onto the porch before killing the engine and tearing up the stairs. Everything's silent. Daisy's not barking. She wouldn't bark at my arrival anyway, but she'd bark if anyone was here who shouldn't be. Unless she *can't* bark.

My brothers would kill a dog. They wouldn't even hesitate.

Terror slicks cold sweat down my spine as I slam through the door, my semi-automatic leading the way. My gaze sweeps the entryway and everything I see is a knife to my heart.

Her scattered purse. The upended table. Her coat and dress and panties on the floor.

They caught her as she came in. Stripped her clothes off. It's too easy to fill in the rest but none of that matters now. Just finding her. Just making sure she's safe.

Then I'll kill them all.

"Anna!" I roar her name and feel my guts come up with it, hot and sour.

A muffled noise comes from the living room. I pivot toward the sound, slipping through the dark hall. Empty, except—there. In the shadows just inside the room. From the chair beside the wall, Anna's staring at me with wide eyes shimmering with tears.

With a tortured groan, I drop to my knees in front of her. Her arms and legs are taped, her mouth covered. Her jaw is swollen, her cheekbone a vicious red even in the dark.

And she's naked in this goddamn freezing house.

Rage and agony forge my lungs into hot iron, each breath burning. "Anna, sweetheart. I'm so sorry." The words are gravel, my throat scraped raw. "I'm so damn sorry. Let me get you out."

I reach for the tape over her lips. There's no help for this, no way to stop it from hurting. The only thing I can do is make it quick. I rip the tape off. Her head falls forward and she drags in air, her hiccuping sobs shuddering through swollen and bloodied lips.

The sight crushes my heart all over again. Shattered from the inside out, I pull my knife from my boot, pop the blade.

"Try to stay still, baby. I'm going to cut this tape away. Ah, Jesus." Her hands are like ice. Briskly I rub my left palm down her legs, trying to warm her skin while I carefully slice through the gray tape around her wrists. "Talk to me, sweetheart. Tell me you're okay."

She doesn't—or can't. Her body shakes violently and I don't know how much is from the shock and how much from the cold. I can barely fucking breathe and only knowing that she needs to hear a friendly voice keeps me talking instead of howling in anger and pain. With soft murmurs, I try to soothe her as I peel away the last wrap of tape.

The second she's free, I pull her into my arms. She comes without resisting, burying her cold face against my neck. Her slim form weighs nothing when I slip my arm under her knees and lift her against my aching chest.

Faint streaks of blood stain her inner thighs. More dark drops stain the pale upholstery of the chair's seat. The agony in my chest swells and hardens into sheer rage as it rises, sharpening on my tongue.

"I'll kill them for hurting you," I swear to her. "I will fucking *end* them."

Even if means finding another way to get to Stone.

Her body wracked by shivers, she nods against my shoulder. Jesus, I've got to get her warm. I start toward the bedroom but a ragged cry from Anna stops me.

"The phone," she says frantically, twisting in my grip to look for it. "I need my phone."

I spot the phone on the floor by the chair. The second I give it to her the tension seeps out of her body and she sinks into my arms again. I expect her to make a call but she just clutches it to her chest as I carry her to her bedroom, a route I've taken in my mind a thousand times but never traveled before.

"We're going to get you warm, then get you to the hospital, all right?" I pull back the blankets and slide her in. She stares mutely up at me from the pillows, and the dull light in her eyes rips through my gut. All the sparkle is gone. As if she's broken. "Just don't move. I'm going to call Zoomie and Jenny."

She'll need her friends. Women who can help.

"I don't need a hospital." She drags the comforter up to her chin, still clutching her phone. Her voice is a rasping whisper. "And don't tell Jenny. Not today."

After her dad's funeral. "You want me to contact your folks?"

I should anyway. Clara will be able to help her more than anyone else.

A shake of Anna's head stops me.

"Sweetheart—"

"No." The response is hoarse but firm. "I expect the Riders to take care of this."

It won't be the Riders. "I'll do it myself."

Her trusting nod is a kick in my chest. I step out of the room, pulling out Stone's phone. Another glance at the photo—my first look at the timestamp—has me gritting my teeth against the anguish tearing through my soul.

Three hours. She was taped to that chair for three fucking hours. While I was sitting on my ass at the clubhouse and feeling sorry for myself, she was sitting here freezing. Sitting here bleeding.

Maybe thinking I wasn't coming for her.

My throat's a solid knot as I send a text to Blowback. *Stone's place. Haul ass. Bring Z.* He and Zoomie left the clubhouse a while ago. They're probably already in town and they'll get the message. I'm about to send the prez a text when I hear the shower start up.

I head back in. In the master bath, Anna stands naked in front of her glass shower stall, her eyes dull, body shaking, teeth chattering. With one hand she tests the water temperature. In the other, she's still holding her phone.

Snagging a thick towel from the shelf, I slip it around her shoulders. "Anna. Sweetheart, wait until later for this."

"But I'm s-so c-c-cold."

"I know." My voice is thick, broken. "But at the hospital they might want to take samples, make sure there's no diseases—"

"I w-wasn't r-raped. And I don't n-need a hospital."

In denial. I sweep my hand up and down her arms. "There's blood on the seat—"

"From my p-period. He *would* have raped m-me. B-but my uterus s-saved the day."

It's a toneless response. She pulls out of my grip when she's done, placing the phone beside the sink and stepping into the shower, where she curls in on herself. Her arms go around her middle as she bows her head beneath the stream of water, as if she's trying to contain all the hurt.

I drag off my boots and kutte and follow her in fully clothed. Maybe she wasn't raped but she doesn't need a naked man pressing up against her now. I draw her back against my chest and she seems to soften against me, as if the hot water and my warmth are melting the brittle ice inside her.

My arms circle her slender form in a tight embrace. And I swear to God, I'm never going to let her go. Because if I'd been holding onto her? If I'd been here?

They'd *never* have touched her.

But instead I left her alone. I left her vulnerable.

"I'm so sorry, sweetheart," I tell her hoarsely. "This shouldn't have happened. I should have ended it a long time ago."

Another shudder wracks her body. Her head's bowed and her wet hair is streaming down the sides of her head in a thick curtain. "I'm okay."

Okay? Probably not. Brave? No fucking doubt. "Anna—"

"He just slapped me around a little. Taped me up. I'm okay." I can't see her face but her voice sounds stronger. Her body shudders again. "And I knew you'd see the message he sent."

My chest hitches against her back and I bury my face against her wet hair. "When I saw that picture—"

"Probably not my best, was it?" She turns in my arms and her shattered gaze lifts to mine. Her eyelashes are clumped into wet spikes. Tears fill her eyes and her voice chokes up. "And you came. Even though I told you to stay away—"

"Stop right there." Gently I cushion her bruised face between my palms. "I'll *always* come for you."

Her tears spill over but a wavering smile curves her lips. The sparkling gold in her eyes lights again, and the broken pieces inside me all slide into place.

Anna's here in my arms. And there's not a force on this earth that could have stopped me as I lower my head. No force except Anna. But instead of pushing me away, she closes her eyes when I kiss the salty tears from her cheeks. I dip lower and her mouth lifts to meet mine. Tenderly I kiss the corner of her mouth. A broken sigh trembles from between her swollen lips.

This is what I should have done before. I died in that brewery. Not when she told me to stay away, but when I lied and said she wasn't anything more. When I denied who I am.

And I'm hers. I've always been hers.

I could have shown her, told her with a kiss. Instead I covered myself in the filth of my lies like tossing dirt onto my own grave. But I tell her the truth now, softly tasting her mouth, giving her my strength, offering my heart, and with every touch, every breath, I begin living again.

I've got more to tell her, though. Because I've always been hers. But now…nothing will stop me from making her mine.

Her lips part beneath the stroke of my tongue. Her fingers curl into my biceps, a low moan reverberating in her chest. I deepen the kiss, claiming her mouth, claiming her—but gently, because she's bruised and naked. Slamming her up against the tile and fucking her would hurt her, scare her.

I'll always protect her, even if that means protecting her from myself.

So I'll be patient. I've waited this long; waiting a little longer is nothing. I won't scare her away by rushing in too fast, by claiming her too quickly. She doesn't love me—because says she doesn't know me. So I'll show her who I am. I'll bring Stone home, and give her everything she needs to trust me again.

She wants a future? I'll *be* that future.

Whatever it takes.

But for now, it will take time—and by the faint rumble of the approaching engines that I'm hearing over the noise of the shower, we've run out of it.

Reluctantly I raise my head. Her cheeks are flushed, her eyelids heavy with arousal. Slowly she looks up at me, the light still in her eyes, soft and warm and glazed with need, a starburst of deep gold and brown.

I stroke my thumb along her jaw, feel the shiver that races over her skin. That shiver's not from the cold. "Got you heated up now?"

A little laugh breaks from her, then she bites her swollen lip, her wondering gaze searching mine. Maybe asking what I meant by that kiss. But she's got reason not to trust my words now. So I'll just show her and keep showing her, until she's ready to believe me when I say she owns my heart. Until she's ready to be mine.

And then I'll never let her go.

But I've got to let her go now. She tenses in my arms, gaze darting to the bathroom door. Blowback's standing there. His empty eyes meet mine. I shake my head, answering his wordless question.

There are no bodies to get rid of. Not yet.

Zoomie strides into the bathroom, tucking away her gun. "Anna! Oh shit, honey." Her gaze slides across Anna's bruised face. "Who did this?"

"I'll tell you"—her voice is still raw as she turns off the water—"as soon as I get dressed. Will you bring me one of those towels?"

Zoomie steps forward, gently wrapping her up in the thick bath sheet. As soon as she's got Anna secured, she grabs another towel and tosses it at my head.

Her flinty gaze rakes down my dripping form. "You got clothes at Stone's?"

Probably. "I'll find something."

"Will you let Daisy out, too?" Anna picks up her phone, clutches it tight in one hand and the folds of her towel in the other. "I didn't get a chance. She's probably desperate by now. Or hiding under his bed in shame."

Didn't get a chance. My jaw clenches and I see Zoomie's face tighten. But her hands are gentle as she picks up another towel, starts rubbing Anna's long wet hair.

"Go on," Zoomie tells me. "We'll meet you in the kitchen. And make her—Anna, do you want coffee or something stronger?"

"Something stronger."

Definitely something stronger. Because when she learns who came after her, I don't know if she'll ever let me touch her again.

FOURTEEN

ANNA

Stronger is coffee that smells as if it's half whiskey. Blowback plonks the steaming mug in front of me when I sit at the breakfast table. His hard gaze searches my face before lifting over my head to look at Lily. Probably thinking the same thing she and Gunner did. They saw my dress and panties on the floor and assumed the worst.

It could have been the worst. But it wasn't. And now I'm dressed again in my favorite Stanford hoodie and fluffy gray pajama pants, my hands wrapped around a mug of hot coffee, my phone tucked away in the pouch of my sweatshirt. I know Stone won't call right away. But it feels like a lifeline connecting me to him—that as long as I keep my phone nearby, he's going to come home all right. I just pray that Gunner can get word to him about what happened before he sees the video of that bastard slapping me.

I take a sip and almost choke. I was right—half whiskey. The alcohol stings my busted lip but the warmth spreads right through me.

I'm warm all over. I have been since Gunner kissed me.

Why did he? Gingerly, I touch my bottom lip. Holding me, warming me, supporting me—those weren't a surprise. But his kiss was. Not because his lips pressed to mine. Even that might have simply been an attempt to soothe me.

But he kissed me as if I was everything. Only hours after he told me I'm nothing.

And I don't know what to think anymore.

I glance over as he pushes through the mudroom door, Daisy at his heels. His gaze immediately zeroes in on my eyes before dropping to my fingertips, still pressed to my lips.

He doesn't look at me the same way he did only a few hours ago, either. The intensity in his crystalline eyes has always been there, but now it's sharper, hotter—and burns with an intent I can't read. But just one look and my heart pounds at a dizzying speed.

Then Daisy's on me, wriggling and wagging, shoving her boxy head against my arm, licking my fingers with her quick tongue. Suddenly tears threaten again. Oh god. I set down my coffee and grab her big dumb head, scratching her ears and letting her slobber kisses all over my face. I'm almost crying over such a stupid little thing — a dog demanding kisses. A stupid little thing…but so important and incredible to be the recipient of such unreserved love and joy. I should never take these things for granted. But I have. So often.

"She was okay?" I ask, looking to Gunner.

Unsmiling, he nods and leans back against the center island. His dark hair is still wet but he found a pair of loose sweatpants and a thin white T-shirt that clings to his broad chest. "She left a mess," he tells me in a voice I barely recognize. Rough like gravel, his sculpted features like stone — and his glacial eyes devouring me whole. "But it doesn't look like they ever got over to that part of the house."

"Good." I give her another scratch and rub my face against her doggy forehead. But although I'd love to do nothing but this, I can't put the rest off. I take a deep breath. "So you want a step by step?"

"Yes." Blowback's the one who answers me, taking the seat adjacent to mine, the sheer size of him seeming to emit a gravitational force that draws my gaze to the emptiness of his dark eyes. Empty like outer space, and Lily is the bright star burning through that cold vacuum as she props her ass against the edge of the table beside him.

"Everything you can remember," she says.

"Okay." I clear my suddenly dry throat, darting a glance at Gunner. His expression is still hard, but his body has gone rigid as if he's bracing himself—or preparing to look into the depths of Hell. "Daisy was barking when I got here. But I assumed she just had to be let out—because I didn't see any cars or bikes around. So if he parked, maybe it was around behind the house or the garage? Or maybe he parked down the road and he walked in. But farther west, because I didn't pass any vehicles parked alongside the road after I drove through town."

"'He,'" Gunner echoes, his brows drawing down with his frown. "Just one man?"

"Just one. He was on me as soon as I got through the door. I just saw a shadow coming and bam!"—I aim a fist at my jaw and mime a punch—"I went down."

A grating sound comes from Gunner. I glance over and he's got his hands locked on the edge of the island counter, the tendons in his forearms standing in sharp relief, his face a bleak, tortured mask.

"And then?" Blowback shoots a dark look at the other man.

Taking another sip of the loaded coffee gives me time to picture the bastard and to beat back the surge of fear the memory conjures. "He was big. And he wore leather gloves and a ski mask. But he had dark brown eyes and—"

"Brown?" Gunner stares at me. "Not blue?"

"Brown," I confirm.

"You're sure? They weren't the same color as mine?"

"Trust me that I would notice if his eyes were like yours," I say dryly, then frown as he drags in a sharp breath, his big body shuddering. "Why?"

"Just keep going," Blowback says but the look he gives Gunner is a warning. No more interruptions. I'm not even sure if Gunner notices. He's staring at me as if still not believing what I just told him.

"Then he told me not to move."

"Did he have an accent?"

"No. Then he made me take off my coat." My voice shakes and I wrap my fingers tighter around the mug, until Daisy whines and nudges my leg with her head. I scratch her ears and it's easier to continue, "And I thought, he's here to rape me. But then he said my brother's too stubborn—that Stone needed persuading."

Gunner and Lily exchange a startled look. But there's no surprise on Blowback's face. "Persuade him to what?"

"Fight." I take a deep breath. "So I realized this was about the cage fight thing he and Gunner have been chasing down. Ever since those guys got to Lily."

Blowback turns and levels a hard stare at her.

She holds up her hands. "I didn't say anything. I told you. The brothers don't keep their mouths shut."

"What else did he say about Stone?" Gunner's utterly focused on me, ignoring the exchange between the other Riders.

"Just that he needed to be persuaded. So I assumed the club business with that girl, Cherry, and whatever's going on in Arizona—I assumed that really he got inside that fighting ring somehow, but he doesn't want to kill someone in a death match. So I told the guy that hurting me won't persuade Stone because he'll assume I'm dead. He'll assume that this fucker made his video and then killed me."

Gunner's face whitens. "Yes. He would."

"So I said he needs to make a deal with Stone—that after he fights, Stone can call me and verify that I'm alive."

Blowback goes utterly still. "He's going to call you after his fight?"

"That's what he said." I'm shaking again. I bury my fingers in Daisy's short fur. "But then he said that if Stone ever loses, he's coming back for me. That I'm only alive as long as my brother is."

"Fuck that," Gunner grits out, striding forward and crouching in front of me, fierce eyes locked on mine. "I swear it's not going to fucking happen."

Nodding, I say, "That'd be great. So if you could let Stone know that it's time to blow that whole undercover thing apart now, I'd be grateful."

No agreement from the Riders—just silence for a long, empty second that rolls my stomach into a tight knot.

Then Blowback says, "You said he had brown eyes. How tall, how big?"

"Um, as tall as Saxon, but, uh, bigger. Rounder. Not soft fat, but hard fat over muscle. Like Widowmaker is."

The Riders' warlord nods. "Anything more?"

Too much more. "I think he had a beard because the mask seemed…pillowy around the jaw." I close my eyes, picturing him. "He had crooked bottom teeth but I never saw his upper teeth. And he took off his right glove when he was stroking himself. He had a word inked on the back of his fingers. *RIDE*. And he was uncircumcised."

"He'll be circumcised by the time we're done," Lily promises grimly. "Circumcised all the way down to his fucking balls."

"The tattoo said *RIDE*? You sure?" There's a dangerous note in Gunner's voice that I've never heard before. Low and cold and utterly terrifying.

"There's lots of bikers with that tattoo, pretty boy," Lily says evenly—as if she's talking him back from the edge.

"But not the whole package." His pale gaze is feral as he looks to Blowback. "That's the enforcer with the Iron Blood. I'm going to tear his goddamn—"

"You're going to do nothing yet," the warlord cuts in, his voice like steel. "We go after Chef and every path to the Cage will vanish."

Gunner abruptly shoots to his feet and paces to the island and back, his jaw locked, every muscle tense. "Who's your contact in the Hangmen? Are they telling us everything they know about the Cage?"

"Unlikely."

Gunner snarls in response to that easy admission. "Then maybe you don't have the balls to do what needs to be done to get the information."

Blowback just looks at him. Lily's staring at him, too, her face a picture of disbelief. Probably because Gunner must have really gone over the edge if the thinks Blowback doesn't have the guts to fuck someone up. I don't know the warlord well but most of the Riders act like they're walking barefoot through a minefield covered in broken glass when they're around him.

Yet they know who this guy is and Blowback is telling Gunner to hold off? Why? And why the hell do they need a trail leading to the Cage if my brother is there, pretending to be one of their fighters?

Unless…my brother *can't* lay a trail. Unless my brother isn't pretending.

Unless Gunner lied to me and Stone isn't doing some undercover thing at all—and instead my brother simply disappeared like all the other fighters did.

A ragged breath rips from my chest as the truth hits me. At the sound, Gunner's head whips around and his body stills when he sees my face. I stare up at him with accusing eyes.

"What really happened to Stone? And don't say that undercover bullshit again. Where is he? Do you even *know?*"

"Anna—" He starts toward me and abruptly stops when I jerk back in my chair. I don't want him coming close. I don't want his nearness fucking with my head—or my heart. A flash of pain seems to tighten his features and he roughly continues, "I told you, it's club business."

"Of course it is. Except fuck you and fuck the Riders. You aren't the only ones who call him a brother. Stupid me, thinking that meant something to you. That maybe me, my mom, and my dad were more than random assholes who just happen to be in Stone's family."

Tension whitens the edge of his mouth. "You are."

A hard laugh bursts from me. "Really?" Because only a few hours ago, I wasn't more. Fingers scrabbling, I dig my phone out of my sweatshirt. "So that's why you did *this*, yeah? Why you lied for a week and then lied to my face when I asked if he was okay!"

"Just to keep you—"

"From worrying about *my brother*!" I shout. Daisy cringes at my feet but I can't hold back the fury. "My brother! Who I have every right to worry about if there's reason to worry! And there is reason, isn't there? I mean, Jesus. I'm not asking for details about the Riders' business. I'm just asking for the truth! *Is he in trouble?*"

His face an emotional wasteland, Gunner stares back at me. And that bleak silence is answer enough.

My throat burning, I look to Lily, whose full lips are pressed into a thin line, her jaw tight. "And you, too." My voice cracks. "Hugging me after the funeral, pretending everything was fine when my brother is…"

Going to have to fight to the death so that some rich fuckers can bet on him. Oh god.

Gunner pushes in front of me, leaning in and bracing his hand on the table, his broad shoulders blocking my view of Lily and the pain in her eyes. "We're going to get him back, Anna," he says gruffly. "And we won't let anyone touch you again."

"Yeah, well. That's what you tell me. But is that true or is it more of this shit?" I lift my phone, scroll back through the messages and read, "'Everything's all right, pipsqueak. Just taking longer than it should.' I can't believe a single word you say."

"Then don't believe what I said here, either." Gently his big hand covers mine, his thumb sliding down the screen. "'Gunner's a useless fucking asshole.'"

A huffing laugh escapes me. Shit. I want to hold onto my anger, because the anger's the only thing keeping my fear for Stone from taking over. But seeing that message, I know exactly what Gunner must have been thinking—all last week, searching for my brother and not finding him, so angry and frustrated…and blaming himself.

Just like he's been blaming himself for everything tonight. But this isn't his fault. And even though I've got every right to be pissed off by his lies, it's not right to lay more blame on him.

I know he'll look for Stone. I know the Riders will protect me. He's not lying about any of that. Maybe everything else, but not that.

Gently he cups my cheek, tips my face up to meet his eyes. "And I'm so damn sorry, Anna. Sorry I lost him. Sorry we didn't see this bastard coming for you. Sorry I didn't get Stone back before you realized he was gone."

I believe all of that. Raggedly I say, "Just tell me the Riders are going to find him."

"We will." His callused thumb sweeps across my trembling bottom lip. "And we'll keep you safe, too. All right?"

I nod into his hand. His pale gaze holds mine for a long moment, steady, as if imparting his promise not just with words but with that look.

Finally he turns his head and says to Blowback, "I'll take Anna to my place tonight, watch over her. You want to update the prez? And maybe you and Zoomie stay here in case that fucker comes back."

"We'll do that," Blowback says.

Lily nods and her gaze is on me, even as she asks Gunner, "You still heading out tomorrow?"

"As soon as Anna's settled." Gunner meets my eyes again, his voice low. "You're all right, coming with me tonight?"

Even though he's leaving tomorrow. That knowledge twists painfully in my chest. But I won't cling to him—even though I want to. Even though I feel so safe with my face cradled in his palm and his eyes searching mine.

Stone is his priority. And I'm just Stone's sister.

"Yes," I tell him. "I'll come with you tonight."

"Good." His hand slips from my cheek when he straightens, and without his touch I feel cold all over, a shiver racing over my skin. Until he turns away and I hear him say softly, "Because I don't know how I'm ever going to let you out of my sight again."

FIFTEEN

ANNA

I jolt out of a nightmare of eyeless masks and gloved hands and into an unfamiliar bed — flat on my back, Daisy's weight across my ankles, and my heart pounding. With sweat-slicked hands I grab the phone laying beside my pillow.

No missed calls. No messages.

It's only three a.m.

At the end of the bed, Daisy lifts her head. With a shuddering sigh, I shut off the phone and stare up at the ceiling with the afterimage of the screen floating in front of my eyes.

I'm in Gunner's bedroom. In his bed.

This wasn't how I hoped to get here. I haven't been to his place before. I knew where it was, of course—a one-bedroom rental at the edge of town. But he doesn't seem to spend a lot of time here. When he's not out riding, he's either working, at the gym, at the clubhouse, or at Stone's place…which really means my place, since Stone doesn't pass a lot of time upstairs and Gunner always comes down with him.

Gunner doesn't *seem* to spend a lot of time here, but he must. Because, Jesus—the books. They're everywhere. He doesn't have much in the way of furniture and everything is clean in the "there's no dirt" sense. But the way the books are shoved into shelves—and on top of the coffee and side tables, and stacked beside the nightstand—the only word for it is "cluttered." This is the house of a nerdy professor, not the Hellfire Riders' lethal sergeant at arms.

How does he fit it all in? Work, the gym, the club, these books? Maybe he doesn't sleep much.

I don't know if he's sleeping now. If he is, he's probably out in the living room. As soon as we arrived, he tucked me into his bed to rest, then told me about Cherry and the drugged beer, about finding Stone's phone in a Dumpster, about spending a week tracking down different clubs and asking for information. All the while he was packing—a small bag of clothes and two long duffles holding weapons he pulled from the huge gun cabinet standing against the wall opposite the bed.

Then the shock and the whiskey caught up to me and I was out. Not for long, though. I don't know exactly what was in the nightmare that woke me but I don't want to expend any mental effort remembering.

My body is making the effort, though. Despite the covers and Daisy's warmth against my feet, despite my hoodie and pajamas, I begin shivering. Clenching my teeth, I roll onto my side —

And look straight into Gunner's pale eyes.

My breath catches. He's not in bed with me. Instead he's crouching beside it, still wearing those loose sweatpants — but he shucked the shirt, revealing miles of tanned skin and sculpted muscle.

"You're all right, Anna." His big hand cups my cheek, giving me a warm anchor. In a voice roughened by sleep, he says quietly, "You're safe."

Teeth chattering, I glance over the edge of the bed. There's a sheet spread out on the carpet under him, and a pillow smashed up against the foot of the nightstand. "Were you sleeping down there? Why not the couch?"

"I'm not going to leave you alone."

Those words would have melted me if I weren't a block of ice. "Then get up here."

"I'm fine on the floor." Tension adds a taut edge to his reply.

"Maybe, but I'm not fine. I'm f-freezing." As if to

emphasize my claim, my teeth click together harder. "I c-can't even t-tell if I'm really cold or if it's just a d-delayed reaction."

"Ah, sweetheart. You're killing me." With a low groan, he grabs his pillow. "Scoot over so I can stay between you and the door."

He had a gun within reach under the bed, I realize when he transfers the pistol to the nightstand. Daisy whines as if I'm torturing her when I roll across the mattress, taking my pillow and my phone with me. Through the dark, I glimpse chiseled abs and flexing biceps, then the sinuous stretch of obliques before I roll another quarter turn, facing the wall. The mattress sags under his weight and I slide right back into him, my spine against his chest. I pull my legs up to make room for Daisy at the foot of the bed, the curve of my bottom against Gunner's rigid stomach. He's lying lower on the mattress than I am—his feet must be hanging off the end.

His heavy arm wraps around my waist. His breath sweeps over my nape as he says gruffly, "Better?"

"Y-yes." So much better. God, he's like a furnace, the heat already sinking into my skin. "Sorry."

"Don't say sorry." He pulls me tighter against him when a shudder races through my body. "You'll be all right. It'd be a damn miracle if this shit didn't hit you hard even after it's done."

"Like PTSD?"

"Something like that. Though hopefully it won't stick

more than a few nights."

His voice is so soothing, so deep. Every word he speaks sends a faint vibration into me, and all I want to do is keep him talking. He's possibly said more to me today than in the past six years combined.

"Did it ever happen to you during your deployments?"

"I had some bad nights," he admits. "And I've had some bad nights since. But it never settled in. I know plenty of others who weren't so lucky."

"Including a couple other Riders." I can think of a few off the top of my head. Some old ladies, too. Though they probably weren't traumatized in combat—more likely by the men in their pasts. A few of the women, I think they hang around the bikers because even with all the fighting and the dangerous shit that goes down now and then, the Riders are still less terrifying than what's in those ladies' heads.

"Yup," he says in the same tone Stone sometimes uses when he acknowledges the truth of something I've said but has no intention of talking about other patchholders behind their backs.

That's all right. I don't really want to talk about any other Riders, either. But I can't dredge up another subject yet, because I can't focus on anything except his hand. He's not moving at all—his long body like a steel beam behind me—but his taut forearm is an iron bar across my torso, only a few inches beneath my breasts. His long fingers curl around my ribcage as he holds me securely against him.

And all I can think is how close his hand is to my breast. Every tiny fluctuation in the strength of his grip, every subtle change in the pressure of his fingertips is an agonizing tease, my nipples stiff and begging for his touch.

Or begging for him to slide his hand south, over my belly, slipping beneath the elastic waist of my pants—

On second thought, maybe not south. Not for another day. A little blood might be great for scaring away would-be rapists. Not so great for sexy times.

But Gunner doesn't move north or south. Just holds me as my shivers slowly ease.

The quiet is killing me. I cast around for something innocuous, something a million miles away from my sensitive breasts and the fire between my legs.

Like something hanging on his bedroom wall. "You really did put up that stupid painting."

There's a smile in his voice. "I did."

Because he has terrible taste, apparently. It's a peek-a-boo landscape I painted almost five years ago and called "Playtime's Over." At first glance, it's just a forest scene. But look close and there's a naked Barbie swinging through the trees like Tarzan. A rabid Furby lurks in a hollow beneath a rotting stump, its glassy eyes reflecting an amber glow. Amid a pile of rocks, a Magic 8 Ball says to "fuck off." It was the first and last painting of its type that I made. It was supposed to be funny but just felt cynical, and I would have painted over it and re-used the canvas if Gunner hadn't offered to take it off my hands.

"I like the fireflies," he adds, and for a moment I can't remember any fireflies at all, until I realize I spelled out *Anna was here* with the glowing bugs. A squeeze of his hand against my side almost distracts me from his, "And now they don't lie anymore."

Because I *am* here. For the first time. But although I smile into the dark, my mind goes straight back to the brewery. Straight back to writing on his chest in lipstick. Straight back to telling him not to come around anymore.

A long, shuddering sigh escapes me. I'm so glad he didn't listen.

"Anna." Concern deepens his voice. "You all right?"

"Yes." Not really. "I was just thinking…at the funeral today, I realized—a gravestone is the ultimate version of that, isn't it? When all of Red's friends are gone, when Jenny is gone, when no one remembers him, that gravestone will still be there, saying, 'Red was here.'"

His grip tightens. "No."

"No?"

Against my neck, I feel him shake his head. "That's not what it says. 'Beloved father and husband' was engraved on it. So when all those people are gone, it doesn't just say he was here. It says he was loved."

Oh my god. I choke up so fast, my eyes fill so quick—and I don't know why. Except that Gunner just ripped open something inside me.

Silence falls as I fight back the tears and Gunner waits for my reply. Abruptly he seems to realize it's not coming.

He sits up. Without his chest to support me, I roll onto my back and suddenly he leans over me, his right hand planted beside my shoulder, his face close to mine — searching my eyes through the dark.

"Don't," he says roughly. "Don't cry."

"I'm not." It's thick and clearly a lie but I don't quit telling it. "I'm not."

He groans and hangs his head. Tension cords the powerful muscles of the arm braced against the mattress and holding his upper body above mine. "What'd I say?"

"Nothing. Just, I don't know—" I'm still working it through. "Maybe that's what I've been doing. Leaving gravestones all over the place. Desperately telling myself that I'm loved."

"Damn it, sweetheart. That's not what I meant for you to take away from that." He sounds tortured. "You *are*—"

"I know." I do know. I'm loved. By my family, by friends. "I'm just tired. And feeling sorry for myself. And a little vulnerable. You know, all that fun stuff."

He nods, his face shadowed, but I can feel him watching me. "So that selfie in the brewery — was that a gravestone?"

Agony constricts my lungs. I strive for a light reply but I only manage a strained whisper. "It was definitely the end of something."

It was supposed to be — the end of hoping I'll ever be anything more to him. But like a vampire or a zombie, the hope keeps coming back from the dead. And I need to remind myself that this hope only returns to suck me dry or to eat my brains. This hope only leaves me feeling empty and stupid.

But it's so hard to remember that when I'm in bed with him. When he's looking down at me. When every gesture and every word says he cares.

Even though he said something else before. *You're not anything more to me.*

His fingers twist around the ends of my hair and a light tug brings me back to the conversation. "The end of worrying about dying?"

"Yes." Let him think that. It's partially true. Then the memory of a fist to my jaw and the blinding light in my face spins that worry around and I can't stop my laugh. "Oh god. Maybe I stopped worrying about dying a few hours too early."

"Don't you fucking say that." Gunner's not laughing. "He'll *never* get to you, Anna. I swear to you. I'll make sure you have your future."

I fall quiet at the ferocity of his response, as if every bit of gentleness was scraped from his voice, leaving nothing but a rough promise. Longing fills my chest. I want to believe that promise. And I do believe he'll protect me. But to give me a future? It's just too much to believe he'll be any part of it. At least, not in a way that's any different from the past ten years.

"All right?" he says, his voice softer now.

I nod, throat hurting too much to speak.

"Good." He lowers onto his side again, his head on his pillow and his arm over my stomach — but now that I'm on my back and we're not spooning, he's not as close. He's not wrapped around me.

A few hours ago, he kissed me. I ache to turn over now, press my mouth to his — seeking comfort in his warmth.

Then seeking more.

But I've done that before. And even though *he* kissed *me* in the shower, I don't know whether it was anything more than what he's doing now. Being here for me. Supporting me. Trying to warm me and soothe me.

It *felt* like more. But how many times have I thought the same thing, simply because he looked at me a certain way? It always felt like more. But it never has been. And after he found me taped to the chair I was so hurt and vulnerable. I might have read too much into that kiss. I might have seen what I wanted to see.

If I turned toward him now and he pushed me away? If he reminded me to keep it simple? I want to pretend I'm not, but the truth is that I'm still hurt, I'm still vulnerable — and that rejection might kill me. And I don't know if I could hide the pain this time. Not when I'm feeling so fragile.

So I won't throw myself at him again. If Gunner meant anything by that kiss, then *he* needs to step over the line between us.

But he doesn't. Instead he lies beside me, his fingertips drawing absent circles over the side of my ribcage. Quietly he says, "I fucked up by sending you those messages."

I turn my head on the pillow, searching through the dark to make out his expression. There's nothing. Just angular shadows upon shadows.

"I don't have a real excuse," he continues and his body is rigid with tension beside me. "Just that your first text came in right after I found his phone and I was still trying to figure out what the hell had happened. Plus you'd just heard about Red and I didn't want to add worry to your grief. I thought it wouldn't matter, just one time, and then I'd find Stone. But I didn't. So it just…snowballed."

I look up at the ceiling. "You still wouldn't have told me he was in trouble, would you?"

"No. I'd have said he was out of touch, on club business."

God, I should have known. Because that's the same thing Stone would have said. But I'm not angry now. I'm hurt that he kept the truth about Stone from me…but I understand it, too. Maybe more than he realizes.

Because I know a lot about what my brother does for the Riders and I never tell my parents any of it. I hide so many things that might otherwise worry them.

And tomorrow, I might be doing it again. Not lying to them. But not telling them all the details, either.

My chest lifts on a heavy sigh and in the dark, I slide my palm across the taut forearm slung over my stomach. The steely tension in his body eases as I say, "I'm glad you sent those messages. Aside from the pretending-to-be-my-brother part. But texting with you last week was a bright spot amid a whole lot of grief and shittiness."

His voice sounds a little hoarse as he replies, "For me, too."

"Okay, then. Unicorn Daddy."

The bed shakes as Gunner's laugh rumbles against my ear. Then my heart jumps as he pulls me closer—but only a little closer, his arm wrapped around me, his fingers tucked against my side. His head's at the edge of his pillow, his breath whispering through my hair. I'd only have to turn my face toward his and his lips would be *so* near to mine.

But I close my eyes. And although my body burns and this endless longing aches in my chest, I'm pretty sure I'm smiling as I fall asleep.

And if any nightmares would have returned, having Gunner so near chases them away.

I MUST HAVE SLEPT LIKE the dead. The sun's high and bright when I open my eyes, and I'm alone in Gunner's bed.

My heart clenches painfully when I realize I'm not *just* alone—the bags of clothes and weapons that he packed last night are gone, too. Did he already take off, then? He intended to leave this morning, to go looking for Stone. He wouldn't delay that. He probably arranged for some of the other Riders to look out for me and then left.

And it's good he did. I'm glad he's the one going after

Stone. There's no one who will risk more to make sure my brother returns.

Still, everything inside me aches as I slowly shuffle into the bathroom. Not just my jaw and my leg. Every muscle hurts, including the stupid one beating in my chest.

Then it gives a wild leap when I walk into the living room and the front door opens. Daisy runs in, tail wagging. Gunner follows her, a tray of coffee cups and a pastry bag in hand, his crystalline gaze sweeping from my sleep-tousled head to my bare toes.

I stop, heart pounding. Sometimes I forget how gorgeous he is. Except I don't really *forget*. It's more like every time I see him, he's somehow more beautiful than the last time I did—even though nothing's really changed. He's worn those faded jeans before and they've always hung low on his hips, always emphasized the long muscles of his thighs. Four years ago, my mom gave him that Henley shirt for Christmas, and although the color has faded from dozens of washings, the dark cotton has always stretched across his wide shoulders and broad chest like that. He's always pushed the long sleeves halfway up his strong forearms, always looked so effortlessly strong and sexy. His jaw has always been hard, his eyes always that glacial blue and surrounded by thick black lashes, and his lips…

God. I can almost feel them on mine. Can almost taste him, the hot thrust of his tongue, the sweetness of his kiss.

Daisy's head bumps against my leg, demanding attention. Moving gingerly, I bend over to greet her.

"She needed out, so I took her up the block." Pushing aside a stack of paperbacks, Gunner sets the coffee on the counter separating the small kitchen from the living room. "And I had Bottlecap run out for breakfast and dog food."

"She'll probably like whatever's in that bakery bag better."

"I figured." Although his mouth curves, his gaze is solemn as he watches me straighten. "The prez wants us to head over to the Den as soon as you're ready. You up to it?"

"Yes." Especially since Saxon isn't just the Hellfire Riders' president. He's my boss.

"You feeling pretty sore? I've got ibuprofen, Tylenol. Or I can get something stronger for you."

"Ibuprofen would be good." The muscles in my shoulders protest when I reach for my coffee. "God. It feels like I haven't just been punched in the jaw or whacked my leg on a table. More like I was beaten everywhere."

His jaw clenches. "I know."

I suppose he would. Sipping my coffee, I watch his gaze linger on my mouth before moving slowly upwards. By the dangerous expression in his eyes, I don't think he's checking me out like that because I'm so dang pretty.

"It looks terrible, doesn't it?"

The huge bruise across my cheek hasn't grown into a full-blown black eye but looks as if it was trying. My bottom lip is split and the left side of my mouth swollen.

Strangely, my jaw hurts the worst but looks the best.

My breath stops when he lifts his hand and gently traces the curve of my bottom lip. "Looks like it hurts," he says gruffly.

"It's not so bad. I'm just not looking forward to seeing my parents."

Abruptly he steps away. "Or them seeing you."

Yes. That's more accurate. They're going to be so worried. But maybe they should be. Not just for Stone.

"Do you think my parents are safe? They're my brother's family, too. Maybe they'll be threatened."

"I don't think so. You noticed Blowback wasn't surprised when you told us why the fucker was there?"

"Yes." Even though Gunner and Lily were.

"He knew family had been threatened after the fighters were taken. Not everyone, but some. So he had Hashtag looking out for you during the nights."

"Really?" I hadn't noticed at all.

Gunner nods, his jaw working. "I didn't know. Just the prez and Blowback did. And Hashtag figured everyone on the executive board was in the know, so when Widowmaker sent him home sick last night, he assumed that you'd be covered. We fucked up."

I shrug. They couldn't have known for sure it would happen. "It turned out okay."

"No." His gaze holds mine before flicking to my cheek, my lips. "Not okay. A fuck up like that could have gotten you killed."

"But not my parents?" I'm doubtful.

"You live out of town. You were alone. Your parents live together and across the street from the goddamn sheriff. Targeting them's not going to be worth the risk to these fuckers."

Is he lying to me so I don't worry again? I can't tell. But I think there's something he probably isn't saying—because another fuck up wouldn't be acceptable. "The Riders are still going to have someone watching over them, aren't they."

It's not a question, and the corners of his mouth quirk up into a smile. "Yup. But you don't know that."

"Okay."

Easy enough. There's a lot of stuff I supposedly don't know.

Stomach rumbling, I pick through the pastry bag. There's a variety, but the variety is all sugar. Bottlecap apparently has a sweet tooth. I like my coffee to resemble syrup but that's about it. I'd have killed for a yogurt or fruit, but I can grab something at the Den.

Frowning a little, Gunner picks up the bag when I set it aside. With long fingers, he tears a blueberry muffin apart and tosses the entire bottom to Daisy, who wolfs it down in a single bite and turns her best *I'm a sad starving puppy* eyes up to beg for more.

He tears off another bottom and feeds it to her, then catches my look and grins. "I like the muffin tops best. Not so dry."

I like watching him eat the tops best. In fact, sipping coffee and watching him share his breakfast with Daisy is the best start to a morning that I can remember in a long, long time.

But it doesn't last. Too soon, he's crumpling the pastry bag and looking over at me. "I packed up the truck earlier. So we'll head out as soon as you're ready."

To the Den. Then Gunner to wherever he's going—and I know better than to ask where that is. I already know the answer. Club business.

With a heavy heart, I nod.

"You want someone to pick up your stuff at your house, or do you want to head out there and do it yourself before we go to your parents' place?"

Oh. Because, right. I probably shouldn't stay alone at my house for now. "I'd rather do it," I say. "And I need to get Daisy's stuff, too. How long do you think I'll need to stay there?"

Gunner frowns. "Where?"

"My parents' house."

"You're not staying there," he says flatly.

"Oh. Then where?"

He regards me for a long, endless moment. I can't read his face, but his eyes—Jesus. Just like last night. Hot. Intense. Devouring me whole.

"Just go get ready," he says gruffly. "And we'll talk to the prez."

SIXTEEN

GUNNER

Hands to myself. Eyes forward.

After ten goddamn years of telling myself the same fucking thing over and over, keeping my hands and eyes off Anna Wall should be as easy as breathing.

But even breathing isn't easy. Because, Christ—I can smell her. She showered before we left my place, and now her thick hair is piled in a messy bun on top of her head, smelling like my soap. It's not her usual perfume, a green tea scent her dad gave her last Christmas, but *my* scent. As if I've marked her. And I'm one second away from dragging her close and burying my face against her skin, so I can breathe her all in and claim every inch. Mine.

One second away. God damn it. I should have more control than this. But around Anna, that control hangs by a thin thread. And every year, every day, every breath — that thread stretches thinner and thinner.

I can't let it break.

Hands to myself. Eyes forward.

My fingers clench on the steering wheel. Hands to myself. Even though her thigh is pressed up against mine. Wearing that big puffy coat, she's buckled into the truck's middle seat so Daisy can stick her head out the passenger window.

A dog on one side of her, and something more feral on the other. Because that bruise on her cheek, her swollen mouth have broken loose a savage part of me that I've kept chained down all these years. Bullets for Chef and every bastard in the Iron Blood wouldn't satisfy my need to kill them. Even a goddamn sledgehammer wouldn't be enough. But my hands, my teeth? I'd bathe in their fucking blood.

My need for her burns just as hot and wild. I didn't let myself fall asleep last night. Not while holding her. Because on this thin primal edge, I might wake up with my thick cock buried deep inside her scalding heat, fucking her with raging ferocity until she screams my name, her pussy gripping me tight as she comes. Or wake up with my face between her legs, devouring her sweet cunt until her juices are slipping over my tongue.

Ah fuck. Just the thought of tasting her pussy makes my cock throb painfully, my balls tight and the head dripping precum. Just imagining sucking on her little clit while she bucks and cries out beneath me leaves me a stroke of my hand away from coming in my jeans.

I'd do anything for a taste. Just one single lick.

I'd do anything except hurt her. And shoving my dick into her only hours after some asshole tries to rape her? After she wakes up shaking from a nightmare?

Not a chance in hell.

But even though the night is over, I can't unleash that savage now. I can't touch her again. Not until we find Stone. Not until my family's usefulness is done. Even though the feral beast inside me is howling that she's mine. All fucking *mine*.

I can't touch her. But I can keep her near me. I don't have to let her go.

That knowledge is the only chain keeping me in control.

We'll talk to the prez. But it doesn't matter what Saxon says. Like it or not, Anna's coming with me. All these endless goddamn years, I tried to save her by staying away—and she got hurt anyway. My brothers already fucked up once, watching over her. I won't take that chance again. Anna's mine.

And she's mine to protect.

Late morning, the Wolf Den hasn't opened yet and

the parking lot is all but empty. Just the prez's motorcycle and a car belonging to one of the cooks, who Anna says comes in early for lunch prep.

She scoots out the driver's side after me, telling the dog, "Stay in the truck. Saxon will kick my ass if you bring the health inspector in." She looks to me. "We're not going to be long, are we?"

"Probably not."

With her key, Anna lets us in through the front entrance. I follow her past the bar and through the employees' door. The prez's office is down a hallway, the door angled open, Saxon sitting at his desk with a pile of paperwork in front of him.

Anna taps lightly on the door and the boss leans back in his chair, telling her to come in with a flick of his fingers. His steely gaze lingers on her cheek, on her mouth. The boss is a hard man to read but I don't need a magic decoder to know what he's thinking.

He wants Chef dead. And he's pissed that bastard's getting extra time to live because we can't rock the Iron Blood's boat while we're searching for Stone.

Anna doesn't waver under that hard stare. "How's Jenny?"

"At the brewery. Working already."

"Of course."

The boss nods. "You need anything?"

"My brother home," she says simply. "And to know my mom and dad will be okay."

"We're taking care of both. You got your phone?"

Wordlessly, she pulls it from her coat pocket and shows him.

"You just keep hold of that. We're going to look after you. I'll get someone in to cover your shifts for the next week or so. You're taking a vacation."

"Paid? Because I *am* your most awesome employee."

She jerks her thumb over her shoulder, indicating the wall behind her, covered by over sixty employee-of-the-month plaques that Anna hung herself. No one could doubt the boss has a soft spot for her, considering that he's got over sixty photos of Anna staring out at him and she's wearing a different silly face on each one.

His mouth twitches. "Paid," he agrees. "Now get the fuck out of here while I talk to Gunner."

She goes with a smile curving her swollen lips. I shut the door.

The boss eyes me and taps the phone laying on his desk. "You gonna explain this message you sent about her going with you?"

"The Riders won't expend resources to protect her, so I'm getting her out of town."

"Bullshit."

Yes. "That's the reason I'll give the Notorious Few."

A speculative gleam comes into his eyes. "They the reason you stayed away from her all this time?" He doesn't wait for my answer, his gaze hardening. "They a threat to her?"

"Only if they think she's more to me than Stone's sister."

"No problem there." Wry amusement fills his voice. "You've been pretending she isn't as long as I've known you. You just keep on pretending."

Even if it kills me. "I will."

The boss nods. "All right. One thing for damn sure, she'll be safer with you than with anyone else, because there's nobody who'll take more interest in protecting her. You'd kill your blood brothers to keep her safe. Tell me I'm wrong."

I can't.

"Yeah. I know exactly how that is." It's said in the same rough tone he uses whenever he's talking about Jenny. "So you're taking her, then. Hell, let her listen around, set her up tending a bar. She might pick up more than you do."

Not gonna happen. If I have my way, my family won't even know she's in the same state. "Anything else?"

He takes a long second to answer, as if deliberating. Finally he says, "That info Blowback is getting from his source in Vegas? The FBI's got someone looking into the Cage."

Undercover? "With what club?"

"The Devil's Hangmen. They're out of favor with the cartel so his info's dated, but I'm telling you for two reasons. One, you trade that information if you're up against a wall. Stone for the cop. Two, try and make sure it doesn't come to that, because he's how we're going to get that trace on her phone when Stone calls. He's more useful to us alive than dead."

An undercover fed with the Devil's Hangmen, who will have a tap on Anna's phone. "Are the feds going to bust the Cage after she gets the call?"

The prez shakes his head. "Blowback's source says there's a leak in the Bureau, and that's why the assholes running the Cage are always a step ahead. When he gets the location he'll hold it close to his chest, so no one tips off whoever's in charge of that show."

"Or blows his cover."

"Or that." The prez's gaze hardens. "But you've gotta assume the more calls she gets, the closer the feds will come, too. And I don't care how Stone gets home, whether it's us or the cops breaking him loose. But I'd sure like to know that the bastards who took our brother never get cozy in a cell. I'd rather see them in the ground."

"I'll put them there if I can," I tell him. Especially the bastard who touched Anna. "And their fucking enforcer is dead, either way."

A sharp nod says he approves of that plan. "Good enough. You got cash?"

"The prize money from last week's fight."

"Hit up Old Timer if you need more."

I nod and head out. Anna's sitting in the empty restaurant, staring at her phone. "Is this going to help—if he calls?"

"We've got friends who can trace the call."

Doubt darkens the golden brown of her eyes.

"Whoever took him has to know there's a possibility the call will be traced. They'll cover their tracks."

"They'll try." I'm sure they will. "But it'll still be more than we had before. And even if we can't trace it, Stone will have time to think of what to tell you, maybe get a message through. So don't let that out of your sight."

"I won't." On a deep breath, she stands. "So am I going to be hidden away at the clubhouse? Obviously it won't be at Jenny's house"—a wry smile twists her beautiful swollen mouth—"because anyone coming after me might get to her, and Saxon wouldn't risk that."

The prez wouldn't risk anyone getting to Anna, either. "How do you feel about a road trip?"

Her eyebrows knit together. "What do you mean?"

"I mean, right now that phone is our strongest hope. And if we hid you away at the ranch, whether you're at Jenny's or the clubhouse, there's a damn good chance you'd miss any call coming in."

Just like I didn't get that picture of her taped up last night until I got some goddamn reception.

"Oh." With a grimace, she clutches the phone to her chest. "That'd be bad."

"Real fucking bad. And we could hide you away on the ranch and keep the phone here in town, but fuck knows what'll happen if you aren't the one who answers. They might think you handed it over to the cops."

"Also bad."

"Yeah." I step closer and watch awareness flare in her

eyes, feel it race through my veins like fire. Christ. I need to get this under control. Everything I say, everything I do can't look like anything but a man watching out for his friend's little sister. "But we don't want you so easy to find if that fucker comes looking again. One solution is to get you out of town. And me, I'm heading out of town. So the answer about where you ought to go is real damn obvious."

Her lips part and she stares up at me. "With you."

"That's right."

She takes a deep, slow breath. Then another. "Okay."

"You sure?" Because it took a damn long time for her to work up to that *Okay*. "It doesn't fit in with your plan to kick me out of your life."

And I'm a dick for even saying it. I know she's not going to run around hooking up with a bunch of assholes, looking for a future while Stone's future is uncertain. But she might look for someone to console her. To hold her through any rough nights.

Better she knows now that even though I'm not a part of her plans for the future, I'm the only one she can go to. Soon, I'll be the only one she'll *ever* go to.

Her eyes are suddenly huge, dark and wounded. "I'm sure. Because I'd rather be safe and have a future where I'm totally alone than have no future at all."

Yeah, I'm a fucking dick. "You won't be alone."

Anna nods, but her expression is sad and tired as she averts her eyes. Jesus, I can't bear that look. Gently I lift my fingers to her face, trace the line of her jaw. Her gaze raises to mine, searching my eyes. I've got to be careful here. So careful. I can't get in the habit of touching her. Even though nothing in my life ever felt so damn good.

But touching her in this tender way around my family might fuck up any chance of finding Stone. Losing him would hurt Anna more than anything my family could do to her. I won't be the reason for any more of her pain.

I withdraw my hand, shoving my fists into the pockets of my jeans. "We ought to get going."

Her voice is husky as she asks, "What about Daisy?"

"Probably best to leave her at your folks' place." On the road, there's too many strangers, too many unfamiliar surroundings. And fuck knows if Anna and I have to take off quick, Daisy might be left behind. "We'll be driving my truck down, but I'll be taking my ride, too — and there's no place for a dog on a bike."

"Yes," she says, then bites her lip and glances away with a stricken look on her face.

Oh hell. I know what that is. "You worried about seeing your parents?"

"Yes." It's a strained whisper.

And I can't help myself. I cup her jaw again, sweep my thumb over her cheekbone, but my gaze touches the bruise on the other side. "We'll go to your place, pack up your stuff, then head to your parents'. And I'll be there with you. All right?"

On a shuddering breath, she nods against my palm. "All right."

SEVENTEEN

GUNNER

About an hour south of Pine Valley, Anna asks, "So where are we heading?"

I glance over. She's been quiet since we left Daisy at her parents' house, where it went just as badly as we both knew it would. Seeing their girl had been hurt tore up both Clara and Paul.

And it went better than I thought it would, because Anna clung to my hand the entire time, using me for support as she told the truth as far as she could—saying the girl Stone was with ended up being more trouble than he thought, and that same trouble showed up at Anna's place the night before. And that now I'll be watching over her until the trouble is taken care of.

I suspect they'd have packed up and tried to come with us if we hadn't pressed Daisy onto them. Having Stone's dog to take care of gave them a way to help their son, gave them some way to be useful — and as it was, Paul wouldn't let us leave until he whipped up a few sandwiches and put together a lunch for us to eat on the road.

Then we left her family and headed toward mine — families that are a hell of a lot farther apart from each other than the miles can measure. Still exhausted and looking guilty as hell, Anna curled up in the passenger seat with her head pillowed against her rolled-up coat and her phone in her lap.

I thought she'd go to sleep. Instead she's looking at me, asking where we're going. That doesn't surprise me. What surprises me is,

"You waited until now to ask?"

She smiles faintly. "Before I found out I'd be going with you, I assumed your answer would be 'club business.' And after I found out I'd be going…I didn't want to know, in case I'd have to lie to my parents. I think they're assuming Arizona. And that's a hell of a drive, but I guess you can't fly with those guns."

No, I couldn't. With my bike, either. "We're heading to Santa Rosa."

"California?" She blinks. "Do you think that's where Stone is?"

"No. My family lives in the area."

"Your family," she echoes and I can feel her astonished gaze without even glancing over. "Really?"

"Yup."

"And are you going to add anything to that? Or are you going to just drop that bomb and leave it there?"

I'd like to leave it there and never touch it again. Never let her touch it, either. But her response from last night wrapped around my heart like barbed wire. Her response to whether she loved me.

I don't think I even know you.

I can't look to a future with her yet. Not until we get Stone back. But in the meantime, I'll give her enough that she'll start thinking of me as a future, too. I need to start building that foundation by letting her know me.

But, Jesus. Instead of falling for me, the shit I've got to tell her might send her running the other way.

"They're a motorcycle club—"

"Your *family* is a club?"

"Kind of. And they might have info about the Iron Blood and the Cage."

She twists to look at the motorcycle mounted in the bed of the truck. "You can't just visit and ask? Because your bike, all those weapons—it looks like you're going in for a long haul."

That's what it needs to look like to convince them

I'm staying. "It might take a little while," I tell her. "It's complicated."

"Do you hate them or do they hate you?"

That came out of nowhere. I shoot her a glance, find her watching me steadily. "What?"

"Well, you never talk about them. And if anyone asks, you change the subject. Plus you never visit them, do you?"

"I try not to."

"See? *You* don't like being there. Why?"

I don't even know where to start. Hands clenched on the steering wheel, I search for somewhere to begin. But there's nothing I want to share with her. Hell, there's nothing I want to dredge up whether I'm sharing or not. I prefer to get by not thinking of them at all.

"Zach." She's using my real name. Shit. If I don't answer her soon, I'm going to have a seriously pissed-off Anna to deal with. "You say they are a motorcycle club. You say you don't like being around them. I imagine you're going to keep me away from them—"

"I'm going to try."

"—but I need to know what I'll be dealing with. Just in case. Because being taken by surprise really sucks."

She touches the bruise on her cheek as if to remind me of the last surprise she got.

I don't need a reminder. And she *does* need to know. Not just because I want to build a future—but because even if I try to keep her away from my family, the chances of making it through this without them seeking her out is zero.

Fuck. Might as well just get it over with. "It's a club but it's not a normal one," I tell her. "That's just how it all shook out after my father started identifying as an outlaw biker about thirty years ago."

"So what is it?"

"It's a cult."

"A *cult*?"

"Yes."

"You're serious."

"Yup."

"A religious cult?"

"No."

"Do they think aliens are coming?"

"No."

"You know, you could help me out here." Her voice is a mix of amusement and exasperation.

"More like…the Manson Family. If my father was Charles Manson."

She sucks in a breath. "With his followers going around murdering people?"

"Not quite. But a lot of the same thinking behind it." Maybe even inspired by Manson. The timing would have been right, and fuck knows my father got inspired — energized — by all kinds of shit. "Believing that the end was coming, that a race war will destroy civilization. My dad wasn't looking to start that war, though. More like survive it and establish a new world order, populated by a pure race that could live in peace."

"Jesus," she whispers.

"Nah. His cult is a lot better than my father's."

Her grin flashes. "What's your dad like?"

"Dead." Cut down like a tree by his own seed. "In body at least. For my mother, his spirit and his purpose live on in her boys. We all look just like him."

"You're kidding," she says.

"No."

"That answers every single question I have, then. Like, why would a cult spring up around him? Was he that charismatic? Nope, he just looks like a freaking god."

Shit. I laugh, shaking my head. Some of my tension eases. My family's fucked up, but she's taking it in stride—not running the other way.

"So how many Cooper men are there?"

"I have four brothers." Still living. "Christ knows how many nephews now, too. But they're all still kids."

"Then are your brothers the only members of the MC?"

"No. My father collected followers." Women, easily. My mother was always the female at the head of the pack, but men followed him, too—partially because the women around my father were available, partially because they liked what he was saying. "He started back in the 70s as the leader of a free love clan—they had a commune on my mother's family farm—but that era was winding down and he knew he needed to evolve. Then he read Hunter Thompson's book about the Hell's Angels and liked what it had to say. About living free and being your own man and fuck the world. So he formed a club and put himself up as prez."

"It sounds a lot like how the Hellfire Riders started."

With Tommy Burns and his friends, including Red Erickson and Thorne. "No. They wanted to ride and fuck. It wasn't about creating a dynasty. The Riders are a brotherhood. The Notorious Few was about my father delivering a new world—and that's how they talk about it, too. About him predicting the end of the hippie era and having the insight to understand how they had become Lotus-Eaters instead of revolutionaries, and how he envisioned a new path. About the string of coincidences that led him to Thompson's book and how that's proof of his destiny. And now it's about his sons leading the way."

"Some might say that's a real brotherhood. Like, literally one."

"My family would say it is." For a long time, I thought it was. "But I've been in the Marines and the Hellfire Riders. I know what brotherhood is. I know what a brother is."

I don't need to name names. Her smile tells me she knows I'm talking about Stone.

She regards me, her eyes curious. "So if your father's dead, what's holding it together?"

"His bloodline—and my mother. It's a cult, like I said. Those commune roots never went away and my brothers have bought into this idea that a race war's coming and that there was something special about our old man. That they've got a legacy to carry on."

"So who's leading them now?"

"My oldest brother, if you ask them."

Her brows arch. "And if I ask you?"

"My mother." I glance at Anna. God, the way she's looking at me, I should have started talking to her like this long ago. There's no judgment. Only genuine interest, as if I'm the most fascinating man she's ever seen.

Then again, that's no surprise. Working the bar, she's always drawn people in and had them spilling their guts. And it's probably best I didn't spill anything before. Because what I'd be spilling was how much I want her lips on mine, tasting her instead of talking. How much I want her sitting on the bar and my head between her thighs. How bad I need to be inside her.

Christ. I shift in my seat, but there's no position that's going to ease the ache in my cock.

Talking about my mother might do it, though. "Maybe she was the driving force behind my father the whole time and was just good at staying in his shadow. Or he was the flame who drew all the moths and she was the one who kept pouring in the kerosene. Because she's still keeping that flame lit — even though, despite all of us looking like him, we're *not* like him. Aside from our faces, we only got bits and pieces."

"What do you mean?"

"That charisma he had, it's a hell of a lot of things — all the traits that draw people in. So he was smart, funny, persuasive, charming as hell. And he was kind, generous — especially if it meant people would feel obligated to him afterward."

"And let me guess — combined with his looks, that all made him as sexy as fuck?" Anna puts in, her gaze sweeping down my length.

That, too. I grew up seeing the way people looked at him. Seeing how obsessed some of them became. "He drew in both men and women with it. But that charisma's also all those traits that hold people captive, make them fall in line. The way he could tear someone down, the way he'd threaten and carry a threat through. The way he'd get pissed and rage, and how he had this icy anger that was just fucking terrifying. So my brothers, some have a few of those traits. The others have a few different traits. Like Adam, he's got the rage. He can be generous. But he's sure as hell not smart. No one has the whole package."

Anna looks at me in bemusement, her swollen lips pursed. "You have the whole package."

Not quite. "I don't need to be the center of everyone's attention like he did. And I'm missing the sociopathic element and delusions of grandeur." My mouth twists into a wry smile when I glance at her again. "Some of my brothers aren't missing those."

Her eyes narrow. "You've read up on this. This personality and cult stuff. Because you talk about it like you've pulled it apart and categorized it all. Like you're looking at it from a distance."

Not far enough. But she's not wrong. "Your mom sent me a package of books after that first visit. They helped me wrap my head around it."

Her brows shoot high. "Mom knew?"

"You're really surprised?" Not much ever gets past Clara Wall. When Anna shakes her head, I tell her, "First time she got me alone, I ended up telling her half of all this without even realizing I was doing it. I guess she figured out the rest."

Anna's soft laughter fills the truck's cab, rolls right over my skin. "I bet she did," she says, then bites her lip.

Which tells me she wants to say more. "Just ask it," I tell her.

"You eventually left—so what prompted you to go?"

Too many reasons to list, starting with David's girl being killed. But all those reasons boiled down to one. "I figured out that wasn't what life should be."

"What do they think of you going? Did they turn their backs on you?"

If only. "No. They've been waiting for me to return. They've got plans for me, and they want me to stop dicking around and fall in line."

Her brow furrows. "So, you're going to…what? Tell them you'll come back home if they help you find my brother?"

I nod and try not to feel the sickness rising in my chest. Because they won't be satisfied with me *saying* I'll come back.

Her gaze searches my face. "So where do I fit in? What do I need to be to you?"

"Just be Stone's little sister. It's important there's nothing else between us."

Shrugging, she pulls her gaze away to stare through the front windshield. "We established last night there isn't."

It's true I said that but her shrug pisses me off. "Just fucking listen. You're important to me. But if I show up with any girl who doesn't—"

"I get it, okay?" she snaps at me, eyes sparking. "You show up with some girl who isn't part of their plan and they might not be as willing to help with Stone—right?"

It's right. It's not my primary reason—protecting Anna—but it's reason enough. "Yeah."

"Because I'm just his sister," she says flatly. "So when you kissed me in the shower—"

"I shouldn't have."

Her breath catches and she looks at me, her expression frozen. "It was a mistake?"

"Not a mistake." Never a mistake. "I sure as hell don't regret it. But I wasn't thinking."

Because I shouldn't have done it yet. I should have waited. Not just because of this shit with my family but because I can't jump the gun with her. Only a few hours before I kissed her, she kicked me out of her life. Said she didn't just want a fuck. So I've got to work up to that. Let her know me first. *Then* kiss her.

Shit. And now I've dug a hole because she's staring

out the windshield again, her body tense. "It was a physical response to the stress," I tell her. "After seeing that picture. Then the relief of knowing you were all right."

She flicks me a disbelieving glance. "Stone said you were one of the coldest bastards he's ever known in stress situations."

I could never be cold, finding her like that.

"It doesn't matter." She slides down in her seat, burying her hands in the pouch of her hoodie. "Just call it a mistake. Because God knows you wouldn't have kissed me under normal circumstances."

Under normal circumstances—in a shower, with Anna naked against me? I'd have kissed her. But I sure as hell wouldn't have stopped at a kiss.

But I don't think that's what she's saying. "What the hell does that mean?"

"It means that under normal circumstances, you wouldn't have even been alone with me. You always make an effort *not* to be—that's pretty obvious. And this is the most you've talked to me in years. So under normal circumstances, you'd never have touched me." Her eyes are glassy and hard when she flicks a glance at me. "Am I wrong?"

Completely fucking wrong. Because if anything about my family and these circumstances were normal, I'd have spent the last ten years touching her. Being alone with her.

Wrong—yet everything she said was true. But what the fuck can I tell her now?

I can't be alone with you because I won't keep my hands off you? Because every fucking second of every fucking day I'm thinking of you? Because the more I open my mouth around you, the more likely I'll say all the filthy things I want to do to you?

Starting with pulling this truck onto the side of the road, tossing her ankles up over my shoulders, then fucking her so deep and hard she won't be left with a single doubt about why I can't be alone with her.

But there's not a damn thing I can say. Not now. Jaw set, I watch the road. Until a soft gasp makes me glance over.

Anna's looking at me with horror dawning on her face. "You thought it was them." Her hand lifts to her bruised cheek. "You thought it was them. That's why you were so surprised there was only one man—and that he didn't have blue eyes. You thought they came after me and raped me. You thought your *brothers* raped me."

I nod, my throat suddenly a constricted mess. Because the distance she was saying I had shrinks to no distance at all, just imagining what might have happened. By the horror on her face, that distance vanishes for her, too. It's one thing to talk about my family. It's another to realize they might have shown up on her doorstep—and what they'd be capable of if they did.

And now we're heading for *their* doorstep.

Confusion replaces her horror. "But…why would they hurt me?"

"Those rumors about you and me." Gravel fills my voice. "My family got wind. So I thought…I thought they might have come. Because you aren't part of their plan for me—and they'll make sure no one fucks that up."

"Oh." Lips rounded in surprise and realization, she stares at me. *"Ohhhhh."*

That's not a good sound. "What?"

Gingerly she asks, "Is that why you never hook up with anyone—because they might come after her?"

No. Because I could have had as many hookups as I liked. My family doesn't care if I screw around. In their eyes, the more women I fuck, the more of a man I am. They'd only go after a woman I was serious about. Keeping the Cooper line pure is what matters.

The only reason there's been no one else is simply because there *is* no one else. Not for me.

There's no one but Anna.

"So that's why it's important they know I'm just Stone's little sister," she says softly. "Or we'd have more to worry about than finding my brother. Right?"

"Yes," I say roughly.

"Well, then." Voice oddly hollow, she looks to the road ahead. "It's a good thing I'm not anything more."

EIGHTEEN

ANNA

After our late start, we don't arrive in Santa Rosa until well after dark. But instead of heading to his family's spread—a farm somewhere in the hills outside of the city—he pulls into the parking lot of a mid-range chain hotel.

As soon as Gunner finds out that the two rooms Widowmaker reserved for us don't have a connecting door, he changes the reservation to a third floor deluxe suite—which turns out to be a regular double queen with a fireplace and a spa tub, separated from a living area by a half wall.

Gunner slings his bags on the bed nearest the door. Ten minutes later, after checking out all the locks and the security of the balcony's sliding glass doors, he heads down to the hotel's weight room.

Unpacking my bag takes up ten more minutes and then I'm out of things to do. Back in Pine Valley, I'm always busy. Either bartending at the Den or working on my house. Even while watching TV, I usually have another project with me—like sketching on my drawing pad or editing my pictures on my desktop computer.

God. I need a laptop. I'm afraid to poke at my phone too much. With my luck, I'd be playing Candy Crush when Stone's call came in and accidentally hang up on him by pressing the wrong part of the screen at the wrong time.

Sprawled on my bed, I aimlessly flip through channels, debating whether to head down to the swimming pool. But I'm tired, and sore enough that I probably wouldn't enjoy it.

Not to mention, I didn't bring a swimming suit. Plus, my phone and the pool? Maybe not a good combination.

Anyway, I know what I'm really trying to do: distract myself so I don't think about Gunner.

Big surprise, I think about him anyway. Story of my freaking life.

With a sigh, I haul my ass off the bed and examine

the spa tub. It looks clean. So I'll trust that the hotel maids bleach the hell out of it every morning and try to soak away some of this soreness.

God knows I've got time. My brother and Gunner often work out together, so I know he's going to be down there at least an hour. Maybe more.

I turn on the tap as hot as I can stand before stripping, then pile my hair on top of my head. My cheek still looks as if an asshole rapist slapped the hell out of me — because, hey, an asshole rapist did — but the swelling on my lips has gone down. Not so bad. The bruise on the side of my thigh has darkened to an ugly purple splotch the size of my fist and hurts like crazy if I touch it.

So of course I bump it against the rim of the tub while climbing in. Teeth gritted, I lean back and close my eyes — and try to mentally sort through the chaotic jumble that has become my life. Which is,

A) My brother has essentially been taken prisoner and will be forced to fight in a cage match to the death.

I don't even know what to make of that. Not really. Do they just fight with their fists? Maybe MMA-style? Or is he going to be like Mad Max, grabbing chainsaws off the sides of the cage?

I hope it's just fighting. I've seen him up in the ring a couple of times. He's fast and he's strong and, from what I hear, he's also very good. But these assholes are probably grabbing other men who are good, too.

And that scares the shit out of me. Because the guy

who attacked me — Chef — made it sound like losing was an inevitability. Eventually.

But that *eventually* is what keeps me from descending into terror, because

B) Gunner's going to find him. And Blowback's looking for him, too. Between them, they'll bring my brother home. *Eventually* will give them enough time.

I don't know what route Blowback is taking to find my brother, but I'll help Gunner in any way I can. Any way.

Right now, that way requires me to wait for Stone's call. And to keep things between Gunner and me as simple as they've always been. Which brings me to

C) Gunner grew up in a cult,

and D) Holy shit.

Because I *still* can't completely wrap my head around it. But it puts a lot of what I knew about him into context. His refusal to talk about his past — and the whole celibacy thing.

Not that he's always been celibate. I know he hooked up with girls when he was in the Marines. But maybe it was different when he was in the service. Maybe his family was far enough away that he felt he could — or maybe it was just that his time in the Marines was a temporary thing. But when he moves into a town to settle down? Maybe he couldn't fuck around anymore because his family would see a more permanent arrangement as a threat.

That eases some of the old hurt — knowing he probably turned me down because of this thing with his family. And it wasn't just me. He turned down every girl who asked. Over the years, there must have been hundreds of hookups he passed on.

But, Jesus. Pussy's a hell of a thing for a young, straight guy to give up. Especially because Pine Valley isn't that special—it's just like any other town in central Oregon. So what's there that's worth settling down and sacrificing sex for? Was joining a motorcycle club and hanging out with Stone really that great?

As much as I love my brother, I don't understand that. But maybe I *can't* understand that. Gunner said he found real brotherhood in the Marines and with the Riders. Maybe after the way he grew up, that brotherhood was worth giving up sex for. Since I wasn't raised in a cult, I can't begin to know how Gunner feels about it.

Anyway, going without sex for years and years isn't *that* bad. I should know. My fingers and toys do a pretty bang up job of getting me off. Like every guy in the world, Gunner probably eases the tension by jacking off—

Oh god. I shouldn't have let my mind wander in that direction. Because now I'm thinking of how he might look when he pleasures himself. Maybe stretched out on the hotel bed, all that male beauty on display. The ropes of muscles in his arms. His corrugated abs. The happy trail leading downward, his strong heavy thighs…his big hand wrapped around his cock.

Maybe going slow, his eyes closed as he imagines a

leisurely fuck. Or stroking harder, his gaze hot and intense and locked on mine.

On the bed, stroking himself—watching me in the bath, where my thighs fall open to the advance of my hand. My fingers glide over my clit and I try not to think of him. I'm quitting all that. I try to picture someone else on that bed but although my mind flits from one sexy actor to another, my imagination comes right back to Gunner.

Maybe that's not a surprise. After fantasizing about Gunner for so many years, my brain is conditioned to associate arousal with images of him.

So just this time. One last time.

And I'm not picturing him on the bed anymore but coming back from the gym, sweaty and gorgeous—and his beautiful face going hard when he finds me in the bath. And he'd stand there for a long second, watching me. And I'd see how aroused he was, his cock rigid and his sweats doing nothing to hide it.

But I'm over him. So I wouldn't feel anything as I stand up out of the bath. Just haughty amusement when he sees me naked, his crystalline eyes going hotter, but it's nothing to me.

Because I'm *so* over him. And I just saunter toward the dresser to get my pajamas.

But the next thing I know his big hands grab my waist and his rough voice growls in my ear, "Don't walk away from me, Anna." And he pulls me hard back against him and his fingers dive straight between my legs, delving into the cleft of my pussy, and I'm so wet, and he's so strong, and I can't stop him from rubbing my clit. And he groans against my ear and says, "You're so damn sexy, sweetheart. I've wanted you for so long and I need you so bad. I need to fuck you."

And I'm going to let him, but only because he's so beautiful. It's just a physical thing. I don't want him or need him. Not anymore.

But before I can answer he shoves me forward onto the bed, and instead of letting me turn around to kiss him, he drags me up onto my knees and I feel him hot and hard behind me.

And he's so desperate. So rough. Because he hasn't had anyone in years, because his family's too dangerous—

no, no, this is my fantasy, so instead I'll dream it's

—because for all these years he only wanted me, and that's what he says as his big cock slams deep inside my tight pussy, so long and thick that I scream, because there's been no one else for me, either, but he's ruthless, just fucking me and fucking me, because he can't control himself anymore and he needs me so much, and his relentless fingers are rubbing my clit, rubbing and rubbing even though I'm too close, too sensitive, and he's leaning over me and with every devastating stroke of his cock he tells me—

I need you, I love you

—and I come hard. So hard, the water sloshing against the sides of the bath and lapping the tight, burning points of my nipples. My chest heaves as I try to catch my breath.

Oh my god. Oh my god. I'm so screwed. Because

E) I'm never going to get over him.

And for such a long time, I tried to protect myself by saying I didn't love him. By reminding myself that I didn't know him. But now I'm finding out more.

With some people, that would kill it dead right there. With some people, the better you know them, the more you realize the things you liked aren't really what you thought. What seemed like a dry sense of humor is just bitterness. What seemed polite is rooted is sexism. What seemed considered and thoughtful is just a dull imagination.

But what I'm finding out about Gunner isn't disappointing me. And I'm still eager to know more. I'm a glutton for pain, apparently.

Or I really just don't know when to quit.

Because even if his family is the reason why he rejected me all those times, he flat out said I'm nothing more than Stone's sister. I can't *be* more than Stone's sister, especially now.

And if I ever *had* been more, he could have taken the risk. *I* would have. Because, God—I spent the last ten years thinking I was going to die soon anyway. So if I thought he loved me, I'd have grabbed onto a chance to be with him and held it so tight. No matter the danger.

But it's been ten years. And in all that time, nothing.

So I'm not worth that risk to Gunner.

So I'll just be his friend's sister. And if my heart is fucked, it's fucked.

All that matters now is getting my brother home safe.

I don't hear Gunner come back because I've got the hair dryer on high, and I don't see him right away because I'm bent over with my head upside down. Then between my legs I see *his* legs, and my heart jumps. I straighten and flip my hair up.

And, good god—it's just like I imagined. I'm out of the tub and dressed in a nightshirt, but Gunner's sweaty and his muscles are ripped and his chest is bare, because he's using his wadded shirt to wipe down his skin. Except he's not wiping anything now, just standing utterly still and staring at me, his face hard, his eyes hot.

But he doesn't say, *I need you, I love you.* He doesn't grab me and shove me toward the bed. Instead he stalks wordlessly into the bathroom, and a second later I hear the shower.

So. Looks like we're back to silence.

Looks like we're back to "don't be alone with Anna."

Looks like we're back to hiding how much that hurts.

NINETEEN

GUNNER

I HAVE TO TAKE THE LONGEST SHOWER OF MY LIFE, jacking off twice before my cock finally stays the hell down. Coming in and seeing Anna bent over like that, her nightshirt riding up to the curve of her ass, playing peek-a-boo with a tiny pair of boyshorts, it was all I could do not to get up behind her and drop to my knees. Or pull those cute little undershorts down to her ankles and bury myself deep.

Sharing this hotel room with her is going to fucking

kill me. If not from whacking off until my dick falls off, then by the loss of blood to my brain. Seeing her bent over like that made me so damn stupid, I didn't even take a change of clothes into the bathroom with me.

I knot a towel around my hips and head out. And, shit—maybe I'm vain as hell or just desperate to see appreciation in her eyes when she looks at me, because I'm disappointed when she doesn't even glance my way. She's on her bed, her eyes glued to the television screen. No matter that she's a short little thing, her legs are goddamn long and sleek, and when I see the small bottle of moisturizer on the nightstand beside her, I realize she was out here smoothing that lotion over her skin while I was busting a nut in the shower. Just picturing her hands gliding over her thighs has my depleted cock stirring to attention again.

I'm so fucked. I pull on my jeans, find my shirt—and watch her not watching me.

She finally looks over when I start lacing my boots. Her brow pleats into a little frown. "You're going out?"

"There're a few joints where my brothers hang out." I'll tell them I've got trouble and need info. But I'm sure as hell not going to show up at the farm, begging for help. Better that they come to me, offering it. "You'll be safe here."

Right now, only Widowmaker knows where we're staying and I know Anna won't open the door to anyone but me.

Still, I'll probably go crazy worrying.

"All right," she says softly. "Just text and let me know where you end up. That way I can tell Blowback where to start looking if something goes wrong."

Nothing's going to go wrong. But, shit. She's trying to have my back — and she looks so damn small over there. When I said I was heading out and leaving her alone, some of the spark in her eyes dimmed, and that just rips at me.

Anna's not meant to be locked away. Not with that light in her, not with all that life. Hiding her away, keeping her in the dark isn't protecting her. It's hurting her.

I can't leave her here. Her body would be safe in this room tonight, but *all* of her would be safer with me.

And my family will find out she's with me soon enough. Might as well bring her out in the open, because keeping her like a secret in a hotel room will only make them think the opposite of what I need them to think.

"You up to going with me?" I ask her and my whole chest seems to fill up with the light from her smile.

"Yes." She bounces forward, heading for the dresser.

"Boots and jeans," I tell her. "We're riding tonight."

I'VE NEVER HAD A WOMAN ride behind me. I don't know if it feels so damn good because of the way she's pressed up against my back, her hands gripping me tight, her thighs cradling mine — or if it feels so damn good just because it's Anna, and the way she holds on like she put all her trust in me, as if I'm her anchor as we ride out of the city, hurtling along the dark highway.

I just know I want to keep going. But all too soon we're pulling into the lot of a roadside bar. There's an equal mix of cages and choppers parked out front. I don't know what my brothers are riding, but the farm's only a few miles farther on. There's a good chance at least a couple of the Notorious Few are here.

Anna pulls off her helmet and swings her leg over the seat when I kill the engine, then stumbles over her feet when she stands. Not used to riding and still finding her legs.

I catch her waist, pulling her back against me. The weather's milder here, so she ditched the big puffy coat and I can feel every slender inch through her clothes. Her hair's braided to keep it from getting tangled in the wind, and she's wearing tall boots, tight jeans that cup her sweet little ass, and a close-fitting athletic jacket zipped all the way up to her throat.

She looks so damn gorgeous dressed up to ride, her cheeks flushed and eyes bright. I should have taken her around before.

"Thanks." Her smile is brief and she bites her lip, her gaze flicking down to my chest and quickly away.

"Say it."

Her solemn gaze meets mine. "You're not wearing your colors."

No, I'm not. I left my kutte behind in Oregon and I feel its absence like I'm missing part of my skin. Like there's nothing covering my back, leaving me raw and exposed.

Having her pressed up against me while we were riding soothed that some. But walking into this bar? Knowing it's the start of wearing another vest?

Flays me right open again.

She must see it. Her warm eyes search my face, worry pinching her brows. "Gunner?"

I shake my head. My throat's thick but this is the choice I made. "I'm not Gunner for now. Just Zach."

"All right," she says but her hand presses flat against my chest, as if stopping me from going anywhere. As if I would go anywhere when she's touching me. Her mouth curves and she arches her brows, whispering, "When we get back to the hotel, just ask nicely and I'll draw the Riders' patch on your back…Gunner."

I fucking love this girl.

But although I want to haul her up and kiss the hell out of her, that can't happen now. So I just roughly say, "Stick close to me."

I head toward the entrance, taking her hand. I should have had my fill of her touch when she had her arms around me on the bike. But instead of being filled, I just get hungrier.

She squeezes my fingers. "People who are just friends don't hold hands."

"You're not my friend," I say and her hand jerks in my grip as if she's trying to pull away, but I don't let her go.

"My family would never believe a man and a woman could be *friends*. They don't think like that."

"You don't hold hands with someone who's just your friend's sister, either."

"Yes, I would, because you're under my protection." Deliberately, I lace my fingers through hers and hold our linked hands up between us. "This? I'm keeping you close so I can look out for you better."

The anger firing heat into her cheeks softens. "I see."

Does she? I tilt my head. "What do you think this looks like?"

"You know what it looks like," she hedges and when I just wait, she rolls her eyes. "It's possessive."

Yeah, it is. "Because you're Stone's sister, and I'm taking care of you. If you were my woman, I'd also take care of you. So it looks the same."

Which is a huge fucking lie. Because if she were mine, we wouldn't be here. We'd be back in that hotel room, her sleek legs around my waist and my cock pumping deep inside her wet pussy.

But the rest of it's true. If they see me with someone who's under my protection, they'll expect it to *look* like protection. It doesn't matter that she's my friend's sister—she's mine to take care of.

Mine.

It doesn't get more possessive than that.

She nods, accepting my explanation. My hand's tight on hers as I lead her into the bar. It's not much to look at inside, dark and smoky, with southern rock crackling through old box speakers hanging from the ceiling. There's a handful of pool tables near the back, a few dozen tables and booths, and at the bar, the line of men sitting on the stools display a canyon's worth of combined asscrack.

Rough, but not the kind of place that'll scare Anna. The Wolf Den's nicer, but she still sees shit go down there. She's seen the Riders fuck and she's seen them fight. Nothing here will make her blink an eye.

I spot a Notorious Few kutte near the pool tables. Not one of my brothers. A wiry bastard, with red hair and so heavily freckled the spots have melded together into an orange tan. He nudges the man next to him. Another one of the Few. Bigger, arms sleeved in tattoos, his bald round head shining with sweat.

They both look me up and down as I come close. Neither one even glances at Anna, which tells me not much has changed around here. Seeing a Cooper brother with a woman? Doesn't matter who she is because there will be a different girl the next time you see him.

"So you're the missing brother." Leaning on his pool cue, the redhead greets me with a grin. The patch on his kutte tells me he's called Chipmunk.

"Not missing any more, considering he's here," his companion says—Chunk. "I think that means he's the projidal."

Prodigal. But although I'd give any Rider shit for that, and these patchholders seem in good humor, it might be taken as disrespect instead of a friendly ribbing. And nothing closes down any biker faster than disrespect.

"It's Zachary," I tell them. "Any of my brothers around?"

"Ayuh." Chipmunk jerks his thumb toward the bathrooms. "Six-Point's in the back, wetting his dick in some blonde. I'd go in and let him know, but he'll be out soon enough. It never takes him long."

So he gets off fast. Either selfish or not good at holding back. Knowing my brother, maybe both. "He got a regular table?"

Chipmunk points to a booth in the corner.

"I'll be there."

Chunk nods. "We'll let him know."

At the table, I have Anna slide into the seat first—a wall on one side of her, me on the other. From this position, I've got eyes on the main door and the bathrooms. It'll do.

"Six-Point?" she asks softly.

"Isiah. The youngest, aside from me." And David.

"So he's the fourth brother? What's he like?"

He's the best one to run into tonight. "Easygoing. Maybe because he's younger and knows he's never going to sit at the top. So he just fucks around and gets along with everyone. And he's impulsive, but not hot-headed."

"Who are the hot heads?"

Keeping eyes on the crowd, I track two other members of the Few as they come in, see them look this way, then look again. Word's going to spread quick. "Adam, the firstborn. And Muncher—he's third. Strawman's got a temper but it isn't hot. He's more controlled. Cold."

"Like your temper is."

Why would she think that? "I don't have a temper."

Her eyebrows shoot high. "You remember last summer when Reichmann got to Jenny? I saw your face. You would have killed him if you'd been the one to find him there."

I would have. Instead the prez almost killed him. But I shake my head. "That's not temper. I wasn't angry."

"What were you?"

"Ready to get shit done."

"So what my brother said was right. You're a cold bastard in those high-stress situations."

"Maybe." Except when I'm kissing her.

Her eyes suddenly narrow, as if she's caught me in a lie. "I pissed you off in Jenny's brewery—telling you not to come over. You were angry then."

"That wasn't temper." Though it probably sounded like it. Just like it does now, my voice hard and sharp, remembering. "That was a knife in my fucking chest."

She goes utterly still, staring at me with wide, shimmering eyes. And, Jesus. This is why I can't be alone with her. Shit that I shouldn't be saying just comes flying out of my mouth.

"Was it?" Her whisper is so strained I can barely hear it over the music. "But I'm just Stone's sister. You said."

And I could say it again now. But I'm not going to lie

to her anymore. "You were kicking me out of your life. So I just said what you wanted to hear."

"That's not what I wanted to hear." Her lips tremble as she draws a shuddering breath. "But I knew you were lying to me about Stone. That he wasn't really okay, no matter what you said. And I was so pissed."

Not what she wanted to hear. There's something pulling loose inside me, tumbling around. I can't grasp all of it so I grab for what I can. "How did you know he wasn't okay?"

Her eyes squeeze shut and she shakes her head.

Fuck, I can't let that go. "Did you hear it from one of the brothers? Was someone running his mouth? I need to know, Anna."

"No. I just know Stone. And I knew he wouldn't ask you to text me and pretend to be him. Because…of reasons."

And she obviously doesn't intend to share those reasons. But the rest? She's probably right. She knows Stone well enough to guess something was wrong. "All right."

Her gaze raises to mine again, searching my eyes. "So I pushed you away. But I didn't think it would really matter to you."

"It mattered," I tell her gruffly. It mattered more than anything.

"So…what are we?" Her expression is shuttered, but her voice holds a note of wary hope. "Maybe I'm not just a friend's sister? Maybe you and I are friends, too?"

Jesus. It kills me how tentative she is. Like she thinks

maybe I'll tell her to go get fucked, when the only thing I want to do is pull her close and never let her go. "You really have to ask?"

"Yes," she says simply. "Because I apparently know even less about you than I thought I did."

And doesn't know me well enough to love me.

Yet.

This seems like a damn good step on that path to knowing me. To her feeling anywhere close to the way I feel about her. "We're friends."

Her smile instantly lights up her face, her eyes. "Good."

I bite back a groan. God, her face. All that joy, just because we're *friends*. I just hope she's as happy when I tell her I want more.

But I can't ask for more now. Instead I have to ask for less. The bathroom door opens and a blonde comes out, hair mussed, straightening her dress. "We're not friends here, remember."

She nods, her gaze sliding past me, eyes widening. "That's him?"

Yeah, that's him. I stand up. Six-Point spots me before Chipmunk and Chunk get to him. He breaks into a grin and gives a whoop that has everyone in the bar looking over, tracking the speed at which he bounds over to the table.

"Zachary!" With another whoop, he grabs my extended hand and pulls me into a strong hug, thumping my shoulders. "Brother. Jesus, it's good to see you."

"You, too." It's not a lie. My chest is both heavy and light as I return the embrace, hands fisted against his back. Adam, Strawman—I could have died happy never seeing them again. But Six-Point is only three years older than me, and he was always closer to me, closer to David. He never agreed with my reasons for leaving but came closest to understanding them. And I've missed him.

I still wouldn't trust him alone with Anna for two seconds.

He pulls back, gripping me by the shoulders at arms-length as he looks me up and down. "So that's why it's so fucking cold in here. You're standing in front of me, so hell must have froze over."

I laugh, shaking my head. "I did say something like that."

"Yeah, you did. Meant it, too. Which is why this is such a fucking surprise." He looks past me, gaze landing on Anna before sliding over the table. "No drinks?" Turning, he shouts, "*Janice!* My brother's been sitting here without a beer? You bring three over here or I'll be tanning your wrinkly ass!"

A gray-haired waitress at the bar turns and gives him a sour look.

"Yeah, we'll get those in about an hour." Grinning, he slides into the booth across from Anna. His speculative gaze touches her briefly before he looks to me again. "Strawman said he saw you."

"He did."

"Also said you told him to fuck off."

"I did."

Six-Point chuckles and his eyes finally rest on Anna. "And you told him that one isn't yours."

"She's not." Even though I'd give anything to have her. "A friend ran into trouble. This is his sister. I'm keeping an eye out for her."

"Sure you are." He snorts out his disbelief and reaches across the table, palm extended. "Six-Point."

"Anna," she says, shaking his hand.

"I know who you are, Anna Wall—you're the prettiest damn thing here." With a wink, he leans back again, turns on the charm. "So you're running around with this asshole?"

She shrugs. "I'm stuck with him, I guess."

"Lucky him." His gaze lingers on her swollen lips, her bruised cheek, before looking to me. "My brother didn't do that to you?"

Her brows shoot together. "No. Of course not."

"Of course." A smirk twists his lips, as if he finds it damn funny that Anna knows I'd never hurt her, but his smile softens when he looks to her again. "I've seen worse. Hell, I've *been* worse. You know how I got the name Six-Point?"

Anna glances at me when I groan, tilting my head back to stare up at the ceiling. Five minutes into seeing him again, and this story comes up. I might as well have never left.

"Do you just wait for someone new to come along to tell this shit again?" I ask him.

With a laugh, Six-Point admits without any shame, "I do. Because it's the only damn story I've got." He looks to Anna. "Can you guess?"

"Um, six points? Something…about a game?"

"Heh, no." He settles in, forearms braced on the table. "So one day me and my brothers are riding up the coast highway. Beautiful day, right? Got the ocean on one side of me, and I'm making love to that road, riding all them sweet curves. The sun's shining down on me, and I'm just enjoying the scenery, minding my own damn business when a six-point buck jumps out in front of me and *BAM!*"—he pounds his fist into his palm—"I wind up in traction for three months."

"Oh my god," Anna breathes. Because she's been around bikers long enough to know that even though he's telling it like a joke, it was no joke then.

"Yeah, but here's the best part." He sits back as the waitress—Janice—sets a Budweiser in front of him, then two more for Anna and me. "Because I'm lying there in the hospital—"

Janice snorts. "This story again?"

"Get out of here, you ugly hag. Before my beer goes sour." He gives her flat ass a swat as she goes. "So I'm lying there, suspended facedown over my bed, with all these goddamn braces on, and this fucker"—he indicates me with a sharp jab of his finger—"comes in with David, and they're carrying this big ass picnic basket between them. And the smell coming from this basket, Jesus. It's like meaty heaven. That's where those fucking terrorists get it wrong with those virgins in heaven, yeah? A man almost dies, he doesn't want cherries. He wants meat. So, David, he starts laying out these paper plates and piling heaps of steak on them. And while he's doing that, Zach here comes over to my bedside with his plate, and he's just slicing through that meat, saying, 'Isiah, it's so fucking juicy. It's sooooo good.' Then he starts eating it in front of me, moaning like he's Muncher on a pussy. Then David joins in. And you know what it is they're eating?"

If Anna's already guessed, she can't say because she's giggling so hard.

"The fucking deer! Our mama fried up all that venison to give to the hospital staff, but these two fuckers bring it in and practically wrap it around their dicks. Zach, he's groaning like it's the best meat he ever had, saying my body slamming into the buck tenderized it real nice for them. And me, I've got my fucking jaw wired shut and I've been sipping pudding through a straw for a week! Fucking deer almost killed me and I don't even get a goddamn bite of it."

Anna's laughing and shaking her head. Six-Point takes a swig of his beer, grinning—but I see the moment where it hits him: that was one of the last times he saw David. He was still hobbling around on crutches when David went after my father with an ax.

His smile fades. "Anyway. So I've seen worse. But I can't say I like seeing it on a girl. Especially a pretty one." Eyes like chips of ice, he looks to me. "You take care of it?"

"Trying to. They were threatening her brother."

"So you're looking for help?"

"Information, mostly."

"Mama's going to ask a price."

"I know. I'm prepared to pay it."

He nods, holding my gaze. "You hear Adam's out?"

"I did."

His mouth flattens. "Seventeen years inside, he's a bigger prick than ever. Muncher and I hightailed it out of there tonight. We're making ourselves scarce while he fucks all that time out of his system."

Knowing Adam, he isn't just fucking. His dick's like a rage barometer. The angrier he is, the hornier he is. "Mama'll keep him in line."

"Yeah, you'd think. Except Strawman is poking at him every chance he gets. He got real comfortable acting as prez and now he has to step aside. So she's come down on him, instead of Adam."

Fuck. Bad enough coming to the family for help. Now we're walking into this. "She must be happy he's back."

"Oh yeah." Six-Point laughs like that's the biggest understatement he's ever heard. "But she'll be happier her baby's back. Adam going to prison, she felt nothing but pride. What he did was for the good of the chosen. You bailing…that's something else."

The ice in his eyes tells me exactly what it was. Betrayal. I turned my back on them at the worst damn point.

I'm not sorry. I'll never be sorry.

But I can agree with him. Me going *was* something else. It was freedom.

What my mama's going to offer is not.

He draws a deep breath, lets it out slow. "She'll be real glad, though. She'll help you. But if you're smart, you'll give it a few days before showing your face. Let Adam work all that shit out of his system."

I would if I had a choice. "We don't have a few days."

"You wouldn't get them, anyway," he says wryly. "Word's probably already reached the farm. Where you staying, if Mama's got a mind to pay you a visit?"

"I'll come out to the farm and see her tomorrow."

The amused twist of his lips says he noticed how I didn't offer the name of our hotel. "All right." He pounds the table with his fist, stands. "I'm glad you're back again. Because it just occurred to me that my favorite story is about my two brothers who are gone. And you've been gone a damn long time."

I was right to go. So that shouldn't twist in my chest. But it does. "I'm here now."

Like it or not.

"Yeah," he says and nods. "See you tomorrow, then. Me, I'm going to get more pussy before my dick's too drunk to stuff one full."

Anna watches him go, then turns wide eyes on

me. "Holy shit. You really do look alike. I thought you just meant, 'We have a strong resemblance.' But it's way beyond that."

"Yes."

Her eyes narrow. "Genetically, you know, that's kind of crazy, because half your genes come from your mom. Does she look like you, too?"

"Not a bit." I take a drink, letting my gaze run over her like it's just for comparison. "She's about your height. Blonde. Although she's got blue eyes, too."

"Like yours? That freakish pale color?"

"Freakish?"

She doubles down. "Yes. Absolutely freakish."

I guess she's spent a lot of time looking at them if she's that sure. "My mother's are regular blue. Like anyone's."

She nods, her gaze never leaving my face as she studies me. "Six-Point's eyes were a little darker than yours. His jaw a little wider, too." Her gaze drops. "His mouth not as…"

She trails off and takes a long drink, like whatever she was thinking made her need to cool down.

Now I'm real interested. "Not as what?"

She bites her bottom lip before saying, "Don't take this the wrong way."

"With an introduction like that, sweetheart, there's no other way to take it."

Her swift grin quickly fades when her gaze settles on my mouth again. "Okay, well, your lips are more…pouty."

"I look pouty?"

"*You* don't. But your lips are…" She touches her own lips like she's imagining the feel of mine. "Pillowy."

"Pillowy?" I echo, with no intention of easing up on her. She's struggling to find words, her gaze glued to my mouth.

My cock's never been so fucking hard.

"Yeah. Soft and full. But they're not, are they? Not soft." Her eyes glaze a little, as if memory. "Just…sexier than his."

"Sexier? I'll take that."

Her low, breathy laugh almost has me coming in my jeans. "Thank God. Because I was digging a hole."

"You dig like that, you can dig whenever you like." But now I'm the one taking a long cold drink. The icy beer doesn't do a damn thing to quench my real thirst or to cool the need burning in me, but it keeps my mouth busy enough that I don't say the rest of what I want to — telling her exactly what I can do to her with these pillowy lips.

And what she can do to me with hers.

A slight flush tinges her cheeks when she finally tears her gaze from my mouth. I'm sorry she does, but it's probably for the best. She keeps staring at my lips like that and God knows what I'll do.

"So, um — " She starts writing on the table, using the water from the ring of condensation forming under her bottle. *Anna was here.* "So there's Six-Point, and Muncher, and Strawman, and Adam. Right?"

"Right."

"Adam doesn't have a road name? Or *is* that his road name?"

"It's Hunter. But everyone calls him Adam. Because he's the firstborn."

Her lips purse as she nods. "And Strawman? Is it because he sets people up and knocks them down?"

That takes me a second. I hear 'straw man' and I think of a scarecrow. But the way she grew up talking with her mom, pulling apart the way people argue with each other and hide from each other, I realize Anna would think of something else. "You mean like a straw man argument?"

"Yeah."

I shake my head, laughing. "No. Nothing that clever. Though he'd like that explanation better than the real reason behind his name."

"Which is?"

"My father got onto him for something. I don't remember what—I was maybe eight or nine years old then. But he did something stupid and my father said his head was stuffed with straw. Then he started calling him Strawman instead of Jacob. So it stuck."

She winces. "Ouch."

"Yup. Especially because—you remember we were talking about those traits that were passed on? Strawman actually got some of the brains."

"You did, too."

For all the good it's done. "Sometimes I don't think

so."

"Oh yeah?" She leans forward onto her forearms, tilts her head and meets my eyes with a challenging stare. "What about all those books?"

I snort out a laugh. "I started reading so I could imagine being anywhere but here. But I'm back here again. So what's that say for brains?"

"That…just said plenty." Her gaze searches my face before she says, "You signed up with the Marines seventeen years ago, right? That's how long Six-Point said Adam was in prison. Was that the reason you left?"

"Part of it." Not him going to prison—he deserved a hell of a lot worse than a cell—but what happened before it.

"What did he do?" she asks, and I can tell she doesn't expect me to answer. Maybe throw some 'club business' at her.

But the Notorious Few aren't my brothers yet and she should know this.

"He murdered a sixteen-year-old girl," I tell her. "He was supposed to be in for life."

Her eyes are wide. "So he got parole?"

I shake my head. "His conviction was overturned."

"Overturned?" She's silent for a long second, just staring at me, and I can see her mind working it over. "But did he do it?"

Throat thick, I just nod. He did it. Killed a girl, and destroyed David. And if the family had any idea how I felt about Anna, he'd do the same to her.

Anna's biting her lip again, watching me. "I won't ask for details, but you and Stone, for the Riders—"

I know exactly where she's going. Because I've killed, too. "There's not a single one I'm sorry for," I tell her. "Each one, I think the world's better off without. What happened to this girl was different."

"The law probably wouldn't think so."

"It wouldn't. But I feel it's so. Now are you going to give me shit about moral relativism?"

"No." Steadily, she holds my gaze. "Because I get it—probably better than you think. Because of Jenny. I mean, Saxon saved her from being raped and yet he had to go to jail for it. And last year when she was being hassled by the Eighty-Eight, the law couldn't have helped her until it was too late. But the Riders did."

"Yes." Helped her by putting down the skinheads running that chapter. Anna shouldn't know that. I shouldn't be confirming it.

But I'm not going to tell her she doesn't know what she's talking about.

"So when I hear some of the Eighty-Eight are dead, I can't pretend that I'm not glad. Of course I wish it didn't come to that. But given a choice between that or Jenny hurt? I'd chose what the Riders did to them every time."

"Me, too," I say easily.

She huffs a little laugh. "Because you *have* chosen it. And my brother has, too. I probably would, too. If my mom or dad or Stone—or my friends—were in danger, I can't say I wouldn't cross that line. I understand protecting your own. And even if it's not right, there's a line between that and murder in my own morality."

"Yes." But I need her to know this, too. "But to my family? Adam killing this girl *was* protecting their own."

"How?"

"She was pregnant. She was Asian. So she'd have fucked up the bloodline."

Horror drops her jaw open. "Oh my god. Did you know her? Was she…your girlfriend? Is that why you left?"

I shake my head. "My brother David's girl. Ivy Tan. He was smart enough never to bring her around the farm, but he was crazy about her. So proud of her. And he wouldn't keep it quiet. He said our family had to be better or he'd leave to be with her." I have to stop for a second. Anna watches me silently. "I liked her. She wasn't a threat, in my mind. But my mind works differently than theirs."

"It's a good difference."

"Glad you think so."

Her faint smile has no real amusement in it. "Six-Point said you were both gone. David took off, too?"

"He's dead."

"Oh." Her slender fingers grip my wrist, squeeze lightly in sympathy before letting go—because she's just her brother's sister. I never hated that line between us as much as I do now. "Sorry."

I take another drink, try to close all the emotion down.

This is why I need to be cold. "It is what it is."

She doesn't look convinced but nods anyway. After a long second, she asks quietly, "My brother…what will the Cage do to him? He has to kill someone in the ring—but not someone who's an enemy in a war or threatening the club. Someone who's basically innocent. What will it do to him? What would it do to you?"

She already knows. Maybe she's looking for another answer from me, but I can't give it.

My throat's tight as fuck. Not cold yet. "It's going to hurt him. It's going to fuck him up bad."

Her eyes go bright, shimmering with unshed tears. "So when I get this call—it'll be after he wins. But it won't really be a victory."

"No, it won't."

There's no winning until we get him home.

TWENTY

GUNNER

I don't sleep. I'm pretty damn sure Anna doesn't, either. I hear her tossing in the other bed all night. And me, I lay motionless with my cock so hot and hard against my stomach I'm surprised the shape of my dick isn't branded into my skin by morning.

When she gets up early, puts on her running shoes and a pair of little shorts, I go with her.

And the exercise doesn't help a damn bit. The past ten years, this is how I got through—always working or working out. Laboring on the maintenance crew. Pounding fists at the gym. Riding with the club. Reading at home. I filled every minute, trying to keep my body and my brain too busy to think of her.

It didn't work, but it helped. I went to bed every night so damn tired, I didn't have to spend many sleepless nights like this. That was pain.

This is fucking torture.

A long sleeveless T-shirt covers the tent in my loose shorts. Running with a hard cock? Not the best start to my morning. So that's a lesson learned. Tomorrow, I'll jack off before we head out for a run.

Shit. The way this is going, I'll be spending the next few days with my hand glued to my dick.

She sets a hard pace for five miles, using her phone to navigate through the city until I realize what she's doing and start pointing out the best route. A block from the hotel, she slows to a walk and finally takes out her earbuds.

"So what's the plan today?"

About a mile in, my cock finally got the message and heeled, so I drag up the hem of my shirt to wipe the sweat from my face. Her gaze drops to my ridged abdomen before shuttling away, but it's enough to get my dick rising again.

I need to get my head in the game. "I'm going to ride out to the farm, get the help we need."

"You really think they'll give it?"

"Yeah, they will." I just don't want her to know what

I'll be trading. "I'll be taking my bike. The truck's yours to use. There's cash in the safe—spend it on anything you need. I don't know if these fuckers from the Cage can trace your cards but there's no reason to risk it. You'll be fine in the hotel or heading out of the city. You've got good hiking that way, ocean that way."

"Maybe I will." She pauses in the hotel lot, bending over and stretching her legs, her body in a long, lean line. Christ help me. "I should have brought my paints."

"Use the cash and get some. We might be here the better part of a week." Maybe even a month, but I don't want to start thinking that yet.

Jesus. The way she's folded over with her hands on her ankles, I'm not thinking at all. Just about how flexible she is—and how I could get her heels up by her ears and get into her so fucking deep.

She straightens up, arms raised high in another long stretch that lifts her shirt above the waist of her shorts, exposing her tight stomach and smooth golden skin. I'm biting back a groan when she looks over her shoulder at me. "I get the shower first."

"All right." And I'll just be pressed up against the bathroom door, fucking my fist.

It'll only take about two strokes to come. Especially if I picture the way she smiles like she is now, playfully catching the tip of her tongue between her teeth before saying, "I'd be your slave forever if you have coffee waiting when I get out."

"Shit. I'm not passing that up."

She laughs and heads in, passing the elevator. We take the stairs up, Anna jogging a few steps ahead, and me in heaven with her delicious little ass bouncing in front of my face.

She reaches the room ahead of me, then waits while I pull the keycard from the zip pocket of my shorts. I open the door and ice races through me, instantly sharpening into rage with a cold, killing edge.

Strawman's sitting on Anna's bed.

I hear her soft indrawn breath as she bumps into the hand I put up behind me, stopping her from coming in.

"Get out."

Strawman's eyes are as cold as mine, his grin like a shark's when he spreads his hands. "My brother. I hope you don't mind. I told the girl at the desk that I'd forgotten my room key and she remembered my face, so she let me have another."

"Get. Out."

He rises but isn't going fast. Anna's hand grips mine and I tug her inside the room, leaving the door propped open and keeping her close beside me.

His gaze locks right onto her. "I just thought I'd have a look around. I see you slept in separate beds."

"Because what's between her and me is just like I told you it was."

Disbelief fills his short laugh. "I don't know what the fuck is wrong with you, brother. Jesus." His eyes go hot as he looks her up and down, lingering on her long legs. "Hello, girlie."

Her chin lifts. "Anna."

"Anna," he echoes with a slow, mocking smile that's going to look real nice smashed against my fist. Until he says the words that remind me why I can't pound his face in—yet. "I hear you've got a brother in some trouble."

Her fingers tighten on mine. "Yes."

"And my brother's helping you out. So tell me why you're not on your knees sucking his dick in gratitude?"

Fuck this. I let go of Anna and head for him, my eyes locked on his, watching for the moment I know is coming.

And there it is. The flicker in his eyes. The one where he realizes that I'm not his little brother anymore. The one where he realizes that my oncoming path isn't a safe place for any man to stand. The one where he realizes that I could come at him without any weapons but my bare hands, and still beat his ass to the ground.

That flicker is doubt and fear and it pisses him off. But pissed doesn't change what's true. He knows it. And I know it.

So I get up in his face and tell him softly, "Are you saying anything worth hearing or are you leaving?"

He responds with a slow grin. "I'm just delivering a message from Mama. Because when you told Six-Point you were coming, it sounded like you intended to visit by yourself. But she wants you both."

I don't let him see how everything in me rejects the

thought of Anna ever going out to the farm. But if Anna's just a girl under my protection, this shouldn't be a struggle.

"All right," I agree easily. "If Mama wants."

"She does." His eyes harden as he steps closer, speaks softly. "Now, you want us to think this girl's nothing? Then you better think about what you're going to do when I ask her to get on her knees for me, considering how we'll be helping her."

"She's not asking for help. I am." If I don't kill all of them first for pulling shit like this. "And she's not *nothing*. I owe her brother my life. I owe it to him to protect her. So you consider what that obligation to her brother means to me before you even think of speaking to her again."

He smirks. "Yeah. Those separate beds aren't nothing." Slapping my shoulder, he heads past me, turning and walking backwards as he continues, "But I'll keep your secret for now. Because I don't want to lose another brother over some impure pussy."

Red swims in front of my vision. I start toward him, and if he doesn't move fast, that red's going to be his blood. "Get the fuck out!"

He holds up his hands, shoots a grin at Anna as he backs past her. "I'm going. And best you pack up your things, bring them out to the farm. Mama will want you staying there."

"No fucking chance."

I slam the door on his grinning face and stand with my palms braced against the doorframe, shaking with rage.

Anna's waiting just inside the mirrored vestibule leading to the bathroom, her arms wrapped around herself, looking worried and small.

Swallowing hard, I try to keep the anger out of my voice when I ask, "You all right?"

"Yes." She bites her lip. "You?"

Fuck no. I bark out a hard laugh and shake my head.

"Gunner," she says softly and I look to her again. Nervously fiddling with her fingers, she moves out into the entryway and leans back against the wall as if bracing herself against it. "I know how these things work in some MCs. If being on my knees is what it takes to get Stone back—"

Anger boils up again. "Don't you go there." Without a thought I'm on her, my fists slamming into the wall on either side of her shoulders, my face right up in hers. Through gritted teeth I repeat, "Don't you even fucking go there."

And my girl doesn't know when to quit. She opens her mouth. "But—"

"Don't." When her teeth snap shut, I rasp harshly, "You think Stone wants to be saved that way? What's the difference between that and the Iron Blood fucker raping you?"

Even in the face of my rage, she doesn't back down. There's not a single flicker. "Well, I'd choose one."

"Bullshit! It's not a choice when someone holds your brother's life over your head and makes you suck his dick. It's what you're forced to do, not what you want. And that's called rape, sweetheart." I lean in closer, my eyes on level with hers, making sure she can't mistake this vow. "And I'll never let it happen in a million fucking years. You got that?"

Eyes huge, she nods.

Not good enough. "I want to hear you *say* it."

"Okay. I got it. No sucking dick." On shaky breath, she licks her lips. "But just so you know, if it comes to that, with you, I'd be all right with it. Like, if you're forced to make a point about how little I mean to you when we go there. I could do it with you, not them. Because with you it *would* be something I want."

All the blood drains out of my head. "What?"

"Well, I mean…" With a tiny frown forming between her brows, her golden gaze searches mine. "Come on. Do you really think I threw myself at you last summer just because I was drunk? I get turned on just looking at you. And, Jesus—when you touch me? It's like I'm burning alive. So if you'd ever shown any real interest, I'd have gone to my knees in a hot second—"

That's enough. Because *Real interest?* That's my mouth claiming hers and inhaling her gasp of surprise. That's me lifting Anna up against the wall and wedging my hips between her thighs. That's me kissing her like a man starving, and groaning when her lips part and her sweet hot taste floods my senses.

And when my mouth's on hers, there's nothing else in the world so right. I knew it ten years ago on the side of a road and I knew it in her shower the other night.

The only difference then was I stopped after one kiss.

Hungrily I feast from her lips, returning to delve deep into her mouth again and again, tasting, devouring. She's frantic against me, her hands fisting in my hair as if she's afraid I might lift my head and walk away, and the sweet pain from her fingers joins the brutal ache of my arousal as I grind my cock between her sleek thighs. But I'd even love torture from her, because her mouth is slick and greedy, as if this kiss is everything she's wanted, needed.

It's all I need. Just tasting her, hot and wet and deep. As if I could make up for ten years of not kissing her, as if I could make this last for ten more years. And I'm still kissing her as my orgasm erupts without warning, coming endlessly hard into my shorts when she boldly sucks on the tip of my tongue, moaning her pleasure as if she needs to suck on *something*, anything.

Chest heaving, I lift my head to get a look at her but her fingers tighten and she drags me back down to drown in the perfection of her mouth.

Wrapping her legs around me, she rocks her hips harder, faster. Soft needy whimpers against my lips become ragged desperate cries. Tension tightens her slim body, her back tight against the wall.

Abruptly she breaks the kiss, her neck arching, her eyes glazed and skin flushed.

Oh fuck, yes.

My cum painting the inside of my shorts, I grind up

between her thighs, my lips against hers. "You about to come?"

The erotic sound she makes sends blood rushing to my dick again. Like she meant to say yes but only a needy whimper emerged. Then she's makes another of those desperate cries when I grip her ass and slow the rock of her hips.

"Shh, sweetheart." I steal another taste from between her lips, and her moan and the way she seeks out my tongue drives me crazy. "I'll take care of you. I'm not going to leave you aching. Is your pussy nice and wet?"

Her answer is to pull my head down for another hard kiss, trying to grind against me—then going utterly still as my hand slides forward over her hip. Breasts pushing into my chest with each ragged breath, she stares up at me, her lips parted, her breath hot.

And she's drenched. I groan when my fingers slip beneath the edge of her shorts, pushing aside her panties, and find her so slick and hot.

Covering her mouth with mine, I swallow her pleasured cry and push my longest finger deep inside her scalding heat. Her body jerks, her back bowing. Jesus, she's so wet and tight—and sensitive, her lean muscles tensing and trembling with the lightest brush of my thumb over her clitoris.

But it's not enough. I kiss her, stroking her slippery clit until her movements become chaotic, erratic, and her low moans rise sharply with each thrust of my hand.

"You want to come like this, on my fingers?" I ask roughly against her lips. "Or do you want more?"

Her fingernails dig into my shoulders. Desire deepens the gold in her eyes, reddens her skin. Her response is a thick moan. "More."

"I'm going to give you more, sweetheart. What do you need?" I know what *I* need — to taste all of her. "You want me to suck on your hot little clit?"

Her inner muscles clench around my finger. Her breath stutters.

"Fuck yeah," I groan against her mouth. "Your pussy says yes. But I want to hear you say it. Tell me you want my tongue all over your sweet cunt. Tell me you want me licking up all this pussy juice. Ask for my mouth."

"Your really *dirty* mouth?" she responds and it's a half laugh, half desperate sob.

"You like it." The way her pussy gripped me so tight, I'd say she loved every filthy word. Slipping another finger inside her, I screw my fingers deeper into her drenched sheath and she cries out, bucking against my hand. "Now tell me what you want."

"Your mouth!" It's almost a sob of frustration and she yanks at my hair. "I want your mouth."

"And my pouty lips, yeah?"

Her body shakes on another laugh, then stiffens again, arching against me. She's right at the precipice, trembling on the edge of release, but I'm not giving her enough.

Not yet.

I ease her feet to the ground and she sags against the wall. She gives a plaintive moan as I slide my dripping fingers from inside her, then abruptly goes still when I grip her shorts and panties and drag them down to her knees.

Sweet Jesus. I should have gone slower, stripping away her shirt first, taking off her running shoes, because the sight of her bare pussy in front of me sweeps away every other thought. Her mound is waxed smooth, her clit and pussy lips flushed a deep pink and peeking from her slit.

"You're so fucking beautiful." I lean in, breathe deep. And Christ, the sweet smell of her is intoxicating. "You keep it bare for yourself or for someone else?"

"For myself." She's breathless, trembling.

"You're so goddamn pretty. I could just look at you and die happy."

"Don't die yet." Impatiently she tugs at my hair. "You said more."

I did.

My hands look huge when I grip her hips, tilting her forward. With her legs trapped by the shorts and panties around her knees, her thighs are barely parted. Her arousal glistens over smooth skin. As I dip my head, her body trembles.

I do, too.

Open mouthed, I taste as much of her as I can all at once, groaning when her tangy flavor hits my tongue. She tenses, fingers digging into my scalp, a tortured little noise breaking from her lips.

"Shh, baby," I whisper huskily, then slide the flat of my tongue over her clit in a long, rough lick. She moans and shakes, pushing her pussy into my face. I can't get much deeper into her slit, not with her shorts hobbling her legs, but I can get at her clit, flicking my tongue, teasing, teasing, before covering her with my mouth.

God, her sweet taste. I could do this forever.

With a hungry moan, I suck on her clit and she gives a gargling cry, her knees giving out. I could hold her up but I want her down. My mouth locked onto her pussy, I ease her to the floor, her back sliding slowly down the wall.

Breathing heavy, I draw back. She looks drugged by her arousal, eyelids weighted, her eyes glassy. Her breath comes in short pants, her breasts rising and falling with each one, her nipples like hard beads beneath the thin cotton of her shirt. I drag her running shorts and panties down over her feet, pulling off her shoes as I go.

"Spread those gorgeous legs for me, sweetheart." My voice is gruff with ravenous need. "Give me room to get in there deep."

Despite the command, I don't wait for her, gripping her knees and pushing them wide. Her pussy lips part and I get a view of heaven, wet and lush and pink.

I tear my gaze away from her beautiful cunt and find her staring at me, her full bottom lip trapped between her teeth. "Anna, baby," I groan, sweeping my fingertips higher up the insides of her thighs, loving her sweet shiver. "Tell me not to stop. Tell me you need more."

Her body shakes on a laugh. "Don't stop. Because I'll kill you if you stop."

"I'll die if I do. God, sweetheart. I'm going to eat you all up. Your pouty clit hasn't gotten enough of my pouty mouth."

"Oh my god." She laughs breathlessly. "I think we settled on pillowy."

"I remember sexy."

Her gaze dips to my mouth, the amusement fading, replaced by burning heat. "Yes," she says. "Very sexy."

"*This* is what's sexy." I push her legs a little farther apart. "Jesus. I'm a second away from coming again, just looking at your sweet pussy. Thinking of how fucking good you taste."

Her fingers curl against the floor. "Gunner, please—"

"More?" I press a kiss to her knee, then higher. "You still needing me, sweetheart?"

"Yes," she breathes. "So much."

"I'm going to take care of you." My eyes locked on hers, I kiss higher, higher, scooting down and stretching out between her legs, bracing my upper body on my elbows. With my lips hovering above her glistening clit, I promise, "I going to make you feel so damn good," before claiming her pussy with a long, slow lick.

And then I lose it. Over the years, I've imagined this moment thousands of times. Imagined how I'd tease until she's begging and screaming my name. How I'd be slow and controlled. But the moment I get my mouth on her fully, there's no control. Instead I'm trying to taste her all at once, fucking my tongue up inside her, pumping two fingers deep and feeling the squeeze of her hot sheath, sucking on her juicy clit and licking, licking. Her fingers fist in my hair and her body rises up in a taut, strung bow, her hips thrashing against the grip of my hands.

She doesn't scream my name. Instead she comes on a guttural choking breath, her pussy convulsing around my fingers, her pussy juices coating my chin. Lips wrapped around her spasming clit, I moan and suck harder, riding through each jerk of her hips, until she gasps "No more" and pushes me away.

I don't go far. Softly kissing her inner thigh, I look up.

Her arousal still burns. Eyes still glazed and heavy, her bottom lip pinched between her teeth, she watches me—half sitting up, her shirt rucked up beneath her breasts, her shoulders crammed into the corner of the wall and the dresser. Jesus. I don't even know how she got there. We're a full six feet away from where we started.

Her hand strokes lazily down the length of her taut belly. "You want to join me in the shower?"

Where I could finally slide my cock deep inside her. Where she could get on her knees and wrap her beautiful mouth around my dick—

And then I have to make my family believe I'm not crazy about her.

My voice is rough. "I shouldn't."

"I think you should."

"This wasn't a good idea." I draw back and scrub a shaking hand through my hair. "Fucking hell. I'm sorry."

"Sorry?" She pulls her knees up against her chest, suddenly looking small in that corner.

I reach down, offering my hand. After a brief hesitation she takes it. I pull her up to her feet. "I shouldn't have — This is the worst fucking thing to do right now. I shouldn't have lost my head."

"Oh." It's a small sound. "So it's another mistake."

"No." Jesus, it could never be. And I've hurt her, goddammit. Hurt her after she just gave me the sweetest possible gift. "Did I say worst thing? Because it was the best fucking thing ever. Just, with all this shit going on, I shouldn't have —"

"It's fine. Don't beat yourself up for losing your head." Her voice high and tight, Anna turns away to gather her things, then opens the dresser drawer and starts picking out more clothes. "What's a guy to do? I threw myself at you again, offered to suck your cock. I'm kind of shocked you didn't immediately push me away, but maybe fourth time is the charm."

"Fourth time?"

"You know. The fourth time I've given you a pretty blatant invitation. But, hey. At least I got an orgasm out of it before you shut us down. So it's okay. We're still friends."

She doesn't sound okay. She sounds hollow. Chest aching, I tell her, "Anna, look at me."

Turning toward me, she offers a bright smile and a

shrug. "Anyway, no complaints here. In fact, I'd say I got the better end of it, considering I came all over your face. So now I'm taking a shower. You still getting that coffee?"

So she'll be my slave for life. But it's already the other way around. "Yeah."

"Great." With that chirpy reply, she sweeps past me into the bathroom. The door snaps shut.

Groaning, I sag back against the wall, drag my hands through my hair. I won't follow her in. No matter how much I want to. I won't slam through that door and demand more. I won't demand that she stop shrugging and start *caring*.

Jesus, but I fucked that up good. I shouldn't have kissed her. I shouldn't have lost my head. I'm on a mission to find Stone—and to protect Anna. This was supposed to come later. After we found her brother. After she knew me better and she could look to a future with me.

But I *did* kiss her and I did lose my head.

And completely fucked it up.

TWENTY ONE

ANNA

Gunner's right. I know he's right. The second he kissed me, it was the best fucking thing. Crazy, explosive need.

But it's just the wrong damn time. Stone needs to come first. If Gunner looks at me like he did out there — if he looks at me like that in front of his family — maybe this won't go as it should.

That's why, even as I'm aching so deep, his pushing me away doesn't hurt like it has before. Because then, I didn't understand his reasons. Keep it simple, sure—I'm only Stone's sister, sure. But I *knew* we were explosive together and it always hurt that I wasn't enough to make him cross whatever line he'd drawn between us.

But now I know why that line is there. Stone's life is on that line. *My* life is on that line. And everything about this sucks so bad. But it doesn't mean Gunner's not interested. It doesn't mean he doesn't want me. It doesn't mean I'm nothing more than Stone's sister. It doesn't mean I'm not good enough, or that I'm lacking something.

It just means Gunner has a job he needs to do. A job that *I* need him to do.

I glance at my phone as soon as I get out of the shower. I left it plugged in last night and the battery's almost full. But I need to buy one of those emergency chargers that you can use even if you're not around an electrical outlet. It would be so stupid if I missed Stone's call because I let the battery die.

And I need to let my mom and dad know I'm okay. Jenny, too. I don't know what Saxon has told her about me leaving, but I'm sure he didn't want to lay too heavy a burden on her the day after her dad's funeral.

But I think I can make her smile, even this far away. With my finger, I write *Anna was here* on the fogged mirror. Turning around, I aim a cheesy grin at my camera, making sure the bruised side of my face is out of the shot. Then another pose, with exaggerated duck lips to hide the swelling.

I send the photo of me smiling to my parents, with a message that *Everything's good!* Then the duck lips to Jenny, adding *Send me $50 and I'll take off the towel.*

And I've got no excuse to linger in here any longer. The hair dryer and a second sink are in the vestibule outside the bathroom, separate from the tub and toilet — and it'll save time if I finish getting ready while Gunner showers. Gathering my courage, I open the bathroom door…and Gunner's not in the hotel room. The coffee maker hasn't been used. He must have gone out to buy some.

Works for me. Especially since I didn't pay attention to what I was pulling out of the dresser earlier, and ended up taking three shirts and no pants into the bathroom with me.

When we leave, I assume we'll be riding his motorcycle again. Quickly I pull on a pair of jeans and a long-sleeved shirt before returning to the vestibule.

Gunner comes back into the room as I'm applying sunscreen and moisturizer to my face, my wet hair in a turban atop my head. He slides a coffee in front of me, along with a cup of yogurt and fruit. A furrow forms between his eyebrows as he searches my features in the mirror. "Did I fuck up unforgivably?"

"No." I rinse my fingers and grab the coffee. "Did I?"

His frown deepens. "How would you?"

"Oh, only because on the day after we establish that we're friends, I tell you I want to go down on you. It kind of crosses a boundary."

Heat and humor light the pale blue of his eyes. "I don't know—I consider any offer to suck my dick pretty friendly."

I grin and turn to face him, head tilting back. God, he's tall. Practically taking up this entire space. "We're okay," I tell him and am so damn glad it's true. "But you're right. Our focus should be on Stone."

Gaze locked on mine, he slowly shakes his head. "No. My focus is on you, too. Getting him back is only part of it. But I'm also watching over you, keeping you safe."

"I know you'll do both," I say, and my breath catches when he gently takes my hand, presses his lips to my palm.

Heart thundering, I can only stare when he lets me go and heads into the bathroom. He pauses with the door open, looking at the mirror.

"Did you take a selfie in here?"

Still recovering from that kiss to my hand, I simply nod.

"You usually send them to your brother's phone."

"He wouldn't get it."

"I would." He slides a wolfish glance my way. "Were you wearing a towel or nothing?"

"A towel," I tell him with a grin. "And I told Jenny that if she sent me fifty dollars I'd take it off."

"I'll give you fifty."

"The offer's only for her." For him, I'd do it for free.

His beautiful eyes narrow. "But I'm your friend, too."

"She's my *best* friend."

"We'll have to rectify that." His voice deepens and the intensity of his gaze feels like a powerful magnet, preventing me from looking away. "I like being on top."

He closes the door then, and I'm left with a racing pulse—and, when I look into the mirror, I see a huge, silly smile on my lips. I'm such a dork. I don't have anything to smile about.

God only knows what's in store for us today. Strawman was nothing like Six-Point, even though they had the same grin, the same easy way of talking. But Strawman was *scary*. Not just dangerous, like Gunner is. And not scary like Blowback, though he looks dead inside and he makes even the hardened Riders uneasy.

With Strawman, it was something more than that. When he was here, I couldn't take my eyes off him—and not for the same reason I can't stop looking at Gunner, though their faces are so similar. With Strawman, I kept watching him not because he's beautiful, but because he was terrifying. It was like sharing a tiny space with a coiled, poisonous snake, waiting for him to strike.

From inside the bathroom, I hear the rasp of the shower curtain sliding across the rod. Oh god. Gunner's naked in there. Turning on the spray. Soon water will be dripping over his skin, sluicing across hardened muscles. Soon he'll be soaping up his lean, strong body, maybe lathering up his hands and stroking his thick cock—

Quickly I crank up the blow dryer and try to drown out every tempting sound.

LAST NIGHT, IT WAS TOO dark to see much while we were riding. Today the sun is bright, with only a few puffy white clouds floating in the blue sky, and the hills we're speeding through are simply beautiful, a patchwork of vineyards and olive groves, huge estates and cozy-looking farms. It almost reminds me of my time in Tuscany, though I was traveling alone then, trying to see as much of the world as I could before my inevitable early end.

This is so much better—pressed up against Gunner's strong back, clinging to his lean waist. And that inevitable end hasn't come for me yet.

I'm not so afraid it will. No matter what his family throws at us.

But that worry must be getting to Gunner. As we turn off the highway onto a long, two-lane road that winds deeper into the hills, the tension in his muscles hardens to steel. I hold him tighter, and for a brief moment he lets go of one of the handlebars to squeeze my hands, clasped together over his stomach.

Maybe thinking I'm the one who needs reassuring.

He slows at a stop sign, preparing to turn right onto another rural road. In the brief lull, when the engine is growling instead of roaring, I call out,

"We can say I have herpes!"

He turns his head as if to look at me over his shoulder, but given how close I am and the difference between my height and his, he probably only sees the top of my helmet.

"We can say what?"

"To your family!" I yell. "If they try the 'If girlie wants something from us, she needs to get on her knees' thing, I can bite the inside of my lips and fake some open sores!"

I can't hear his laugh over the rumble of the engine, but I feel it shaking through his back. He doesn't respond, just grips my clasped hands again before taking off, but the tension in his back isn't so rigid now.

The family farm isn't what I expected. Though I don't know *what* I expected. Maybe a cross between the old farmhouse from *Children of the Corn* and the creepy village from *The Wicker Man*, tended by empty-eyed women in long dresses. But the entrance to the property is a huge open gate, with "New Eden Organic Farm" spelled out on an elegant sign overhead. A smaller notice beside the gate reads:

New Eden Organic Farms welcomes visitors from March 1st–Thanksgiving Day. The Farmer's Market and New Eden's Farm Store are open daily, 6am–8pm. Food Pavilion open Saturdays and Sundays.

It's the Monday morning before Thanksgiving, but it doesn't look like they're winding down soon. A few dozen vehicles sit in a huge gravel parking lot facing a red barn. Customers mill between stalls of colorful fruits and vegetables. A picnic area, a small playground, and concession stand lie near the barn's entrance, which is topped by a sign announcing "Farm Store."

Gunner slowly rides through the lot, and when I realize he's not stopping here, I tap his left side—our signal to pull over.

He pulls into a parking space and kills the engine. "You okay?"

"Yeah. I just want to wrap my head around this first. *This* is the Cooper family farm?"

Nodding, he slides his gaze over to the barn. "There wasn't quite all of this before I left, but it was what Mama was working toward. Inviting other local farmers to set up those produce stalls, and it's where she gets all the ingredients to use in the pavilion on the weekends. What produce doesn't sell, Mama buys up and either cans it fresh or makes jellies out of it to put in the store."

Smart. "I bet that creates a lot of local goodwill."

Something that must be incredibly valuable if a motorcycle club is also running out of this farm.

"It does," he says and the wry note in his voice acknowledges the same thing. "But they get people in from the city, too. In the summer, they've got a petting zoo and things like hayrides to bring in the families with little kids. There's a small vineyard up on the east side of the property, so they get the tourists who come through the area visiting wineries. And come October, they set up a haunted corn maze and pumpkin patch, put up a beer garden and stay open until midnight. That's when you can't even find parking here."

"They must rake in the big bucks then."

"I think they do."

"That's seriously impressive. Most of the farmers who

come in to the Den are struggling." And I'm never sure if the drinks I serve make it worse or better.

"Mama probably had a leg up, because this land came from her family and they had some money. But this"—he tips his chin toward the barn—"that's all her. My father just wanted a self-sustaining farm, something like what he planned to live on after the world was rebuilt, but she's the one who turned it into this."

"And you grew up working the farm?"

He chuckles softly, like that's an understatement. "Yeah, I did."

"On a farm called New Eden…and you and your brothers all have Biblical names? Are you sure it's not a religious cult? Was your dad's name Joseph or Solomon or something?"

His laugh deepens. "I'm sure. And my father's name was Leonard."

"Really? That's kind of a let down."

"His road name was Prophet."

I snort hard. Gunner is wearing a grin as he fires up the engine again. Although he said there was a vineyard on the east side of the property, I didn't realize how big the place was. After we ride past the public area and the barn, we pass a pasture full of grazing cows, an orchard and an olive grove, and a few more barns—each one more modern-looking than the quaint old barn housing the farm store. And even though Gunner had told me the clubhouse was at the back end of the property, it's not until we come across a tall, imposing gate that I understand how separate the club is from the farm. A big NO TRESPASSING sign and security cameras posted above a chain link fence topped with razor wire are as far away from the farm's warm welcome as it gets.

Gunner pulls up to the gate, and we sit idling. Waiting for someone to see us through those cameras, I realize.

"The club members all come in on a different route off the main road," he tells me. "Only family comes through this way."

So he's claiming that privilege. "Is this where everyone lives?"

He shakes his head. "Mama's house and all the brides' houses are up on the east hill."

The brides' houses? That doesn't sound creepy at all.

An electric hum sounds, then a loud rattle as the gate rolls open. Nothing's as neat or as nice here. The ground is bare dirt with a few patches of dried grass struggling through. The clubhouse is a long, low building shaped in an 'L', like an old-timey ranch house. The stucco had once been painted a warm brown, but the paint is cracked and peeling away, revealing the gray plaster beneath.

About two dozen motorcycles form a double line in front of the long porch that wraps around the clubhouse. Gunner rolls up beside them as the clubhouse door opens. Strawman, I recognize, and I assume the other is Muncher, because he looks slightly younger than the man at his side—though on a dark night, I'm not sure I'd be able to tell the difference.

Except there *is* a difference, and it's not just the tiny variations in jaws and lips and eyes. It's in the way they look at us. Strawman's wearing his broad grin that seems like it's all teeth. Muncher watches us with unsmiling mouth and unreadable eyes, as if he's not too pleased to see his younger brother.

Not as friendly as Six-Point, then. But also not as scary as Strawman—though Gunner said he was hot headed, so maybe that's coming.

I'm not really sure I want to meet Adam.

And I'm nervous. I wasn't before, but now I am. I can't reach for Gunner's hand, though, or go looking to him for support.

I'm just Stone's sister. Gunner wasn't supposed to kiss me as if he was starving for my taste, or eat my pussy with such devastating hunger. He wasn't supposed to make me laugh, or tease me about my selfies, or sweetly press his lips to my palm.

But, oh my god, I'm glad he did—because it makes this a lot easier, makes me feel a hell of a lot safer, even if he can't touch me now.

Except he does. He takes my sweaty hand in a firm grip, and I remember what he told me last night—that they expect him to be possessive, because I'm his to take care of. But he doesn't look at me; for all the attention he gives me as we start toward the clubhouse entrance, I could be a sack of dirty laundry that he's carrying at his side. His profile is hard, his eyes like ice. Heart pounding, I follow right behind him as he approaches his brothers, half-running to keep up with his long stride.

On the porch, Strawman leans his shoulder against a post, the wooden surface pocked and splintered, as if it's not just used as a leaning post but has taken on its share of knives and fists. "You stop at the house first?"

"I didn't." It's not just Gunner's face that's hard and cold now—his voice is, too.

"Mama's not going to be happy about that."

"Mama'll live with it."

Big arms crossed, Muncher fixes his pale eyes on me. "That one's supposed to be up at the house. She can't stay with you if we're talking business."

"What I have to tell you isn't anything she doesn't know." Gunner stops at the bottom of the porch stairs, his gaze zeroing in on Strawman. "You made an issue of her coming. I told you she's mine to protect. So she's with me until I feel she doesn't need to be."

Strawman pushes away from the post. "All right."

Gunner lifts his chin, indicating the clubhouse door. "She going to have any problems in there?"

"No," Strawman says. "I told the others she's off limits."

Gunner narrows his eyes and looks to Muncher, who nods.

"He told us she's under your protection and not to be touched." Muncher's lips curve a little but it doesn't reach his eyes. "Because you've got a friend who you feel more obligated to than you do your family."

"And without that friend, I'd be in the ground and you'd have one less brother."

The other man tilts his head as if considering that, before offering a slow nod. "All right, little brother." His gaze is slightly warmer when it shifts to me. "Welcome to the Notorious Few, pretty girl. You might want to close your eyes."

TWENTY TWO

GUNNER

There's nothing Anna hasn't seen before—in small doses. Because she gets an eyeful of all kinds of shit at the Den, but she's never been to the Hellfire Riders' clubhouse.

It's a weekday, so most of the Few who hold down day jobs are gone. Those that are here, either they're on security duty or they're enjoying what the club has to offer—pussy, drugs, liquor. A smoky haze swirls near the ceiling. The odors of weed and sweat and sex thicken every breath.

Anna's fingers tighten on mine. Her gaze is darting everywhere.

There's a small group gathered in front of a widescreen television, idly watching a recorded UFC event—last year's championship. Chunk's on the couch, a bottle of beer in hand and a redhead bent over his dick. He tips the beer at me as we pass by, before looking to the screen again. Two heavy patchholders are spit-roasting a tiny blonde between them, grunting like they're in a race to come.

Maybe they are. First woman I ever went down on, it was in this room, and it was a race—the first Cooper brother to make his pussy come. Muncher won, because he's got his name for a reason. But I was so fucking proud to place second, so fucking proud of the way my father clapped me on the back and told me job well done.

Now I wonder if the woman I was with faked her orgasm just to get an inept fourteen-year-old boy off her. It sure as hell never would have occurred to me then. Not when I grew up hearing how every woman was gagging for any Cooper's touch, that they'll always come on our cocks. I didn't learn differently until I was in the Marines and hooked up with a few women who didn't hide their disappointment with my performance—which was a far cry from the wild, crazed moans of the women I fucked here as a teenager.

But listening to similar moans now, it all sounds about as real as a porno—and the memory feels like a crust of filth on my skin.

Anna shouldn't be clinging to my hand. She shouldn't even be touching me. I sure as hell shouldn't have touched her.

And it never felt like this with the Hellfire Riders. I never touched any of the club pussy there, but it didn't turn my stomach seeing and hearing and smelling the other Riders with their women. Hell, more often than not, I was hard as a rock, watching it all go down and picturing Anna with me.

But *this* fucking place. None of it feels right. Knowing the girls are free to come and go, but that my brothers use their faces to draw them in—and once they're in the club-house, they're fair game to every member of the Few. They can say no, but if they do, they're out permanently. So a lot of them don't. Not with my brothers sweet-talking them into staying, making promises they don't keep, making them feel special just long enough to persuade them.

We follow Strawman toward the back of the club-house, toward the rooms reserved for the Coopers and the club pussy they've chosen.

Adam's chosen a dozen—all lying naked around the room, some tangled together, most looking exhausted. He's got a brunette bent over the arm of a sofa, pounding into her, his jeans hanging loose off his ass and sweat drip-ping down his bare back. His fingers are fisted in her long hair. Abruptly he pulls her head back and grunts, his body a solid wall of muscle as he comes inside her.

We head across the room toward the table in the back. Sprawled on the sofa bed in the far corner, Six-Point stirs awake between a pair of nude women.

Adam spares us a glance as he pulls out of the brunette. Absently he strips off his condom, tosses it onto a heap of used latex on the floor, then points to another girl. "You. Suck until I'm hard again, then I want your ass." He points to a pair cuddled together on a recliner. "And you two. Start eating each other out. Get your pussies wet for me."

The brunette stumbles away from the sofa on shaky legs. Muncher crooks his finger at her, and she actually lights up as she changes course toward him.

He catches her around her waist, nuzzling her ear. "My brother didn't take care of you real well, did he? Just plowed your pussy and left you wanting."

She only dips her head. Probably too afraid to say aloud that she didn't have an orgasm with Adam inside her.

Chuckling, Muncher swats her ass. "Get up on that table, then, and I'll have myself some breakfast." He looks back at me. "She's a squirter. It's fucking amazing."

I bet. I squeeze Anna's hand, letting her know I'm still right with her, despite the line we've drawn; she squeezes back. Doing all right, in the middle of all this.

She's fucking amazing.

The table's a circle, so I can't sit her away from the others. My jaw clenches when Strawman takes the chair on her left side, and his grin widens when she scoots a little closer to me.

I study her face. Her eyes are wide and her cheeks flushed, and she's looking everywhere but at Adam. Then the brunette spreads herself across the table, her head within arm's reach of both Anna and me, and Anna's gaze settles on the woman's tits, then her pussy, then Muncher's mouth between her legs.

There's nothing fake about the way the woman starts moaning.

"Take your time," Strawman tells him. "It doesn't look as if the firstborn is in a rush."

Six-Point joins us, dragging on his shirt and carrying a half-empty fifth of whiskey. He grins at Anna. "Hello again, sweet thing. I don't suppose you want to be *my* breakfast?"

"Fuck off," I tell him.

"Oh, and someone's in a bad mood. It's okay, baby brother. We could share her." He winks at Anna. "That'd probably make him feel better."

The only thing that would make this better is getting the fuck out of here.

"If not her, you sure you don't want to pick out another one?" Six-Point turns and indicates the women spread around the room. "They can change your mood quick. They're all real good at sucking dick."

They probably are. "I suppose it's easy to suck you off when you've barely got enough cock to fill their mouths."

Muncher snorts out a laugh, his face still buried in

the girl's pussy, his mouth riding the wild undulations of her hips.

Six-Point grins and drops into the chair next to him. He looks across the girl's writhing body to Anna again. "So what's your story? Strawman tells us you were sleeping in different beds. So why the hell aren't you fucking my brother? You prefer women? Because if you do…" He indicates the room with a sweep of his hand. "We've got some for you."

Anna shrugs. "He's pretty to look at, but…I don't know. He was never interested. I asked him out once and he said no. So I moved on and we just kept things simple."

"You said no?" Eyebrows shooting together, Muncher lifts his head and stares at me. "What the fuck is wrong with you?"

"There's a whole damn list," Strawman says. Lips tight, he stares at Adam, who's rolling on another condom and smearing lube down the length of his cock. "Get her off and let's start talking. We're not waiting for the firstborn. He can catch up later."

Muncher and Six-Point exchange a glance. In the next second they're both on the brunette, Six-Point fucking her mouth with his tongue, fingers plucking at her nipples while Muncher redoubles his attentions to her pussy. Within seconds she's coming, her screams muffled by Six-Point's mouth and Muncher groaning as he laps her up.

They're both looking damn pleased with themselves

as Muncher helps her down off the table and steers her toward the nearest couch.

"I just realized," Anna says suddenly. "None of you guys wear tats."

Strawman stares at her. "That's what you're thinking about after watching her pussy squirt all over my brother's face?"

I'd never admit it, but I was marveling at the same damn thing.

"Well, I mean"—she waves dismissively at the table, where some of the girl's juices are still pooled in front of Muncher—"I see that kind of thing on my bar practically every day."

Not even close to every day. But I'm happy letting my brothers go on thinking that if she wants them to.

She continues, "But what I *don't* see is five bikers together and not one of them inked. Not that I've seen every inch of your skin, but—"

"Hell." Six-Point stands up, unbuttoning his jeans. "We can fix that."

"Sit your ass down," I growl at him while Anna laughs, shaking her head.

"No need. I've already seen you without your shirt. I've seen Zach without one. Adam." She points to where he's working his cock into the girl's ass, then looks to Muncher. "And there's nothing on your arms, where it's most common to see some ink. But you don't have any. Unless I'm wrong?"

"Not wrong," Muncher says, wearing a slight smile.

"We were born looking this way for a reason. So we aren't messing with that." Smile fading, he eyes me. "Unless you did while you were gone?"

I shake my head.

Strawman looks so pleased by that answer, I wish I'd had another to give. "Then maybe you weren't gone all that far—which makes it a hell of a lot easier for you to come back. So why don't you start telling us about the trouble her brother is in?"

"And tell us who did that to her face," Muncher says.

I do, laying it out in broad strokes. The missing fighters. The rumors about the Cage. How Strawman's comment at the rally got me looking at the Iron Blood. Then Stone going missing after he just happened to win a fight against Paladin—and how a man resembling their enforcer showed up at Anna's place.

Six-Point and Muncher both study her carefully then, and I know what they're thinking: the same damn thing I did when I saw the blood between her thighs, on the chair. And they're wondering if that's why I'm not fucking her—because she's been hurt too bad and is still recovering.

Strawman doesn't give a shit whether she was raped. He's sitting back in his chair, looking at me as he works it over. "So you're here because you want to go through us to get to the Iron Blood."

"I don't want to fuck up the business you've got going with them. I just want info on the Cage so I can get Stone out of there." And our friends in the Bedlam Butchers, too, but my brothers won't give two shits about that.

"And helping you with that won't fuck up our business?" He scoffs. "You're asking a hell of a lot for someone who isn't wearing our colors."

"I know it."

Eyes narrowed, he leans forward. "You willing to wear those colors? And not just until your friend's out. You willing to wear them permanent? Because that's what we'll be asking from you in return."

I know Anna's staring at me, holding her breath, but I don't glance her way. One look at her and I don't know whether I could force this out of my mouth.

"I'm willing."

"Shit yeah!" Six-Point crows. "Then we'll get your boy back. Hell, we've got a run with the Iron Blood coming up—"

He abruptly falls silent as Strawman raps his knuckles on the table and looks to Anna.

"That business isn't for outside ears," he says. "And our brother's not wearing our kutte yet."

Muncher smirks. "That won't take long. Mama had one made up for you years ago. Just waiting for you to come back."

"Then I guess I'll be wearing it soon enough."

"And about fucking time," Strawman says, then points to the whiskey bottle at Six-Point's right hand. "Why don't you pass that around and we'll drink to that."

"Should we get Adam over here first?" Muncher looks over his shoulder, calls out, "Heads up, firstborn! We're sharing a round. Zach's gonna be putting on his vest."

"Is that right?" Abruptly he pulls out of the girl's ass and pushes her away from him, stripping the condom off his still-erect dick. His flat gaze is on me as he heads to the table, hauling up his jeans and tucking his cock away but not bothering to fasten up. Bringing with him the bleached odor of cum and sweat, he reaches for the bottle Six-Point holds up for him, then tips the neck toward me in a salute. "Well, then. Looks like Mama's got all of us home again."

He takes a swig, tosses the bottle across the table to Strawman. Going in order of birth. I'm last, and by the time the whiskey reaches me I can barely choke down a single swallow. But that's easy to cover when Six-Point is grinning and thumping my back.

I glance at Anna. She's watching me give my life away, her eyes dark and troubled, and slowly shakes her head when I hold out the bottle to her.

"No thanks," she whispers in a strained voice. "This looks like a family thing."

But what she's really saying is she won't drink to that. I nod, thankful that someone won't, and she averts her gaze, staring blindly at the wall.

Adam swipes the whiskey out of my hand, takes another drink, his hot eyes focused on Anna. Still gripping the bottle, he extends his forefinger, points to her.

"I want that one next."

Her head whips back around, face paling.

My blood runs to ice. Six-Point might joke and tease her. Adam fucking means it. I surge to my feet, get right in his path, so he's pointing at me, instead—and so he'll have to get through me to get to her.

That'll never happen.

"You turn that finger in another direction, brother." The cold steel in my voice is a warning.

But Adam's always been stupid. So instead of turning that finger away, he pokes it into my chest.

"You brought her in here, brother." His smile is thin, cruel. "It's been a while since you left, running away from here like a weak fucking pussy, but it's not so long you've forgotten the rules. Because I've been in a goddamn *cell* that same amount of time, and I still know the rules. You bring a woman in here, and unless she's a bride, she's for all the brothers to share. Are you saying she's a bride?"

I'd love her to be. But if I said that, I'd have to kill him where he stands. "She's not mine," I say, and because it protects her, the lie comes easy. "She's just mine to protect."

With a hard laugh, Adam drops his hand away from my chest and gets up in my face—maybe thinking that'll intimidate me like it used to. He's always been the tallest, the biggest. And he's only gotten bigger in prison, as if he spent most of his free time pumping iron.

I've gotten stronger over the years, too. But more importantly, I've learned to fight a hell of a lot smarter.

From behind me I hear Strawman tell Six-Point, "Get all the other pussy out of here. Now."

Though I don't take my eyes off Adam, I'm aware of Six-Point heading for the brunette, her scrambling over to the other girls, their frantic whispers, the rush to the door.

Adam ignores it all.

"So you're protecting her — and that means protecting her from my cock? You come here asking for help from the Few and then treat me like a threat?" Rage is building in him, hardening his face. Years inside have faded the tan from his skin, but now he's going tomato red, a vein throbbing in his forehead. "Are you denying me what's rightfully mine to take?"

"Yeah, I'm denying you." I say it easily, as if I'm telling him he needs to tie his shoe.

His eyes bulge. "Muncher, start getting her pussy wet for me. If he's worried I'll hurt her, then we'll make sure she likes it. Fuck, she'll be begging for it. And you, little brother, stand aside. That's an order from your goddamn president."

My wide grin isn't enough to express how glad I am he said that. Because, "You're not my fucking prez. Not yet."

The roundhouse swing I anticipated finally comes. Fingers still wrapped around the neck of the whiskey bottle, his fist flies at my head.

Smoothly I duck under his arm. A sharp jab to his stomach doubles him over. A knee to his chin sends him stumbling back, spitting blood. The bottle drops from his hand and thunks to the floor.

But he doesn't go down. Good. Because I've been waiting seventeen fucking years for this.

Face red, nostrils flaring, he charges like a bull. Stepping out of the way would send him right into Anna so I meet him head on, gripping the back of my chair and hauling off on him, whipping the solid pine straight into his path.

Wood splinters in my hands. Knocked sideways off his feet, his head bleeding, Adam roars and rises to his knees, swinging at me though I'm out of reach. A red haze swimming in my eyes, I toss the broken chair aside and then I'm on him, cracking my fists against his jaw, knocking him back down every time he attempts to rise.

Though the haze, I barely hear Strawman say, "Pull him off,"—I just feel the hands that touch me aren't Anna's, and send Six-Point flying. Because Adam's still trying to get up, but David's never getting up again.

So I'll keep going until Adam stays down.

I hear Six-Point's wild laugh, then Muncher's "Holy shit, that's brutal," and they're both on me, struggling to get a grip, dragging me back, then grunting in pain as my fists and elbows connect with muscle.

"Stop this!" A familiar voice cuts sharply through the din and the pounding of my blood. "What is going on here? Stop!"

Muncher and Six-Point freeze, abruptly releasing

me. Hand still tangled in Adam's hair, fist poised to snap another blow at his face, I look up. Mama's staring at me, anger and disbelief crackling in her blue eyes.

Reluctantly I let him go, then glance over my shoulder to where Anna's sitting at the table, hands clamped over her mouth as if to stop a scream, her eyes wide with horror—and with Strawman's fingers wrapped around her upper arm, as if he's holding her in place. Or holding her back.

I only have to look at him and he removes his hand.

"Zachary?" Mama's voice drags my gaze back to her. She's shaking her head. "Adam? What in the world is this about?"

Adam sits up, wipes blood from his mouth and grins. "We were just saying hello to our little brother."

That's what a boy says when under fire from his mother. And we're not boys anymore.

"No," I say coldly. "You were disrespecting me and disrespecting this woman. It doesn't mean a fucking thing if you call me brother if I can't trust you to have my back and to help care for what's mine to protect. And Anna Wall *is* under my protection. If you can't respect that, if you can't respect my obligations, then I'll be heading right out the door with her. And I won't be coming back again."

Mama comes closer and I see she's carrying a leather vest folded over her forearm—my new kutte. So she was that sure of me.

Her gaze slides past me, lingers on Anna. "This is the

sister to the Marine who fought beside you for so long? The sister to the man who saved your life?"

"Several times over."

"Then your obligation to him is ours, too. No one touches her." She stops to lift her hand to Adam's face, frowning at the cuts on his brow bone, his mouth. "There are plenty of other girls for you, my son."

He winces as she prods at his jaw. "I didn't know we were making exceptions."

Frowning, Mama looks to Strawman. "You didn't explain this to your brothers?"

"I did," he says flatly. "I told everyone she was off limits. I don't think Adam listened."

Disappointment thins her mouth. "Your father never had any trouble making sure everyone heeded his voice. Adam has no such trouble, either."

Strawman's jaw whitens but he nods.

"Well. I'm sure you boys have club business to discuss." She gives the kutte to Muncher and turns to me. "Come up to the house later, Zachary, and I'll greet you properly. For now, your Anna can come with me. We'll find something on the farm to keep her occupied."

I'd rather not let Anna out of my sight, but Mama has said that no one is to touch her, and her word carries more weight than Adam's and Strawman's together. She'll be safe.

And better she's on that part of the farm than in the clubhouse when I'm patched in and the celebrations begin.

I glance over at Anna. "You all right with that?"

"Yes," she says, her response quiet but strong. Quickly she collects her jacket and joins my mother, who watches her with a warm smile.

"Come along, then," she says and looks to me. "It is good to see you where you belong again."

I nod, and watch her leave with Anna, at whose side I truly belong. Strawman comes up beside me, quiet until they're gone.

"Adam's going to be picking pieces of that chair out of his head for a week." His voice is low and amused. "You still going to say that girl's not yours?"

No. I'm not going to say a thing about her. Not now. Not when I'm about to cover myself in more filth.

"We've got the fucking kutte," I tell him. "So let's get this shit done."

TWENTY THREE

ANNA

That inevitable end is coming again. I can feel it. But that end doesn't look like cancer this time. Instead it looks like Gunner's brothers. It looks like his mother.

But it's not my end. It's Gunner's.

I can barely breathe as I leave the clubhouse with his mother, heading past the motorcycles toward a flatbed Ford truck. A few words of small talk pass between us —*Please, Anna, call me Marian.* and *Have you been to this part of the country before?* and *Are you returning home for Thanksgiving*

Day or are your plans not yet known?—then she has to take a call on her cell and I'm left alone to my thoughts, where I desperately try sorting out everything I just saw.

But there's nothing to sort out. What happened was clear.

Gunner traded his life for my brother's. He traded his *future* for my brother's.

And I don't know what Gunner wanted his future to be. But I know it wasn't this. Not after everything he said about his family. I don't know exactly what made him leave here in the first place—something about his brother David and the girl Adam killed—but he said that his reasons had boiled down to one: he figured out this wasn't what life should be.

But now it's what his life *will* be.

God. I can't let it happen. I can't.

I should call Saxon now. Tell him to order Gunner to pull out. Tell them we'll find another way to get to Stone. There has to be another way. Because my brother wouldn't want this for his friend, either.

I know what the response would be, though: a flat "no." That is, if he even bothered with a response. More likely it would be "It's club business."

Or maybe Saxon would tell me I should respect the choice Gunner made. He basically jumped on a grenade for his friend.

Or maybe I need to trust that Gunner has a way out. Or that he'll *find* a way out. There has to be another way.

So I won't do anything but go along with what we planned. At least for now.

And that means watching every word I say, every move I make. His mother seems friendly and warm, but that's not the woman Gunner described to me. He described someone with a will of steel and a purpose that she shapes with iron fists.

Iron fists in gardening gloves. They're lying on the seat between us, covered in dirt. Mud is caked halfway up the feet of her tall green rubber boots. A flannel shirt with rolled-up sleeves looks soft and warm, perfect for a mild fall day. Graying blond hair is swept back into a chignon and secured with a big claw clip. She's beautiful, which isn't a surprise, yet doesn't look anything like her sons. Her finely drawn features and petite frame seem almost absurdly delicate compared to her sons' aggressive masculinity.

"My apologies for that," she says, ending the call. "Unfortunately life on a farm means that not everything runs according to a schedule. In this instance, that means a draft horse that's taken sick."

"I hope nothing serious."

"Colic, most likely. But of course it requires additional care—and cancelling the wagon rides this afternoon. But such is life." She smiles at me. "If everything always went according to plan there would be few pleasant surprises. So we do our best to weather the unpleasant ones."

An unpleasant surprise like me? But I won't assume

she means the worst. Not yet.

"You have an amazing setup here," I tell her. "I'll admit that I pictured something smaller. More traditional. But what Zach described is incredibly forward-thinking."

"Yes, well. The Coopers have always looked to the future. And everyone on the farm works hard, contributing as much as they can." She slows as the farm store comes into sight ahead. "I understand that you're a bartender?"

And I *still* won't assume she means the worst by that, just because it came right after her comment that everyone on the farm contributes something—as if bartending doesn't contribute anything. It could be a natural question to ask after mentioning the work people do.

"I am," I tell her. "It suits me."

"Hmm, yes. That is fortunate. We should all be so lucky to know so young what our place and our purpose is."

My purpose isn't bartending. It's a job that just happens to suit me. But I don't think I'm imagining things now. She's very elegantly and subtly cutting me down.

She can try. And when I get back home, my mom and I will have a nice long laugh over the thought of a few softballed insults finding a mark. I have to care for someone before I care about their opinion of me—and Marian Cooper just doesn't qualify for the 'caring' part.

Downshifting as we approach the barn, Marian suddenly huffs out a breath, shaking her head. On the asphalt drive behind the farm store, a heavily pregnant blonde pushes a wheelbarrow piled high with golden hay toward a small paddock.

"Johanna! You put that down!" Marian calls through the open driver's side window even before the truck is stopped. She throws me an exasperated look as she opens the door. "I swear, these boys," she says before climbing out. "Come along."

These boys are apparently Gunner's nephews, who were supposed to be taking the hay out to the goats in the paddock. Instead their mother is doing it.

Johanna offers a few protests when Marian takes the wheelbarrow from her, then seems to accept the futility of arguing and looks to me with a welcoming grin. She wipes her hands on her bulging apron front before extending her palm.

"Johanna," she introduces herself.

"This is Anna," Marian says before I can. "Anna, Johanna is Jacob's wife."

Strawman's wife. I wouldn't have guessed in a million years that this friendly woman with her sharp, curious eyes was married to that scary bastard.

I take her hand. "Hello."

She has a warm grip and an easy smile, which turns into a laughing shake of her head as Marian begins pushing the hay toward the paddock. Johanna and I walk along beside her.

"Anna will be visiting for a little while," Marian adds. She comes to a stop at the fence and turns to face her daughter-in-law, hands on her hips, her voice stern. "And you are taking too much on yourself. If the boys run off, ask the other wives for help. That is what family is for—to share and ease one another's burdens."

Johanna spreads her hands. "But they are swamped, as well. Everyone is so busy."

"We are *always* busy. A little more work should be taken in stride. But *you*, my dear—at this stage, you should keep busy with less physical labors." Marian looks to me. "Johanna is our resident agricultural expert and currently writing an article about increasing soil fertility through the introduction of almond trees into our olive groves."

Ah. Not just a hay pusher or a drink slinger, but someone who contributes much more. "I see."

Marian's gaze turns dour. "That is, she *should* be writing it. Not feeding goats."

"Yes, Mother." Johanna's pretty lips press together as if she's repressing a laugh. Smoothing her hands over her huge belly, she says to me, "You might say fertility is my speciality. Oh! and there are my errant sons. Mother, leave the hay in the wheelbarrow—I'll run the boys down."

"You will run nowhere," Marian tells her. "Anna and I will send them over. We are heading in that direction anyway—I'm needed at the horse barn, so will be leaving Anna in Grace's capable hands."

"Oh, that will be fun for you, Anna," Johanna tells me. "Grace is lovely."

I'm sure she is. But I also suspect Johanna is the sort who would think everyone is lovely—even her mother-in-law.

Quickly we catch up with two dark-haired boys of about eight and ten years of age, where Marian extracts a promise from them to help out their mother more often. As they scamper off, we strike out toward the front of the barn.

Marian slides me a sideways look. "I hope you did not take Johanna's remarks about fertility in the wrong way. She meant no offense."

What offense would there be? "I didn't."

"Ah, good. It struck me that her comments might have unintentionally pained you. I know some women are very sensitive if they cannot have children of their own." She catches my quick frown. "I'm sorry, my dear. Zachary happened to mention your inability when he spoke with Jacob this past week."

A dull pang strikes through my chest. "He said that?"

What context could such a thing possibly be mentioned in?

"Hmm, yes." She stops at the corner of the barn, her piercing gaze steady on my face. "I won't dissemble, dear. Before you came here, I had some concerns about the nature of your relationship with my son. But Zachary assured us that, since your cancer left you barren and your birth mother was likely a drug addict, he would not consider you a suitable life partner."

"Oh."

It's all I can manage. Because I don't care about her

opinion of me. But Gunner's? God, I care so much.

And I know she's trying to tear me down. I know it. But this information couldn't have originally come from anyone but him—and having my guts ripped out would have been less painful than knowing he'd told his family *that*.

Her expression becomes a picture of remorse. "And now I've upset you by mentioning things you'd rather not be known. I'm sorry, my dear. You can, of course, rise above such unfortunate circumstances. I understand you were very fortunate in your adoptive parents."

Those parents are the only reason I'm not biting her face off now. Only the thought of the agony on my mother and father's faces if Stone doesn't come home is keeping me from walking straight off this farm—and tossing a match behind me.

Faintly, I agree, "Yes, I was very fortunate."

She smiles. "And you do seem a resilient sort of girl. I imagine you'll make the best of your shortcomings. Even your infertility must seem like a blessing in disguise, since you don't know who your birth parents are. Goodness knows what you might pass on to any children you had."

Indeed. "They could be monstrous."

Her smile tightens. Obviously not appreciating my light response when having unknown birth parents is *so* tragic—or perhaps unhappy that I'm rallying instead of bawling on the ground.

But the thought of showing this woman how much

this hurts me? I'd rather crawl back to the paddock and start eating goat shit.

She starts off again and I keep pace beside her, waiting for her next lob. What'll it be? My hair's too brown, my skin too naturally tan? Maybe she'll gently inquire whether I'm Latino, or maybe Italian, or perhaps mixed race?—Oh, my dear, I'm so sorry. Of course you wouldn't know.

Checking her watch, she says, "I'm sorry that I must abandon you so soon"—*but hey, you're used to being abandoned by women like your birth mother, right?*—"but Erin is expecting me at the barn. She is Adam's wife—and our resident veterinarian."

I smile. "Very convenient."

"We are very lucky to have her, it's true"—*because she's so useful, unlike a lowly bartender*—"and while I'm gone, Grace will take very good care of you. There she is. Grace, dear!"

Beside one of the produce stalls, a willowy blonde is chatting with a lemon vendor. Like Gunner's mother, she's wearing tall rubber boots and jeans, but with a puffy red vest over a long sleeved shirt to keep her warm instead of a flannel. At Marian's call, she glances over before starting in our direction.

"Grace is a third-year medical student," Marian says, watching the other woman with a fond smile. "She rarely has any free time available, so we're fortunate she could be with us today. Grace, my love! Come and meet Anna."

"Hello." The other woman's greeting is friendly, if

slightly more wary than Johanna's. "It's lovely to meet you."

Yes, everything here is lovely. "You, too."

Marian lays her hand on Grace's arm. "Zachary is here, dear."

Grace nods and glances at me. "So I gather."

"Grace is Zachary's intended bride," Marian says to me. "And since you are familiar with him, I thought that would give you plenty to talk about while you are together today. Grace, dear—do you mind showing Anna around the farm?"

Grace's steady blue eyes haven't left my face. "I'd like that."

"Of course." With a glance at me, Marian says, "I'll see you both up at the house later."

"We'll be there," Grace answers and she watches Marian go before turning to me. Her voice lowers in concern. "Are you all right, Anna?"

No.

And I'm trying to rally again. Desperately trying to. It was all I could do to stand upright with a pleasant look on my face after *intended bride* passed Marian's lips. Everything inside me is bawling on the ground, curled up and bleeding.

Because *this* is also what it means for Gunner to trade his life. This is what it means for him to fall in line.

Did he know? This morning, when he kissed me. When he had me on the floor, his head between my legs and devouring me whole—did he know?

He must have. All the other brothers have brides. He must have known one was waiting for him.

And suddenly the *mistake* and the *shouldn't have* take on a new meaning. Maybe Gunner said he shouldn't have touched me not just because we have to draw a line between us so his family will help him get to Stone — but because Gunner knew he had a gorgeous medical student waiting for him. Someone who isn't barren and adopted and cancer-ridden.

Just when I started to believe that he hadn't drawn the line between us ten years ago because there was something wrong with me. But he's always known about the cancer. I told him about it the first day.

No wonder he pushed me away. Not because his family might have come after me — that first day, I never asked for more than a hookup. Nothing different than he'd had before with other girls. And he hadn't settled in Pine Valley yet. He didn't until four years later.

This explains so much. I've never been good enough for him.

No. I draw a shuddering breath, force my soul up off the ground.

If Gunner thinks that, he's not good enough for *me.*

Awkwardly, Grace shifts her weight between her feet and tucks her fingers into her pockets. "So what's Zachary like?"

"He's an asshole." And I'm the stupid idiot who fell in love with him. "Just a giant, soul-sucking asshole."

"So he's just like his brothers?"

Despite my devastated heart—or maybe because of it—I can't stop my laugh. But it only lasts a second, and my throat is thick when I nod and say, "He apparently is."

Her face softens, and she tilts her head toward the barn. "Let's forget Zachary Asshole Cooper for now. The farm closes down this week, which means we're going to be swamped with people coming in to pick out their turkeys and their pumpkin pies. My girl Shari is minding the register, but she's a little overwhelmed right now." She slants me a wry look. "She's an engineer, which I'm sure Marian wants you to know—and also Benjamin's wife."

Muncher. Who I just watched go down on another woman. Having his breakfast while his wife works in the store.

I don't know if knowing that makes me more sick or angry—but I'm leaning toward angry. It's a lot easier to deal with.

"I can be useful in a store," I tell her.

"Good." Catching my hand, she pulls me toward the barn entrance. "Watch out for the lemonade. It's crazy addicting. I'm pretty sure that if the boys are into dealing crack, at least some of it ends up in there."

I purse my lips. "It's probably Mama Cooper's way of keeping people coming back."

Grace laughs. "Honestly? I wouldn't put it past her."

TWENTY FOUR

GUNNER

Before the hour is out, I'm introduced to the others at the clubhouse and patched in as a member of the Notorious Few.

Patching in doesn't happen that fast in any other club. With the Hellfire Riders, I busted my ass as a prospect for the better part of a year before officially getting my colors. I *earned* that vest. Anyone who's not a Cooper earns his Notorious Few kutte in the same way, and they have to wait for a club meeting with everyone present, too. But my brothers skipped right over that for me because—as Adam said to the others while he was sliding the kutte into place over my shoulders—I was literally born to wear it.

Maybe I *was* born into it. But it just feels like a vest. The Hellfire Riders' kutte feels like my skin.

What I've been born with and what I've earned—I know which one I'd prefer to define me. Just like I've got the brothers I was born to, and the brothers I've earned, and I know which I'd rather spend my time with.

As soon as the backslapping peters out, Strawman asks how I want to celebrate. I know they're thinking I want to fuck and drink, but I don't want either of those. Instead I want to do what a motorcycle club is supposed to do: go for a goddamn ride on a roaring hog.

The air tastes better as soon we hit the highway. Five hours south at a beachside diner, I toss some poor fucker out of his seat to make room for Adam. Two dozen of the Few sit and eat and make assholes of ourselves before heading back up the coast highway. Before turning east toward home, we stop at a beach and stand around a couple of burning barrels, beers in hand.

And I finally get a chance to learn more about the Iron Blood. By unspoken arrangement, only the Coopers are standing at this barrel. Strawman's standing with me, Six-Point's getting his dick sucked on the other side of the fire, and somewhere up on the grassy dune behind us, Muncher and Adam are fucking the club pussy they brought along. I guess ten hours without getting off is about their limit.

I take a sip of my beer—just nursing one, because I've got no intention of staying overnight at the clubhouse or at the farm, and Anna will be riding back to the hotel behind me.

Remembering the feel of her arms around my waist gets my dick stirring more than the slurping moans coming from Six-Point's girl ever could. And thinking about the taste of her? Jesus. My cock is practically spring loaded.

Eyeing Strawman, I ask, "So you going to tell me about the Iron Blood or am I going to have to knock it out of you?"

"You're wearing that kutte. That pussy isn't." He gestures to the girl on her knees.

I look to Six-Point. "Take that somewhere else, brother."

But he's already coming, gripping her hair tight until she swallows, then patting her head before pushing her off. "That was real nice, darling. Now go and warm up one of the brothers for me. Chipmunk over there looks pretty damn lonely."

"So does our little brother here," Strawman says, smirking as he eyes the bulge of my stiffened cock behind my zipper. "Looks like watching that show got you pretty damn excited. You sure you don't want to use her first?"

"I'm sure." I'm only hard because I was thinking about Anna holding onto me, then about the sweet taste of her pussy, and she's the only one I ever want to relieve this need. "How'd you run into the Iron Blood?"

"They ran into us." Suddenly his tone is all business. "Came looking for a favor."

"A favor?" If he'd said they'd rolled up in a Scooby Doo van, I'd have been less surprised. Asking a favor from a friendly club is pretty damn rare. Asking a club that's a stranger to yours? Almost fucking unheard of. Because asking a favor carries a heavy obligation to pay it back—and you *always* pay up, no matter what the other club asks in return.

Strawman nods. "A couple of years ago. They come to us because they have a patch in the prison upstate—the same pen Adam was in. That patch caught the attention of some wetback gangbanger, and the Iron Blood want Adam to take out the gangbanger from inside, so they can get him off their boy's back."

So that's why they asked a favor from an unknown. There's no other connection between the clubs, so no one knows the Iron Blood set up the hit, and they don't stir up any shit on the outside.

"You weren't worried about it coming back on the Few?"

With a shrug, Strawman says, "The firstborn did it quiet. Don't think they ever figured who took the bastard out. All that mattered was Adam timed it so the Iron Blood patch wasn't anywhere near, and no one ever looked at him for doing it. And the patch was out a year later."

I don't give a fuck about the patch. "You still got your favor coming?"

Because this will be real easy if he does. We'll just ask for Stone back.

Taking a drink, he shakes his head. Yeah, it being that easy was probably too damn much to hope for.

"We heard some chatter about MCs escorting different cargo around the region—doing it in relays. You provide security for one leg of the route, pass the cargo off to another MC, then pick up a hefty paycheck. And Six-Point heard from skinhead trash in the Eighty-Eight that the Iron Blood was a part of that network. So my favor in return was letting the Few pick up some of those relays, earn a place in the network."

Skinhead trash. He says that without a hint of irony, even though the Notorious Few can't claim to be any better.

"You escort anything yet?"

"Not yet." He tips his bottle at Six-Point. "As our fucking loudmouthed brother shouted out this morning, we've got our first run coming up. That's why I was in Arizona last weekend—finalizing the details. We had to be cleared through their higher-ups first, and the Blood'll be riding with us on our leg. That first time, anyway."

Shit. That's not much of a connection to pull information from. "But they mentioned the Cage—and warned that anyone who wins a fight on the circuit might be grabbed?"

Strawman gives a slow nod. "They did."

"You think you can follow up on that?"

"I can."

"Who gave you the warning?"

He sucks on his teeth for a second, eyeing me. "You going to jump the gun on this?"

And go beat the answers out of the bastard? No. If that was an option, I would already have had Chef's head in a meatgrinder. But I can't risk the assholes running the Cage to pack up their toys — and Stone — and vanish.

I shake my head. "I'm not going anywhere."

"It was a fucker named Paladin. The same patch Adam helped out inside."

The same fox-faced fucker Stone fought that night.

But that's damn good news. Because that means he might feel a personal obligation to the Notorious Few — it's probably why Paladin gave him that warning to begin with. And if there's a personal obligation, Strawman has a better chance of getting more out of him the next time.

Muncher trudges in out of the dark, fastening his pants. Six-Point tosses him a beer and he twists off the top, looking expectantly at Strawman. "You ask him yet?"

"Not yet," Six-Point says. "It's been all real boring shit. But you better ask now before the firstborn finishes."

Beer poised at my lips, I realize some shit's about to go down. "You asking *me* something?"

"We want you to take Adam out of commission," Strawman says bluntly. "He's no good for the Few."

I stare at them. What the fuck is this? Some test of my loyalty? "You're fucking with me."

"No," Muncher says. Dead serious.

"His temper's dangerous," Strawman says. "He's got no control. You see how many of the Few are gone today? Some had their jobs to be at. But some, he already laid out on their backs—or worse. Our secretary is out with a broken jaw for touching the girl Adam was going to fuck next. We've got a good prospect with a busted wrist because he spilled a beer that he was bringing to Adam. The beer didn't even spill *on* him. And you saw him with your girl. He loses his shit for the stupidest reasons."

"And that's just a few days outside a cell and spending most of his time in the clubhouse," Six-Point says. "He starts throwing that tantrum shit around other MCs? Out in public? We're going to have every biker and gangbanger gunning for us."

They're not wrong. Jesus. Some club presidents can pull shit like that—but only if they're the biggest MC in a region. And even then, the prez would have to watch his back.

"Adam never led the Few before he went to prison," Strawman says. "Not for one fucking day. I always told Prophet he didn't have the head for it, but our father put him up as his second anyway. Maybe with more time, Prophet would have seen Adam wasn't suited to be president—"

"Or maybe he wouldn't have seen it," Six-Point puts

in dryly. "Because Mama sees the firstborn through the magic filter that makes him look perfect to her. Maybe Prophet had one of those filters, too."

"Or maybe Prophet just didn't get that time," Strawman says, his voice sharp as a knife's edge and tossing a warning look at Six-Point — but before I left, words like against our father would have earned Six-Point a beating that wouldn't stop until he was pissing blood. "So now the firstborn has taken the place Prophet gave him, and if he continues like this, he'll bring the Few down. Unless you take him down first, little brother."

I won't argue with their reasoning. It's the last thing I expected, but they're right. I just don't know why the hell I was picked for it. Not because of the fight today. I beat Adam's ass, but together they could do it. And Strawman's smart enough to come out on top if he took the firstborn on alone.

"Why you looking to tap me for it?" I look to Strawman. "Seems like it'd be your place, as VP."

"Mama," they all say in unison.

Strawman goes on, "You're the baby, you just came back, and you look just like David. So you're the only one she'd forgive for it. And we're not talking killing him. Just making sure he can't ride again."

Because if he can't ride, he can't lead the MC. Even Mama couldn't argue with that.

But this is a hell of a thing to drop on me. And I still don't trust it. "So what is this?" I ask, eyeing each of them in turn. "Is this what it's really going to cost me to get Stone back?"

"You earned that help when you put on your kutte." Eyes unblinking as a shark's, Strawman's gaze doesn't waver from mine. "You do this, we'll run interference with Mama and put Anna in your house as your bride."

Everything in me goes utterly still. Anna. In my house. In my bed.

Mine.

Just the thought burns through me like an electric shock, tightening every muscle, prickling my skin, stiffening my dick.

But I don't show any reaction. Because I still don't trust this. They've been pushing hard, trying to make me admit I feel something for Anna. For all I know, this is Mama's idea.

And even if it's genuine, I'd cut off my balls before moving Anna permanently to the farm. A few days around this shit? She'll be all right. But there's no way in hell I'd let her live in a home where everyone around her thinks she's not pure enough to be there.

"There's nothing like that between Anna and me," I say evenly.

Strawman smirks, but it's Six-Point who answers. "We figure you and David are more alike to each other than all the rest of us — and not just because you're twins. You both got that 'one woman' shit locked down tight. So if you do this for us, we'll do that for you. We'll protect her from Mama."

Right. I huff out a laugh, shake my head. "Let's just focus on that run with the Iron Blood. If I get information that points me to Stone, maybe I'll do something about Adam. *Only* for the good of the Few," I stress. "Not to get Anna."

Laughing, Muncher starts, "All right, brother, if that's how you want to play it—"

His abruptly stops talking like he never started, tipping his beer up for a swallow.

Adam comes out of the dark, arms spread, breathing deep. "Ah, that fucking sea air. It's damn good to smell it again."

"The smell of freedom, brother," Strawman says and bumps his fist.

Six-Point draws in an exaggerated breath, lets it out. "Freedom smells like pussy."

"That's because you're standing downwind of Muncher," I tell him.

Six-Point crows out a laugh. "True that."

Adam grins, then rolls his shoulders, cracks his neck. "I'm ready to ride again. So let's get the hell home. We've got brides who need fucking." His gaze lands on me. "And you've got one to break in."

Fucking goddamn hell.

I'd forgotten about the girl. I never forgot that Mama hopes to hook me up with some woman of her choosing, but I'd forgotten that Strawman told me she already had one picked out. That means the woman is working at the farm, living in my bride's house, being groomed to become my wife.

And knowing Mama—if she thinks there's any chance that the relationship between Anna and me isn't what we say it is, she'll parade that girl in front of Anna all goddamn day, hoping to break her heart.

The Anna who is just Stone's sister wouldn't care. The Anna who's just my friend might not, either. And that's where she is now—calling herself my friend, because she still doesn't know me well enough to love me.

If that's all there was, I wouldn't be riding toward the house with this sick dread festering in my chest.

That's not all there is, though. Because this morning, Anna kissed me like she could never get enough. She spread her sleek thighs for me and came on my tongue. This morning was the sweetest gift anyone's ever given me.

But after Mama walks her intended bride out in front of Anna, what's she going to think this morning meant to me? By now Anna must have met all the wives. She'll know my brothers were screwing and eating club pussy and those girls didn't mean a thing to them. She'll think I'm no different than Muncher laying the brunette out for breakfast while his wife works up at the farm.

If Anna thinks she knows this about me, that's it. She'll be done. No chance she'll ever love me. I know how she feels about the Riders who cheat on their wives. She thinks they're pure fucking trash.

If Mama made it seem like I've had a wife waiting for me, Anna has reason to believe I am, too.

My heart's racing, and I'm in a near panic by the time my brothers and I split off from the rest of the Few, taking the main road up to Mama's house instead of heading back to the clubhouse. I'm telling myself it won't be that bad. That Anna will know I've never even met this girl. That she'll know I have no intention of marrying this girl. That she'll know I'd never touch anyone but her.

But how can she know? I never told her.

I never fucking told her.

Right away I know it's as bad as I feared. Because Mama greets us at the door with a triumphant gleam in her eyes that isn't just from seeing me in the Notorious Few's colors for the first time. She's got everyone except for the kids rounded up in the farmhouse's big living room, and while she makes noises about how glad she is all her boys are back together, I try to get Anna to meet my eyes.

And she won't. Sitting on a sofa between two of the brides, her gaze just slides over me like there's no difference between me and the brothers I'm standing with.

She's never done that before. Not ever. Sometimes she doesn't look my way. But when she does, her eyes always stop on me. They always stop and linger, and I never knew how bad I needed her gaze on me—and how bad it hurt not to have her eyes meet mine—until they slip past me like I'm covered in pig grease.

Insistent fingers take my arm. Mama's tugs me away from my brothers—and there's a young woman right next to her, looking as if she's trying hard to smile.

Mama's smile isn't forced. It's watchful and expectant. "Zachary, this is Grace."

And Anna's eyes are on me now. My chest an empty ache, I glance over and she's staring at me and Mama and the blonde, and her eyes are as hard as they were in the brewery, just before she told me to get out of her life.

This is *not* happening.

"Mama," I tell her softly. "Let's talk in the other room."

Her face brightens and she pulls Grace forward. "Oh, yes. You'll want time to talk alone. I'm sure you'll—"

"No, Mama. You and me."

It's still quiet, because although rage and frustration are howling through me, I'm not going to humiliate this Grace woman in front of the family. I know exactly how that would go. Mama would blame my rejection on the girl not being good enough, decide that she's chosen wrong and just needs to find another, instead of listening to what I say. I know she would, because it's what she did with the girl she pushed at David, trying to pull his eye away from Ivy Tan.

"All right." Mama gives the other woman a reassuring pat on the arm. "We'll be just a minute, dear."

I head toward the kitchen, the old floorboards squeaking under my feet in the same spots they always did. The kitchen's all the same, with the big pine table where we ate our informal meals, the pots hanging above the butcher block island, the fresh flowers in the window above the white enamel sink.

Mama doesn't like anything to change. But it's about to.

I just have to figure out how to lay it out for her without jeopardizing Anna's safety. Because I'm not taking a bride.

The night Anna sent me away at the brewery, I walked out of there thinking that I'd have to. That I'd have to take a bride as part of falling in line. But the moment Anna ripped my heart out, I also thought it was the end of my fucking life. It wouldn't have mattered if I was forced to be with someone else if Anna never wanted to see me again. Nothing matters when everything inside is dead.

But since the moment I saw that photo of her mouth taped and her face bruised, I haven't given a single thought to any bride. And I started living again when I kissed her in the shower.

Since then, there's not been a single moment where I've considered any other option for my future. Because other women don't exist for me—and I won't touch anyone but Anna.

Ever.

But saying that would make things harder for Anna here than they already are. So I have to come at it another way.

"Mama." Just inside the kitchen, I turn and face her.

She hasn't changed much, either. Just a little gray in her hair, just a few faint lines around her eyes. And still seeing everything the way she wants to see it. "Do you think I give a fuck about a woman when Stone is out there, still missing?"

Disapproval thins her lips—because I said *fuck.* All the rest is nothing to her, because it doesn't fit with her agenda. Me refusing to be with this girl is just something to be rolled over. "You cannot do anything for your friend at this moment."

"I can keep his sister safe while he can't."

"*We* can do that. Don't return to the city tonight. Anna can stay with me. And you can finally take your place in your own home, start creating your own family."

Jesus. It always comes back to this bloodline shit. "I told you the last time I was here—I can *never* start a family. You didn't believe the report I gave you showing my sperm count? All right. Erin's in that living room. She's still inseminating the cows? Then she can take a good look at my sample and tell you it wasn't a damn lie. You don't trust my doctors, you can believe her word. And she'll tell you that I could fuck every bride every night from now until next Christmas and you still aren't getting a baby out of me."

She sighs. "Even if it's true, we will simply ask your brothers to step in after you've claimed her."

"Then why don't you ask Erin to inseminate her with their cum now? You want a breeding program, might as well treat her like one of the cows."

"Zachary!" Voice sharp, she frowns at me. "You insult Grace with such talk. And you insult me."

I grit my teeth. Because that's where this always goes with her. She won't address the point I'm making—that we're nothing but sperm donors and baby incubators. She'll just take offense to the way it's said. "If you intend to send all my brothers into her bed, you could do that now. You sure as hell don't need me to marry her first."

"You do need to marry her. Because if she's chosen to continue your father's bloodline, then she deserves the honor of his name and the protection of his son."

"There's a simple solution to that," I say, my voice hard. "You need to go up in front of a judge who'll change her name to Cooper, and ask my brothers to extend their protection. Unless you're saying my brothers are too weak to take care of more than one woman?"

The way I see it, they aren't taking care of their wives at all. They're just fucking them. It's Mama who's taking care of them.

She lifts her chin, ready to redouble her arguments.

Before she opens her mouth, I tell her softly, "Mama, I'm *here*. I'm wearing this kutte. That's as far as I'm willing to go. Either you'll accept that it's enough or you won't—I don't give a fuck. But it's all you're getting from me."

Anger snaps through her eyes. "All right. But you stay on the farm tonight. Don't mate with Grace, if you don't want her. But you *will* stay at your home. I'll keep

Anna with me and we'll keep her safe until your business regarding her brother is done. There's no need to waste the time you could be using to find him by watching over this girl."

So she's shifting the blame. But not to Grace. It's coming down on Anna.

I pinch the bridge of my nose, struggle for calm. "We're not staying here. Not in a place where she wouldn't be safe if the end comes." It's a stupid argument, but if Mama's going to stick so hard to these beliefs of hers, this need to see me at home and breeding, then I'll use them against her. "Unless you can tell me she'd be safe here if that race war started up overnight? You going to tell me that you'd trust her not to side against the brides and their children, betraying you before running off to join her own kind?"

Silently she stares at me, rage pressing her mouth tight. But she doesn't contradict me. Because she *does* believe it. She'll shelter Anna right now. But if all the shit they're waiting for came down? That protection she promises would disappear fast.

"Yeah, I thought so." I sound so damn tired. I *feel* so damn tired. "So you need to accept this: I'm not taking a bride, and I'm not staying at home. *Ever.* What you've got now is all you'll be getting out of me. And that has nothing to do with Anna—it has everything to do with you, and you pushing your breeding nonsense on me. It has everything to do with David, and how he died because of all the bullshit this family believes."

Flinching away from me, she draws a shaking breath. Tears spring to her eyes—and that pain's real, and it hurts me to see it, but I'm not sorry she's feeling it.

She thinks I should be sorry, though. "You say that to me? You don't think I paid enough when I lost my *son*? You don't think I paid enough when my own son killed my *husband*?"

"I don't think any of us have paid enough." We brought it all on ourselves. "Maybe we deserve how much it hurts. But David didn't. And Anna doesn't."

Mama just shakes her head, turning away from me, breath shuddering. And I can't stop myself from wrapping my arms around her, holding on until her crying stops.

I stroke her soft hair, say quietly, "I'll be at the clubhouse again first thing. But I'm leaving now. I'm tired and I'm sure Anna's tired. I'll bring her again tomorrow if she wants to come—and if you're still willing to look out for her on the farm."

Mama pulls away, wiping her face. "I said we'd look out for her. Whatever else you think of me, Zachary, I won't go back on my word."

I know. That's often the problem. She always follows through. No matter who it hurts.

But I only tell her "Goodnight, Mama," and head for the hall.

"Zachary." Her bleak voice stops me at the kitchen door. "The next time you boys feel the need to wrestle, perhaps for my sake you will refrain from hitting Adam in the face. Of you all, he looks the most like your father."

As far as I'm concerned, that's all the more reason to hit him. But I simply nod and go.

And pray I can persuade Anna to start looking at me again.

TWENTY FIVE

GUNNER

Anna still doesn't meet my eyes when I collect her from the living room and we head out to the motorcycle. The need to make her look seethes in me, the need to put my hands on her and force her to face me, but I can't say to her what I need to say now. Not with the family looking on.

So instead my gaze eats her up as she silently buckles her helmet. She *does* look tired, her eyes dark and hollow, her movements slow, as if her entire body feels heavy. I expected a little argument from her inside the house, that maybe she wasn't ready to go, but she just mutely got to her feet.

"You all right, Anna?"

Her shoulders lift on a shrug and her mouth curves into an unconvincing smile. "Of course. I'm fine."

She's not fine. I know she's not. If she was, then when she swung her leg over the bike and settled in behind me, she wouldn't be sitting with an inch of space between us instead of scooting up tight. I start the engine, waiting to feel her hands on me and realize she's leaning back instead, gripping the seat behind her for support and balance.

Holding onto it instead of holding onto me. As if she can't bear to touch me.

Pain slams through my chest and shoves out a harsh command. "Put your goddamn arms around me."

She touches me then—but just her hands gripping my sides, not wrapping her arms around me and clasping her fingers over my stomach like she did this morning. Behind me, her body's rigid. Because I hurt her. I swore I'd never do it again, but I did. By keeping my fucking mouth shut so tight.

I open the throttle, eyes fixed on the splash of lighted road ahead, my chest a burning ache. I hurt her—

And she shrugged.

She *shrugged*. As if it didn't matter.

But it does. Because I can see it matters. She's just pretending it doesn't.

Jesus Christ. How many times has she pretended not to be hurt? How many times has she shrugged and smiled?

So many times. And I know every single one because they're seared into my brain. I hated every single goddamn lift of her shoulders, because she shrugged and smiled every time I had to push her away. As if it was nothing to her, even though I was tearing out my heart each time.

But that shrug is a fucking *lie*.

Now there's hope filling the empty ache inside me. So much damn hope. Because I hurt her—I never wanted to hurt her—but she *is* hurt.

I couldn't hurt her if I didn't have at least a small piece of her heart. Attraction, that's something else. I knew that was always there.

But she *cares*. I don't know how much. Maybe that piece of her heart is tiny. There hasn't been enough time for her to love me yet—and shit, after today I'll have to work my ass off to regain any strides I might have made there.

It doesn't matter if she doesn't love me, though. What matters is that a tiny piece of her heart finally belongs to me—and that she cares enough that I could hurt her.

What matters is never hurting her again.

So that's the end of this, then. The end of holding back. The end of keeping my hands off her. The end of hiding from her how I feel. I was waiting to let her get to know me, but hell—loving her is all that I am. It's all she needs to know. And I was waiting so we don't jeopardize our chance to find Stone—but Anna's smart, she's careful. I will be, too. If we're at the farm, if we're being watched, we can make sure no one sees anything we don't want them to see.

But as soon as we get back to the hotel, get up to our room, she's going to know how I feel. And I'm not letting her leave that room until she's mine.

It won't be easy. She's closed herself off, shut down. It'll be a fight.

So it's only fair that I give her some warning.

The rumble of my engine echoes through the concrete hotel lot as I pull in next to my truck. She's off the bike almost before I've stopped. She's fast, but I'm faster. I catch her hand.

"When we get up to that room, we're going to sort this through," I tell her. "After it's sorted, I'm going to lay you on my bed and kiss every sweet inch of you, until you're as wet and as hot as you were this morning. Then I intend to fuck you all damn night—slow, then hard, then real slow again."

Her golden brown eyes stare at me, stunned and wide, before abruptly narrowing. With a furious hiss, she yanks her hand out of mine. "You're never going to touch me again!"

Spinning away, she takes off toward the hotel.

Seeing her run from me rips a hole through my chest. Right now she must think I used her this morning like my brothers use their girls. But that's not what it meant to me and she's damn well going to know it.

I lock down the bike and follow her. The elevator doors are closing when I get inside the hotel lobby, giving me a disappearing view of her defiant eyes and compressed lips before sealing her inside. Helmet dangling from my fingers, I head for the stairs. She's pushing through the room door when I hit the third floor landing and emerge into the hall. For a second I think she's going to swing the interior security latch closed and I'll be shouting what I have to say through the door for everyone to hear. But when I insert my keycard, the room door opens instead of catching on a latch.

Anna's sitting on the end of her bed, taking off her boots. The defiance is gone and in its place is pleasant cordiality. There's nothing about her expression or posture that says anything different than it did this morning, when she was confirming we were still friends.

We're not going to be just friends anymore.

I make sure the door's closed and secure the latch. After Strawman's appearance this morning, we had our room keys changed but I'm not taking any chances that my brothers will walk in and see what I'll be doing to Anna tonight.

She opens her dresser, grabs her nightshirt, never looking my way as I toss my helmet and kutte onto the luggage rack. Never glancing over as I cross the room, leaving her a hand's breadth of space.

Though I'm crowding her, Anna doesn't look up. "So, I

met Grace," she says like she's my buddy. "I liked her."

"And I don't give a shit about her."

"Your mother chose well."

"I'm not marrying her."

"She'll make a good wife."

"To someone else, because the only woman I'm ever going to touch is you."

"Really?" Her voice cracks but not on a sob—instead it's rage breaking through, as if she was containing it behind that mild expression but she can't anymore. She turns to me and her eyes swim with so much hurt I can't fucking breathe. "But I'm not a suitable bride. I'm barren. And full of cancer. Oh yeah—and my birth mother was probably a crack whore."

Ice splinters in my chest. "Did Mama say that to you?"

"Whether *she* said it to me doesn't even matter. Did *you* tell Strawman that I can't have kids because of my leukemia treatments? That I was adopted?"

Oh fuck. "I did, sweetheart, but only because—"

"No! There is no 'because' that can ever make it better!" Glittering tears fall from her lashes but she stumbles back when I reach for her, as if my hands are poisonous blades. "Those are things I always thought made me a better person, stronger. Adoption gave me the most amazing family. I had cancer, and I fucking *survived* it. Those are the most incredible things in my life. So what if it means I can't have kids? I never thought that made me less of a woman. Never in my life have I *ever* thought I'm less of a person because of those things."

"You aren't—"

"But you *said* those things made me worthless! You took something gold and said it was shit. You think I care whether you were saying it to mislead them? You throw shit on my face and I'm supposed to say it's okay because, hey—the bigoted psychopaths in your family don't like a woman who is covered in shit, so at least they won't threaten me now? I knew what they would think about me, say about me. But to have you *tell* them to think these things? To have you put the shit in their hands so they can throw it, too? *You?*"

Her voice breaks and all at once she's sobbing helplessly behind her hands, her shoulders hunched, and the devastated sounds she's making are like bullets tearing through my gut.

Her anger was never about the brides. What she's thinking of me now is so much worse.

"Ah, Jesus. Anna, please. I don't think any of that makes you worthless. I don't think anything like that. I fucked up. I'm sorry for it." And I can't blame her for not wanting me to touch her. But I can't bear her pain. Throat clogged, eyes burning, I catch her up against me, bury my face in her hair. Hoarsely I whisper, "I'm so fucking sorry. I was just thinking of protecting you and I fucked up."

A harsh laugh breaks from her and she shoves at my chest, twisting away. "Yeah, you did. Because you seriously have a messed up idea of what protection is. 'Hey, let's give shit to my family so they can throw it at Anna! Hey, I'll just lie to Anna for a week, using her brother's phone!' Like you think protection is standing between me and a threat and then punching me in the face."

"Oh, sweetheart, you have no idea." My chest a solid rotted ache, I fist my hands at my sides so I don't reach for her again. She doesn't want it—and she doesn't even know the extent of how I've failed. Staring at her fragile shoulders, I tell her grimly, "I've messed up protecting you for ten goddamn years. If I'd protected you right, I'd have made you mine when I met you instead of staying away."

Her head whips around and she looks disbelievingly at me, tears glistening on her cheeks, her arms wrapped around her stomach as if holding in so much hurt. "What are you talking about, ten years?"

"From the first second I saw you. You grinned at me and flashed me your tits and told me about your cancer and I wanted you so damn much. But I pushed you away, afraid of what might come for you. But you are the only one for me. You've been the only one for me since the day I pulled over to change your tire."

"You've wanted *me* since then?" Her short, incredulous laugh hurts—but it's the wary hope in her eyes that destroys me. As if she wants to believe, but I've hurt her too much for her to trust my words now. Wildly she shakes her head. "No."

"You think I'd lie about this? You think this is what I *wanted*?" I blast the question at her, all the pain and frustration of a decade pushing me forward, until I'm right up in her face. This time she doesn't run away—just lifts her chin, her soft lips quivering as I grind out, "Before you, I had more than my hand to fuck. I planned to live free and easy for a long, long time. Then you come along and I can't touch you because of my family, because they'd see how much you mean to me. And I can't touch anyone else. For ten fucking years!"

"Gunner," she whispers, searching my eyes. Searching for truth.

The truth is in the word she just spoke. "You know why my road name is Gunner? Do you know why Stone started calling me that in front of the other Riders until it stuck?"

"Because you were a gunnery sergeant when you left the Marines."

That's the reason everyone assumes. But I shake my head, my voice softening. She's listening now. She's with me. "Back then, he called me Zed. You remember?"

"Yes."

"Right after I left the service, I had a vasectomy. And your brother started calling me Gunner because I was shooting blanks."

A little laugh slips from her. "That's awful."

"Stone's jokes usually are. But ask me why I had the operation."

"Why?"

Gently I take her hand, bring it to my chest. Her gaze

drops to our linked fingers until I start talking, then her golden gaze locks with mine again. "Because I only knew you for a goddamn week, but after that first visit, I couldn't touch another woman. Four years later, your brother was heading home to Pine Valley—and I knew you were there, so I went, too. I knew my family would still be a danger. But I thought: If I can't continue the bloodline, maybe they'll let me go. Maybe I'd have a chance to be with you the way I wanted."

That wary hope shimmers in her eyes again. "You did?"

"Yes. But Mama didn't believe the evidence I put in front of her," I say, and when Anna smiles wryly in acknowledgement of how unsurprising that is, I raise her hand to my mouth and press a kiss to her palm. "So getting snipped didn't work. But I never once regretted it. Now ask me why."

"Why?" So quietly, it's nothing more than a movement of her lips.

Mouth grazing the soft skin of her inner wrist, I feel the wild fluttering of her pulse. "Because the only woman I wanted to be with couldn't get pregnant. So what did it matter if I was shooting blanks?"

Her eyes well with new tears, her trembling lips parting as she stares up at me, still so afraid to believe.

Slowly I pull her closer. "You were the only future I ever wanted, Anna. You were the only future I could see for me, even if having you was impossible. But I figured if it ever became a possibility, and if we ever wanted kids, we'd adopt. Because both you and Stone were, and you had the best damn family. A family I wanted so badly to be a part of. So adopting our own seemed like a good option to me."

Tears dripping over her lashes, she tentatively raises her hands to my face, fingers tracing my jawline—and if that's all she ever gives me, that small touch, that small hope, that small trust, I'll take it.

But I'm still going to fight for more.

Though my movement mirrors hers, there's nothing tentative in the way I cup her face in my big hands. Nothing tentative in the way I smooth my thumbs across her cheeks, wiping away her tears. Nothing tentative in the way I bring her closer, until her slender frame is flush against me and there's no distance between us. A tremor races through her and she presses closer with a shuddering sigh.

I lower my mouth to hover above her swollen lips, my voice roughened by my need for her—need for her body, her heart. "And all that time, I stayed away. Never alone with you because I wanted you so fucking much. Afraid I'd open my mouth and say too much and my family would come for you. Afraid you'd get hurt. But you got hurt anyway. And now I'm alone with you and can't keep my hands to myself. Now tell me you don't want me to stay away anymore."

"I don't want you to, but—" Her fingers sink into my hair, halting the descent of my head. She's panting softly, her quick warm breaths bursting against my lips. "What about Stone? Your family?"

"Out there, it'll still have to be the same. For now."

"And when we're alone…we'll be more?" A tinge of doubt colors the question.

Soon, she won't have a single doubt. "You've always been more, sweetheart," I tell her gruffly. "So much more. I've belonged to you for such a damn long time."

And it's long past time to claim her. To make her mine.

I just need one word. "Tell me yes, Anna. Tell me you belong to me, too."

She shudders against me. And even as I'm on the verge of taking her, she gives me everything.

"Yes," she whispers. "I do."

TWENTY SIX

ANNA

This must be a dream.

In real life, I must have fallen off his bike during the ride back to the hotel. I must be lying on the side of the road with my head cracked open, because Gunner can't really be here, telling me I'm the only woman he's wanted, looking at me as if I'm everything, carrying me to my bed and kissing me so hard, so deep. As if his entire life depended on this kiss.

Oh god. This is the best dream I've ever had. And I

don't want to wake up.

Fully clothed, he presses me into the bed, settling between my legs. Mouth devouring mine, he pins my wrists over my head with his left hand and braces his weight on his right, groaning when I arch beneath his strong body, pulling against his grip, desperate to touch him.

With a cry of frustration, I turn my head. "Gunner, please!"

"I'm not rushing this, sweetheart." His voice is rough against my mouth for the length of a harsh breath. "I've waited so damn long. I'm going to take my time and do everything I ever dreamed of doing to you."

Then his tongue strokes between my lips again, sliding across mine in a slow, erotic taste. I can't get enough of him. I can't get enough, but he's only giving me this kiss, his weight between my thighs, his rigid cock lodged against my pussy but with too many clothes between us. It's everything I've ever wanted from him but I'm desperate for more, my body aching, my skin on fire.

Hungrily I return his kiss, rocking my hips beneath his, trying to push him harder, trying to drive him wild.

But whatever iron control allowed him to keep his hands off me for ten years must be serving him well now, because I can feel his desire, feel how hot and hard he is, but he still takes his time — sipping gently at my mouth before devouring me again. Groaning as I suck on his tongue and wrap my legs tight around him. Licking into my mouth, teasing, until I'm whimpering and chasing down his lips for another heady taste.

Softly Gunner kisses my upper lip, then the fullness of my lower lip, before raising his head.

His voice is gruff when he says, "I'm sorry for this," and I don't know what he's apologizing for until he gently kisses my lower lip again, still slightly swollen and the split not yet completely healed.

I shake my head. "It's not your fault."

"It is." Gently his mouth grazes the line of my jaw, then the sensitive tendon at the side of my neck. "I should have been with you. All these goddamn years. I should have been with you."

My heart swells and tightens. "You're here now."

His dark head lifts, hot crystalline eyes meeting mine. "I'll *always* be here."

I knew this was a dream.

Still the best one, though he won't let me touch him. Instead I can only beg in helpless frustration and pull against his grip on my wrists when he drags my shirt hem up over my belly, then higher, exposing my breasts.

A shudder wracks his powerful form as he looks down at me, and I groan as the quake through his body forces his stiff cock to rub against my clit in delicious little tremors.

"Shh, Anna," he hushes my tormented moan, as if *he's* the one being tortured here. Strain pulls his voice tight as he whispers, "Jesus, you have the sweetest fucking tits."

Abruptly he lets go of my hands. But I don't have a chance to run my hands over his skin—only grab at him wildly when he suddenly sits back and bodily lifts me straight up, my legs still wrapped around his waist, his face level with my breasts. My fingers find anchor on the bunched muscles of his biceps just as his mouth opens over my right tit.

I cry out as scalding heat engulfs my small breast, as he sucks hard and draws back, his teeth scraping across my stiffened nipple before taking me deep into his mouth again—sucking hard and drawing back before biting my throbbing nipple in another soft pinch that I feel like an electric jolt to my clit. My fingers sink into his thick hair and I hold on, my head falling back, the world suddenly spinning. I've never thought my breasts were particularly sensitive, but he's overloading my nerves with intense sensation, with shocking heat and gentle pain. And the sounds he's making. God. As if I'm the best thing he's ever tasted, and it's driving me wild, until I'm writhing against the corrugated muscles of his abdomen.

Suddenly he stills, his groan deepening. "You've soaked through your jeans."

Oh god. I have and I'm rubbing all over his stomach. But when I try to jerk my hips away, he just forces me back tighter against him, his forearm locked around my ass.

"You're so fucking wet." His voice is a soft growl against my reddened breast. "Getting your pussy juice all over me."

Cheeks burning, I duck my head, but he's staring up into my face, his eyes glowing with need. As he watches me, his lips close over my nipple and his cheeks hollow when he sucks hard on the sensitized flesh. Whimpering, my fingers clenching in his hair, I can't stop myself from moving against him again.

"Fuck yeah." He quickly kisses my scar, then abruptly tips me back, my shoulders hitting the mattress with Gunner on his hands and knees over me. Amusement joins the heat in his pale gaze. "This morning, I got so damn excited, I came in my shorts when you kissed me—and I didn't care. It just made it all wetter and hotter. So don't be embarrassed, Anna. Because knowing you're this hot and wet is all it takes to get me about ten seconds away from coming again."

"Ten seconds?" A breathless laugh shakes from me. "That's a good thing?"

His grin takes the little breath I have left. "Real good. Except"—all at once he pulls back, off the end of the bed—"maybe we can't go as slow as I planned this time. Now take that shirt off."

I do as fast as I can, greedily ogling the flex of his triceps and the sexy crunch of his abs as he reaches behind his head to pull off his own T-shirt. In record time, he toes out of his boots while I tug the elastic from my braid and drag my fingers through my hair, pulling the wavy strands forward over my shoulders, the tips teasing my erect nipples.

Then his hands go to his belt and I can't hold back anymore. "Let me," I tell him huskily, scooting forward to the end of the bed, my gaze fixed on the bulge behind his zipper. "Let me see, let me taste—"

"Taste?" Groaning, he catches my wrists before I can touch him. "I won't last even ten seconds if you do that."

"Then you can come again later."

With almost no effort, he pulls my hands up over my head, holding me captive. His pale eyes burn with need when they meet mine, but his touch is gentle when he presses his free thumb to my bottom lip. "Wrapping your mouth around me would only hurt you, sweetheart. This needs to heal up more first or you'll start bleeding again."

From the split in my lip? I giggle. "You're that big?"

He grins again. "You'll need to back up the length of the bed before I unzip."

A laugh bursts from me but I do, scooting back across the bed until I'm up by the pillows again, anticipation burning over my skin. Good lord, he's gorgeous. From his tousled dark hair and those incredible eyes to the stubble on his sculpted jaw. His broad shoulders are wide enough to carry the world, his arms strong enough to hold it steady. And his stomach, god—every ridge of muscle so perfectly defined, with a dark trail of hair leading beneath his waistband. But it's his big hands that I can't look away from, his long fingers that hold me transfixed as he slowly unbuckles and unbuttons and unzips.

His hands, as he pushes his jeans down his hips. His hands, as he fists his cock and slowly gives it a long, hard stroke.

Oh god. He wasn't really kidding. Not that I needed to back up—although maybe it's good that I did, because I can barely stop myself from reaching for him now—but sucking on his length really might have split my lip again, because he's long and thick, but simply rubbing against him before, I hadn't realized *how* thick.

So incredibly thick and hard and just as gorgeous as the rest of him.

His big hand strokes his heavily veined shaft from balls to crown, and a soft moan escapes me when I spot the precum glistening at the broad tip.

His voice is low and dark. "You like the look of my cock, Anna?"

So much I can't tear my gaze away. "Yes."

"You going to take this thick cock inside you?"

My inner muscles clench hard, as if his explicit words were a touch and he knows just how they affect me. Oh god, I'm aching all over, shaking.

"Yes," I answer breathlessly.

"How deep?"

"So deep." Desperate, I pull my knees up against my chest and slide my trembling hands between my thighs, squeezing them tight. The crotch of my jeans *is* soaked but I don't care, because all that wetness will ease his way. "I'll take all of you, Gunner. I need to. Except—"

With the fluid ease of a predator, he eases onto the mattress and starts coming for me, that big cock pointing the way. "Except?"

Licking my lips, I lift my gaze to his. "I know we're tossing slow out the window—but maybe, at first, slow would be good. Because it's been a really long time for me, too."

"I know." Kneeling, he stops in the center of the bed, stroking his cock, gliding his thumb through that pearly drop of precum. His expression is sharp and feral as he looks at me. "Because you didn't want to sort out the good guys from the useless assholes."

No. Because all I wanted was him. "Something like that."

"I just thank God you chose *this* useless asshole."

"Me, too," I laugh, but it falls silent a moment later. Breathless tension tightens around me as his next words drop like stones between us, a hard command.

"Lie back and take off those jeans."

Fingers trembling, I do, aware of his hungry gaze ravenously taking in every inch I reveal. Shucking my jeans and panties over the side of the bed, I lean back and boldly spread my legs, my feet beside each of his knees.

But he's not looking at my pussy. Instead he's bracing his hands beside my hips and bending his head over my thigh—over the giant bruise—and gently pressing his lips against the edge of the contusion.

"This, too," he says gruffly, and I know he's adding to his earlier apology, but I can't even think. Not with him so close. Not with so much skin and heat.

Pushing against the headboard, I shimmy down the

bed, sliding my body farther under the muscular torso braced above me. "Gunner, *please*."

"Please?" He catches my hands again and avoids my seeking lips, his pale gaze locked to mine, his big body motionless over me. "Ah god, sweetheart. I've dreamed of this for so long. Tell me what you need."

Hoarsely I answer, "Just you."

For so long.

Groaning, he captures my mouth. His steely thighs push mine wider, and I feel the length of his shaft sliding through my wet folds, hot and thick.

Abruptly he stills and hangs his head, body shivering like iron struck by a sledgehammer. "Anna?"

My fingernails dig into my palms. "Hurry."

"Tell me I can fuck you bare." His voice sounds strangled. "Because I don't have a single goddamn condom. But I was tested for STDs before my operation and I swear to God there's been no one else since I met you."

No one for me, either. And I can't get pregnant.

"You can," I say and all at once he's kissing me again, claiming my mouth with deep, drugging thrusts of his tongue between my lips.

Fucking my mouth. I need him fucking *me*.

Kissing him back, whimpering with need, I arch my hips toward his. And suddenly can't breathe when I feel the blunt tip of his cock parting my slippery folds, pressing against my entrance.

Gunner breaks the kiss and groans against my ear,

"You're so fucking wet. Sweetheart, you feel so good and I'm not even in you yet."

And *not in me* isn't enough. Desperately I push against him and his groan deepens. He shifts his weight, his back flexing but the pressure just builds and builds, until I'm panting in sobbing breaths against his mouth.

"You're so tight, Anna. So goddamn small." But he's not stopping, thank god, not stopping and he releases my hands to reach down and grip my hip, tilting me up at a new angle and bearing down.

And I'm not small or tight—he's just thick, so thick, forcing my body to stretch and yield to his, pushing inside and claiming me inch by inch, so slowly and completely that he's utterly possessed me before I've taken half of him.

He rears back, braced on one strong arm. His face is a rigid, beautiful mask above me, his glacial eyes blazing. Through gritted teeth, he grinds out, "Anna. Let me in."

I'm trying. But he's so big all over, surrounding me with his powerful body and filling me with his heavy cock, and I'm tense and shaking and letting him in isn't so easy.

Then all it takes is a look—between us, at my thighs spread wide beneath his, at that thick gorgeous cock sinking into my pussy and all at once he slides deeper, deeper, until there's nothing left for me to take.

Another harsh groan rips from him and he claims my mouth, his body unmoving as he leisurely kisses my lips, as if letting me adjust to the feel of the massive length lodged deep inside me.

But I'll never adjust to this. Never get used to the feel of Gunner holding me tight, kissing me in this tender way. Even if I welcome him into my body and my bed every night for the next fifty years, I don't know how I'll ever feel anything but the disbelief and wonder and sheer joy that are coursing through me now.

Then he lifts his head, fingers tangling in my hair. And his gaze burns into me as he says, "I love you, Anna Wall." His voice sounds thick. "I know you don't love me back yet. But if you let me, I swear I'll give you any future you want."

I thought this was a dream. But I was wrong.

I'm dead. And this is heaven.

Silently I stare up at him, hope and fear and joy and all the old hurt building up so high, until he laughs and groans at the same time, gently kissing my lips, then the corners of my eyes.

"No tears, sweetheart. We're going to fix what hurts. I'm going to make you feel so good. Is my cock deep enough?"

So deep. Breath shuddering, I nod.

His fingers tighten in my hair and he says roughly, "But I'm not as deep as I can be," then shoves forward, bottoming out inside me.

I cry out, my back arching, my pussy gripping him tight, so tight.

"Fuck yes." He pushes into me again, so long, so thick. "That good?"

"Oh my god. *Yes.*"

So good I'm sobbing with pleasure against his lips. It's never been like this. I don't know if it's because my delicate tissues are swollen with such fierce arousal or because he's so thick, but my inner muscles are clenched around him, the ache inside me so sharp, as if I'm on the verge of coming, but I never go over. Instead I just hang there on the edge, his cock making it better and worse with every long thrust. My fingers claw at his shoulders. Jaw clenched, he grinds against me before setting a slow, steady pace until I'm begging, writhing beneath him.

"That's it, sweetheart." Neck taut with strain, he bends his head, tastes my panting lips. "Now tell me when I get you just right. When I'm sliding against your clit. When my cock's giving your pussy what you need."

His hand wedges under my ass, lifting me—and I don't have to tell him when he gets it just right. His cock pushes inside me at a new angle, the thick head rubbing hard across the nerves lining my upper wall. My entire body stiffens and clenches, a strangled cry breaking from my lips.

"Just like that, Anna," he groans. "Oh fuck, your pussy squeezes my dick so tight."

His mouth crashes down on mine, kissing me hot and hard, fucking me like he can't get close enough, holding me tight and his cock pushing deep, deep, deep. But I can't take it anymore, and my lips tear away from his, my hands clenching and unclenching on his shoulders.

"Gunner! Please, please—"

He doesn't cease his relentless thrusting. "You going to come, sweetheart? Then come on my cock, baby," he urges roughly. "'Cause when I feel you go off, I'm going to come right up inside you. All my hot cum up inside you. You want that?"

"Yes. *Oh god.*"

Groaning, he licks my open mouth. "Just look at the way I'm filling your cunt. I've never seen anything so damn beautiful as your pussy stretched around my dick, your sweet clit so wet and swollen. Does your pretty clit ache, sweetheart? Do you need more?"

I'll die from more. Each filthy word is like a lick across my clit, and he knows it, he knows it.

"I can't, Gunner—"

Then his fingers are there, too, sliding over my clitoris and his voice like the rasp of a rough tongue. "You like this, Anna? Me playing with your hot little clit with my thick cock pumping deep inside you?"

So deep. With my pussy so tight and I still can't get enough, and I can't make any response but a desperate stuttering moan, my head thrashing as if I'm saying no but he knows I'm not, because he's still fucking me and fucking me.

Harder now, each thrust sharper. "You like me filling you up with my big cock? Filling up every inch of your pussy?"

Yes. But I can't make a sound, my body stretched taut

like a bow and shaking, shaking.

"Then come on me, sweetheart. Let me feel you squeezing me tight so I can fill you with my cum. Because I'm going to come inside you, Anna. I'm going to come so fucking deep inside you — Oh, fuck yes, baby. Like that. You're so fucking beautiful, Anna."

Then he's not talking, but groaning deep as I begin convulsing around him, my hips locked in wild gyrations as if trying to ride his cock harder, deeper. But he's still fucking me, pounding deeper and deeper until his mouth covers mine and his body stiffens and I feel him come, the thick pulse of his cock spilling hot semen deep inside me, triggering more convulsions through my inner walls.

I'm still shaking when he collapses over me, my breath shuddering, crying a little, laughing even more.

Burying my face in his sweaty neck, I wrap my arms around him. "Oh my god, Gunner. I'm a cum slut."

Laughter rolls through his big body as he pulls me over, lying on his back with me straddling his hips — and with his thick cock still a delicious pressure inside me.

"You're *my* cum slut, sweetheart. Because you love everything that comes out of my pouty, filthy mouth." Fingers tangled in my hair, he kisses me, long and deep, then holds my gaze when he lowers his head again. "You're beautiful. And I love you so fucking much."

My heart so full, I stare down at him, my fingers tracing his lips.

"No, Anna. No tears." His beautiful smile flashes, then

he catches my fingers, presses a kiss to my palm while his other hand slides down my back. "I see I'm going to have to make you feel good again."

Swiftly, he rolls me over and claims my mouth in another deep kiss.

And once again, he lasts a hell of a lot longer than ten seconds.

TWENTY SEVEN

ANNA

I DO FEEL GOOD. BETTER THAN I EVER HAVE, MY ENTIRE body boneless as I lay in Gunner's strong arms, our skin covered in sweat. I'm almost half asleep when I force myself to roll over off the bed.

Big hands catch my hips and pull me right back. A deep voice in my ear says, "I still have a real slow one planned."

I grin, tilting my head to rest against his shoulder. "I have to clean up."

His palms slide up the sides of my ribs, cupping my breasts, and I hear the smile in his voice when I shiver against him. "Why? We're just going to get dirty again."

"Okay, well—'clean up' is actually a code phrase for 'I have to pee.'"

"Then stay and we'll get *really* dirty."

Oh my god. I start giggling so hard it might be out of my control in a second. Then he lets me go with a playful swat to my ass, and I get moving, picking up my nightshirt along the way.

"You won't need that," he calls after me, so I turn at the bathroom vestibule to flip him the bird.

And stop, because Gunner naked in bed? Holy shit. I've fantasized seeing him like this a thousand times but the fantasy's not even close to the real thing. He sees me staring and a slow smile spreads over his lips. His big hand slides down his taut stomach to grip his hardening cock.

Arousal and amusement deepen his voice. "You going to stand there and watch?"

I want to. But I really can't.

Rushing into the bathroom, I pull on my nightshirt so I won't freeze while going through the necessary. Then I *do* clean up, washing my hands and using a washcloth between my legs, where I'm sticky and tender.

This definitely isn't heaven. Or a dream.

Because I've never had to wipe away drying cum from the inside of my thighs after dreaming about him. In my fantasies, my face isn't bruised and my lips swollen by anything except his kisses, and I never imagined knowing what I'd smell like with Gunner's scent all over my skin.

And I never thought he'd be so fun and filthy and sexy and intense.

I've imagined him saying *I love you* a billion times, though—and even that was all wrong. Because I had no idea it would feel like this. I imagined triumph and happiness. And there *is* happiness, but also fear and hope and doubt.

Because this *isn't* a dream. But right now, what Gunner and I are sharing doesn't extend beyond the walls of this hotel room. So I'm not even sure if it's real.

I don't know if it ever will be real outside of this room. Not when there are so many factors still keeping us locked in. His family. Finding Stone.

And what happens when I go back home?

But I'll worry about that another time. Right now, I'm grabbing onto this opportunity—grabbing onto him—while I can.

While it lasts.

I brush my teeth and finish up my nightly routine. I'm not sure if he really does have another round in mind, but if he does, I intend to pass out from exhaustion afterward. When I emerge from the bathroom, Gunner's moved to his own bed, sitting up against the pillows with a thick paperback in his hand. I hesitate for a moment, until he throws the covers back and invites me in.

"No wet spot to fight over," he says. "But you have to

be on that side.”

So he’s between door and me. Snapping off the entryway light, I slide between the cool sheets. “That can be our humping bed and this can be our sleeping bed.”

“Nah, I’m pretty damn sure they’ll both be our humping beds.” He draws me closer against his side, his arm coming around me as I pillow my head on his shoulder. “But that’s the beauty of maid service. No dried spots to avoid tomorrow.”

God, he’s so warm. I snuggle in closer. “I guess it’ll also help to throw off any of your brothers who come in and inspect the number of beds we slept in. This way, they’re both used.”

“Yeah.” On a deep sigh, he reaches over and sets the book on the nightstand but doesn’t turn off the light. Instead he settles against the pillows again, his hand smoothing up and down my back. “I’m sorry you had to deal with all that. *All* of it.”

“It could have been worse. I liked the brides. They were nice. And I really liked Grace. Which was *almost* the worst thing—not being able to hate her. Because I kind of wanted to.”

A hint of teasing colors his reply. “Jealous?”

“No.” Not really. “Just…it wasn’t so awesome. Realizing what they had planned for you. And because of this morning.”

Because it hurt so much thinking he’d touched me before heading off to meet his intended wife.

Gunner must realize it, because his amusement's gone. "There's no one but you, Anna. I didn't even think about a bride until earlier tonight. I forgot you'd meet one. I'd have prepared you. I'd have told you all I felt for you before you met her, if I'd realized. And I told my mother that wearing a kutte's as far as I go. I'm not taking a bride."

I believe him. Nodding against his shoulder, I trace my fingers along the defined edge of his pectoral. "How's your family going to react to that news?"

Expecting a quick answer, it surprises me when he takes a moment, then says slowly, "I'm not sure—at least not sure about three of my brothers. Adam, he'll keep pushing me to fall completely in line. Mama will, too. She won't give up."

That sucks. I pull in air through my teeth for a second, then tell him, "I don't think Grace was all that thrilled you showed up."

"I had the same impression—that she was at least uneasy. Which wouldn't be surprising."

"No, it wouldn't be." Meeting some guy and knowing his mother would push you into his bed that same night? That would make any girl uneasy, even if the guy looked like Gunner does. "What really surprises me is that she buys into the whole cult thing. That *any* of the brides buy into it. Because they're all super smart. Which, I realized, is great for the farm. If the end of the world comes, your mother is going to have a doctor, an engineer, a vet, and an agricultural expert who specializes in soil fertility and sustainable crop production. So if one group had to rebuild society…jeez, your mom picked the right women."

"And the men are the muscle."

"Yeah." Suddenly lying against him and only feeling his reactions isn't enough. I come up on my elbow and turn to meet his eyes. "In so many ways, it's kind of awesome. Not to get all 'girl power' about it, but—"

He grins and wraps a strand of my hair around his fingers, tugging gently. "Get all girl power if you want to."

Easy to do. "It's like your mother knows that the world is basically screwed if the important shit is left up to the men."

A laugh shakes through him. "Yes."

"But…oh my god. It's so bad, too. Because it's all based on something so awful."

"Yes." His smile fades.

"So I can see why these women might buy into it. I mean, that place. It's like a utopia. You just have to put up with husbands who stick their dick into anything and who think they're chosen for some special destiny, and also buy into some pretty hefty racism. But, you know, aside from *that*…" I trail off, rolling my eyes.

"Aside from all that," he agrees with another smile, his pale gaze never leaving my face, as if he's enjoying watching me talk almost as much as he is listening to my observations about his family.

"And even the racism is weird. Not even so much, 'I'm superior to you' or 'I'm afraid of you' but like 'You're just fine, but there's no place for you in a peaceful and perfect world.' Oh, and 'Your kind has to be eradicated from this earth before we'll have a true widespread utopia, because there will always be strife between different races. So sorry, no offense. That's just the way it is.'"

"It's self-evident, right?" Shaking his head and grinning, he says, "While we were sitting at lunch Muncher began laying out all this shit that's happened since I've been gone—because, not living on the farm, I wouldn't see the truth of how everything taking place is fulfilling my father's vision of the coming race war. Everything going on overseas, the riots here, illegal immigration. So he's telling me all of this, reminding me that my father was just speaking the truth that no one else wants to hear or has the balls to say. About how it's going to come down to us and them."

"And I'm a them," I say wryly.

"No offense, though. Right?" His tone is light, but he cups my cheek in his big hand, and the warmth there slips through every part of me.

"Right," I agree just as lightly. "But your brothers believe it, don't they? Like *really* believe it. Your mom, too."

"They do."

I study his face for a long second. So like his brothers… yet so different. And I don't know how he did it. He grew up just as they did. "So how'd you get out?"

His gaze searches my eyes, and I don't miss the slight hesitation—as if he isn't sure whether to say.

As if he isn't sure of my reaction.

I press a kiss into his palm. "You don't have to tell me."

"I can," he says. "It's just that there's a long story and a short one."

"The short one first?" I suggest, playfully walking my fingers up the center of his chest. Maybe I'm not quite as tired as I thought I'd be—and I want him to know I'm here, that he doesn't have to be uncertain with me.

"It's not the kind of story that makes you want to fuck after hearing it." There's no anger in his voice. Just something tired and heavy. "Come here."

I scoot closer and he slides his arms around me, pulling me back down to pillow my head against his shoulder again. So I *can't* see his face, I realize.

His hand slips into my hair, brushing it back from my cheek. So he can watch me, judge my expressions.

Maybe worried what I'll think of him.

I spread my hand over his heart. Wait for him to start.

"The immediate reason I left was David," he says after a minute. "I told you Adam killed his girl."

"Yes."

"Shot her on her way home from school. Left her in a ditch. No witnesses. And no one looking at him—they looked at David for a minute, but Adam made sure it wouldn't come back on him. He did it when David and Mama and me were in San Francisco one day. But David guessed, or he figured it out, or maybe he overheard something. I don't know how. But he knew. And it just fucking broke him."

His voice is deeper, rougher. I slide my hand across his chest to curl around his side and hold on tight.

"And those days we were always working our asses off. Always some chore or another. That afternoon we were out at the woodpile up behind Mama's house, splitting logs into firewood. Which means I was the one working, because by then everyone except me and David were patched in to the Few. That meant my older brothers and my father sat around smoking and drinking while David and I worked. Sometimes David and I bitched about it, but it was essentially how we served our time as prospects."

In the club hierarchy. "So David wasn't there?"

"Not at first. But he does finally come out our way. And I'm tired and hot, and I know he's torn up bad over Ivy but one way we've always gotten through shit together was working so hard we didn't have time to dwell on what hurts. So I tossed him the ax. And he went after our father with it. Chopped halfway through his neck."

Oh my god. "Killed him?"

"Yeah. After a minute or two, bleeding out."

"Why not Adam?"

"Because my father was the club's prez. David knew that even if Adam fired the gun, he wasn't acting on his own initiative."

So the orders came from their father. "Did David go after Adam then?"

"Maybe he would have. But Adam's hauled off and

knocked him down. Benjamin and Jacob and me are trying to save Prophet, and Isiah's on his crutches and shouting for Mama. Then she comes running out, and Adam goes to intercept her, because he's thinking that she doesn't need to see what's happened to our father. But of course nothing's keeping her away from him. And in that time David picks up that ax again and heads for her, shouting that he knows she made the decision. But before he can get to her, Adam pulls his gun and shoots him. Three bullets in his chest and gut."

His voice is thick and I don't know what to say. So I just keep holding him.

"So I go to him. Everyone else is around Prophet, though he's already dead, and my mama's screaming for him to come back to her, but David's lying there bleeding on the fucking ground—"

Abruptly he stops. His chest shudders on a breath. Once. Twice. My eyes burning, I press my lips to his shoulder.

He starts again. "So I go to him. And he's choking and can barely say anything—I tell him not to say anything—but he does. He tells me, 'Promise me you'll find something better.' And I know he's talking about leaving the farm. Because we'd talked about it so many damn times. I don't know if I ever would have, though, without him."

"But you did," I whisper.

"Yeah, I did. Signed up with the recruiter that same

week. Left as soon as I graduated." His lips press to the top of my head. "So a good thing came out of it. The other good thing is that's how they got Adam. His gun went missing after he shot my brother and the ballistics weren't solid, but the cops put two and two together quick, and matched the bullets that killed Ivy Tan to the ones Adam used to stop David. It's only bad fucking luck that the science they used then is shit now and his conviction was overturned."

"Yes." And he's right. That's not the kind of story to have sex after. "And the long story?"

"Not longer to tell, really. Just it took place over a longer time. Because I was trying to get out before I ever left."

I remember what he said before. "By reading?"

"Both David and I did. We were twins, did I tell you? Not just looking like each other. Shared a room up in Mama's house, always passing what we're reading back and forth. So we were both thinking outside what my father was saying—but I don't know if I could have done that by myself, either."

"Why?"

"The way my father was—he wanted us reading. Wanted us challenging him. So we did and he got a kick out of it. And he could always, *always* twist whatever we were saying back around until it supported what he believed in. Today, talking to him, I could probably see how he did it—how he builds up straw men, uses so many false equivalencies, stacking the deck with facts that suit him. But to a couple of teenagers trying to poke holes, it was like nothing ever touched him. And without being able to talk with David after, trying to unravel some of the bullshit—maybe I'd have just accepted it all. But we did talk. Especially about leaving."

"And then you did."

"Yeah." A soft chuckle rolls through his chest. "And then I just stayed quiet."

"What? Why?"

"Because I was never sure what would come out of my mouth." When I tilt my head to look up at him, he drops a kiss to my lips before sitting back again. "When you grow up, thinking one way, sometimes you don't even realize you think things you don't want to think. So you start trying to change it. But it's an effort."

"Like renovating a house." Or close enough. "Because maybe the wallpaper is pretty but the plaster beneath is rotten. And you don't know until you start peeling away that wallpaper that you've got a hell of a lot more work to do than you thought."

"Yeah. That's exactly it." He pauses. "The Marines was the farthest thing from the pure community at home as I could get. And the shit that popped into my head some-times…it was all those years of living on the farm. Not anything I actively thought or believed in, but was just sitting there in my head. Like my first deployment, there was this Arab guy in my battalion. Real good guy. But now and then these thoughts would just get into my head that he was going to turn on his brothers. Because I grew up hearing it. And shit, we were in Iraq. So there's my father's voice saying, 'He's going to side with his own kind.' But this Marine, he was *so* fucking loyal. I knew it. So I'd watch every word that came out of my mouth, and make sure it was what I wanted to say, not my family saying it for me. And I spent years being uncomfortable in my own fucking head."

So he wouldn't make anyone else uncomfortable. "Are you still?"

"Not so much. Now and again, sure. Shit pops up and I wonder where it came from. Sometimes it's me. No one's that fucking perfect and there's all kinds of noise slipping in."

"Like calling girls 'club pussy'?"

"Yeah." His lips twitch. "Sometimes that's to piss off Zoomie, though."

"But not always."

"No, not always," he admits. "Sometimes that's me. And other things, sometimes that's me, sometimes it's that old shit."

My chest is tight. How much of that old shit? "You were always quiet around me."

"Yeah, I was."

"What pops into your head that you don't want to say?"

"Things like, I bet your pussy tastes real damn good after you've come around my cock."

My gaze flies up to meet his, pale ice burning with humor and need. Instantly a familiar ache deepens between my legs. "Really?"

"That's just to start. So, Anna, sweetheart"—abruptly he flips me over onto my back, begins sliding down, kissing his way past my navel while I try to catch my breath—"Hush now. Because I've got a decade of being quiet to make up for."

LATER, IN THE DARK, WITH exhaustion pulling me down, what pops into my head are doubts. So many doubts. Remembering all those years of Gunner staying away from me. Wondering what's so different now, if he loved me then, too.

Was it just because I was hurt and Chef threatened to come back again? But what happens when I'm back home and his family is still a threat? Will he stay away from me again to keep me safe?

It just doesn't seem like anything has changed. The only difference is here, in this hotel room.

"That's a heavy fucking sigh," Gunner says quietly, pulling me closer. "You all right?"

"Yeah. Just…wondering how this is going to work. After we get Stone back."

"You worried I'll ask you to stay here—near my family? Because I wouldn't. We'll be going back home."

"So you'll be with the Hellfire Riders again?"

He's quiet. Not because he's holding something back,

I realize. But because the question hurts him.

"Gunner?"

"I can't," he says, his voice thick. "I gave my word when I patched in with the Few. I'm a member permanent."

Pain twists through my chest. A trade he made so they'd help find my brother. "Then how are you going back home?"

"They need something from me. They were willing to offer something else in exchange but…it's no good. So I'll ask for nomad status in return."

So he'd still wear the Notorious Few's kutte. He just wouldn't live here. "But you still wouldn't be a Rider."

"No." A hard kiss presses to the top of my head. "I'll be a member of the Few, keeping up my part. Wearing the kutte. Coming here when they need me. Doing the jobs they need me to do. But having you, having Stone back safe — it's worth it."

But will still hurt him, because it will be a line drawn between him and the Riders who've become his brothers.

Throat aching, I nod against his shoulder. "And your family? You said your mom and Adam would never accept you being with me."

Voice harsh, he says, "And if there's a single fucking threat—"

My phone rings, the screen lighting up on the night-stand. For a second I look at it stupidly, wondering who the hell is calling at this hour, then my heart jolts up into my throat.

Oh my god.

I leap for it, my hands trembling, and I hear Gunner saying behind me, "Record, Anna," and I go through the motions we practiced after installing the app that will record a phone conversation, pressing the right number on the keypad to activate the recording before hitting the speakerphone.

"Hello?" The word trembles and a brief pause has my heart rate spiking with panic and fear. "Stone?"

His familiar deep voice suddenly comes through. "How you doing, pipsqueak?"

A sob rushes out of me but I can't stop to cry. "I'm all right and I love you. Daisy's okay, too."

"Good. Now tell Gunner that me and Crash had a real bad argument, and I—"

And silence. I wait breathlessly but there's nothing more. Just the phone disconnecting after the silence continues for a few seconds.

I turn wild eyes on Gunner. Tension whitens his jaw and every muscle in his body is rigid. "What did he mean—him and Crash? He crashed? Or does that mean a person that he fought with?"

A real bad argument.

"It means a person," he says hoarsely and pulls me close, buries his face in my hair. I'm shaking uncontrollably against him. "And it's nothing good. But this call will make it better, all right? I need to tag Blowback, get this trace started."

I nod and he pulls back, cupping my face.

"You did good, sweetheart. You told him just what he'll need to hear."

I hope so. I just pray it's enough to find him.

TWENTY EIGHT

ANNA

"I thought I'd find you out here," Grace calls out.

I look away from the canvas I'm working on and see Grace walking up the hill toward Gunner's truck, where I've got an easel set up in the truck bed. Her cheeks are flushed with cold and her vest zipped all the way to her chin.

"Yeah, I'm here," I call back, smiling. Because the alternative right now is being in Marian's house and that's not so fun.

But Grace's company is more than welcome. It's been almost a week since we arrived in Santa Rosa, almost a week since Stone called. Almost a week since he told me he loved me. And each day since I've been driving Gunner's truck out to the farm, with him tailing me on his motorcycle until he heads out to the clubhouse.

I miss riding behind him on his bike, but he's been on and off the property since patching in, and having his truck gives me the option to leave whenever I want to—and gives me the option of bringing in canvases and paints, parking the truck up away from the houses and working on my landscapes.

In the afternoon, at least. In the mornings, I'm usually helping Johanna with her chores—an arrangement that suits us both, since it gets Marian off her back and makes me feel like less of a lazy interloper.

And keeping busy helps keep me from worrying…a little. We haven't heard anything yet about the trace on my phone.

But hopefully Gunner can learn more today. I don't know many details, but he and the other Few headed out early on a run with the Iron Blood—and Gunner thinks they have a connection to the Cage.

Grace climbs up into the truck, parks her butt on the tire well. "Nice," she tells me, nodding to the painting.

I like it, too. But then, it's inspired by an amazing view—the olive groves rolling down into the shallow valley, the stark afternoon light.

"But not particularly useful," I say.

She grins and passes over an insulated mug, which I take gratefully. The coffee's more bitter than I like but my hands are chilled, and warming my fingers up on the sides of the container is worth about a thousand sugars.

"So dinner yesterday," Grace says in the way I've come to understand isn't actually the beginning of a remark, but *is* the remark. Just her way of opening up a subject.

And dinner yesterday was Thanksgiving dinner at Marian's house—though it wasn't technically Thanksgiving. But the farm store was open through Thursday, so the family has a tradition of celebrating the holiday on Sunday, instead.

"It wasn't too bad." Kind of fun with the huge family there, all the kids. Everyone loud and getting along.

"You and Zachary left early."

"Yeah, we did." I take another sip before handing her the coffee. "It was hard. Missing my mom and dad. And Stone."

And because Gunner and I wanted to spend the rest of the evening in bed. Which we did.

This week, we've been going back early to the hotel as often as we can. And he hasn't once run out of dirty things to say.

Grace slides me a wry look. "I suppose Marian didn't help."

"Maybe not." She hasn't given up on pushing Grace in his direction.

She picks at a stray thread at the hem of her vest. "He's not such an asshole."

Everything inside me tightens. "You think so?"

"I guess that's why he was gone. He's not like them." She glances up at me, then suddenly sits up straight, shaking her head. "Oh no. I don't mean it that way. Okay, maybe I shouldn't be saying anything, but—there's something between you two, isn't there?"

"No." At least not that I'm going to share. Because I really like her. I think I could trust her. But I'm not risking Stone.

"Yeah. Okay. You're afraid to say, and I don't blame you. So I'll give you something." She leans back against the side of the truck bed, stretching her arms out along the rail. "I'm not here to be a bride. You know why I'm here?"

I shake my head.

"My girl Shari met Benjamin about five years ago. And she started coming out here a lot, and so I was here, too. Then three years ago, I was finishing up my four-year degree, looking ahead at med school. And I realize Marian's starting to…treat me a little different. So she comes to me and basically says, 'I have a son who will eventually be coming home. I think you'd be a great match for him. So here's a house you can live in for free—and, oh yeah, we'll pay for med school, because we'll need a doctor around. You just can't screw any other dudes before he comes back.'"

My jaw is somewhere near the floor of the truck bed. "Seriously?"

Eyebrows arched high, she nods. "Not in so many words, but… Yeah. And I would have said no, except that it seemed—aside from Marian—that everyone else believed Zachary was never coming back. So I figured what the hell. And the bonus was, I could be here with Shari."

Sharon—Muncher's wife. Who's sweet and quiet. Every now and then I glimpse a few sharper, tougher edges in her, but mostly she just looks tired and sad.

Which isn't really surprising.

Eyeing Grace carefully, I venture, "You know what goes on in the clubhouse?"

"Yeah. Not just the clubhouse." She takes another sip before passing the coffee to me again. "Benjamin and Jacob slept with Erin while Adam was in prison to make sure she got pregnant after her conjugal visit with him—slept with her at the same time, so there was no telling who the father was. Any baby would just be Adam's. And while he was gone all the brothers regularly saw to her needs. They just used condoms so a baby wouldn't come at the wrong time."

My jaw is down around my feet again.

"And Shari asked me to join her and Benjamin." With a brief grin, she watches me struggle to figure out how to react to that, then laughs and continues, "Shari and I have been close before. In *that* way, yes. Exactly as you're thinking. Marian knows it, too. But as long as I wasn't with a man, I was still suitable. And still a virgin because *this* doesn't count."

With a wicked grin, she holds up two fingers and pumps them up and down.

I'm laughing and still dumbfounded. "You're really serious."

Grace nods. "Right? They're so open-minded in some ways and so bigoted in others. It's kind of dizzying. But it's so easy to get sucked in. Shari met Benjamin and that was it. Bam. Just crazy for him. And we were together then but were more like friends with benefits and…"

She trails off with a shrug.

"Yeah." I know what the shrug means. I've done it myself a couple of hundred times.

"Anyway, they all felt that I should be taken care of while waiting for Zachary to return. And I figured, what the hell. The only rule was no penetration, which is fine. Because guys don't do it for me, really. But Benjamin, Jesus. He can suck on a clit like a hungry baby on a bottle."

I've seen him. But… "Is that supposed to be a *sexy* image? Because babies and clits? No."

Her laughter rolls out hard and she shakes her head. "I guess not. I have babies on my mind lately. Not my babies." All at once her amusement's gone and she looks out over the groves. "Shari's having a rough time lately."

"Because of the cheating?"

"Kind of. I mean, you would never know he was. The way Benjamin is around her, I'd have said he'd never touch someone else. But he's like, I'm born this way."

Give me a fucking break. I don't say anything but she glances over with a look that says exactly the same thing I'm feeling.

Then she sighs. "The thing is, it's hard. Because Shari and I both have had people tell us, you know, being with other girls—that's a choice, not the way we are. They say we weren't born this way. So sometimes it feels like, Okay, yeah. Maybe Benjamin's born without that monogamous trait. And other times it's like: That's not the same as being attracted to a certain gender. That's just not having enough self-control to keep from jumping everyone you *are* attracted to, so maybe you could try a little fucking harder."

Yep. But I just nod.

"And she knew about the club girls before they got married. There wasn't any deception on his part. It was just, that's at the clubhouse, this is the farm, they're separate parts of his life." Pausing, she looks down at her cup, absently swirling the contents. "Then she had her second baby about a year ago and kind of went into a funk after. We all thought it was postpartum depression. And she's seen people for it, gotten care for it. But, you know…I think she's just unhappy with how things are."

I would be. But again, I only nod.

This time Grace seems to realize it. "I'm unloading on you, aren't I?"

"It's okay." It helps her to talk and I like learning more about the Cooper family. "It makes sense. You don't want to unload on Shari, maybe make her burden worse. But telling anyone else? How would it make sense to them?"

"Yes. It helps that you understand." She slants me a laughing glance. "But that's not the only reason. Unlike some of the brides, I also know you're not going to tell Marian."

"No, I'm not," I agree, laughing.

She grins in response but it quickly fades.

Watching her, I carefully say, "What happens if Marian knows? Are you afraid of her interfering? Or just afraid?"

A sigh is joined by the helpless spread of her hands. "A little of both. Because Shari hasn't *said* she's going to leave Benjamin. But there have been a few times when I felt as if she was *this close* to saying something like it."

"And that worries you—what the family will do?"

"Yeah. No." She licks her lips in agitation. "I don't know. There was another bride, Emily. She was Isiah's wife."

"I did wonder," I admit, because I've heard her name mentioned but she was never around. "I just figured she was an astronaut or neurosurgeon or maybe out being a superhero."

"No." Grace's smile fades quickly again. "An accountant. Smart as hell with numbers, and pretty, but in a quiet way. Kind of on the mousey, timid side. So Isiah blows into her life."

Six-Point. I can imagine how that went. "He's hard not to like."

Grace nods. "Yeah. And before you know it, Marian's got them sealed up tight. But right away it starts going bad. And you know what, I'll give him credit where it's due. He tried. He did stop fucking around."

"Really? How do you know?"

"Because the others gave him crazy shit for it. Apparently he wasn't touching any of the club girls. So I think he did care about her. As much as he could."

"But it still didn't work?"

"No. For a while, it seemed, maybe it would. Then she got pregnant and she was unhappy because he was on her too much. Always needing to fuck. So he backed off but he was frustrated and angry, and she was angry and trapped. And the fights, Jesus. You could hear them shouting at each other. Emily yelling how she would leave and take the baby. Then Marian steps in and—she's a lawyer, did you know?"

"No. But at this point, I'm not really surprised."

Grace laughs. "Yeah, I guess not. She doesn't really have a practice, just keeps her license current and she advocates for local farmers, property rights, pro bono work for neighbors, that kind of thing—and she represents the Few when they get into trouble. Anyway, she went to Emily and basically said, go ahead and get your divorce. But try to take the baby, and Marian would make sure she was ruined professionally, declared unfit, and Isiah given full custody. And she knows all the local judges, and so on."

"Holy shit."

"She scared the crap out of Emily. But pissed her off, too. Then she had the baby and a week later she was gone. Just up and left. She wasn't waiting around for the divorce or for Marian to ruin her."

Holy shit again. I stare at her. "So what happened?"

"Isiah was just…hurt. And I think kind of pissed at Marian, because he said she scared Emily away with that custody talk. Marian's pissed, too, because the baby's gone, but Isiah was only talking about Emily. Asking, *What could I have done?*" Grace pauses, bites her lip. "I don't think there was anything. It just wasn't going to happen. But he wanted to go after her, and Marian told him, no no—let your brother go. You're too emotional and you'll just fight again. She's mad at you but your brother can talk her into coming back. So she sent Jacob after Emily."

Oh god. Strawman? My skin prickles with dread. "What happened then?"

Grace spreads her hands again. "I don't know really. He came back with the baby, and some papers signing over custody—Johanna's raising him as her boy now. And Jacob said Emily told him that she didn't want Isiah anymore, that she wasn't coming back. And she didn't want custody because she didn't want any reminder of her time on the farm or with Isiah. So she was going to get as far away as possible and to never contact her again."

Because I feel it coming, I say, "But?"

"That's just it. I don't know. Maybe it was just like Jacob said. And if it was, I can't blame her. I've looked her up, you know. Googled her. But she was a Jones. You know how many Emily Joneses are out there? Even if she kept her married name, Emily Cooper, there's still so many. And that's *only* if she didn't deliberately start using another name so Isiah couldn't track her down." Her lips press together and she shakes her head. "But maybe there's nothing left to find."

"Jesus." I was thinking it, but she came out and said it. I'm not sure if that's brave or stupid, outright saying Strawman might have killed her.

Or maybe she just doesn't know MCs that well.

"Yeah." She gives me a look that says she knows exactly how crazy the idea is—and how not-crazy it is. "And Jacob, you know—he doesn't make a move without Marian giving the okay. The only time he crosses her is when it's about Adam. Jesus, he hates Adam."

"I've seen that." And the look of intense pleasure on his face when Gunner was pounding Adam's head in.

"But regarding anything else, Marian's the last word. So what would she have told him to do? If Emily was going to fight for her baby?"

I don't answer, but I know. Marian would tell him to do the same kind of thing that Gunner was afraid would happen to me all of these years. The same kind of thing that happened to Ivy Tan. Because Marian is determined to carry on her husband's legacy—and if Prophet ordered Adam to kill a woman who threatened the children in their bloodline? I have no doubt Marian would tell Strawman to do the same thing.

Grace is studying my face, and whatever she sees there doesn't reassure her. She lets out a long breath, as if she's finished getting all that off her chest. "Yeah. So anyway. I don't even know what to do about Shari."

"I do."

She looks to me, waiting.

I pull out my phone, text my mom to give her a heads-up. "First, I'm going to give you a number to call. You or Shari. It's my mother's cell. You can call her any time, absolutely any time. If you just need to talk this through again, or if you need to discuss options, she can help. And if Shari decides to go, if she needs protection, there are places that can shelter you, okay? I don't know their names but my mom can get them for you. And then Shari can be supported while she's negotiating all the other stuff—custody, divorce, whatever."

"Okay."

"The second option is—if she doesn't want to try negotiating, or thinks Marian's going to pull some crazy legal shit, just drive her and her kids straight to Pine Valley, Oregon, and this place called the Wolf's Den. Maybe I'll be there and working. If not, ask for Saxon Gray. Say you're my friend, you need help and that you need to disappear. He'll do it." He'll give me a whole lot of shit for springing someone on him, but he'll do it. "And you can either disappear forever or just until Shari gets her life back together enough to figure out what to do then."

Grace is slowly nodding as she listens, her eyes shimmering. "Thanks," she says thickly. "I don't know if it'll come to that. But it helps to know there's something."

"I know what it's like to feel helpless." Cancer is a different reason, but the fear is the same. "Having options always helps."

She wipes at her eyes. "I can tell it's not your first time."

"Hah, well. I work at a bar. Some people who come in need more help than a bottle can give. And my brother has a habit of attracting girls who need it, too."

Sighing, she nods, then her gaze sharpens. "Any word on him? I know it's club business, so they won't say much. But...?"

"Not much," I say softly. "But I hope soon."

TWENTY NINE

GUNNER

Stone's call is a dead end. It came from a burner phone purchased three years ago with cash, and made from a location along an empty highway. So the fuckers probably drove Stone out into the desert, let him make the call, then drove a few hours back to the Cage in whatever direction they'd come from.

And I didn't expect much from the trace. Not when every single MC around uses burners. But I'd hoped Stone would get a chance to get a message out.

Instead, Jesus—I just hope I misunderstood him.

Tell Gunner that me and Crash had a real bad argument.

Because if it means what I think it does—that if Crash was the man Stone went up against in the Cage—then it means Stone had to kill a Bedlam Butcher.

He had to kill a friend.

And we've been through some shit together. But nothing that could rip a man's soul out like killing a friend would.

But I'm hoping I'm wrong. So I haven't even told the Butchers yet. Instead I'm riding through some back roads in northern California, escorting a van loaded with shit we aren't supposed to ask about—and trying to keep my mind occupied, so I don't reach for the weapon holstered at my side, aim it at the Iron Blood fucker who's riding point, and blow a hole through his goddamn helmet.

Chef. Who should have been dead within hours after touching Anna.

His day's coming. But the bastard's got a few more yet.

And goddamn fucking Stone and his goddamn useless message. That's what he shares? He and Crash had an *argument*? I didn't expect him to rattle off map coordinates but I thought for damn sure he'd give more than that. I've even had Blowback ask some of his intelligence contacts to look for any coded shit. Not that Stone's that damn clever.

It eats at me, though. Because he's not going to talk

in code. But Stone *is* smarter than that. Maybe he couldn't get enough of the message out and they cut him off too soon for it to make sense. I don't know.

I just feel like I'm missing a big flashing arrow — especially because he told Anna to tell *me*. Not to tell the Riders or Saxon, though he had to know that after she was attacked the Hellfire Riders would be looking out for her.

He couldn't know Anna was with me. Stone would assume I'm away from Pine Valley and away from Anna, while looking for him. But he wanted her to give that message to me.

And somehow I'm failing him.

But I'm on the right road. Because when we hit the end of our run, we hand the van off to the Desert Kings. Shaggy, the source Stone and I were supposed to meet in Cactus Gulch — the source who never showed — rode with the Kings.

Shaggy's not riding with them now.

So dead, maybe. Maybe just got scared and ran off. But the dots are all lining up. I just can't see where they're pointing yet.

ON THE RETURN TRIP WE stop at a roadside joint to seal the new alliance between the Few and the Iron Blood — a suggestion made by Strawman, and with the Iron Blood more than happy to go along as soon as he said the Few would be footing the bill.

Shit. So that's where I learned that. Open up a tap,

get people talking, make them start feeling an obligation to you. Something I've done more than once as the Hell-fire Riders' sergeant at arms. But it was straight out of Strawman's playbook.

But it's not my play tonight. It's all his.

Instead I sit with my brothers and try not to stare a hole through Chef's big skull. I've got other shit to manage. Adam's restless. No girls came along on this run and I can see him slowly tensing up, and he's looking through the local women. A lot of them are looking back, but when he gets in a mood, he doesn't just want to fuck. He'll want to fight. So he'll go after a woman who's already taken so he can fuck up the man she's with before he fucks her.

Across the bar, Strawman's talking to Paladin as planned. But he's only chatting a second before he goes from Paladin to Chef.

So what happened there? Did Paladin point him to the Iron Blood's enforcer to get more info?

I don't fucking know. But I'm going to keep my ass in this chair, because if I get that close to Chef, there's a damn good chance the Iron Blood and the Notorious Few will be walking out of here as enemies instead of allies.

Those of us that walk out at all.

Adam gets up and heads to the bar. I glance at Muncher, who sighs and follows him.

Alone at the table with me, Six-Point says, "So you give any thought to our problem?"

The only problem I care about is finding Stone. But

he's talking about Adam. They offered me Anna in return for taking him down. But I'll be asking for a nomad's patch, instead, because after this is through I don't want Anna anywhere near the farm.

But I only say, "Yup"—because now is not the time to be discussing it. I've got eyes on Strawman and Chef. Shit looks real easy between them. Not how I expected it to look if Strawman's poking him about the Cage. But maybe he's winding up to it. "You ever deal with Chef?"

Six-Point shakes his head. "Strawman's the only one who does."

"So he has before?"

"Chef's the one who came to Strawman asking the favor."

Asking Adam to get some fucker off of Paladin's back while they were in prison. "Is Chef the one who's bringing in the Few on this relay thing?"

"That's my understanding."

We both shut our mouths as Paladin comes over, gestures with his bottle to the empty chair next to Six-Point. "All right if I sit?"

"Knock yourself out, man." Six-Point reaches out to bump the other man's fist. "We're here to make friends."

Paladin grins, sits. Then looks to me, his sharp little eyes narrowing. "Weren't you wearing a different kutte the last time I saw you?"

"Me?" I shake my head. "You ain't ever seen me or this vest."

He scoffs and takes a drink, eyeing my kutte. "You sure? Because I've seen your face before. And that leather's pretty fucking new."

"Because my last kutte pretty fucking saved my life. And if you've seen my brothers, you've seen this face."

"Yeah, that's for fucking sure." He looks to Six-Point, grins. But he's not letting it go. "What'd you mean, it saved you?"

"What I mean is, last month I was out riding, and some asshole in a cage tossed his bottle out the window—one of them fucking sissy tea drinks that looks like kangaroo cum juice. The neck of the bottle got up in my front wheel and just"—I jerk my hands to the side like my handlebars are being wrenched out of my grip—"right into a fucking guard rail. Next thing I'm flying over the embankment and into this tree. And I'm fucking hanging there, on this broken branch, because when I hit the branch the fucker snapped. And the sharp end turned the whole damn thing into a spear this fucking big around. But instead of going through me, by some goddamn miracle it went right up here along my side and through the back of my kutte. So I'm hanging there like I'm on a meat hook. And this lady who was in a cage behind me and saw the whole thing is calling from the side of the road, 'You alright, mister? You need some help?'"

I shake my head, finish up. "No, lady. I'm just fucking hanging in a tree, having a good time. Don't need any goddamn help."

Paladin's laughing, shaking his head. Because there's nothing any biker likes better than hearing about some crazy wrecks — especially the ones a rider walks away from.

"Anyway," I tell him, "I've got that kutte framed and hanging up. These bastards said to just patch it up, but I like it up on my wall. I figure I'll put it next to a picture of that tree and memorialize the whole miraculous event. Besides," I lower my voice, lean in. "It was some cheap fake leather shit. This one's better."

He nods. "These runs work out for you, no worries there. You'll be picking up a lot better."

With plenty of money coming into the club.

I glance over at the bar. Adam's not talking up any girl. He's looking back at us — then heading our way, Muncher behind him.

Six-Point leans in. "Is there a lot of work available? Because this was a fucking cakewalk. We'd sign up for a lot more of this."

"There's more of this. And better jobs up the line. Me, I'm working up to the enforcer's spot." With a lift of his chin, he indicates Chef across the way. "He's the one who gets the good jobs."

Something in his tone and the lift of his eyebrows hints at what's good about those jobs.

And Six-Point's all over it. "You talking girls?"

"Sometimes. Especially when someone needs persuading. Jesus, his last one? He tells me he plowed her so hard he made her bleed. Enjoyed it so fucking much he didn't take the video he was supposed to. Just showed her crying after. The sweetest face, the sweetest tits." He shakes his head and has no fucking idea that I'm sitting across from him, thinking about how easy slicing his throat open would be. "Shit. I would have liked watching that one."

Hard hands clamp down on my shoulders. Muncher. Maybe heard enough to know that holding me down right now is real fucking smart or real goddamn stupid.

Adam drops into the vacant chair, a hard smile on his lips. "You talking about other jobs? I hear mouthing off got you into trouble before."

"Nah," Paladin says, but he's looking a little uneasy, tossing a quick glance over toward Chef. As if the enforcer might be able to hear him talking club business. "Your brother was telling me about hanging from a tree."

His fingers still digging into my shoulders, Muncher says, "The fucking bottle story?"

"I was telling him why I needed a new kutte," I say flatly. They know the story well.

It's Prophet's story. And more proof that he was chosen for a special destiny, because he should have been dead. Instead a tree saved him.

"Shit," Muncher says, his voice carefree and his hands locked on me like bear traps. "You know the best part of that story? That lady who called in for help, we go to her house later to say thanks. Take her some flowers." Which is what he and Prophet really did. "And she's looking at us up and down, and he's all, ma'am, let us thank you another way. And she did let us. Jesus, she had the sweetest fucking pussy."

Paladin grins appreciatively before running his gaze over us. "How many are you?"

"Five brothers," Adam says.

"And another up in Oregon? Patched in with the Hellfire Riders?"

Adam's face tightens. "He's not our brother. He left to ride with another club. He's dead to us."

Six-Point looks surprised by that. His gaze flicks up over my head—looking at Muncher, whose hands loosen on my shoulders.

So maybe just dead to Adam. I can live with that real easy.

Paladin's nodding as if he's not surprised. "So you're making him pay? I like it."

Six-Point looks at him in friendly confusion. But Six-Point isn't lacking any brains and he's rarely confused. "Making him pay how?"

That fox-like face closes up. "You know. Shutting him out. That's hard on a brother. Anyway—" Abruptly he stands. "I'll let you all get back to it. Nice riding with you."

Fuck. I push up out of my chair.

Adam's hand on my arm stops me. "No, brother. He's a cop."

"What?"

"Either a cop or in a cop's pocket." He leans back in his chair. "That bastard they had me go after in the pen?

I was curious about why they needed him gone. Because he beat up Paladin a few times?" He scoffs. "It's fucking prison. A beating is like saying it's Tuesday."

I sit back down. "So how do you know?"

"Like I said, I was curious. So I told the poor fucker I'd make it quick if he told me. He did. And apparently, he was saying what I just told you—that little Paladin fucker is either a cop or he's squealing for one. Because Paladin had a cell mate who was saying things inside and it was going into ears outside—and feds were raiding shit they shouldn't even know about. A whole lot of busts, a whole lot of territory shifting hands. And the Iron Blood ends up with plenty of it. So either Paladin's building his career or he's building someone else's. So you be real fucking careful around him."

I nod. Better to be. But, shit—that's real interesting.

If he's a cop, and he knows where the Cage is but he's not giving up the location? Then he's a real dirty cop.

And if he's just an informant, those favors might be going both ways. Like someone in the FBI telling him when to look sharp and when to cover and run. The prez told me there was a leak somewhere. That's why Blowback's source was playing this tight to his chest.

So I'll pass that info to Blowback. He might be able to squeeze something out of the bastard, because it doesn't look like I'll be touching him.

I've got someone else to focus on. I look to Chef. "Does Strawman know about Paladin?"

Adam shrugs. "Don't know. And I'm not going to share."

Like fucking little boys. Not brothers.

I sit back and shake my goddamn head.

THIRTY

ANNA

Gunner gets back late. He sent me a text around midnight, telling me they were still a few hours out. So I went to bed and tried to sleep but just lay there, thinking I should just give up and grab one of his books or turn on the TV, but then telling myself that if I give it a few more minutes I'll fall asleep.

But a few more minutes turns into three hours, and I'm still lying awake when I hear the soft knock at the door.

Because he's got a keycard, but after Strawman got in simply by asking for a card at the front desk, we've been using the security latch.

Lightly I run to the door, praying he got the info he needed. One look at his expression tells me he didn't.

"I'm sorry, sweetheart." Strain and exhaustion shadow his face. "Strawman couldn't pull anything out of the fucker. Nothing about the Cage, nothing about the fighters."

And he must be *really* tired if he's telling me that—giving me details instead of vague bits of info. But although my heart drops, I don't show it. Just draw him into the room.

"It's okay," I say. "We'll still find another way."

His nod is barely a dip of his chin. And by now he'd usually wrap me up in his arms, even if he is tired, even if we are heading straight to bed—to sleep. Instead he's pulling away, dragging his hands through his hair.

"I need to head down to the gym. Get a workout in."

Really? He works out like it's a religion. Stone does, too. But this is the kind of day they'd usually sin and be well forgiven for it.

I glance at the clock. "I'm pretty sure the weight room closes at midnight."

"A run, then." He tosses his kutte onto the luggage rack. His Hellfire Riders' kutte, he'd have hung up. His T-shirt's next. "I got to get this shit out of me."

"What shit? Gunner"—I stop him with a hand to his arm. "If you need to work something out of your system…I'm right here."

His pale eyes flare before he closes them. "I'm fucking filthy right now, Anna. Seeing that fucker who hurt you. Watching him laugh and drink and knowing he told his brothers what he did. Knowing he showed them that recording he made. Knowing all that, seeing him right there, and not being able to—"

His hands clench so tight there's no doubt what he needed to do. And how he's feeling like a failure now. For not taking out Chef. Because they didn't learn anything new about Stone.

But he's blaming himself for a whole lot of shit that isn't his fault.

Slowly I sink to my knees. "Gunner."

I wait until he looks down at me—his powerful body going utterly still, his expression stark with sudden need.

"My lip's better," I tell him. "You won't be too big for me now."

"Anna." My name is a feral growl through lips whitened by tension. "Unbuckle me, then."

Eagerly my hands go to his belt. Oh god. I've been waiting for this.

And Gunner started out behind me but he's catching up fast. His cock is already hardening. With my cupped palm, I rub him through heavy denim as I work his belt free with my opposite hand.

Roughly he says, "You look hungry for my cock, sweetheart."

Oh shit. Just his voice and I'm clenching my thighs together, holding back a moan. Through my lashes, I glance up at him. I'm not sure which is hotter—the burn of his pale eyes, the thick length of him, or every damn word he says. Maybe it's good he never talked to me at the bar or my house before. I'd have spent the past ten years as a quivering, walking orgasm.

Which, okay. Doesn't sound too bad.

His breath hisses through his teeth as I slowly lower his zipper. "Jesus, Anna. I've dreamed of this."

So have I. Though I never had any idea he was so thick, or that he'd fill my hands like he is. And sometimes I'd fantasize that I'd do this and just overwhelm all of his defenses with sheer need, until he was putty in my hands. And other times I pictured him losing control, needing me, dominating me, forcing me to swallow as much of his cock as I could. But always one of us taking, the other giving.

But it's already both. Already giving pleasure with my hands. Gunner already telling me, "You want to taste that precum, baby? You want to lick it right off me?" as if he knows just how each word pulses through my inner core on a hot erotic beat. And I take a taste for me, and for him, and it's giving and taking and it's so much better than anything I ever dreamed.

"Ah fuck," he groans from low in his chest. "I'm not going to fucking last."

That's what he always says. But he always does. So

I take my time, licking up that broad shaft. Tracing the heavy veins with my tongue, stroking the wet path with my hand.

"You want to suck on me now, Anna?"

Oh god. "Yes." It's a low moan against the wide tip of him just before I open my mouth and take as much as I can. It's not as deep as I want, he's just too thick, but Gunner groans, his abs clenching as he hunches over, his hand in my hair and holding the long strands away from my face.

Watching me suck his cock.

"You like the way I taste?" It's low and rough, then abruptly he adds—"Fuck no, don't answer that, sweetheart, because you'll have to stop."

And I have to stop anyway because laughing chokes me a little, and he's grinning when I'm done coughing and he guides my mouth back to his cock.

"All right?"

My answer is to take him as deep as I can again, loving his groan and the way he thrusts his hips a little before his body tenses again, as if he needs to fuck my mouth and is barely controlling himself.

"Christ." He's staring down at me, arousal etched starkly on every line of his body. "This is better than I ever fucking dreamed. The only thing better is licking your pussy. God, I love sucking on your sweet clit and getting you so damn wet before sliding up inside you. But now I'd get up inside you then have you on your knees again, so you could taste yourself all over my cock. Would you want that, sweetheart?"

I groan around his shaft.

"Fuck yeah. But it's a real bad plan. Because once I get into your pussy I'm not coming out again." Laughing, groaning, he tightens his hand on my hair. "And the next time I'm in you, Jesus—baby, this is how it's going to be. I'm going to have you on your knees, your ass up high. And you'll be screaming into the pillow because I'm going to get so fucking deep."

Oh god. Like he was last time. Desperately I suck harder, my fingers sliding between my legs.

"You just let me know when, sweetheart. You let me know and I'll stuff your sweet pussy full of my thick cock. Or just keep doing this. Just give me a sign and I'll fuck your throat so deep. You want to drink my cum— Oh fuck, no."

Abruptly he's hauling me up against him, his fingers snagging my wrist. Deliberately he brings my hand to his mouth.

My knees almost give out when he sucks the arousal from my wet fingers, one at a time.

"This"–my index finger–"is"–middle finger–"my"–ring finger–"job." And finishing with a long slow lick down my pinky.

I grin at him. "I'm capable of multi-tasking. Plus, I'm good at it."

"At fingering yourself?" Hands on my hips, he starts

walking me back toward the bed. "Why?"

"I did a lot of it in the past ten years."

"Thinking of me?" He's wearing a teasing grin — teasing, because he's playing. He has no idea. "Imagining me fucking you while you rubbed your pretty clit?"

"Yes," I tell him and watch his face darken.

And I don't know why. Don't know why there's the sudden storm in his eyes. But it's there and he's claiming my mouth, kissing me hard, harder, before suddenly whipping me around and pushing me onto the bed.

Just like he said. My ass in the air and —

I scream into the pillow when he roughly fills my pussy, so thick, so deep.

So *good*.

Fingers digging into my hips, he fucks me hard, our skin slapping wetly with every brutal thrust. "Is this better, Anna? Better filled with my cock? Better than alone?"

"Yes." It's a wild moan. "Yes."

"God, it is. Now are you going to come for me? My cock's digging so deep. I want to feel your pussy clamp right down on me, sweetheart. Then I'm going to fuck your mouth, with your sweet pussy juice all over my dick, smearing all over your lips."

Oh my god. His cock slams deep again and I come, not screaming into the pillow but biting it, moaning as my pussy clenches around him again and again, his thick cock stretching me so tight.

I'm huffing against the sheets when he slides out of

me. Ready to taste us both on his cock, I turn toward him, but he just pushes me onto my back and spreads my legs wide.

I cry out as his cock slides into me again. Arms braced beside me, Gunner groans as my pussy envelops his thick length.

"I lied, sweetheart," he says and his voice is like gravel. "I just said that to get you off."

My laughter is just soft and brief because he's moving inside me and I'm so sensitive and already can't get enough again.

"Because your pussy, Anna"—he kisses me long and deep, his tongue stroking into me with the slow ride of his cock—"your pussy, after you come… Christ, you're always so wet and tight but after you come your pussy's even wetter and tighter. Like it needs to come again."

I groan when he grinds deep inside me, arching up against him. "I do need to come again."

"You've got a greedy pussy, sweetheart. You know what a greedy pussy gets?"

I meet his eyes, my hands sliding through his hair. "It gets you."

"That's right. My big thick cock to fill it. And more."

Slowly he sits back, but doesn't take me with him. Instead he grips my hips and hoists my lower body up, my shoulders against the bed, his cock still deep inside me—and his eyes all over me, my hair spread over the pillow, my nipples so tight, my entire body laid out before him.

"Now play with your sweet clit, Anna," he commands, his voice low and harsh. Holding my hips immobile, he slides back and then deep inside me again. "Play with it just like you used to, when you were alone."

Oh god. I do, reaching up. I'm so wet and I can feel him sliding past my fingertips, pushing deep inside me on every stroke.

"But you'll never be alone again." Gaze locked on mine, he fucks me harder, harder, and my fingers work faster, faster. "Never alone again."

Never alone. On a shuddering gasp, I come hard, my body tensing and my clit convulsing beneath my fingers. I have to stop rubbing, it's too much sensation, but he doesn't stop fucking me, groaning as he rocks forward again, his mouth claiming mine for a long endless kiss until he's coming, and I moan as my pussy clenches with every hot pulse of cum his thick cock releases deep inside me.

Breathing harshly against my hair, he rolls over and brings me with him. Quietly I cling to him, savoring the feel of his sweat-slicked skin, his thickness inside me. I'm almost asleep when I feel the sweep of his hand down my back.

His fingers come to rest at the base of my spine. "You have paint on your hands. Did you work on the landscape today?"

"A little."

"Any problems?"

On the farm. "No. I talked some with Grace."

He stiffens. "You okay?"

"Oh. Yes. That wasn't— She's not at all interested in you."

"Good. Easier that way."

"Yeah. She says Shari's not happy."

"Muncher's bride?"

"Yes."

"Are you surprised?"

I smile against his neck, shaking my head. "No. But Grace is a little scared of what might happen if Shari says she wants to leave."

"Did you give her Saxon's info?"

Throat suddenly burning, I hold him so tight. "I was afraid you might be a little pissed—giving a woman advice about how to leave your brother."

"Shit, Anna." His chuckle is low and deep. "I ran away from the farm, too. I'd be giving bus tickets away to every woman there, if I could."

I huff out a silent little laugh.

"You ran away, too," he says.

I lift my head to look at him. "When?"

"All over the world."

"Maybe. I didn't really look at it like that." But I guess it might be considered running away from the future that was coming for me—which I was certain would be sickness and death.

"Then you stopped." His callused thumb brushes over my lower lip. "You stopped and went home. Why?"

"Money, partially. Mom and Dad helped me out with a lot of the traveling expenses to begin with. Then I didn't want them to spend so much—so I'd come back, work tables and save up, go again. But I didn't think of it as running away. I was just…trying to live. You know. To see so much and cram life in."

He nods, his gaze searching my face. Waiting for me to go on.

"But I was going all these places, and none of them were mine. I had *Anna was here* on a million pictures, but me being there was just transient. And everything I cared about most was back home. My family, Jenny. So I went back to stay. And I realized that I didn't need to make a wide mark all over the world—I could just make a deep one in a single spot. And when Stone and I bought that house, it seemed like the perfect way to *really* make something mine. To put myself all over it. Except for his rooms. And, you know, wherever Daisy makes a mess. That's all his."

A quick grin flashes over his perfect mouth. And I can't resist—I lean in for a kiss.

God, I love being here with Gunner like this. I'd stay in this hotel forever, if I could.

I fold my forearms on his broad chest, prop my chin on my rolled fists. "Anyway. I guess Stone's the opposite, isn't he? He doesn't care what I claim. Because that house,

I couldn't wait to get my name on it. But even a house, he didn't want that. He really doesn't like leaving a trail, does he?"

"No, he doesn't." He watches me with an unreadable expression. "Partially to protect you."

"What?"

"There's always danger of someone like him making enemies. If there's no paper trail, it's not so easy to trace back to where he lives. Someone can ask around in town, right? But nothing he leaves anywhere would direct them to you. And if anyone asks the Riders, they'll be pointed toward the clubhouse. He doesn't bring girls to the house. And he lives with you, so if you have any trouble at the Den, there's someone looking out for you at home."

I stare at him. Some of that was obvious — like Stone not wanting any enemies to find him. But protecting me? "You're serious."

He gives a solemn nod.

I laugh a little, because it does sound exactly like Stone. Then I quiet because I realize, "The Iron Blood found me really quickly."

"Yeah, they did." A frown pulls his dark brows together. "Though maybe that was easier. They were looking for you, not Stone."

"And they could find me in public records?"

"Yeah." That comes out like an agreement, but his frown is deepening, and he's sitting up.

I slide off his chest, kneeling on the bed beside him.

"Gunner?"

"Just thinking." Staring across the room at nothing, his hand absently stroking my back. "Just thinking about bad arguments. And how they found you so quick. How they knew to even *look* for a sister. Because Stone would have never given them that. Not your name, not nothing. Not even to Cherry, if she'd been fishing for info. He was always careful. Especially with you."

Dread prickles my naked skin. "And what you're thinking isn't good, is it?"

"No, sweetheart. Not good at all," he says roughly and when he meets my eyes, the pain there is a razor across my heart. "I'm thinking you need to tell me everything else you've heard while you've been around my family."

THIRTY ONE

GUNNER

The sun is low in the sky when I reach the farm. I wonder if this is how David felt, riding up to Mama's house that last day — thinking about how your own family hurt the person you love more than any other. Seeing her face bruised and mouth bleeding. Seeing her fear for her brother, and knowing he's going through fucking hell, and that's on your family, too.

Every second, hoping you're wrong. Every second, knowing you're not.

And all the while filled with a hurt and rage so fucking deep, it'd be easy to pick up an ax. It'd be easy to swing it.

But today I'm swinging something a hell of a lot stronger.

Three dozen Hellfire Riders roll in behind me, led by Thorne. Three dozen Riders at my back, even though I'm wearing a kutte boasting the wrong damn colors. Three dozen Riders, sent without hesitation after a single call to the prez early this morning.

The only delay was the miles between us.

Mama's out on the porch when we ride up the east hill, frowning and shading her eyes against the sun as she watches us come. Maybe preparing to rip the skin off Adam's ass for bringing the Few to this side of the farm before realizing she's looking at a different club. Then her gaze settles on me, and she waits quietly as I cut my engine, walk up to meet her.

There's relief in her eyes when her gaze flicks down to my kutte, but her smile is tight. "Friends of yours?"

"Yup. Just riding through and wanted to see how I was doing," I tell her. "So I invited them up to meet my brothers. I just texted Six-Point, so they all ought to be on their way."

And it's all quiet now behind me. Every engine off, and I know without even looking around that they're all just sitting on their bikes. Watching me, waiting for a signal.

I don't want to give it. But I will if I need to.

"Let's have a seat, Mama." I point to the porch swing. "The sunset's going to be real pretty."

Her fingers are clenched as she sits. A little uncertain, but mostly angry. "What is this, Zachary?"

"Just doing my job as a member of the Notorious Few," I say and set the swing into gentle motion. When my brothers arrive, at first they'll just see the Riders sitting there. But the movement will draw their eyes here, which is where I need them to be looking to make sure shit doesn't get ugly real fast. "Because the Few promised to help get info regarding Stone's whereabouts. So that's what I'm doing—getting info regarding Stone's whereabouts."

Her cheeks are pale with high spots of color on each one. "From whom?"

"From Strawman, I figure." And I should have fucking known a week ago. *A real bad argument.* Just like Anna, Stone wouldn't automatically associate the name with a scarecrow, like I do. 'Straw man' would mean something else to him. "But how badly I have to hurt him before he tells me what I want to know will be up to you. Because he does love you, Mama. And he'll keep his mouth closed until you tell him to open it."

She stares at me as if never seeing me before, then turns her face away on a deep, shuddering breath. "This is my fault."

"Because when he called you up from Arizona and said he know a way to bring me home—you told him to do it?"

Have his friends in the Iron Blood grab Stone, then make sure I know there was a connection between him and the Cage. But what Grace told Anna about him consulting Mama before every decision was likely true—he would call up Mama first. Not just for permission but for approval.

I don't think any of my other brothers knew—like little boys, not sharing—but Mama would have.

"No," she says softly. "My fault because whatever this weakness is in you, it must have come from me. Outwardly, you are so much your father. But inwardly, you are nothing like him."

"I'm not sorry for that."

"And David was, as well." She looks at her wrist, fingers tracing the veins beneath the fine skin. "Some weakness in me. Some poison."

"That's a good thing, then. Because if a disease is bad enough, sometimes they use poison as medicine. And the way I see it, Prophet was a cancer. So if your blood is what poisoned me and David, I'd also say that's what saved us."

"Your *father* a cancer?" Her laugh is hollow. "If anything is, these girls are. What they did to you, to David."

"So now it's the girls at fault—and not your blood?" I shake my head. "I imagine you'd say anything is at fault, as long as it's not Prophet. So let me give you someone to blame, straight out: Me. I'm at fault for the way I am. And I'm not sorry, because everything you've got here on the farm sure looks pretty, Mama. But it's nothing except racist ideology festering on Prophet's corpse," I tell her evenly.

Her chin goes up, eyes snapping anger. "This is how you talk to me? Your mother? How you talk about your father?"

Of course. I sigh, pinch the bridge of my nose, then look up as the sound of my brothers' bikes draw nearer—then revving higher as they spot the Riders.

Led by Adam, because Strawman wouldn't be that stupid. He'd have slowed down, looked for Mama and made sure she wasn't in immediate danger, then called in for reinforcements from the rest of the Few at the club-house. But Adam, he just opens the throttle and charges in.

Gravel flies under their tires all the way up the house. Then Adam's off his bike, roaring, "What the fuck is going on here?"

I'd get up from the swing, but I'm not sure whether Mama would find a way to stab me in the back.

"Had some friends come by," I say evenly, and he's instantly turning that rage toward me. "Because we were interested in what Strawman had to say about one of their brothers who went missing."

That was not what Adam expected. He shoots a glance at Strawman.

Who knows exactly why I'm here. His gaze is steady on Mama, waiting.

She's not looking at him.

"Because I think he knows where Stone is being

held—or at least the general vicinity. I think he's a little friendlier with Chef than he lets on. What I also think is that he's not going to say a word until Mama here tells him to."

"What the hell, Zach," Six-Point spits out, his entire body tense. "You're going to hurt Mama?"

"Hell no. Thorne there"—I point to the Riders' veep—"is going to blow a hole through Strawman's knee unless he starts talking."

Muncher's shaking his head. "You're threatening your own brother? While wearing that kutte?"

A laugh rocks me forward. I meet his eyes, then look to Six-Point—the only two brothers I even give a damn about. "You're fucking kidding me. You remember what favor you asked of me only a goddamn week ago?"

"That's different," Six-Point says.

"No. The only difference is that I'm asking the same favor from the Riders." I lean back again. "But Mama just has to say the word and our brother doesn't lose his leg."

Still straddling his bike, Strawman's just staring at her. Waiting.

I look to Thorne. "Count of three."

The older man drags the shotgun out of his scabbard on *one*. Pulls back the hammers on *two*.

Just before *three*, I say, "Point it at Adam's knee, instead."

And Mama shoots forward off the swing, crying out, "Tell him, Jacob! Tell him what he wants to know! He wants to call other men his brothers? Let him. And he will never again be welcome back to this home because this impotent devil is no son of mine!"

Good enough. Rising from the swing, I remove my kutte. On the steps of the porch, Adam's looking at me in angry confusion.

"You're patched in, little brother."

"You said permanent!" Six-Point explodes at me, stalking closer. "You're not fucking leaving now."

"I'd have stayed on as one of the Few. I would have fucking *stayed*," I tell them. "I came in on good faith and one fucking condition: that my obligation to Stone had to be respected. But he"—I jab my finger toward Strawman—"broke that faith from Day fucking One. By sending that trouble to Stone in the first place, so I'd be forced to come here for help."

Six-Point stops midstride to stare at Strawman. Muncher's up off his bike, shaking his head.

"You did that?"

His face tight, Strawman looks to Mama before nodding. "I did that."

"Goddammit, Jacob!" Dragging his hands through his hair, Six-Point yells at him. "Our brother was here with us! Making us better!"

"He's not our fucking brother anymore," Adam says coldly, walking back to his bike. "You heard Mama. So I'll leave you to tell him what you need to tell him, Strawman, and he needs to get the fuck out of here. Six-Point,

Muncher. We're heading back to the clubhouse."

Expression torn, Six-Point looks helplessly at me.

Muncher doesn't move. "I think we'll stay until these Rider bastards are gone, brother. Make sure Mama's safe."

"Suit your fucking self." Engine roaring, he heads out.

The house's screen door slams. So Mama's gone, too, and as soon as she is, Strawman's shoulders slump a little.

Probably he would have preferred having his leg blown off than seeing how Mama leapt to Adam's defense, but was all too willing to sacrifice him.

But I can't be fucking sorry. I walk over to him, toss my kutte over his handlebars. I don't need it anymore. "So you got something to say?"

On a short breath, he nods. "There's a property just east of the California-Nevada border, not far off Highway 395."

I pull out my phone, call up a map. "You show me exactly where."

It takes him a minute, following some tiny route he zooms in on. Finally he points out a location and I drop a pin.

"So here's what's going to happen," I tell him. "You're going to give me your phone and you'll be the special guest of a few of my friends until we've got Stone home. Not one of them will touch you; I just don't want to have to worry about you giving Chef a heads-up, yeah?"

He huffs out a laugh. "Yeah."

Because it's not like he has a fucking choice. I look

to Muncher and Six-Point. "You got any issues with that?"

"No," Muncher says.

"All right," I say before turning to Strawman again. "Not one of them will touch you. But *I'm* not one of them. And you sent Chef to rape *my* woman."

His eyes widen — then my fist slams into his jaw and he flies backward off his bike, drooling blood, spitting a tooth. Rolling over on the ground, he holds up his hands. "I didn't, brother!"

"Fucking bullshit." I advance on him, wishing I had that fucking ax, but my fists work just as well and will take a lot longer. More pain for him. Better for me.

"*Think,* you little shit!" Strawman's laughing on his back in the dirt. "Why'd you bring her here? Because she got hurt! And the last fucking thing Mama wanted was her coming with you! I had no idea they'd sent someone to rough her up."

I pause. That has the ring of truth.

He still deserves to have his ass beaten to a pulp, but I forgot this about him — he *will* keep laughing. Laughing and enjoying every bit of pain. So I either make it quick or I don't do it.

I crouch beside him. "Just so it's clear, brother — you not knowing is the only fucking thing saving your life now."

He spits blood, wipes his mouth, still grinning. "Yeah. I figured."

"Give your phone to Muncher, then the Riders will escort you to where you're going." Quickly I frisk his legs, take his knife, his gun. "Don't give them any shit."

"Hell, I'm looking forward to a vacation."

I bet. I wait until he's on his bike again, then glance at Thorne. The Riders all start their engines. The roar is deafening and calls to my blood, calls me to ride. But I'm not done here yet.

With a wave, Thorne pulls out. Strawman falls in and I watch them until they vanish round the bend in the road.

Then I head over to Six-Point and Muncher.

Muncher's eyes are locked on mine. "We didn't know. And we could still use you, brother. No matter what Mama says. You're good for the Few."

"Maybe," I tell them. "But being here isn't good for me."

"Fuck." Six-Point links his hand behind his head, turns in a taut circle as if containing all his frustration in that small space. "Because we just saw what you have—and they didn't even have to say one goddamn word. Every single one of those fuckers was ready to die for you, and kill for you. The rode four hundred goddamn miles for you. But they're not your blood and you weren't even wearing their kutte. And facing them, most of the Few would have scattered. Hell, they wouldn't even come around if it weren't for the pussy. So what do we got to do?"

It's real simple. "You've got to open up your goddamn eyes and look at what's outside this farm—not just go along believing everything you're told. You gotta look and see what brothers really are. Because it's not this. This is just blood. The legacy of a dead man. A brotherhood is a living, changing thing. And Mama says you're looking to the future but you're not. This whole place is chained to the past and to Prophet. So if you want to ride free? Really ride free? You gotta break those fucking chains. You've got to bring in good men who aren't Coopers, give them a real place in the club. You've got to start making brothers who aren't blood. You gotta start listening to your wives instead of to your dicks, especially if you care about them at all—because figuring out what matters to you after you've already lost it is a shitty way to keep moving forward. And all that's only where to *start*," I tell them.

"Shit." Six-Point rubs the back of his neck, laughing. "I like things easy."

"It won't be. It'll be real damn hard to keep going. But it'll be worth it—and I got to tell you, just by admitting that you like it easy, you've already got a jump ahead, because you know all the rest is work. You can't pretend it's not. But there's a lot of fuckers who say they want to live free, yet what they really mean is they want everything to be easy. Easy riding, easy pussy, easy beer. But that shit's the *reward*. And anyone who isn't willing to work for it, you've got to boot them the hell out of your club—and that includes brothers who get everything handed to them easy, just because they're firstborn."

"Jesus. Hell knows we got to try something or Adam's going to run us into the goddamn ground." Muncher hauls in a deep breath like he's fortifying himself for a fight ahead, then grasps my hand in his strong grip before yanking me into a hug. "Good seeing you, brother."

"He's not a brother anymore," Six-Point says but it's with a grin. "Didn't you hear Mama?"

"Some brothers are earned." I bump his fist. "And if you ever need help, I'll give it."

"Same back," he says then laughs. "And I goddamn *knew* you were lying about her. 'My woman.' Shit."

Almost mine. I just need her heart.

And to find some way to convince her to give it.

THIRTY TWO

ANNA

I'M ABOUT TO STEP INTO THE BATH WHEN A MESSAGE from Unicorn Daddy pops up on my phone. Gunner, still using Stone's cell.

It's me.

The knock that follows explains that. I wrap a towel around my naked body and rush to the door, flipping the security latch open. I didn't expect Gunner to be back already—although, really, I didn't know *when* to expect him back. Last night, he never really went to bed. I told him about my conversation with Grace and everything else that I'd picked up in a week's worth of talking to the women at the farm, then he held me as I feel asleep. But I was vaguely aware of him sliding out of bed not long afterward.

And today we didn't go out to the farm after our morning run. We went for a ride instead, heading out on his bike with my arms wrapped tightly around him, stopping for lunch in a little bistro overlooking the San Francisco Bay—and although he didn't say a single word about what was going on, after his questions the night before and the way he was keeping me away from his family, it wasn't hard to guess.

He thinks his family was involved in Stone's disappearance.

I can't imagine how that must hurt—no matter that he and his family had a strained relationship, at best. But if he didn't want to talk about it, I wasn't going to force him to. So I just held on tight on the ride back to the hotel, and held on tighter when he carried me to bed.

Then late in the afternoon, he received a text and left a few minutes later, reminding me to secure the latch behind him.

And whatever he's been doing the past few hours, wherever he went, I can't really tell. Because the second I open the door and he sees me in the towel, a wolfish grin widens his beautiful mouth.

"Fifty dollars and you'll drop that, right?"

Nope. I let it drop where I stand.

"Oh shit." Laughing, he hustles me back into the room, kissing me, closing the door behind us. His hand slides down to grip my ass. "No one else gets to see this, sweetheart."

"Pfft. They wouldn't have seen my ass anyway. It was full frontal, baby."

He laughs into my mouth, his smile wide against my lips. "They don't get that, either."

"Not into sharing?"

"Not at all."

The smile's still there but that's deadly serious. And I don't mind. I'm not into sharing, either.

Raising his head, he looks me over, tweaks the big messy bun on top of my head. "Did you take a bath?"

"I was going to. But now…" I slide my finger down his chest and abruptly realize—"You're not wearing your kutte."

After wearing it all day. After wearing it all week. Although wearing the Few's colors wasn't his choice, he *had* been wearing them as often as he used to wear his Hellfire Riders kutte, displaying them as if he were just as proud to bear them. Not just on the farm. Everywhere.

His smile fades. "I'm not." Pressing a kiss to my forehead, he says, "Go ahead with your bath. I don't mind sitting my ass down for a bit, and watching you will be a good way to pass the time."

"Okay." Especially since passing the time with him

usually means talking. And god—I love talking with him. It's so easy. As if we never spent ten years barely saying anything to each other.

I scoop up my towel and head back to the big tub filled with bubbles and steaming water. Gunner draws a deep breath.

"Is that the bomb stuff you bought today?"

"The bath bomb, yeah."

"You're going to smell so fucking good."

I grin and slide in. "That's the idea."

Actually, the idea was to shave my legs and sip wine and find a cheesy movie to rent, but this is better. And watching his perfect ass in those jeans as he drags the desk chair over beside the tub is a thousand times better.

"Grab a cup," I tell him and point to the bottle of pinot noir sitting on the edge of the tub. I've already filled one of the hotel's paper coffee cups half full. "We're extra fancy tonight."

"Shit. I'm even fancier than that." He reaches for the wine and takes a swig straight from the bottle. "We might have something to drink to."

I go still, watching him. "Oh yeah?"

Slowly he nods. "You hear anything from the farm?"

I shake my head. Grace and I have been texting lately, but nothing today. "I think Grace has classes all day."

"I'll be real interested to see how Mama spins it to her," he says. Then, "We might have Stone's location."

It's so unexpected I can't do anything, just stare at

him—then finally say on a shaky breath, "Really?"

"Really."

And I still can't read him. I can't tell if he's being careful not to get my hopes up too much, or if his family's involvement simply destroyed any good feelings he would otherwise be having, after finally getting a solid lead.

Carefully, I tell him, "Whatever your family did… Stone's not going to blame you."

And I think I hit that nail right on the head. As if in pain, he closes his eyes, lips pressed flat. Roughly, he says, "Anna—"

"I don't blame you for Chef, either."

"Jesus." Voice hoarse, he shakes his head and his chest lifts on a deep, ragged breath. Finally he looks at me, his gaze tormented. "I should have done something about it. A long time ago."

"Like kill all your brothers? Kill your mom?"

His gaze doesn't waver. "Maybe."

"And I think that would hurt a lot more than this does." Fingers dripping, I reach for his hand and love that he leans forward without hesitation and takes mine. I squeeze his fingers tight. "It's done. We'll find Stone. It'll be okay."

Another long, deep breath—then he nods, leans back in his chair again. "I'll be heading out tomorrow morning. Saxon is flying a Rider down to drive you back to Pine Valley in my truck."

"I can drive it back."

"Not alone. Not until this is finished."

"Okay." It doesn't matter if I drive or sit. Either way, I'm going home.

Which is good. Because it means we're that much closer to getting Stone.

So my heart shouldn't be hurting like this.

I reach for the wine, take a sip, try to ease the pain in my throat. It doesn't. Trying to swallow just makes it worse.

So does saying, "Good," while nodding and nodding. "It'll be good to get Stone back."

Watching me, Gunner says softly, "Then why that look?"

Oh god. I can't even hide from him anymore. He always sees when I'm hurting now.

So it doesn't do any good to lie. "I just…I'll be sad to leave here."

"Santa Rosa?"

"The hotel." My voice is so thick. "It was…a good vacation."

"Yes, it was." Leaning forward, he takes my hand, lifts it to his mouth. His intense gaze never leaves my face, even as touches his lips to my wet fingertips. "So maybe you've come to love me a little, if leaving this place makes you sad? That's good, sweetheart." His voice is thick, too. "If I've got a little bit of your heart, I'll figure out how to get the rest."

A little bit of it? I want to laugh but I can't, because my

chest is so tight—and I'm scared. So damn scared. Sitting in a warm bath with the man I love, who's overwhelmed by the thought that I might love him a *little*. By the hope I might one day love him more. And I'm sitting here, terrified that everything so perfect about this moment and this past week will vanish the moment we leave.

So tiny and scared and afraid of being hurt if I expose my heart. But I need to.

Because I think he's scared, too. And he shouldn't be. I can't bear that he is.

My hand trembling in his, I say, "Do you really think you won't get the rest?"

His eyes close, and his hand holds mine tighter, his lips press harder to my fingers. "Maybe. If this information isn't good… Or if we're too fucking late—"

"For Stone?" The very thought makes my heart tighten more.

"Yeah." His voice is a strained rasp. "I promised I'd bring him home. And if shit goes wrong…I lose you both. Because there's no fucking chance you'll keep falling after that."

"You're wrong." Holding his hand so hard, I shift around to face him in the bath, bracing my elbows on the edge of the tub. Carefully I cup his clenched jaw in my palm. "You won't lose us. And you'll never lose me. I want you to see something. Can you grab my phone?"

He almost seems glad that I've told him to do something—as if he can distract himself from these tortured thoughts. Letting go of me, he snags my phone from the table where I left it.

I wave my wet hands at him when he holds it out to me. "Just open the photos, swipe back through them. I'll tell you when to stop."

Leaning back on the edge of the tub, he turns so I can see the screen as he begins rolling through my photos. The reference photos and landscapes from the farm. A picture of me in a towel—

He pauses. "This is what you sent Jenny?"

"Yeah."

"You need to send it to me."

"I'll send you naked ones. Keep going."

"I'd rather take the naked one now—" Abruptly he stops, his body rigid with tension. "Why the hell did you keep this one?"

The picture that Chef took of me, bound and bleeding. "I don't know. I just…don't like deleting photos. Even bad ones."

"Yeah, well. Anna didn't need to be here." His voice is harsh. Without hesitation, his blunt fingertip taps against the trash can, then confirms the deletion.

And…okay. That one I don't really mind losing.

"Did you delete it from Stone's phone, too?"

He doesn't answer. Because the photo I wanted him to see is the next one. It was taken the same night—less than a half hour before I got home and Chef snapped the other photo. And Gunner's already looking closer, not sharing the screen anymore but peering closely at it, his eyebrows drawn and his face tense, as if he's not sure what he's seeing.

But what he's seeing isn't what it really is, anyway. "I don't like showing anyone how much I'm hurting," I tell him softly. "So this is hard. Because that selfie…when I took it, I was hurting more than I ever have."

And it shows. Maybe the photo that Chef took didn't bother me very much because I've seen myself looking more hurt. Not bloodied or bruised but just broken, eyes shattered and without a single shred of joy or hope anywhere in my expression.

He swallows hard but his voice is still thick rasp when he says, "It doesn't say what I thought. In that heart. On my chest."

"What did you think?"

"Anna was here."'

"No," I whisper, and all at once my eyes fill with tears, as if I'm still writing what I did.

Anna was never here.

But I was. I didn't know it. But I was.

A shudder rips through him and he tosses the phone onto the bed as if he can't bear to look at it anymore. Turning, he catches my face, tips my head back to look up at him. "You said then it was a reminder. A gravestone." The gravel in his voice rips at my heart. "Sweetheart. What the hell made you look like that?"

"Because I thought it was true," I whisper and my

tears slip over. "Because I'd hoped and hoped for so long that I'd be more to you than just Stone's sister. But I knew you wanted simple and it hurt *so* much. So I told myself, 'That's it, Anna. No more.' And I needed to remind myself why I couldn't keep hoping. That I had to stop."

"No, sweetheart. No. Ah fuck." A tortured groan rips from him and he buries his face in my hair, his arms sliding around me to lift me from the tub but he just holds me, my wet body to his chest, and the tortured sounds don't end. "No. Ah fuck, no. I'd have stopped it, Anna. Ah sweetheart. I'd have stopped you hurting. Ah fuck. *Fuck*."

Abruptly he pulls back. My face cupped in his hands, his gaze desperately searches mine, his eyes glistening. "You stopped hoping?"

"Yes."

He's absolutely still. "How long did you hope?"

"Gunner—"

"How long?"

A pained breath shudders from me. "A long, long time. Since I met you. But I tried not to. Because every time you pushed me away and—"

"I didn't know it hurt you when I did." Face bleak, he shakes his head. "I didn't think it mattered to you. Why did you never say it did?"

"Because what was I supposed to do? Slice my guts open in front of you? Every single time, I was the one coming on to you. Every time. I invited you into my bed. I invited you out. I threw myself at you. Each time you pushed me back. How many times do you have to shoot me down before I'm afraid of being shot again? How many times do I throw myself at you? Fifty? If a guy did that to a girl, he's a fucking creep. Why do you *think* I didn't say?"

"So you didn't want to hurt. And I'm not blaming you, sweetheart." His gaze tender, his thumbs slide over my cheeks, wiping away the tears. "Why would I blame you for protecting yourself when everything I did was to protect you, too? Are you still afraid of being hurt?"

Under that intense gaze, I can't even pretend to hide this. "I'm afraid this will end when we find Stone."

"This?" Gently, he kisses me. "No."

His sweet confidence has my eyes filling with tears again. Because I can't be so sure, yet the way he holds me without any doubts of his own makes it easier to say, "But nothing has changed. Your family is still—"

"No," he says softly and kisses me again. "Not an issue anymore."

Good. Good. And I'll make him tell me more soon, but—"And the next time there's a threat? Will you draw the line between us again to protect me? Because you loved me, but apparently never enough to step over the line. I was never enough for you to take that risk for. Not until some fucker beat me up."

His brows lower, darkening his features. His fingers tighten. "You were enough. You always were."

"No. Because it was ten years, Gunner." Pain tightens my throat. "Ten *years*, you left that line standing between us. I know now it was about protecting me. To keep me from getting hurt. The thing is, you knew I might get sick any time. You knew that death might come from right from inside me—that your family might be the least of my worries. I was running around the world because I was so afraid of it. And you knew that, too. But you *still* never stepped over the line."

"Sweetheart." With another groan, he pulls me completely out of the bath, swings me up in his arms. "You wanted to live as much as you could. You think I could risk shortening that? But here's the selfish part of me. I thought all you wanted was sex—and that wasn't worth risking you. But if what you're offering is your heart? I'll do anything. So if you're wondering what's changed? It's this."

Gently he lays me on the bed, kissing me as his hands work between us, belt buckle clinking, zipper rasping. Then he's deep inside me, and I'm gasping with the pleasure of it.

"What's changed?" The raw emotion in his pale eyes burns straight through me. "Is that now you're mine. And I'll *never* give you up."

"Gunner—" I whisper but the hard thrust of his body breaks his name into a sharp cry.

"And this." He rocks against me, his gaze locked to mine. "Now I know you were hurting because we weren't together, and I'll *never* hurt you again."

But this hurts. In the best way. Panting, I wrap my

legs around him. "Please—"

Fiercely his mouth claims mine, his cock thrusting deep, harder and harder, until I'm gasping and poised on the edge.

Then he stops and growls against my lips, "Now I know you love me, Anna. And that changes *everything*," before fucking into me again, and I'm coming hard, so hard, clinging to him with everything I am as he comes to his own release deep inside me.

His mouth softens, and gently he kisses away the tears at the corners of my eyes before raising his head to look down at me. "Knowing you love me changes everything," he says softly again. "And all of these years, Anna—If *you* had known why I was staying away, that it was just to protect you, that I was dying for wanting you…what would you have done?"

It would have changed everything for me, too. "If I'd known you loved me? I'd have gone after you. I'd have worn you down. And I'd have never let up."

"Then are you going to let up now? Are you going to let this fear get in the way? Because it'll fucking kill me if you walk away," he says hoarsely. "You going to do that to me now?"

"No," I whisper on a shuddering breath. "And if you ever told me that we have to go back to being what we were—to keeping it simple—it would kill me."

"I'll never tell you that. Never. I'm going to give you that future you want, sweetheart. And whatever is in that future…in *our* future, we'll face it. Together. No more lines between us. All right?"

I only nod and kiss him, because my throat's too tight to answer with words.

"Now," he says and reaches for the phone. "This photo. You look so fucking hurt, baby. It kills me just to see it. You want to get rid of it? Because you don't need this reminder anymore. We should do another picture, maybe one of your pussy, and I'll write 'Gunner was here' with my tongue."

Giggling, I snatch the cell before he can trash the picture. "No. Because here—this is what I wanted to tell you. To show you. Because in this photo, you already had my heart. Even not really knowing much about you. That's how I kept a tiny piece of it to myself—telling myself that I didn't really know you. Just a tiny piece that I tried so hard to protect. Because the rest of my heart was yours. And now…knowing you, you have that tiny piece of my heart, too. You have it all. And that's the difference between this…" I extend the phone out over our heads, snap the picture. "And this. Look at us. Look how much I love you."

"Ah fuck," he says and his voice is hoarse again, but he's not looking at the photo. He's staring at me, his eyes glittering, his hand clamped to his chest. "Shit. This is why you started crying when I said it. Oh my fucking heart. Say it again."

"I love you." When he groans and clutches his pec, I

grin and lean in, flicking my tongue against his lips. "Does it hurt? Don't worry, baby. I'm going to make you feel real good again. Maybe I'll be the one who goes down and writes 'Anna was here' with my tongue."

With a laugh, he claims my mouth again.

And grabs my phone.

THIRTY THREE

ANNA

When the knock comes on the hotel room door early the next morning, I'm already dressed. No need to wake up—neither Gunner nor I slept last night. Now I'm sore and tired and more hopeful than I've ever been, happier than I ever dreamed.

Gunner opens the door. I don't need to see his face to know he's grinning when he greets the huge man standing there—Bull, the Hellfire Rider who'll be escorting me home.

But apparently Bull didn't only come to pick me up—he also brought Gunner's kutte with him.

"The prez said you'd need this," the big man says. "The other brothers are waiting for you down in the lot."

Gunner's throat works as he takes the Riders' colors. He turns to face me when he slides into the kutte, his pale eyes blazing, and it's like everything in the world settles into place when that leather settles over his shoulders again.

And I do more than hope. For once, I trust that everything will be all right. Because Gunner's wearing that kutte again, so it has to be.

My throat a thick lump, I give him a thumbs up. "Looking damn good."

Looking as he should.

With powerful strides, he crosses over to me, catches my face in his callused hands. "I'll bring him home, sweetheart."

"I know." I do.

"And everything will change for you and me."

I'm too overwhelmed to speak, so I nod, then he's kissing me long and deep.

Too soon he lifts his head, says hoarsely against my lips, "I love you, Anna."

"I love you, too," I tell him, and he kisses me hard again.

"I'll carry that with me," he says.

Then I watch him go—and it's not just the kiss he's

taking with him.

He's got my heart, too. And I know it won't beat again until the next time I see him.

THIRTY FOUR

GUNNER

Stone's being kept on a fucking horse farm.

At least, what used to be one. In two days, I haven't seen a single horse. Just motorcycles belonging to members of the Iron Blood and a few vehicles that circle the property on regular patrols.

For two days Zoomie, Blowback, and I have been taking turns lying out in the goddamn desert, seeing what we can of the layout. It's making me as impatient as hell, but the surveillance is necessary. If we rush in without knowing where Stone's being held, he could be dead before we get to him. But we're on a tight timeline here, because even though we're out square in the middle of nowhere, up on a bluff with our eyes trained on the compound, the longer we watch the place the greater the chance we'll be discovered. And hell knows when another fight will be held—or whether Stone might go up in the ring again.

From what I can see, the Cage itself isn't here. Just two barns where the fighters are kept, and a clapboard farmhouse that isn't home to a family but where the guards sleep and eat.

Most of those guards aren't Iron Blood. Not wearing kuttes, at least. Most likely they're hired guns, and the Iron Blood just picks up the fighters at the rallies and provides extra security.

The second morning, I see Stone being herded toward an old racetrack with three other men.

Exercising them like they're fucking animals. A tower overlooks the track and through the scope I can see the guards up on the platform, rifles slung.

Animals in a goddamn prison.

"Easy, pretty boy." Lying on her belly beside me, Zoomie nudges my leg. She's watching through her own scope, her gaze flat and hard. "I know you're excited to finally see your boyfriend, but keep your head down."

I'm keeping my fucking head down, and keeping eyes on Stone. He's moving smooth, quick. Not injured from his fight—not in any way that shows.

After a half hour, they're herded back to the east barn. Got him.

But he's not the only one we're after. We wait through more exercise rotations, only a handful of men at a time—some faces I recognize as bikers who've gone missing, some I don't.

"All that muscle to push around," Zoomie says softly. "Not enough guards on duty to handle all of it at once."

Good news for us. "You seen Crash yet?"

She shakes her head.

And we don't see Crash. Just Handlebar, coming out of the west barn and heading toward the track. So we'll need to hit both barns.

Almost noon, Blowback returns from his recon on the north side of the property, listens as we fill him in on the location of our two men. "Tonight, then?"

"We going to have trouble with the Iron Blood swooping in?" A part of me fucking hopes so.

Blowback shakes his head. "They're on a relay run. So it'll just be the guards on site."

Two dozen guards, by our count—with only a third of them on duty at any time, and the rest taking their ease in the house.

Chef won't be here. But that'll keep.

Zoomie looks to me. "You want me to call everyone in?"

"Everyone" is the Butchers, the Riders. Each of them holed up in different towns a few hours' ride away, waiting for word from us. And when we give that word, that'll be a hell of a lot of bikers converging on one point. We run the risk of someone noticing and pulling the plug on the stables before we get our boys out.

Blowback, Zoomie, and I could go in quiet. Pull out Stone, then get to Handlebar, and get the hell out before the guards take notice and the shit hits the fan.

Or we can bring everyone in and burn the whole fucking thing down.

"Call 'em in," I tell her.

I suppose kicking through the door of a guarded facility is what Anna might call a stress situation. The sort of situation where Stone told her that I've got fucking ice in my veins.

Doesn't feel like ice. Not when the explosion the Butchers set off in the main house sends heat racing across my skin.

And ice is glacier slow. I'm not. My finger is lightning on the trigger. One, two, three bullets—and three guards down, each one looking surprised that there's a big fucking hole in his skull.

Inside, the horse barn…looks like a horse barn. A high peaked ceiling opens over a long central aisle lined with stalls. Steel bars reinforce the sliding doors, and men are charging against those doors now, their yells joining with the increasing noise from outside. Gunshots. Roaring engines. Shouting.

It's dark—overhead lights went out two hours ago, at ten—but recessed lighting along the central aisle provides more than enough light to see by. I snag the keys off a guard's belt and toss the lot to Zoomie. "Start opening the cages. I'll clear the road."

"There's a faster way." She heads toward a small office off the right side of the entrance. Looks like a horse barn but more like a prison, I realize, with central controls for the cell doors.

Doesn't smell like a barn, either. No hay, no horseflesh. Smells more like a hospital.

I head down the aisle, ignoring the men shouting at me to let them out, looking for one face.

He's in the fourth stall, standing at the sliding door with his arms crossed over his chest, wearing just a pair of sweatpants—and not a bit fucking surprised to see me. And this isn't ice in my veins when I reach through the bars and clasp his hand in a tight grip, my eyes locked on his.

Roughly, I say, "Good to see you, brother."

He returns my grip, holding tight. "And me, I'm always glad to see your girly mouth."

Not girly. Just pouty. But I've only got time for a grin before an electric hum sounds and the door rolls open.

All at once there's men running everywhere. No more guards yet but they might be coming. I pull my extra piece from its holster and toss the gun to Stone.

"Ready?"

He's not. Years of fighting at his side means I can read him fast, and he's not focusing on the exit. Instead he's tilting his head. Listening.

Then taking off running deeper into the barn. I keep up easily. Most of the fighters have cleared out, heading the opposite direction, and despite the noise echoing through the barn I hear it —

The clatter of metal. A muffled scream.

A *woman's* scream.

He heads for a door, what looks like an old tack room. Wordlessly he signals. He's going low.

I take high, slamming through the door, gun sweeping the room. Clean, white, an exam table, medical equipment scattered over the floor. Movement in the corner. A big fucker on top of a smaller figure — tearing off her panties.

Then the fucker collapses on top of her, the top of his head gone, Stone's gunshot still echoing around the room. With a shriek, a strawberry blonde scrambles out from under him, wearing a tiny nurse's outfit and thigh high stockings splattered with blood.

Stone starts for her and she cringes back against the wall decorated with the fucker's brains, holding out her hands as if to ward him off, begging.

"Please, please! I don't care what you do to me. But please first let me find my b —"

Scooping the panties off the floor, Stone shoves the wadded fabric into her mouth, then rips a white stocking off her leg, using the nylon to tie the gag around her head.

Wildly she fights him, trying to rip off the gag and speak, but he traps her hands behind her back and binds them next.

What the fuck? He's been through some shit, but Jesus Christ—treating a woman like this? Shaking my head, I step forward and her panicked gaze swings over to me.

Emerald eyes lock on mine.

Cherry. Without the big red wig.

I back off, let him finish whatever the hell he's doing.

Without a word, Stone picks her up and throws her facedown over his shoulder. Expression savage, he turns toward the door.

Outside, everything is chaos. The fire's blazing in the house. They've started the west barn burning. I spot Spiral at the wheel of my truck, signal to Stone.

He tosses Cherry into the back, leans over and warns through clenched teeth, "Don't fucking move or I'll round up every single man you caged up and bring them over here to use your pussy."

Stalking away from her, he heads toward a group of bikers—the Bedlam Butchers. They've gathered around Handlebar, the Butchers' VP.

One of their VPs. Crash was the other.

Uneasy, I shake my head. "Maybe not the best time, brother."

The Butchers are friends but this is a hard fucking thing to ask anyone to take in. And while hurting?

In his place, if I was hearing Stone was dead, and a friend was the one who killed him? I don't know that there'd be any ice at all. Just fire until his blood ran in rivers over my hands.

But I see Stone's eyes as he heads over toward the other men, and I know that look. I've seen it in broken men. Stone doesn't give a fuck what they do to him. Maybe even welcomes their worst, if the worst is easier to deal with than the shit in his head.

So I'm tense as fuck when Handlebar sees him and all the laughter and backslapping around him stops. The Butchers are watching Handlebar, too. Maybe just waiting for a signal as Stone halts in front of the other man.

"I'm so fucking sorry, man." Stone's voice is hoarse as he spreads his hands out wide, exposing his bare chest. "I'll take whatever you got. Fists. Bullets."

Slowly Handlebar approaches him. He's a massive fucker, with a thick beard, ink, piercings. He looks fierce as hell but I know him as a big, laughing man always ready with a joke.

That laughter is gone, his expression bleak as he grips the back of Stone's neck with one hand, pulls him close and bows his head. Stone does the same, his mouth near the other man's ear. I can't hear what he's saying—just see Handlebar's nod and the wet sheen in the big man's eyes.

They pull away from each other, hands clasped. Then Stone turns and heads back to the truck. I jump into the truck bed after him, watching as he crouches next to

Cherry.

Harshly he says, "You're going to pay for every fucking lying word that came out of your mouth. You understand?"

She's not even looking at him. Instead she's staring at the burning buildings, her emerald gaze wildly searching the flames.

Roughly he catches her chin and forces her to face him. "You understand?"

When she frantically nods, he releases her, then looks to me. "Anna?"

"Safe," I tell him.

"The fucker who touched her?"

"Taken care of." Or same as, because he will be.

He exhales a long, shuddering breath. Closes his eyes. "Thank you."

"I love a goddamn bonfire." Wearing a huge grin, Zoomie swings over the side of the truck and takes a seat on the tire well. "But we forgot the fucking marshmallows."

"Next time," Stone tells her.

"Aw. Look at you, you big asshole, promising to get kidnapped again just for me." With as much affection as she ever showed any of the Riders, she rubs her hand over his short hair before shoving at his head. "Who's the nurse?"

"Cherry," I tell her, then rap my knuckles on the cab's back window, letting Spiral know we're ready to haul out.

"Cherry?" Zoomie echoes, her eyes narrowing. "So why aren't we roasting her instead of a marshmallow?"

"Because I've got something else in mind for her," Stone says and turns his grim gaze toward the woman, who cringes away from his stare. "And I'm going to take a real long time to do it."

His voice—so fucking cold.

And for the first time that night, my blood finally runs like ice.

THIRTY FIVE

ANNA

My heart seizes up when Daisy suddenly starts barking, running back and forth across the floor of my studio. Since coming home, I've been keeping a gun nearby when I'm alone. I grab it now and head to the window overlooking the front drive.

Gunner's truck is pulling in.

My heart gives a wild leap and I'm running, almost tripping down the stairs in my hurry. I burst through the front door and onto the porch just as Stone gets out of the driver's side.

Laughing, I throw myself at him. God, and he catches me and hugs me so tight. Daisy's barking wildly, rubbing up against his legs, and he pulls back to look at my face.

"Aw, pipsqueak," he groans. "Don't cry."

I'm trying not to. Pulling my long sleeves down over my hands, I wipe my leaking eyes. "I was just so happy to have the house to myself. I'm sad I have to share it again."

Stone smiles, but it's not like the quick grin and laugh that such a response would have gotten before, and it fades so quickly. Jaw hard, he cups my cheek.

Looking at where the bruise used to be—because he saw the video of Chef hitting me.

I reach up, grab his wrist. "I'm all right."

Nodding, he lets me go.

"Daisy is all right, too," I say.

He barely looks down at the dog, who's going wild with happiness over his being home, and my heart starts aching.

Gunner said that fighting and killing an innocent man would hurt him. That it would fuck him up bad.

And Stone is home. But he's not the same Stone.

Gruffly now he tells me, "You might be by yourself a little longer. I've got some business out at the clubhouse that I'm going to be taking care of for a while."

"Okay." A lot of the Riders do that now and then. "Have you seen Mom and Dad yet?"

"Not yet." Abruptly he walks past me, toward the side

entrance — instead of using my door.

"I told them you were coming back." I follow behind him, watching Daisy dancing around his feet and desperately trying to get his attention. "But maybe you should stop by."

"I'll get around to it."

God. Stone never just *gets around to it* when it's regarding our parents.

But he just needs time. He just needs time.

And his friends. "Was Gunner with you?"

"No. He said he had some shit to take care of." He climbs the stairs to the mudroom, Daisy trotting behind him.

"Did Gunner say anything about…me and him?"

Stone shakes his head. "Not a thing."

He heads inside — and the screen door slams shut in Daisy's face. She barks at the door, tail wagging, before looking over at me, where I'm standing numb, rubbing my arms, feeling so damn cold.

Gunner didn't say anything to him about me. But that doesn't have to mean anything. It doesn't mean Gunner and I are going back to how we were.

I don't know how we could ever go back. I'm not just a friend's sister. But my brother — his friend — is broken.

And nothing's simple anymore.

THIRTY SIX

GUNNER

Inside Chef's darkened living room, I wait until the big fucker closes his front door before putting two bullets into his knees. The silenced shots sound like an old woman's hacking cough. He crashes to the linoleum floor in the entryway. My boot cracks across his jaw, quieting his agonized scream.

His eyes roll back.

By the time he comes to, I've got him taped to a chair and his mouth sealed shut. I don't need him to tell me anything. I'm the only one who'll be talking.

I press the end of the barrel against his forehead and show him the picture of Anna taped and crying. I sent it to myself before deleting it from Stone's phone—and only kept the picture for this purpose alone. "I just want to make sure you know what this is for," I tell him. "You remember her?"

It takes a moment before recognition sharpens his eyes—as if he's taken so many of these pictures that he has to think it through. Finally he nods.

"Good," I say and pull the trigger.

THE HOUSE BURNS LIKE THE stables did. Blowback's waiting outside.

I delete the picture from my phone, then mount my bike. Unscrewing the silencer from the gun's barrel, I toss the weapon to Blowback. He'll dispose of it better than I ever could.

"You heading home?" I ask him.

"I'm thinking about having a conversation with Paladin first," he says like he's just going to talk to the man instead of whatever he's really got planned. "You going back now?"

"Not yet," I say and fire up my engine.

I've got two more things to take care of first. One for me.

One for Anna.

THIRTY SEVEN

ANNA

Sunday night, I'm back at the Wolf Den. It's not my usual shift—this is typically the night I have off and when Jenny, Lily, and I go out to dinner—but I need to keep busy, and Jenny's still in a rough spot. Not ready to go out, not so soon after losing her dad. But we'll slowly get her there again.

And we'll get Stone where he needs to be, too.

"Hey." Her pale blond hair a little longer than the last time I saw her—too long to be called a buzzcut anymore—Lily bellies up to the bar. "Good to see you back."

"When did you miss seeing me here?" I raise my brows. "You were gone, too."

With a narrowing of her gray eyes, her gorgeous face instantly turns dangerously mean. "Don't fuck with me. I can't take this kind of emotional shit. So tell me right now—are we okay, you and me? Because if not, we're going to hash it out, right now."

I blink in absolute confusion before it hits me. *Ohhhh*. Because I was so pissed at her the last time I saw her—because she hadn't told me about Stone being missing, either.

But, holy crap. That was like two weeks ago. She thinks I'm still mad? And she's freaking out because she thinks I am?

"We're okay," I say.

"Oh. Good." The tension visibly leaves her body, and she grins at me. "Beer?"

I've got one better. Stepping up on a small footstool, I reach for her favorite bourbon on the top shelf.

"Aw, that's a cute little footstool. You want me to get that for you?"

"Shut up." It's not my fault I'm not a giant like she is. Or that I'm so short I actually have to go up on tiptoe, even standing on the stool.

She snickers. A little mean, but I like that about her.

And not always mean. Not if she cares about you.

Watching me pour the bourbon, she says quietly, "So what are we going to do about Jenny?"

I'm pretty sure we just have to give it time. But Lily knows more about this than I do. "What did you do after your dad died?"

"Got drunk. Rode my bike. Fucked a bunch of girls and boys. Became a tough biker. Drank some more."

I grin, trying to imagine Jenny doing any of that. I can't. "She'll be okay," I say. "Nothing will be the same. But we'll just ease her back into it."

"Sounds good."

Yeah, it does. I wait for a long second, then say as casually as I can, "Have you heard from Gunner?"

"Yeah. He's in town, somewhere." Her eyes narrow again, but not angrily this time. More like she's wondering if I just turned stupid. "Ever heard of texting?"

"I don't have his number."

"You're joking."

Nope. "He had Stone's phone. So we just used that."

"You idiots." She snorts and tugs her phone from her back pocket. "I'll give it to you. Or, never mind. He can just give it to you himself."

Because he's coming through the door. Looking so damn beautiful, dragging off his helmet and sliding his hands over his thick hair. He's already spotted me behind the bar, his crystalline gaze locking on me and never wavering, and he doesn't slow his steady pace in my direction even when some of the other Riders come up to bump his fist and congratulate him. Because it seems now everyone knows that Stone was gone.

And they know who brought him back.

My heart's overflowing when he stops at the bar, his hands braced flat on the countertop.

A grin curves his gorgeous lips. "Hello, sweetheart."

"You brought my brother home," I say and my throat is so thick.

"I told you I would," he reminds me, but his grin falters a little, and I know why that pain flickers through his eyes. He glances over at Lily, who seems to read his silent message. She bumps his fist and heads off.

"He seems…not good," I say quietly when he looks to me again—gently taking my hands, holding them clasped in his at the center of the bar.

"He'll come through." Gunner sounds sure of it. "It'll just take time."

I nod, my heart pounding so hard, my breath like a bellows in my chest. "So what now—for you and me?"

"Well." Those pale eyes are so steady on mine. "I thought we could make it simple again."

And my heart's just…gone. My chest empty.

I wonder if this is what it's like to die.

But it can't be. Because death, you don't start hurting again. Death, you don't pull your hands from his and blindly turn away.

"Anna? Where you going, sweetheart?"

I don't know. "The Philippines, maybe." My voice is

thin, broken, almost unintelligible. "It doesn't matter. As long as it's not here."

In the mirror behind the liquor shelf, I catch a glimpse of Gunner's white face. I see the powerful flex of his arms as he shoves against the countertop, vaulting over the bar and into the service area with me. And I haven't run fast enough because his strong hands snag my waist, drag me back against him.

"All right, sweetheart," he says hoarsely in my ear. "If you want to go, we both go. The Philippines it is. Although it sounds like a damn good place for a honeymoon, instead."

Something stutters in the empty cavity of my chest. "A what?"

"I love you, Anna. You love me. So this is *really* simple. Not the kind of simple we had before. I said it all wrong. So I'm just going to let this speak for me."

His fingers thread through mine. But not just to clasp our hands. He turns my palm over, presses his lips to the center before dropping a glittering ring onto the same spot.

A ring. My voice is high, thready. "Gunner?"

"I just need one word from you, Anna," he says gruffly. "So tell me yes. Tell me you'll belong to me."

"I already do."

I feel his huff of laughter. "One word."

"Why are you complaining? I gave you three." My heart so full, I turn in his arms. "And here's three more: I love you."

"I'll take those," he growls against my lips, then his

strong hands capture my face and he claims my mouth in a deep kiss. Behind us, a few cheers echo through the bar, then grow louder, and along with them are Riders shouting suggestions about what Gunner can do to me next.

Laughing, he breaks the kiss, then says in my ear, "Now you've got two choices. I can either sit you up on that bar and lick your pussy in front of everyone, or I can take you into the back."

"Back," I say breathlessly and easily ignore the new shouts and cheers as Gunner swings me up and carries me toward the employee door, his mouth fastened to mine.

Down the hall, he kicks open the stockroom door. Saxon's going to kill us but I don't even care. Wildly I kiss him, pushing at the shoulders of his leather vest, then drop my hands to his belt when I realize there's no reason for his top half to be naked.

But Gunner is stripping out of his kutte, carefully putting the folded leather aside before catching my hands.

I groan, looking down. He stopped me with his zipper half undone and the pressure of his thick erection against the fastening is slowly, slowly unzipping the rest.

"I love you looking at my dick, Anna. You always look so damn hungry and impressed." He's grinning as he turns his back to me. "But look at this first."

Gathering the back of his collar in his fist, he drags his shirt off—and there's ink on his skin now.

The Hellfire Riders' emblem stretches from shoulder to shoulder.

Mouth parting in astonishment, I step forward and lift my fingers toward the tattoo before abruptly stopping. The skin around the edges of the emblem is still an angry red, the inked surface gleaming with ointment. He must have gotten this today. And it's so big, he must have been sitting under the needle for most of the day.

Voice thick, I say, "I thought Cooper boys didn't change what they were born with. That you all look like you do for a reason."

"I'll look how I want to look and for my own reasons. This reason says I'll always be a Rider." His voice deepens before he faces me again. "And the reason for this one is that I'll always be yours."

There's new ink on his chest, too—right over his heart, a thick red script, as if written in lipstick across his steely pectoral.

Anna will always be here.

"Gunner," I whisper, then he's kissing me, turning and lifting me up against the stockroom door. My arms circle his neck as his big hands drag my jeans down—just far enough for him to spread me open and sink deep.

Filled completely, I cry out at the deliciously thick intrusion, my head falling back. His hot mouth fastens to my neck and he fucks me with powerful strokes that rattle the doorframe and shiver through the shelves.

Then abruptly he stops, holding me pinned against the door, his cock so deep. "Put on the ring, Anna. Let me see that you're mine when I come inside you this time."

The ring is still in my hand, clenched in my fist. Hands shaking, I slip my arms from around his neck.

"I swear to you, Anna," he says and emotion roughens his voice. He takes the ring from me and slides it onto my finger before curling my hand into a fist—as if to keep the ring on tight. "I'll give you any future you want."

"Just one that's long and happy." But I'll take whatever I get with him.

"Long and happy." He grins. "At this moment, that describes my cock."

Still buried inside me. His mouth captures mine when I start to laugh, until need begins to take over. Then, with a groan, he tears his lips from mine and swears solemnly,

"I'll give that future to you, sweetheart. I'll give you everything."

With a shuddering breath, I touch his jaw, his lips, before cupping his face in my hands—and the pretty diamond sparkling in my ring can't compete with the beauty of his pale eyes when he's looking at me, so hot and fierce and in love.

"You've already given me everything," I tell him with my heart overflowing. "Because now I have you."

And in the end—it really is that simple.

THE END

STONE

I HEAR THE CHIME OF AN INCOMING MESSAGE ON MY phone at the same time a knock sounds at the cabin door. A soft whimper comes from the slight form on the bed.

"Not a fucking sound," I warn her.

Even though, out here on the clubhouse property, I don't have to worry that whoever's at that door is anyone except another Rider. And when I open it—only six inches, enough to look out and with my body blocking the view of everything behind me—Beaver is standing there in the rain, holding out a wad of cash.

"You won," he says.

I eye the money warily. I haven't won anything worth having lately, so I sure as hell don't trust that this cash is something I want.

"What's that for?"

"Gunner just jumped over the bar after your sister and kissed her in front of everyone before dragging her off to the back rooms. That's public confirmation of them hooking up. You picked this week on the calendar, so you won the pot."

Aw, yeah. I always figured it would be the holidays that would get to them. All those fucking awkward silences at my mother's house. So a week after Thanksgiving sounded about right.

"She came out wearing a ring," Beaver adds.

That makes me smile—the first smile in a long time that actually feels like one.

But it vanishes when Beaver's focus shifts past me, as if he's trying to see more beyond the small slice of door I've got open.

"Anything else?" I ask.

"No."

I snatch my winnings out of his hand and slam the door shut.

The cash, I toss onto a small table under the shuttered window. The cabin's rustic—just a single room with a little bathroom off the side. Two chairs, a small potbellied stove, a double-wide bed, and a naked woman tied to it.

I feel her emerald eyes on me as I check the messages

on my phone. This cabin's far back on the property and one of the few places that seems to get better than sporadic reception. Still I'm surprised it came through, because it's not a simple text. It's a picture. Anna's smiling up at me, her head pillowed on a familiar chest—except now *Anna will always be here* is inked into Gunner's pectoral. An engagement ring glitters on her finger.

About damn time, I text back.

I drop the phone onto the bed, beside a long slim thigh. She's tied with her arms straight up over her head and her legs wide apart, ankles bound to the bed posts. Her pointed nipples are flushed a deep rose, the soft skin of her breasts abraded by whisker burn. Thoughtfully, I rasp my palm over my jaw. Don't really feel like shaving. So those inner thighs will soon be feeling the same burn.

Gazing down at her, I reach into the front of my sweats, drag out my hard cock and give the shaft a long, rough stroke. Eyes wide, her gaze follows the path of my fist.

She makes a soft, plaintive sound, her full lips stretched wide around a ball gag. I've got use for her mouth—Jesus, I've got so much fucking use for it—but no use at all for the lies coming out of it.

"You remembering how it tastes?"

Her brilliant green eyes shoot back to mine. Wide and shimmering, they're pleading with me now, and the sight of her desperation just makes my dick even harder.

"You think I'm going to fuck you? Nah, not yet. We've

still got a long way to go before that, making sure you get every bit of punishment you deserve."

She's watching my hand again, her sweet tits rising and falling with each panting breath. Her rosy nipples stand stiff at attention and the soft curls guarding her pussy are glossy and wet. She doesn't want to love this.

Oh, but she does.

Hunger roughens my voice. "This looks real fucking familiar, doesn't it? Except it was me tied up while you sucked on my cock. But what's *real* similar is how you're about to discover how goddamn hard you can come, even when you hate the fucking sight of the person who's getting you off."

A low moan breaks from her. Her red hair whips around her face as she wildly shakes her head, the long strands clinging to sweat-slicked skin.

The end of the mattress dips under my weight as I kneel between her bound legs and slide forward, stretching out between her sleek thighs. God, her scent. Musky and sweet. Holding back a groan, I lower my head, my hot breath stirring those dampened curls. "But here's the difference in this scenario: Men, we only come once. Twice, if we're real lucky. But you? You're going to come over and over again. Until you break and give me what I fucking want."

Frantically she pulls against her restraints, the long muscles in her pale thighs trembling, her fisted fingers yanking desperately against the rope over her head.

My big hands clamp down on her bucking hips. With broad thumbs, I spread her glistening pussy lips and expose her sexy little clit. My mouth waters with need and I don't hold back, claiming her cunt all at once, groaning at her hot flavor, savoring the agonized pleasure in her muffled scream and the rush of wetness that greets my tongue.

Payback never tasted *so* fucking good.

* * *

I hope you enjoyed this sneak peek of Stone's book! This scene also appears in that novel, but from the heroine's point of view — and her feelings and motivations are not quite what he assumes they are...

ABOUT KATI

Kati Wilde is a tight-lipped, loose-hipped woman of indeterminate age and low breeding. She writes romantic fiction to assuage her darker urge to write Transformers erotica. You can reach Kati at kati@katiwilde.com or any of the Club authors (Ella Goode, Ruby Dixon, and Kati Wilde) at 1theclub1@gmail.com.

www.katiwilde.com

Facebook: www.facebook.com/authorkatiwilde
Instagram: www.instagram.com/authorkatiwilde
Twitter: www.twitter.com/katiwilde

www.katiwilde.com/newsletter

CONTENT WARNINGS

All of the Hellfire Riders stories include swearing, violence, explicit sexual content including references to group sex, sex in public and voyeurism (some main characters only watch while others participate), references to alcohol and drug use, sex trafficking, illegal cage fighting, and murder (mostly only bad guys, but there are exceptions.) There are no cliffhangers and no cheating.

For this particular book:

- the heroine had childhood leukemia

- the heroine is assaulted and threated with rape

- both the hero and heroine are infertile (no magical cures here)

- death and grief

- the hero's family is part of a cult established by his father, who was a charismatic figure similar to Charles Manson. The family-based cult/motorcycle club operates under the belief that an inevitable race war is looming and are concerned with racial purity; in the past, the hero's father ordered the death of a young woman who was dating the hero's brother.